SKELMERSDALE

23 JUL 2010

1 8 JUL 2014

FICTION RESERVE STOCK LL60

DARK SKIES : THE
AWAKENING

Lancashire County Library

30118087889246

D1352402

Lancashire
County Council

LANCASHIRE

DARK SKIES™ THE AWAKENING
A BANTAM BOOK: 0 553 50619 6

First publication in Great Britain

PRINTING HISTORY
Bantam edition published 1997

Copyright © 1996 by Columbia Pictures Television, Inc.
All rights reserved.

Foreword copyright © 1997 by Bryce Zabel

Dark Skies™ The Awakening is a novel by Stan Nicholls based upon
the teleplays, 'The Awakening' written by Bryce Zabel & Brent V.
Friedman, 'Mercury Rising' written by James D. Parriott, 'Moving
Targets' written by Bryce Zabel & Brent V. Friedman and 'Dark Days
Night' written by Bryce Zabel & Brent V. Friedman.
Based upon the television series created by Bryce Zabel
& Brent V. Friedman.

Condition of Sale
This book is sold subject to the condition that it shall not, by way of
trade or otherwise, be lent, re-sold, hired out or otherwise circulated in
any form of binding or cover other than that in which it is published
and without a similar condition including this condition being imposed
on the subsequent purchaser.

Set in 10/11pt Linotron Sabon by Deltatype Ltd, Birkenhead

Bantam Books are published by Transworld Publishers Ltd,
61–63 Uxbridge Road, London W5 5SA,
in Australia by Transworld Publishers (Australia) Pty Ltd,
15–25 Helles Avenue, Moorebank, NSW 2170,
and in New Zealand by Transworld Publishers (NZ) Ltd,
3 William Pickering Drive, Albany, Auckland.

Reproduced, printed and bound in Great Britain by
Cox & Wyman Ltd, Reading, Berks.

NORTH LANARKS
DIVISION
JMO 12/04

FOREWORD

It is appropriate that *Dark Skies: The Awakening* is being published in 1997. This is the 50th anniversary of events that took place outside Roswell, New Mexico, in July of 1947. The supposed crash of a UFO there has received so much publicity in the last ten years that it probably feels familiar to you – like an open secret that's not so much of a secret any more.

Guess again.

Dark Skies – first as a TV series and now as this book – seeks to make everything new again by digging through the history books and unearthing alternative explanations to almost everything. The premise is simple. Our future's happening in our past.

Consider this. If Roswell was a UFO instead of a weather balloon, then it logically follows that there must be an entire suppressed history of alien contact. Not only that, because of the enormity of the secret, events which on the surface would seem to bear no relevance to the flying saucer phenomenon may, in fact, have been deeply affected by it. These events could be as serious as the Kennedy assassination and as seemingly benign as the Beatles' appearance on Ed Sullivan.

Paranoid? To be sure.

Speculation? Without a doubt.

True? Anything's possible.

Dark Skies, then, is a bold alternative history which isn't

5

afraid to create what can be called the 'Unification Theory' of UFOs. In other words, co-creator Brent Friedman and I have built a framework in which there is a consistent explanation for such disparate events as crop circles, abductions, Grays, Nazi saucer blueprints, variable descriptions of aerial phenomena and even cattle mutilations.

Also, as you read this excellent novelization by Stan Nicholls, you will be introduced to an entirely new vocabulary of alien contact as well, including the Hive, cerebral evictions, the A.R.T. and Singularity. You'll meet historical characters from Bobby Kennedy to John Lennon interacting with our main characters, John Loengard and Kim Sayers. You'll also meet key players in the world of ufology like Betty Hill and Jesse Marcel. It's a rich stew of history, intrigue and science fiction.

We chose the 1960s as the place to begin this epic story for several reasons. First, this decade is clearly the most colourful in recent history. This is also the time when the entire phenomenon began to be treated more seriously. Flying saucers became Unidentified Flying Objects. Little green men became extra-terrestrials. Contactees being hosted to an afternoon trip to Venus became abductees who were taken like lab animals and subjected to bizarre medical experiments. And, in the *Dark Skies* universe, the crash at Roswell was eclipsed in importance by the discovery of Patient Zero in Boise, Idaho on 12 February 1962.

Don't think you have to believe in UFOs as an extra-terrestrial reality to enjoy all of this. As I've told the staff of our series, belief is not a requirement of employment. Neither is it a requirement of readership. If you're a sceptic, so be it. Look at *Dark Skies* as as parallel universe where the events you are about to contemplate were true. Then, when you've finished, go back to your own universe and your own life. Be warned, however. You may never look at the news headlines in the same way.

And, on the other hand, if you do believe – welcome to

the *Dark Skies* resistance. Do not be afraid. The fight for Humanity demands your courage.

Bryce Zabel
Co-Creator, Executive Producer
20 March 1997
Los Angeles, California

Prologue

Sixty thousand feet over Peshawar, West Pakistan
1 May 1960

He had no way of knowing he was about to fly into history.

The palms of his gloved hands were clammy. He was clutching the joystick much tighter than strictly necessary. Behind the cumbersome face mask his breathing was laboured.

Craning his head, he peered into the surrounding gloom, anxious to locate the target before he was spotted himself. At this height the atmosphere was thin, but still dense enough to buffet the aircraft. The dimly lit instruments danced a little jig. He gently nudged the controls and his flight path steadied. It was cold as Hades out there, but beads of perspiration trickled through his crew-cut and sweat dampened the armpits of his blue-grey USAF uniform. Yet despite the tension, and the fear, the thrill of the illicit remained. Piloting one of the world's most advanced airplanes in a game of hide and seek was exhilarating.

Only this was no game. Unlike the dozens of simulations he'd undergone in training, it was real. And the stakes were life or death.

There was some small comfort in knowing his matt black aircraft bore no navigation lights or markings of any kind, making visual recognition that much harder. The jet's speed and altitude capabilities were additional assets. But none of that meant he couldn't be detected, or was any less vulnerable to a Russian missile.

He accelerated, intent on the search.

Time to report. He keyed his throat mike. 'Majestic, this is Talon. I've got a tally-ho on the bogey. Eleven o'clock, manoeuvring. I'm on a heading of zero-three-zero with Mach-two.'

Several thousand miles and two continents away, the military communications facility buzzed with purposeful activity. Decked out with state-of-the-art technology, and hidden beneath the capital's streets where day and night had no meaning, Majestic HQ was classified ultra top secret.

Its operations crew were about equally divided between those wearing civilian clothes and personnel in air force or naval air uniforms.

The pilot's message arrived on a tide of static. Leaning forward, Chief of Operations Phil Albano punched his transmission button. 'Roger, Talon.'

'I've never seen a Russian aircraft quite like this before,' the speakers crackled.

Two men stood at the far side of the bunker, engaged in a whispered conversation. Captain Frank Bach, the younger of the pair, may have been outranked by a good third of the people around him, but he had the air of someone who was clearly in charge. Abruptly he held up a hand, cutting off his companion in mid-sentence. Then without a word he turned his back on him and strode toward the control area.

Allen Dulles, head of the Central Intelligence Agency, fumed silently at so casual a dismissal.

As Bach reached the banks of radio equipment, the pilot's tense voice boomed out again. 'Majestic, if I maintain this heading I'm gonna be over Soviet airspace. Advise, please.'

Bach snatched Albano's microphone, thumbing its switch. 'Talon, this is MJ Command. How long before you're compromised?'

The momentary delay before the answer came seemed an eternity. 'I'd say about ninety seconds. That's if I can keep up with him, Majestic.'

Absently scratching his cheek, Bach paused for thought. Dulles pushed forward. 'We can't go in, Frank! Ike has a summit conference with Khrushchev in two days.'

Bach regarded the bureau chief with something very much like contempt. 'I have larger concerns,' he told him coldly. He returned his attention to the mike. 'Talon, you are authorized to break the border.'

Dulles flushed with anger, a pulse beating in his temple at the prospect of an incident that could easily melt the cold war to red hot conflict. 'This is insanity!' he hissed.

'If you're not on board, Allen,' Bach said, 'maybe you should leave.'

The CIA man met Bach's eyes, saw the unbending determination there and bit back his rejoinder. He gave a tiny resigned nod and sank into a chair.

Bach ignored him and turned to address the shift, many of whom had abandoned their work stations and were watching the exchange with stunned expressions. 'This is why we're here, gentlemen,' he reminded them. 'You have your orders.'

They hurried back to their positions.

Albano moved to a transmitter housed under an enormous screen showing a world map. He activated the mike. 'Incirlik tracking, this is Washington. We need high-band telemetry in Section A, vector seven.'

An illuminated line appeared on the map, its trajectory taking it directly towards the Soviet Union.

In his cramped cockpit at the atmosphere's edge, the pilot's only attendants were frigid glittering stars, sharp against the ebony backdrop. Glancing hull-down he could just make out the Earth's curve, an inky half sphere with the mighty Himalayas reduced to dark wrinkles. Behind him lay the faint gleam of Bombay and Calcutta, and the charcoal velvet of the Indian Ocean. Ahead, a crescent of milky light girdled the horizon, ambassador of the rising sun on the globe's far side.

Then he saw it.

Out in the empty night, port side, something shone with an eerie radiance. Something he couldn't identify. He banked, bringing the aircraft round for a closer look.

A trail of strange blue fire marked the enemy's wake. The young pilot homed in, his puzzlement increasing. He couldn't figure out the class of airplane he was approaching. All he could see was an indefinable silhouette.

The snowcaps of the Hindu Kush rolled below as he dredged every erg of force from the jet. His concentration was so focused he didn't even notice he was grinding his teeth.

Little by little he seemed to draw the target craft towards him.

Then he saw that its tail lights weren't tail lights. The craft had no tail. And as he got nearer, he began to make out its shape. It was oval. Different coloured lights rotated around its hull. It looked for all the world like a jewelled Fabergé egg.

'Base, I know I got one of the best planes we build, but whatever this guy's got, I want one too.'

Suddenly the craft shot upwards at fantastic speed, seeming to transform instantly into a flash of light.

He blinked, stupefied, and fought to control his excitement. Sheer professionalism kept his voice calm. 'Majestic, I've just witnessed an impossible vertical ascent. Loss of visual contact . . .' he glanced at the control panel '. . . and my radar screen is clear. Fuel level less than two thousand pounds. Advise.'

In Majestic HQ, Bach was visibly enraged, disappointed at having lost his quarry. He jabbed the mike button and muttered, 'Stand by, Talon.'

Dulles was talking on a telephone. He covered the mouthpiece. 'My people say the Soviets have no idea we're up there yet.'

Bach nodded. 'All right.' He snapped an order at

Albano. 'Get NATO on the horn. See if Turkey will clear our boy for landing, and—'

A blast of sound from the radio cut across him. The pilot was shouting 'Oh my God! Base, we got a real problem up here!'

High above Russian territory, he was near panic. His original target had vanished and been replaced by something else. Another craft, at least half a mile in length.

As he gaped at it, the massive object dropped into his path. It was pulsing with energy. His cockpit flooded with blinding light.

The craft hung in front of him, the size of a dozen football stadiums, brighter than Times Square on New Year's.

Pulling back on the throttle, the pilot arced his aircraft into a bone-crunching evasive manoeuvre. He yankd hard on the joystick, putting himself into a dizzying climb. Thermals ripped at his wings. G-force pummelled his chest. The aircraft wasn't designed for these kind of aerobatics and he risked stalling. But he had to get away.

Over the headset he heard a flurry of background audio from Majestic's controllers.

'I don't know what I'm looking at!' he yelled. 'But it's the size of three cruise ships!'

The bunker was alive with frantic activity. But in truth Majestic's operatives were helpless to do anything except listen.

'Oh, God.' The pilot's voice was barely audible. 'This is . . . incredible!'

'Talon, what is your altitude?' Bach demanded.

'Base, everything's gone crazy. My instruments. Everything. I'm breaking apart!'

'We need a recovery team out of Wiesbaden and in the air,' Bach ordered. 'Now!' As subordinates rushed to obey, he returned to the microphone. 'Talon, man down security code Two Alpha. Repeat, security code Two Alpha. Do you read?'

'Mayday! Mayday! Mayday! I'm in a flat spin. I must eject. I repeat, I'm ejecting from this aircraft!'

Bach listened to the pneumatic whine of the ejector seat, followed by the high-pitched whistle of the aircraft in free-fall. In seconds, static drowned out the sound.

Then the radio died.

On the other side of the world, the U2 spy plane screamed to oblivion.

And for Francis Gary Powers the terror was just beginning.

1

Washington DC
3 October 1961

The green '57 Chevrolet convertible slowed to a crawl as it drew level with the White House. Soft autumn sunshine bathed the president's official residence. Trees on the lawn beyond the gates were turning fiery reds and rusty golds. To Kimberly Sayers, the scene was like something from a fairy tale. 'It's *beautiful*, John,' she whispered.

The driver behind them sounded his horn and broke the spell.

John Loengard grinned. 'Sure is, Kim.' He jabbed a thumb at the following car. 'But that guy doesn't appreciate us rubbernecking. How about we park and take a look around?' Checking the mirror, he edged the Chevy back into the stream of traffic.

'Yeah, and maybe find someone to take a photo of us for the folks back home.' Her eyes were bright with excitement. 'Who'd have thought we'd end up here in Washington?'

Loengard gave her an affectionate glance. An Alice band held her shoulder-length bronze hair off her forehead before it rose in a backcombed crown. It was exactly the same style the First Lady favoured.

'Well, knowing how much you admire the Kennedys,' he replied, 'I guess anybody could have worked it out.'

Kim smiled at his teasing. 'Either that, or they found out

what a hotshot you were at UCLA. Then they knew Congress just couldn't get along without you.'

'Me?' he responded with mock innocence. 'I'm only going to be an aide to an aide to a congressman. You're the one that's going to be working with Jackie K.'

Her eyes sparkled again. 'I know, John, and I still can't believe it. It really *is* like Camelot around here. Anything can happen!'

In his quieter way, Loengard's enthusiasm equalled hers. 'You're right. If two college graduates can make it to government in one easy jump, we might really make a difference.'

She gently touched his arm. 'Why don't we leave the tourist bit for now? Let's go home.'

Home.

The word had a special ring to it, which not even their difficulty in finding the place again could spoil. After all, they'd only seen it once, on that far-off day in summer when they flew out from California for their interviews.

It was near sundown when they finally drew up outside the four-storey, slightly down-at-heel house in George-town.

Their first home together.

Kim slid out of the car. Mindful that the Chevy was John's pride and joy, she took care not to slam the door behind her. Almost running, she led him along the path and palmed the heavy doorbell. Half a minute passed, and she was about to ring a second time when the landlord, Mr Chesney, appeared. Pushing late middle age, his vaguely shabby, threadbare appearance aptly matched the house. But as on their original meeting, he was amiable enough.

They exchanged pleasantries and followed him to the second floor. On the gloomy landing he fumbled with a bunch of keys. When at last they got into the apartment they were faced with mounds of boxes, most piled on the furniture heaped in the middle of the floor. A worn couch was the only thing not completely covered.

'They delivered it all yesterday,' Chesney explained. 'Said if anything's missing you should make a list.'

Kim wandered across to the big bay window overlooking the street. John stayed with Chesney while he disentangled a set of keys from the many on his ring and handed them over.

Then the landlord stepped to one side of the small mountain of possessions and called, 'You need anything, Mrs Loengard, just ask.'

Kim turned and favoured him with a bright smile. 'I will, thanks.'

Chesney lingered for a few awkward seconds before leaving them to it.

As soon as he'd gone, they fell giggling into each other's arms. Kim scanned the room, ignoring the faded paint and peeling wallpaper, choosing instead to admire the graceful ceiling mouldings.

'Compared to my dorm', she decided, 'this place is a palace.'

John laughed. 'Nothing's too good for *Mrs* Loengard.'

'Oh, don't worry. So long as we pay the rent on time, he won't ask any questions.'

She pecked at his cheek and wandered off to explore the bedroom.

Loengard began sifting through their heaps of belongings and soon retrieved the familiar square-boxed red and cream record player. Along with the Chevy it was his most prized possession. He placed it on a crate, plugged it in and reached for the packages of discs. Popping open the lid, he flipped through the stack of 45s until he found the song above all others that he wanted Kim to hear.

The deep bass throb of the introduction to Ben E. King's 'Stand By Me' was all it took to bring her back to the living room and into John's outstretched arms.

He held her tightly, the top of her head nestling below his chin, as he quietly mouthed the lyrics.

She looked up at his handsome features, a mischievous

expression on her face. 'You know what? We should have made new wallpaper part of the deal.'

He said nothing, but started to sway in a close, mildly erotic dance.

Kim slowly joined in, letting the long hard strength of his body thrill her. 'You amaze me,' she said. 'I'm thinking about decorating and you're already right at home.'

He moved subtly against her, caressing her back, then brought a hand up to stroke her cheek. 'We could just get married, you know.'

She tenderly kissed his nose. 'You really don't want to lose this apartment, do you?'

'What I really don't want to lose is you.'

'That'll never happen, John.'

'You know, most women wouldn't want to pass on an opportunity like this.'

He said it in a jokey way, but she knew him well enough to sense the serious intent beneath his words. She made her reply just as light. 'Well, I admit the chance to smash chiffon wedding cake all over your face *is* tempting.'

'So what do you say?'

Kim grew thoughtful, her playfulness evaporating. 'John, if we get married now, then I really am "Mrs Loengard". First I have to be Kim Sayers. And I haven't quite figured out who she is yet. I want to marry you, I really do. But we have all the time in the world.'

He registered the fierce sincerity in her voice and took a different tack. 'You know what I love best about you?'

'Everything,' she beamed. And added, 'You know what I love best about *you*?'

He shook his head.

She stretched to whisper in his ear and a smile lit his features. They sank to the couch.

The record finished, the player's stylus clicking repetitively in the groove surrounding the label.

They didn't notice.

*   *   *

The next few weeks seemed to hurtle past at breakneck speed.

Kim settled into her duties in Jackie Kennedy's office and John was quickly absorbed by the routine of working for Democratic congressman Charles Pratt on Capitol Hill.

But he wasn't content.

He found himself used as a glorified gopher, spending most of his time on menial errands. As for Pratt, Loengard considered him little more than a fat five-termer with a perpetual farmer's tan who never thought past his next election. If you could call that thinking. It was getting to the point where he would have given anything for a real job.

On an afternoon when the chill of late Fall was sharp enough to turn his breath into huffing clouds, Loengard sprinted up the steps to the congressman's offices. He bore yet another cardboard tray of coffee and doughnuts, and brooded, not for the first time, on how there had to be a better way of employing his talents.

He sped along the hallway and through a swing door. The usual chaos greeted him. Too many people trying to work in far too crammed a space. A cacophony of voices bawling into telephones, the scene swathed in a fog of cigarette smoke.

He placed a polystyrene cup on the nearest desk and winked at the harried secretary. 'There you go, Renee; one coffee, cream, no sugar. You seen Simonson?'

In the middle of the phone call, she gestured with her chin.

Mark Simonson, Loengard's immediate boss, was a dishevelled thirtysomething who wore a permanently harassed expression at the best of times. Right now, at Pratt's side as they pushed their way through the crowd, he looked even more stressed. John dumped the tray and hurried over to join them.

They were only dimly aware of his presence. Simonson, his patience fraying, was trying to explain to the congressman what line to adopt in an upcoming vote. Typically, Pratt seemed not to be taking it in, and it was obvious from Simonson's tone that he'd run through his briefing at least half a dozen times.

'This is the *amendment* to the Housing Bill,' he recited, as though addressing a backward child. 'We are *against* the amendment and *for* the bill.'

Pratt gave an almost imperceptible nod. Then as they were about to pass the front desk he noticed a manila envelope and his manner darkened. Snatching up the slim package, he brandished it angrily at his chief aide.

'What the *hell's* going on around here?' he demanded. 'This was supposed to be delivered an hour ago!'

Simonson glared back at him. 'Congressman, I happen to think that getting this amendment defeated is more important than constituent tickets for a tour of the US mint.'

Crumpling the envelope in a meaty fist, Pratt shoved his ruddy face close to Simonson's. 'Son, you think about this: those people gave me a lot of money for my last campaign. A *whole* lot of money!'

Loengard saw his chance. If he played his cards right, he might end up as more than a lowly office boy. He drew a deep breath.

'Mr Pratt, sir, I can take that now.' He slipped the envelope from the congressman's hand and turned to Simonson. 'Sorry, Mark. I should have delivered this yesterday. Like you asked.'

Pratt's plebeian features brightened. 'Loengard, you make sure these people know that I *personally* called in their favour.'

'Yes, sir.'

Without further word, the beefy congressman elbowed his way from the office. He reminded John of a bulldozer cutting a path through a stand of saplings.

'Thanks, Loengard,' Simonson said. 'I owe you one.'

'Just trying to help out. Not that I don't enjoy catering to Fresno's favourite son.'

John's boss put a hand on his arm. 'Look, I know you're being wasted. Welcome to Washington.' He started to walk away.

Loengard's heart sank. On impulse, he added, 'You know I could make things easier for you.'

Simonson stopped and looked back over his shoulder. 'I'm not sure I'm ready to have Pratt killed just yet.'

John smiled. 'Look, you're overworked and I'm bored. C'mon. Just give me a shot.'

Simonson tilted his head to one side, silently considering the offer. Then he said, 'OK. Follow me.'

Not quite believing his luck, John trailed him to his desk.

'The congressman has a budget subcommittee meeting at the end of the year.' He tapped a stubby finger on a stack of bulging files. 'He wants to nominate one of these programmes for the hit list. Knock out even one project and we can save quite a bit of cash. So I want to find out what they're doing and what they're spending. You can do the reports, Loengard. Make 'em three pages, typed. And don't use any big words. He's a farmer.'

'Mark, you won't regret this. Thank you.'

Simonson was already rushing off. 'Just don't forget that package!' he reminded him.

Loengard carted the files to his own desk and sat down to examine them.

The first report was a dry as dust summary of the activities of an obscure government department he'd never heard of and whose function wasn't immediately apparent. The second was just as cryptic, and contained as many meaningless target objectives and figures. Sighing, he tossed that aside, too.

It was the third report that would change his life for ever.

2

Wright-Patterson Air Force Base, Dayton, Ohio

As soon as he read the content of the third file, Loengard had booked a flight to Wright-Patterson.

The report concerned a USAF agency that meant nothing to him. It was called Project Blue Book. And when he leafed through it, he was amazed. Because it seemed Blue Book's function was to study UFOs.

Unexplained aerial phenomena.

Flying saucers.

It just had to be baloney; a crazy programme using public money to investigate the delusions of cranks and fruitcakes. There were even references to people claiming to have seen little green men. Or more accurately, little *grey* men.

In fact, the Blue Book programme wasn't enormously expensive in governmental terms. But if Loengard could show its work to be nonsense, and recommend the project's cancellation, he'd earn brownie points with Pratt and maybe further his own career. The way he saw it, that justified a trip to Ohio.

Once he produced his congressional pass, he got into the Blue Book offices with surprisingly little fuss. He was allowed access to the project's records with similar ease, although he had to share the room with a lieutenant acting as a minder. At first, Loengard found it slightly uncomfortable to be watched as he examined the mounds of paperwork, even though the young officer was quite personable, but he was soon absorbed by what he considered the amusing absurdity of much of the material.

He was allowing himself a brief fantasy, in which President Kennedy thanked him personally for saving the taxpayers millions, when the lieutenant leaped to his feet.

'Major Friend, *sir*!' He directed a smart salute at the door.

As he swept in, Friend gave the impression of a crisp, no-nonsense military career man, all razor creases and broomstick back. His face was firmly lined, his dark hair streaked with silver. He returned the salute and strode to John's desk, offering his hand.

'You must be Loengard. Major Robert Friend. Been running Blue Book since fifty-eight.' He took in the masses of paper. 'Why has Pratt sent one of his eager beavers to dig through our files?'

A little taken aback by the man's directness, John was hesitant. 'Well . . . I . . . uh . . . I think he's just interested in seeing the taxpayers get their money's worth.'

'Really?' He made no attempt to hide his scepticism. 'You know how many cases we had last year?'

Loengard checked his notepad. 'Five hundred and fifty-seven.'

The major raised his eyebrows slightly, impressed by the diligence. 'Divided by exactly three field investigators. Son, we're the biggest bargain around.'

'I think he's more concerned with whether we should be spending anything on investigating, er, you know . . . flying saucers.'

'You're not a believer, I gather?'

John thought it prudent to avoid a direct answer. Clearing his throat, he said, 'If I could, I'd like to look through the most recent files you've got on the DC vicinity. You see, my boss wants me to check out some of these people himself.' He shrugged. 'Who knows? Maybe after I

23

see what kind of a bang-up job you're doing, I can convince the congressman to get you more funding.'

The major was unimpressed. 'I won't hold my breath.' He paused for a second, then nodded at the lieutenant. 'Give him what he needs. We've got nothing to hide.'

Portsmouth, New Hampshire
11 December 1961

A faint dusting of snow fell as Loengard steered his beat up old Chevy through the suburban streets.

It was dusk. Frost lay thick under the naked trees. Coloured lights outlined plastic sleighs, artificial snowmen and dangling decorations on the porches of the houses he slowly passed. He almost overshot the one he was looking for, a nondescript residence identical to all the others, except its adornments were a little more discreet.

Shivering, he brushed aside the road map covering his briefcase of Blue Book reports and the small carton Kim had given him. As he locked the car, he was aware of curtains twitching in nearby houses. He walked to the front door. A Christmas wreath was hanging on it. Absently, he spent a second straightening his tie before knocking.

The door opened just far enough for him to make out the person on the other side. He hadn't known quite what to expect, but after spending so much time delving into the Blue Book files he imagined being met by attention-seeking slobs whose favourite reading was the *National Inquirer*.

If first impressions were anything to go by, he was wrong. The middle-aged woman he saw had strong handsome features. She wore the kind of sober outfit favoured by the professional classes. Her dark eyes gleamed with innate intelligence.

'Mrs Betty Hill?'

She stared at him, coolly suspicious, and made no reply.

John tried a smile. 'Hi. I'm John Loengard. I just came from Wright-Patterson Air Force base and—'

The door began to close in his face. 'I wish you people would leave us alone,' she hissed through the crack.

'No, Mrs Hill, I don't work for the air force. We talked on the phone, remember? I'm from Congressman Charles Pratt's office.'

The door was stayed, then half opened again. She waited for him to say more.

'Look, if you feel like talking', he rushed on, 'my girlfriend baked this fruit cake for us.' He held out the cardboard box, almost dropping it in his haste.

She caught it before it fell.

John thought he was winning. Then a well-built, dark-skinned man appeared behind her. His expression was hard, verging on hostile. 'Is there a problem here?' he wanted to know.

'No, sir. I was just telling your wife that there's some new information about the sighting you reported.'

The Hills exchanged a glance Loengard couldn't read.

'If that's true,' Barney Hill asked, 'how come you need a cake to talk your way in here?'

John felt like a schoolboy caught in some embarrassing act. 'Good point, sir. Probably was a dumb idea. Look, I'll be honest with you. I was sent out to prove the air force investigation is a waste of money. But right now, let's just say I have an open mind.' He grinned. 'And this *is* a damn good cake.'

Somewhat reluctantly, they invited him in.

Loengard was ushered to a chair by the living room's blazing fire. After checking that they had no objection to him taping their conversation, he set up his recorder on a small telephone table. Using the lights of the Christmas tree to see by, he clicked a fresh spool on to the spindle, fumbling awkwardly under Barney's silent, unwavering gaze. Loengard was grateful when Betty arrived with mugs of coffee and plates of cake.

The atmosphere started to lighten.

Mrs Hill was the first to respond to John's initial questions about their experience. Her voice was low and punctuated with occasional pauses in which she looked up at him, apparently trying to gauge his reaction.

'We were returning from a vacation in Canada, down US-Three through the White Mountains to Portsmouth,' she recounted. 'It was after midnight, pretty close to a full moon. There weren't any other cars and all the motels were already closed.'

She turned to Barney. He stayed silent, so she went on. 'I saw it first. It looked like a big light that was following us, and then when I looked through the binoculars, I saw a double row of windows. Real windows!' Again she turned to her husband.

This time Barney heeded the mute appeal and took up the story. 'I thought she was crazy, but she made me stop the car anyway. I went out into a field with the binoculars . . .' He swallowed audibly. 'When I looked through those windows I saw . . . I saw about a half dozen . . . living beings . . . looking back at me.'

'You mean people?' Loengard said.

'I mean *living beings*.' The reply invited no argument.

'What did you do then?'

'I panicked. I thought I was going to be captured so I ran as fast as I could back to the car.' The veneer of his tough exterior was wearing thin.

Quietly, John asked, 'Were you actually . . . captured?'

Barney gaped at him helplessly. It was Betty who said, 'We don't know what happened. Next thing we know we're back in our car. But it's two hours later!' There was an unspoken plea behind her words. She wanted desperately to be believed.

Loengard considered himself a fair judge of character, and despite the fantastic content of their testimony he was starting to accept that the Hills sounded authentic. Even if there was only a shard of truth in what they were saying, this was potential dynamite.

He eyed his tape recorder. The reels turned steadily as their tale unfolded.

None of them remotely suspected that Loengard's

recorder wasn't the only mechanical witness to their conversation.

Attached to the underside of the phone was a round black plastic disc, approximately the size of a silver dollar. The listening device picked up every sound in the room and fed it directly into the telephone line. This ran to a pole further along the street, where a makeshift cable snaked down from a junction box to a parked truck bearing the name of a bakery. The vehicle was all but invisible in the fading twilight.

Inside the van, two men hunched over a stack of electronic equipment. They were dressed in white jackets with the company logo, and each wore headphones. A soft glow from an array of illuminated dials lit their intense faces. The spools of a bulky tape recorder rotated silently.

A little tinny, but quite audibly, Loengard's voice filled their headsets. 'Pratt won't be able to ignore this.'

The eavesdroppers exchanged a sombre gaze. The older of the two whispered, 'This is not good news.'

Betty was saying, 'I think he should do one of those congressional investigations, that's what I think he should do.'

'I don't know about that,' Loengard replied. 'You'd probably have to testify. And people might . . . say things.'

'I'm a black man married to a white woman,' Barney interjected. 'People already say things. If I can find out what the hell I saw and where I was, I'd tell my story to the whole damn world!'

The younger of the phone-tappers directed a quizzical glance at his colleague.

His face impassive, the older man slid a hand into his jacket and drew a snub-nosed service revolver. He flipped out the loaded chamber and gave it a spin, then snapped it back in place with a purposeful click.

3

Light snow was falling as Loengard powered his beloved Chevy along the quiet country roads.

He checked the passenger seat for the fifth time to make sure the vital spool of tape was still there. The Hills' testimony could be his passport to freedom, an escape from menial jobs. But it was more than just that. If there was only a fragment of truth in what he'd been told it would represent one of the most exciting developments in human history.

Snapping out of his reverie, John put his foot down, racing as fast as he dared through winding empty lanes. With the soft drone of the radio his sole companion, he was aware of how sparsely populated this part of the country was. The bustle of Washington could have been on another planet.

Scorching along the bottom of a valley, he passed rows of ghostly birch trees. As he topped the rise they gave way to moon-silvered pines.

When he realized the silvery glow wasn't moonlight he was at first baffled.

His puzzlement turned to alarm as something black and bulky sheered overhead.

A beam of light stabbed down from the craft, bathing him in blinding radiance. He struggled to control the car, one hand shading his eyes. Static drowned the radio. Blinking into the sky, he could make out a hovering, ebony shadow. A deep thrumming sound pulsed from the object. On either side of the road trees quivered and bowed in its downdraft.

The craft swooped, heading straight at him.

Hearing about aliens was one thing, being captured himself quite another.

Palms slick with moisture, heart pounding, Loengard tried to evade the thing. He swerved hard to the left, then the right. The Chevy bumped on uneven ground, skidded and slewed to a halt. Its engine died.

Near panic, mind racing, he scanned his surroundings for signs of the aliens the Hills had reported. He fumbled with the ignition key, stamped hard on the accelerator.

Nothing.

The dazzling light grew more intense as the craft slowly sank to the road in front of him.

He tried to restart the engine but it was useless. Even if the object hadn't disabled his electrical circuits, John knew he'd flooded the carburettor. He flung open the door and scrambled out. The craft rocked as it settled, giving out a roar so deafening he felt dizzy. He took a deep breath and fled into the darkness.

The wind lashed at his coat, hampering him, and he almost fell as he stumbled and blundered over the rough terrain. But somehow he reached the shelter of the trees. Crouching low in the flailing undergrowth, his chest felt banded with iron and he panted for air. Only then did he dare look back.

A hatch had opened in the craft's side. Four figures, indistinct silhouettes against the glare, were spilling out of it with frightening speed.

John hunkered lower, afraid that the hammering of his heart would give him away. Who knew what detection devices these aliens might have?

The quartet of creatures moved swiftly in his direction. As they got nearer he began to make out some detail. In a matter of seconds they were close enough to see what they were.

Men.

Men dressed in black.

Men with guns.

Now he recognized the noise the craft was making. It was the thudding rhythm of a helicopter's rotors.

John took off, leaping fallen branches and crashing through brambles tangling his feet. Under the savage force of the wind, swaying trees reached out as if to grab him. Casting a desperate glance back over his shoulder, he toyed with the idea of stopping and trying to talk his way out of this nightmare. But the guns were too forbidding a bar to conversation.

Sweat freezing to his face, he struggled uphill. All around, darts of platinum light pierced the shadows, making it hard for him to see where he was going.

His pursuers didn't seem to have the same difficulty. The leader was so close that Loengard could hear the man's harsh breathing and the rustle of ferns being swept aside.

Drawing from the strength terror lent, John put on a burst of speed.

Scrambling over a ridge, he found himself in a clearing. If he could only cross it he might lose himself in the denser woodland at the bottom of the slope. Then it dawned on him, horribly, that the road had made a dog-leg. He was back on the tarmac.

Before he could duck for cover again the man behind tackled him. John smacked to the tarmac. He managed to rise to his hands and knees. Another black-clad pursuer smashed him down again. His second attempt to rise was halted by the sound of multiple revolvers being cocked. He froze.

One of the men entered his field of vision, his features lit by the 'copter's searchlight. He had an uncompromising profile, a widow's peak and thinning, windswept hair. There was no gun in his hand. Cold confidence gave him all the authority he needed.

The man reached down. John flinched, then felt foolish when he realized he was being offered help to stand. He hesitated for a second, then took the outstretched hand and was hauled to his feet.

'Very impressive.' The man's voice was just loud enough to be heard above the helicopter's idling engine. His accent was standard, if crisp, Eastern Seaboard. 'You've got a real talent, Mr Loengard.'

'How . . . how do you know who I am?'

The man made no reply. Instead he gestured at one of his gun-toting cohorts and said, 'Get the tape.'

John turned his head a little and saw the subordinate dash over to the Chevy. He wanted to protest, but the guns kept him silent.

'Let me set the record straight for you, John,' his captor told him, his tone almost reasonable. 'Betty and Barney Hill saw an airplane go off course. They're not going to testify before Congress, or Pratt, or anybody else. Is that clear?'

Anger was beginning to outweigh Loengard's fear, and he figured that if these people were going to kill him they would have done it already. 'Why not?' he replied. 'Who the hell *are* you?'

If he thought his display of aggression was going to impress them, he was wrong. The other men moved closer, radiating an almost tangible menace.

Their leader shrugged. 'I'm a figment of your imagination, John. I do not exist.' He paused to nod acknowledgement at the henchman returning from John's car with the stolen tape. 'This incident never happened,' he went on. 'You drove home uneventfully. Tomorrow you'll file a report with Pratt telling him Blue Book doesn't cost enough to merit his attention.'

Another of the gunmen addressed his boss. 'You want me to put him to bed, Captain?' He stepped closer to Loengard, revolver raised.

Suddenly, shockingly, the minion loudly released his gun's bolt an inch from John's ear, making him recoil.

The fear was back. He fought not to show it.

Like a gaping tunnel, the gun's barrel moved to fill John's gaze.

The gunman smirked and pressed the weapon to Loengard's forehead. It felt like the cool kiss of death. The man's finger tightened on the trigger.

'What are you *doing?*' John yelled. 'I haven't done anything! *Help!*'

The hammer clicked on an empty chamber.

Robbed of strength, John's knees gave way. The henchman grabbed his collar in one beefy gloved hand and yanked him upright.

The man with the widow's peak, the one they called Captain, thrusted his face into John's. 'Mr Loengard. *Mr Loengard!*'

As though from a great distance, John heard himself mutter, 'What?'

'Keep your nose out of our business. Or next time we'll make a house call.'

Abruptly, as though he had lost all interest, he walked off towards the chopper.

The tough with a stranglehold on John's collar remained. His thin lips stretched in a twisted rictus of pleasure. A lust for violence lived in his eyes. 'You're lucky, college boy,' he snarled. 'The man says you get to stay up late.'

He let go his hold and delivered a piledriver punch to Loengard's stomach. It was followed by a sharp crack of the pistol barrel against the side of his head.

Jagged lightning forked through Loengard's brain. Near retching, he doubled over and curled into himself, submerged in a universe of pain. By the time his head stopped spinning the gunmen were climbing into the unmarked helicopter. Loengard watched it rise noisily and fade into the velvet sky.

'What have I gotten myself into?' he whispered.

It was almost nine in the morning when he reached Capitol Hill.

He didn't dare use the staff car park outside the Congressman's headquarters, instead he pulled in behind a supermarket. Even then he couldn't bring himself to enter his place of employment and slipped into the diner opposite.

Sitting with a coffee and untouched doughnut in front of him he watched passers-by trudging through the snow outside. Across the street, people were going up the stairs and into the building where he worked. They were clinging to the handrail, trying not to slip. John's fears were much worse than a tumble on the ice.

Washington DC, capital of the free world and bastion of democracy, felt dangerous and oppressive.

The diner was crowded, its windows steaming up, and there was a line of customers at the counter. He knew he couldn't sit there for ever. No sooner had the thought occurred than a young, gum-chewing waitress appeared and snapped, 'You having another coffee, bud? Only I want the table.'

He got to his feet reluctantly, but knew he couldn't put off going into work any longer.

As he crossed the street a helicopter flew over and instinctively he ducked. It was an ordinary USAF flight. He felt an idiot, his discomfort compounded by the odd looks people were giving him. Head down, he hurried on.

Once inside, he scooted to the office, mumbling tight-lipped greetings as he made for his desk. Hanging his coat by the photos and clippings of JFK adorning the wall, he slumped into the chair. His head still throbbed and his hands were trembling slightly. He need not have bothered with the aspirins for all the good they'd done.

A stack of papers and folders were waiting for him. On top was a manila envelope bearing his name. He opened it with apprehension. It contained a report headed, 'Project Blue Book'. There were three closely typed sheets with a budget chart attached.

He hastily read through the summary. It exonerated Blue Book in exactly the way the so called Captain had demanded. The document credited him as its author. But he hadn't written it.

Somebody slapped him on his shoulder. He dropped the report and whirled around.

Simonson leaned over and took it. 'Hey, Loengard, this is great,' he beamed, riffling the pages. 'Project Blue Book. Don't you sleep? I was going to give you to the end of the week to compile this.'

'Uh, Mark, can I get that back, please?'

His boss was too busy examining it. When he reached the conclusion, he read aloud, ' "In summary, Project Blue Book is not only a viable organization, but a detailed cost analysis shows this programme to be an insubstantial line item cut." ' His eyebrows arched in surprise. 'Pretty bold for your first memo.'

'You don't understand. I didn't write this.'

Simonson took a hard look at Loengard's face, then glanced around the bustling office. It seemed no-one had heard. He jerked his head and without a word led the way to a conference room. At this time of day it was empty, the polished tables bare. Simonson moved swiftly to the room's only window and drew the blind.

'Sit down before you fall down. You look like hell. Now what's this all about?'

Hesitantly, Loengard related the story. Simonson listened without interrupting, his expression neutral. At the finish he said, 'Helicopters, armed paramilitaries, and you suspect wire taps. Do you have any idea what you've stumbled on to, John?'

'The Hills definitely saw something. What it was, I don't know.'

'Probably some secret weapon we're going to surprise the Russians with.'

'In *New Hampshire?*'

'Test flight? I don't know.' Simonson was quiet for a moment, concentration furrowing his brow. 'But this explains all the stories I've heard about the Black Ops budget.'

'Huh?'

'Operations that don't show up in the budget.

34

Someone's diverting funds, and you caught them red-handed.'

'I didn't catch anybody, Mark. They caught *me*. And I think these guys are dangerous.'

'They just wanted to scare you.'

'They managed that,' Loengard commented drily.

'So consider this your chance to get even.'

The door flew open, banging the wall and startling them both. Congressman Pratt stormed in, beefy face mottled with anger. 'Simonson, what the hell's going on? Or is my ten o'clock briefing at ten-thirty these days?'

Simonson casually slid the report back into its envelope as though it were of no account. 'I was just going over Loengard's trip, Congressman. I'll be right in.'

Pratt directed a testy look at John. 'So is this Blue Book worth its salt?'

'I'm, er, working on the report now, sir.'

The congressman grunted and took himself off, pointedly leaving the door open.

John nodded at the envelope. 'What are we going to do about that?'

Simonson walked to the door, checking that Pratt was out of earshot. 'We do nothing.'

'Nothing? You heard him. He wants it now.'

'This is our chance to score points for us, not him.' He glanced outside again and added, 'I'll stall the farmer. Whatever you do, keep your head down.'

Then he was gone.

Loengard sat quietly, mulling over the events of the last twelve hours. He had no idea what was going on, and even less of a clue as to the identity of the mysterious Captain who had taken such an unpleasant interest in him.

4

In the days that followed, Loengard's terrifying experience played on his mind. The enigmatic Captain and his gun-toting hoods might turn up anywhere. He thought of Kim, alone in their apartment or walking the unfamiliar streets of Washington, and he was afraid. So afraid that he couldn't stop digging in the hope of discovering something, anything that might indicate who the Captain was.

Night after night, John burrowed through mountains of files at the Library of Congress. Old newspaper cuttings, records of flying-saucer investigations and military personnel files going back decades were all scrutinized. He even followed leads that had him lying to old ladies so he could plunder their dead husbands' possessions.

It was in the suburbs of Delaware that he finally hit pay dirt when a kindly widow took him through to her garage and let him loose. She smilingly brought him tea and cake, and it was as if she were heaping coals of fire on his head. John had never thought he could sink so low. But the guilt didn't stop him searching her late husband's military trunk.

Among the crumbling documents he came across a memo headed 'TOP SECRET/MAJIC'. It was stapled to a yellowing copy of the *San Francisco Examiner* dated 14 July 1947. The newspaper's lead story concerned rumours about the recovery of a crashed flying saucer in a place called Roswell, New Mexico.

John forgot the cramp in his legs, the cold that had his

breath whitening in the air. So absorbed was he that he didn't even notice the black Sedan slowly gliding to a halt opposite the open garage door.

Then he found something even more significant. Tucked into the paper was a brittle black and white photograph. The subject was in military uniform. He was much younger, of course, with more hair and fewer lines on his face. His cheeks were fresh and free of the bags that would later appear under his eyes. But there was no doubt. It was the man who had stolen his tape and left him bleeding on a lonely country road.

On the back of the photo someone had written 'Captain Frank Bach'.

Loengard couldn't wait to tell Simonson.

It was late when he got back from the congressional offices. Kim was already asleep, which temporarily solved the problem of keeping secrets from her. John hated to do it, but the more she found out, the more she'd be at risk.

Loengard spent the night restlessly, his mind churning with speculation. Why was a navy captain so interested in flying saucers? And why had he singled out him for such vicious attention? When dawn seeped through the bedroom's cheap curtains, John gave up on sleep and quietly slipped from Kim's side.

Later, as he was blearily adjusting his tie, Kim swept into the bathroom. She kissed his cheek and surveyed herself in the mirror. Her make-up was immaculate, her hair teased back in soft wings that curled around her face. She pirouetted, showing off her neat tailored suit and white blouse with its delicate fall of lace at the throat.

'You look great,' John said. 'Where are you going?'

Preening in the mirror, adjusting first one earring and then the other, she replied teasingly, 'Oh, nowhere you'd care about. Just the White House.'

Before he could respond, she swept out. Bemused, John followed her into the living room, watching as she collected her keys and purse.

Finally, Kim took pity on him and said, 'Remember that lunch with Lisa Bentley you thought was going to be a waste of time? Well, she referred me to Barbara Collins, who I called, who referred me to Jennifer Ruehmann, who knows Alicia Burnside, who's an assistant to the First Lady.'

'Another ruthless power grab! Wish *I'd* called Lisa Bentley.'

'Well, you can see her tonight. We're making lasagna. If you're good, you can have some.' Kim glanced at the stacks of paperwork John had left scattered over the dining table. 'Oh, and you can give us a place to eat by taking some of this stuff back to the office.'

'Uh, yeah. I'll clean that up. It's really just extra credit. I've got a new angle on something I haven't told anybody at work about yet.'

Busy organizing her handbag, she didn't notice how ill at ease he sounded. 'Just don't go overboard, John. I know how you can be. You never know when to quit.'

'That's what they told Kennedy when he was investigating labour racketeering. Didn't hurt his career.'

The phone rang. Kim ignored it. She grabbed her watch off the kitchen counter. 'I gotta go. Wish me luck.'

She kissed him and hurried out, slamming the door. John smiled. Then the phone shrilled again.

He snatched the receiver. 'Hello?'

'Simonson here. Turn on your TV. Channel Six.'

'Just a minute.' John crossed the room and clicked on the set.

The TV was showing news footage. A young man with a military haircut was walking briskly towards the camera. He was on a bridge, and behind him armed guards with long coats and flat-topped caps guarded a barrier. Someone else, back towards the screen, was walking in the opposite direction.

'An update on that high-level American-Soviet spy exchange of February tenth,' a newscaster announced. 'The pictures you're seeing from earlier this week are of

Lieutenant Francis Gary Powers, the American U2 pilot shot down over the Soviet Union two years ago, walking across the Glienicke Bridge towards freedom in West Berlin. He's passing Soviet spy, Colonel Rudolph Abel, heading toward the Communist-held Potsdam sector of East Berlin.'

Then the camera showed the man escorting Powers. It was Frank Bach.

Simonson's voice crackled over the telephone. 'That's your guy, isn't it?'

John was incredulous. 'Yeah, that's him.'

'Later this morning,' the reporter continued, 'Powers speaks to a closed-door session of the Senate Armed Services Committee. In other news . . .'

'Mark, we gotta get to Powers,' John insisted. 'He has to be involved in this too.'

'Stop right there. If Powers is involved, so is the president. Who do you think made the deal with Khrushchev?'

'This isn't just some military budget scandal any more.'

'That's the understatement of the year. This is quicksand, Loengard, pure and simple. You can count me out.'

'But Mark, this is the break we've been waiting for!'

'Not me. I've got a wife and kids. I'm out. It's over. You hear me? *Over.*'

The line went dead.

John slowly replaced the receiver. Then he slung his briefcase on the table and started cramming papers into it.

Inside Congress, he hurried along a marble corridor. Here and there people sat waiting and talking on the benches to either side. He scanned them nervously but they all seemed wrapped up in their own affairs. But he couldn't help wondering if any of them were secretly watching him. Since this thing had started, paranoia had become his normal state of mind. He tightened his hold on the precious briefcase of evidence.

He rounded a corner and stopped dead in his tracks.

Someone bumped into him and yelled, 'Hey, watch it!' John didn't even notice. He was transfixed by the sight of someone coming out of the elevator opposite.

Frank Bach.

Dressed in military uniform with a chestful of ribbons, Bach's demeanour was purposeful, even a little threatening. The lines on his face sagged downwards and the pouches under his eyes were dark with fatigue. But the eyes themselves were alert, and clamped on John.

He strode forward. Loengard tensed.

Then the lift disgorged several army officers. At their centre was Gary Powers.

The other elevator's doors opened and a mob of reporters surged out. Three TV crews barged their way along, frontmen shouting questions. Cameras flashed and a handful of radio reporters jostled to get their microphones under Powers' nose.

John felt a little safer with the press around.

One of the reporters bellowed, 'You had a poison needle! Why didn't you use it?'

Bach moved forward to shield the pilot. Strained, his face pale from months of captivity, and perhaps worse, Powers held up a hand to still the uproar.

'During everything I said or did over the past two years, I kept the best interests of the United States government in mind. I'm looking forward to telling my side of the story to the US Senate. Thank you.'

Bedlam broke out again as the reporters hurled more questions. Powers ignored them and pushed his way through a door marked Senate Armed Services Committee. A sign had been posted alongside reading 'Closed Session'.

Half the reporters peeled themselves away from the throng and dashed off, presumably in search of telephones. Others sat phlegmatically on the padded benches by the elevator, awaiting further developments.

Bach settled on a seat where he could keep an eye on the closed door. He reached a hand into his pocket and produced a pack of cigarettes. As he lit up he directed a smile at John, part ironic, part menacing.

Loengard took a deep breath to calm his thundering heart. After a long moment, he decided to act. He walked to the bench and sat beside Bach, clutching the briefcase to his chest. The Captain seemed unperturbed.

Loengard indicated the cigarette in Bach's nicotine-stained fingers. 'There's a new report from the surgeon general says those things can kill you.'

'All our days are numbered.' He took a drag and added pointedly, 'Some more than others.'

'I'm a member of the congressional staff. You can't rough me up here.'

'How's your "extra credit" coming along, John?'

The colour drained from Loengard's face. Bach couldn't have known about that phrase unless his and Kim's apartment was bugged.

'Not bad, *Captain Bach*,' he responded through clenched teeth. 'And let me tell you that although I don't know exactly who you work for now, I'm pretty close to the truth.'

Exhaling, Bach appeared to watch the smoke spiraling under the artificial lights, but Loengard was well aware that the man was covertly weighing him up.

'The truth? The truth is overrated, John.'

'Maybe. But what you're doing can't stay hidden for ever.' He had a sudden inspiration. Slipping his fingers inside his jacket, he pulled out a paper just far enough for Bach to see the edge of it. 'I've got a subpoena here from the US Congress. But if you agree to co-operate with me now, I'll protect our conversations. You'll not be named as a source in any hearing or investigation.'

John didn't get the reaction he expected. Bach grinned. Then he got up, dropped the cigarette butt and resolutely ground it under his heel. The symbolism of the action was obvious. 'Your faith in the power of Congress is touching.'

He started to walk away.

Loengard caught up with him in two strides. 'I've read

about Roswell. I know about Project Sign and Project Grudge. I already know a lot more than you think I do.'

'What else do you think you know?'

'Flying saucers don't come from outer space. You're building them, aren't you?'

Glancing back to make sure the reporters were out of sight, Bach grabbed Loengard by the shoulder. With a speed that seemed unnatural in one of his bulk, he reached a hand into John's inside pocket and removed the slip of paper. It was a dry-cleaning receipt.

'Subpoena for a Chinese laundry.' Bach crumpled it. 'You really got an iron set of 'em, don't you, son?'

'When I have to.'

'You have to understand, Mr Loengard, that truth has a price. All you've got to do is decide if you're willing to pay it.'

He turned and walked into the waiting elevator. As the doors swished shut, John stepped in beside him.

Loengard found himself in the passenger seat of Bach's nondescript sedan. As they pulled away he remembered a hundred movies about the Mafia and victims being taken for a ride. He had put himself totally in this man's power.

It was the rag-end of winter, and thin rain was falling as they cruised the capital's streets. Bach chain-smoked, lighting each new cigarette from the glowing butt of its predecessor. John tried opening the window, but found it was locked. He chewed his lip and kept his uneasiness to himself.

Bach flicked a smile at him. It wasn't comforting.

Entering a part of town Loengard was unfamiliar with, they eventually came to an unprepossessing concrete and glass structure typical of Washington's many government office blocks. Not that there were any signs indicating its function. The sedan slowed, turned and bumped down the slope leading to an underground car park.

John surreptitiously applied a little pressure to the door handle beside him. That was locked too.

Bach nosed the vehicle into an empty bay and killed the ignition. He came around to the passenger side and let John out. Then, taking the lead, he made for a robust steel door bearing a sign that read, 'Authorized Access Only'. John arrived just too late to see the code he punched into its electronic lock. The door slid aside for them. Loengard paused, weighing the options. Was he really ready to put his head in the lion's mouth?

'You already decided to go through this door,' Bach told him. 'Don't act like you have to think about it.'

John stepped through the entrance.

Inside, under harsh white light, an armed guard saluted Bach and frisked Loengard with meticulous thoroughness. They boarded an electric utility vehicle, Bach at the wheel, and began navigating what turned out to be a bewildering maze of harshly lit tunnels.

At length they came to a long window showing a crowded operations room. Towering banks of computers housed reels of spinning magnetic tape as big as dinner plates. Men in headphones, men at radar screens or typewriters, men at machines whose purpose was obscure, were working as busily as ants in a nest. Most of them were in uniform, jackets open at the neck or slung over chair backs. One stood, obviously shouting over to a lieutenant at a global display map. But the scene was eerily silent.

Bach tapped the glass. 'Bulletproof,' he explained. 'This is Majestic-Twelve, the highest level security organization you've never heard of.'

Both fascinated and apprehensive, John could only nod.

The vehicle took off again down the endless corridors. They pulled up beside a waiting military policeman. Massively built, his white cap a good 6 inches above the top of John's head, he was holding a black attaché case.

Bach took a key from his pocket and unlocked the handcuffs connecting the case to the MP's wrist. Not one word was exchanged. The case was stowed on the floor of the vehicle. They resumed their journey, taking a sharp left at the next intersection.

'Where are you taking me?' Loengard asked.

'You said you wanted the truth.' Bach pointed ahead. 'The truth is down there. Third door on the right.'

Loengard didn't exactly know what he was expecting when Bach ushered him through the door, but this wasn't it.

The room was dingy. Under the dusty odour of neglect he picked up a dry cold chemical smell that reminded him unpleasantly of pickled rats in school labs.

Bach switched on the lights, revealing something like a surgery crossed with a morgue. Banks of glass-fronted cupboards lined the walls, some displaying arcane medical equipment. A high metal table stood in the centre of the room. His footsteps ringing hollowly, Loengard walked over to it. Its polished surface glared under the merciless lights suspended above. He recognized it as an operating table.

His stomach contracted. He had never liked hospitals. He wasn't too keen on the deep drawers which lined one wall either. Wondering uncomfortably if they held bodies, he came to the sick realization that one of them might well end up holding his. He wished with all his heart that he'd never got into this.

Bach dumped the attaché case on the opposite side of the table. 'When I was your age,' he said, 'I had my sights set on admiral.'

It was an unexpected statement. John flicked a glance at the plump, middle-aged figure. He looked nothing like top brass now. Yet John recalled the old photo of Bach in his dress whites, and thought that maybe the idea wasn't as preposterous as all that. Not when you had felt the power of the man as he had on that lonely road.

Unlocking the case, Bach continued, 'But a covert navy incident unexpectedly landed me at our only nuclear bomber base. Roswell.'

'So those stories were true?'

Bach shrugged non-committally, opened the case and rummaged through the contents. 'Nothing is *all* true. It depends who you ask. If you ask Mac Brazel what crashed on his farm on 3 July 1947, at one point he probably would've told you it was one of these ships.' He skimmed a glossy black and white photo across the table. It showed a flying saucer, smooth except for the part where it had crumpled on impact. And it had windows.

John gazed at it in disbelief. 'The news said Brazel changed his mind. That it was really a weather balloon.'

'The news is irrelevant.'

Not yet trusting himself to make a judgement, John picked up the photo and examined it. He noticed distantly that it trembled in his fingers. He looked for wires, for papier mâché, for any clues that it was some sort of fake. There weren't any. 'Blue Book doesn't have any of this stuff?'

'We confiscate all physical evidence before they get to it,' Back confirmed.

'So Blue Book is only . . . what? A front for Majestic?'

Bach nodded, ducking his head slightly as he removed a chain from around his neck. John noticed that the crown of his head was gleaming damply through his thinning hair. Silently Bach held out the chain, and the small flattened box suspended from it.

Loengard accepted it gingerly, suspecting anything from poisoned darts to truth serum. But the container seemed harmless enough. He rattled it but it made no sound. 'Dog tag?'

'Go ahead. Open it up.'

John hesitated. 'Go on,' Bach urged. 'Take it out.'

46

It?

Reluctantly John sought and found the catch. The top of the container slid off. Inside was nothing but a tiny folded triangle of something that looked like foil, just like they had at home in the kitchen. It didn't seem to smell of anything in particular. Feeling foolish for his suspicions, he lifted the thing out by one corner.

It unfolded all by itself.

Startled, he dropped it. It fell.

Upwards.

Astonished, Loengard reached out to grab it from the air. At the touch of his fingers it floated away. Still triangular, the soft diaphanous metal wafted in the breeze. There seemed to be some kind of pattern on the surface, but he couldn't quite make it out. He gently touched it again, watching it gleam under the harsh lights. It spun, reflections dancing from it.

Bach seemed to tire of Loengard treating it like a toy. He snatched it and wadded it back into the container. 'It's from the Roswell crash. I wear it to remind me that whoever does build these ships, their knowledge is formidable.'

'You think it's the Russians?'

Bach turned away to click in a combination on one of the morgue-style drawers. 'You tell me, Mr Loengard.' He slid open the drawer. A frosty cloud of white mist rose from the body bag inside. Bach unzipped it. 'Does this look Russian to you?'

John reeled back, gagging.

The chest and abdomen of the body in the drawer were criss-crossed with thin deep groves. They might have been incisions that had been stitched up after an autopsy to stop the guts spilling out.

But it wasn't that which sent him stumbling back against the table.

The body wasn't human.

It scarcely seemed adult. At just 4 feet long it appeared childlike, and it lay huddled almost foetally. Skeletally thin, it had grey skin, but what really struck home was the tortured expression on its face. Eyelids puckered over the huge eye sockets as if the thing had wanted to shut out some terrifying sight. The small mouth gaped in a silent scream.

John slumped on the operating table, fighting the waves of nausea swamping him.

'Don't be embarrassed, son,' Bach said smugly. 'Most people have trouble digesting the truth.' He allowed that to sink in before adding, 'Here's the way it works, John. No-one who joins Majestic can talk about this to anyone outside. It's a very exclusive club.'

'Wait a minute. I haven't joined anything!'

'Haven't you? Every day you pursued us was another knock at the door. Take a look at these.' He tossed over a file. It had a label reading 'Loengard, John'.

Loengard's face moved from disbelief to anger as he shuffled through the sheaf of photographs it contained. They showed him during his supposed covert investigation in the Library of Congress and outside the Hills' home. There was even one from the widow's garage in New Hampshire.

'You see, John? You recruited yourself. I'm giving you the chance to serve your country in a way few pople ever have.'

'What if I say no?'

'You can't.'

Bach had a cloaker drop Loengard off in Georgetown.

A cloaker, the Captain had explained, was the informal name Majestic personnel used for field agents. The one giving the lift was called Steele, the chisel-faced, sneering thug who put a gun to John's head the night this all began.

As Steele drove away, John couldn't connect somehow with the normality around him. He walked along his street, seeing the children playing, hearing the inconsequential chatter of passers-by, and none of it was real. He felt he no longer belonged in his own neighbourhood.

There wasn't an area of his life now that Bach and Majestic didn't touch. And it was all his own fault.

It took him two attempts to turn the key in the lock of the apartment. Before he managed it, Kim flung the door open and wrapped her arms around him. Her upturned face was as excited as a kid's at Christmas. Her kiss was intense and passionate.

She had never seemed so far away from him.

John embraced her mechanically and heard her say, 'I met her today! I met *Jackie!* I'm working on this TV special, and it's just temporary, but isn't that the biggest news you've ever heard?'

'Congratulations, Kim. You deserve it.'

She was so wrapped up in her wonderment she didn't notice the flatness in his voice.

'I hope you're ready to celebrate. Lisa should be here any minute. Now hurry up and tell me how your day went.'

John took off his tie and threw it over a chair-back. 'Oh, you know, nothing special.'

Every word of the lie cut like razor blades in his throat.

6

From the moment Loengard was recruited by Majestic he lived from day to day, constantly sick with worry that something was about to happen. But for two weeks nothing did.

Then one day, as he and Simonson were coming back from lunch, he sensed he was being watched. Once or twice he turned, but the streets around the Capitol building were too busy for him to spot anybody behaving suspiciously.

Simonson, who had never again referred to Loengard's tangle with an obviously covert operation, was talking about a favourite TV show he'd watched the night before. 'You can't trust Casey. You know he wants that other doctor, Maggie, but he won't make a move on her. Now why is that?'

John glanced over his shoulder again. 'I don't know,' he said absently. 'He probably has a lot on his mind.'

Simonson was so wrapped up in his evaluation of hospital soaps that he didn't register Loengard's tension. 'I'm going back to *Doctor Kildare*. Besides, the staff of Kildare's hospital seem far more competent.'

At that moment John had confirmation that his instinct was correct. They were standing in front of the steps leading up to the Library of Congress. Two secretaries walking down suddenly stopped, engrossed in conversation. A man behind them had to move to get past, stepping into plain view. It was Steele.

Loengard interrupted Simonson's prattle about TV shows. 'Mark, I'm going to go over to the library, take care of that research. Meet you back at the office.'

Simonson raised his eyes at his protégé's brusqueness but all he said was, 'Sure. See you later.'

Loengard ran lightly up the steps.

Steele watched him approach, staring down his thin ratlike nose. John remembered how his face had looked with a gun behind it and the unwholesome glee in his eyes as he pressed the barrel to his temple.

'Well, well. It's the college boy.'

'What do you want, Steele?'

The cloaker pulled a plane ticket from his coat and handed it over. 'Got your diploma right here.'

Steele was already walking away when John called, 'Hey! This is only one way. When am I coming back?'

There was no answer.

'What am I doing? *What's the job?*'

Steele ignored him and melted into the crowd.

In a matter of hours Loengard found himself in an unmarked helicopter more than 30 miles outside Boise, Idaho.

Bach was there, wearing a rumpled charcoal suit, but he still hadn't given an explanation of their mission. Steele and two other cloakers were also present, though none of the trio spoke to John. Maybe they were embarrassed to be working with a man they had harassed and beaten up, but he wouldn't have bet on it. They eyed him with suspicion the whole way. When the pressure of silence got too much he took out a pack of gum and offered it around. Nobody took it.

Forced in on himself, John stared out of the windows at the serene fields of winter wheat. They were flying over rolling croplands, sprinkled here and there with clumps of evergreen bushes. Over the distant crests of sharper hills the sky was high and blue with a scattering of thin cloud.

Without warning, Bach pointed and yelled, 'Outside! Nine o'clock!'

One of the cloakers, who went by the name Popejoy and was marginally less hostile than the rest, threw the door open. It slammed along its track and through the gap John gazed down.

He saw a strange symbol, a triangle with whirling curves, carved out of the golden crops. It was so big its tail crossed a dusty metalled road. The intricate pictogram was somehow disturbing. John felt it meant something, but had no idea what.

Popejoy had a question. He had to shout to make himself heard over the 'copter's engine. 'Why would anybody smart enough to make one of those be so dumb as to put it out there for the whole world to see?'

'They didn't,' Bach yelled. 'We're thirty miles from nowhere. Last week a private pilot who got lost reported it to the local sheriff's office.'

'Why didn't the farmer who owns the field report it?' John asked.

Bach nodded. 'Good question. All we've got is a name. Grantham. Elliot P. Grantham.'

Steele's eyes glittered. 'We gonna roll him at his house or take him on a field trip?' He was grinning at his own little joke.

'Neither,' Bach replied. 'John here is going to pay him a visit and sweet talk some answers out of him.'

For the first time that day, John felt good. At last he was doing something useful.

Steele snorted his derision.

After the reconnaissance flight, Bach had them taken to the local Cattle Baron Motel. They took two adjoining rooms and Bach immediately hogged the shower in the bathroom separating them.

It was a little after noon. Dust motes shone behind the

closed net curtains as Popejoy wired Loengard with a microphone unit. He stuck a receiver onto John's chest with a circle of plaster and tapped it a couple of times with one immaculately manicured nail.

'Wanna say something for 'em?'

Loengard felt stupid. For a moment he couldn't think what to say. After a second he came up with a lame, 'Testing.'

From the room next door Steele called, 'Breaking up!'

Popejoy spun John around and fiddled with the transmitter in its harness between his shoulders. 'Try it again.'

Loengard shrugged back into his jacket. 'Testing. This is John Loengard. Testing. How's that grab you?'

Steele's cynical voice came back sharply. 'Tell Romeo not to broadcast his name, not even on a mike check.'

Through the open bathroom door Bach growled, 'Loengard!' The criticism in that one word would have done a drill sergeant credit.

Popejoy pinned a black plastic badge on Loengard's lapel. It bore the legend 'Fred Grabar, County Extension Agent'. 'Fred Grabar, that's you. Don't sweat it. Boss wouldn't have picked you unless he thought you could do it.' His tone was almost friendly.

John wasn't so sure about the sweat bit.

Popejoy winked and propelled him towards the bathroom where Bach was now shaving with a cut-throat razor. Face half lathered, he talked out of one corner of his stretched mouth, 'Procedure. You're here to ask questions. Whoever put those markings in that field is probably long gone by now. We need a solid witness. We'll be nearby in case things get hairy.'

John didn't answer.

'You got a problem with that?'

'My girlfriend.' John looked distinctly uncomfortable. 'She thinks I'm out of town on government business.'

Bach's razor hovered. 'Yeah?'

'But I told my office my uncle died.'

The razor went back to its business. After a last couple of strokes Bach towelled off his face and picked up his chain and the container with the triangular alien artefact tucked inside it. 'John, no. You tell everybody the same story. You keep it simple and you stick to it.' As if he were some favourite uncle he patted Loengard's shoulder. 'Don't worry about Kimberly. She'll be all right and we'll take care of Pratt for you this time.'

A quarter of an hour later John stood in a phone booth with Steele and Popejoy watching him intently through the glass. Acutely aware of their presence, Loengard dialled the White House. It didn't make him feel any better that he had the number written down in his address book beside a photograph of Kim.

He got through.

'First lady's Office. Kimberly Sayers speaking.'

'Kim?'

'John? Is that you?' The line crackled so much he could hardly distinguish her words. 'This is a horrible connection. Where are you?'

'I . . . uh . . . I'm sorry I didn't call you sooner. It's a real mess.'

'You sound weird. Are you in trouble?'

He bit his lip. He hated lying to her. 'It's . . . Pratt. Turns out he's got some . . . mistress . . . Back in Fresno. The papers are on to it so he's got me out here trying to kill it first.'

'You don't have to do that sort of thing for him, John.' He could hear the indignation in her voice.

'Look, Kim, the main reason I called is, you just can't call the office. Most of them don't know what I'm doing here.'

Her reply was crisp and professional. 'Thank you for the update, John. I've got to go.'

He didn't know if someone important had come into her office, or whether she condemned him for what he said he was doing.

He was glad to get out of the hostile atmosphere of the sedan when they reached the farm.

Loengard walked up to Grantham's ramshackle red barn. Passing a broken-down harrow, he went in through the big warped doors. A blues station wailed from a radio in the shadowy interior. He could hear metal graunch against metal as someone, presumably Elliot P. Grantham, used a wrench under the hood of the filthy truck that stood beneath a single dusty light bulb.

John cleared his throat. 'Mr Grantham?'

An old man straightened, broad and menacing. Peering against the daylight from the open doors, he came forward, a long screwdriver held threateningly in one hand. 'Who wants to know?'

John stopped himself backing up. He shoved one thumb behind his badge and spoke loud enough to be heard above the singer on the radio. Once he got started, the speech he had been practising came easily enough. 'My name's Fred Grabar. I'm from the County Extensions Office.'

Grantham was as hostile to authority as most farmers who barely scraped a living from the land. 'I didn't call you.'

Loengard's gaze was fixed on the shiny screwdriver inches from his nose. He tried a winning smile, but from the inside it didn't feel very convincing. 'My office got a call saying there's some kind of strange formation in your field. They sent me out here to investigate.'

Magic words. Grantham turned away, taking his screwdriver with him. Bending over his truck's innards, he said, 'I ain't talking about it.'

'Well, sir, you might want to change your mind about that. You see, the law says if you've incurred any kind of crop loss as a result of vandalism, and I have to assume this is vandalism, then my office is obligated to inform you that you qualify for government subsidies.'

This time Grantham did look at him, but the leathery old face was giving nothing away. 'You mean you'd pay me money?'

'That's right.'

The farmer's rheumy eyes didn't soften, but he grabbed a rag from the front fender and used it to wipe the grease off his gnarled hands. 'We'll take my pick-up. Field's too far for walkin'. Get in.'

The vehicle had once been dark green with seats to match. Dust puffed up from the cracked upholstery as Loengard climbed aboard. Grantham said nothing as he slammed the hood and swung up behind the wheel.

John hadn't expected it to be this easy.

All the way to the field, he couldn't get it out of his head that Grantham was secretly laughing at him. The squat farmer didn't say a word but there seemed to be more going on in his head than the hope of government money.

Ten minutes later Grantham nosed the truck over a rise. In the dip below them, the swirling triangle lay open to view, its contours shifting a little as a breeze combed the yellow wheat. Where the design crossed the road in a sweeping curlicue, the dirt surface was white.

They pulled up. Loengard got out and stamped about, raising the powdery whiteness in puffs under his tread. Grantham watched him sardonically, sitting in the pick-up with the motor running.

John learned nothing from the road so he put on his best investigative manner and stooped to examine the fence. Where the design passed underneath it, the wire had disappeared. The ends of it just stopped, hanging in little strands that crumbled when he took off his gloves to touch them. There wasn't so much as a splash of molten metal on the ground underneath.

Grantham still sat stolidly in his truck. It looked like he could sit there all day.

Loengard walked along the design. The strange pattern looked as though someone had carefully woven the brittle stalks together to form a mat, which led the gaze into the distance and uphill. To either side the wheat grew above knee height. Awestruck, he whispered into the microphone, 'This thing's huge.'

He knelt to finger the plaited stalks. No footprints, no tyre tracks. Nothing to indicate what had made this design. Or what it meant.

He tramped back to the truck and asked, 'Do you remember the first time you saw this, sir?'

The elderly farmer, one arm leaning on the window of the cab, shrugged and revved his engine as though he were bored. 'Last week, maybe. I don't come down here much this time of year.'

'Why didn't you report it?'

'Ain't no law says I gotta do that.'

'You see any strange lights in the sky over the last month or two?'

'Why? You seen some?'

Loengard felt something antagonistic in Grantham's tone, but put it down to the natural antipathy old coots like him felt for the government.

He wandered back to the strange pathway, trying to work out what it meant. At the top of a small swell his heel clicked on a half-buried object. Kicking the wheat aside, he uncovered a small triangular metal plate.

'I found something!' he hissed into the microphone.

Dropping to his knees, he whisked the dirt away with his fingers. In moments he had unearthed a three-cornered pictogram that was the large design in miniature. He lifted the artefact to examine it more closely.

'Whatever it is, it looks like it's made of *gold*,' he mumbled into his mike.

The farmer's pick-up revved again, louder this time. John ignored it. Then his attention was caught by a movement at the edge of his vision. He looked up and saw the truck plunging toward him.

His first thought was that Grantham was just coming up to see, but he must have been doing 50 miles an hour. John was rooted to the spot. The truck came at him squarely, its driver staring fixedly ahead, his knuckles white on the wheel.

At the last possible moment Loengard threw himself aside. The fender swept by him a hair's breadth from his shoulder. 'Help!' he yelled. 'He's trying to kill me!'

Grantham had already slewed the truck in a circle and was barrelling back at him.

John dived into the corn, scrambling, running, trying to escape the murderous machine.

Suddenly the truck skewed to one side. He couldn't work out why.

Then he heard the shots. He ducked, peering through the waving wheat to see Bach's sedan closing in on the truck. Bullets slammed into the pick-up. Grantham spun the wheel and streaked down the valley in a plume of dust.

The sedan drove past John, blurred with speed. All he could see was the rat-faced cloaker, Steele, leaning out of the window, gun gripped in doubled fists. More shots rang out.

Grantham's truck fishtailed. It swerved wildly, was brought back under control and sent darting along a cross track. The sedan hared after it, swishing through the corn. Steele sent three bullets in rapid fire through the window of the truck. The sound was deafening.

Grantham jerked, slumped forward. The pick-up careered sideways and began skidding. Popejoy stamped on the brakes of the sedan, just managing to miss the other vehicle's backswing. He wrestled to steer the car to a halt without crashing into it.

The pick-up struck a ditch and bounced into a somersaulting arc. Landing heavily, it rolled side over side. One of the windows sprayed rainbow shards of glass. Inside the cab Grantham's body flapped and juddered. Metal screamed and the truck finally came to a standstill in a cloud of dust.

Bach got out of the car and plodded to the wreck, Popejoy at his heels.

Cautiously the Majestic chief leaned in through the broken side window, gun at the ready.

Loengard arrived in time to hear him say, 'Dead. Let's get him to the lab, Popejoy.'

7

All the way back to Washington Loengard sat silently staring at the back of Bach's neck and feeling unpleasantly aware of Steele's mocking gaze. After witnessing the farmer's death he couldn't help thinking how easy it would be to wind up on the operating table in that lab himself. It didn't take too much imagination to picture his own frozen cadaver stored in a drawer.

And what about Kim? If Bach thought he'd told her any of this, her life was up for grabs too.

The sombre mood was still with him when they arrived at Majestic HQ. His sense of looming disaster grew worse as Bach told him to flank the gurney carrying Grantham's corpse. Popejoy and Steele also walked alongside, and there were armed MPs everywhere. John thought the security a bit excessive for a dead farmer.

As the procession neared the lab it was joined by a man in a surgical gown and black rubber apron from neck to knees. John didn't feel comforted by the sight. He took in the man's security pass, which identified him as Dr Carl Hertzog. It bore a much higher level of security clearance than his own.

'What's going on, Bach?' Hertzog demanded.

At a nod from the Majestic controller, Popejoy threw open the lab door and the group entered. Two military policemen stationed themselves outside. Only when the gurney had been parked alongside the shining metal table did Bach bother to answer.

'No, it can't, Hertzog. This isn't your ordinary man. Ordinary men do not try to run down complete strangers with their pick-up trucks. Do it now.'

On Bach's command, Steele, the round-faced Popejoy and Loengard lifted the body bag from the gurney to the table.

With morbid fascination John watched as the scientist unzipped the body bag. Hertzog didn't seem to find anything untoward in manhandling a dead body. He set to slicing at the abdomen with reckless abandon, extracting a bloody organ dripping from several arteries and slopping it onto a pair of scales.

Popejoy retreated to the far wall and leaned against one of the drawers. He looked nauseous. John wondered if the cloaker knew what was in those drawers, and whether he would have seen them as such a haven if he did.

Hertzog was fiddling around in the corpse's chest cavity. 'Your man Grantham smoked and drank, but only in moderation.' His manner was abrupt and to the point. 'Otherwise no cancers, no surgeries, no major hospitalizations.'

'There must be something,' Bach said.

Almost cheerfully, Hertzog selected a hand-held rotary saw. He seemed delighted at the chance to disgust Bach's group. 'I'll just remove the cranial cap, see about a tumour.'

Clutching a handkerchief to his mouth, Popejoy stumbled from the room.

Steele smirked at what he perceived to be his colleague's weakness. Bach appeared unmoved. To Loengard it was one more piece of evidence that Majestic was totally lacking in humanity.

He slipped out to check on Popejoy and found him on the other side of the corridor, shakily lighting a cigarette.

'You OK?'

Popejoy dragged deep on his smoke and nodded. He managed a weak smile, the most open contact he had yet shown.

John smiled back, sympathetically. 'Yeah, right. If we'd wanted to be doctors, we'd have gone to med school.'

There was nothing else he could do for the man so he passed the MPs and went back inside.

Hertzog had switched on the rotary blade, the jagged edge a spinning blur. It sounded like a dentist's drill. Taking a deep breath, which he instantly regretted, Loengard came to the end of the table to watch.

The doctor scraped aside Grantham's hair and sliced down through the thin flesh until he met bone. He pegged the flap of scalp out of the way. There was surprisingly little blood. Hertzog finished his long curving incision and peeled away the shard of skull. It came free with a sharp crack.

Bach wasn't deterred. 'There!' He pointed to the base of the brain, oozing red from the greyish matter. 'Look! What's that?'

Hertzog polished his glasses and bent to peer more closely. Under the lights his dark eyes held a fierce glitter. He touched a scalpel to something clotted and thin. 'I don't know.' He began to sound less impatient. 'I've never seen a mass like that.'

'Take it out.'

Fascinated, the doctor gripped the thing with strong retractors and began to tug.

'He moved!' Steele exclaimed, staring wide-eyed at the corpse.

'Nonsense!' Hertzog continued pulling against the dead flesh.

But John had seen it too. He retreated a step.

Grantham's face grimaced. Spasms activated the facial muscles, the eyes and mouth trembled and convulsed. A trickle of blood welled up in the hollow of his right ear.

An inch or two of something crimson came loose under the scientist's surgical tongs. Then Hertzog jumped as the

62

retractor was almost dragged from his fingers. The crimson mass retreated. Hertzog yanked harder.

A few more inches of wriggling clots spurted from the wound. The drops of blood flew free to reveal a multi-legged insect-like creature that squeaked and chittered inhumanly. It was the colour of diseased intestines, but worst were the spiky articulated jerkings of its limbs. The thing squirmed and pulsated horribly. Nothing on earth moved that way.

Bach mouthed a curse and dashed from the room, yelling, 'Popejoy! We are now officially Red-Ultra. Secure the entire sector. Go to cold storage A3 and bring in the Roswell brain specimen.'

The military policemen unslung their weapons. Their colleagues along the passage, seeing it, pelted towards them.

Bach rushed back inside.

Hertzog was still wrestling the leggy arthropod. Its hard-shelled, tentacular limbs snapped and tiny claws gnashed as it emitted a shrill scream. Steele stood beside him, pistol cocked in his shaking hands, staring at the thrashing beast.

'John!' Bach snapped. 'Get me a container. Something with a lid.'

Steele sidled, trying to keep a bead on the brute. Dr Hertzog shoved him aside to struggle with the hellish creature. Almost 2 feet of the ravening monstrosity had been drawn out and was still fighting the doctor's retractors.

John ran over to a shelf and snatched a glass specimen jar. Returning to the table, he unscrewed the stopper and held the jar in readiness. Hertzog was winning his battle with the shrieking creature and nearly had it free of Grantham's gory brain cavity.

Abruptly the thing's caudal claw was torn from its anchorage. Hertzog staggered backwards as the creature contracted. Its slimy, jointed body slid loose in the jaws of the retractor, but before it could break completely free

John jammed the container up and over its lashing tail. Like a hunted crayfish the beast thrashed wildly. Several of its claws shot up to grip the rim of the jar, but Hertzog renewed his grip and plunged downwards with all his strength. The beast crashed against the bottom of the glass so hard John feared it would shatter.

Bach thrust one hand into his leather glove and pounded the creature down below the rim. 'John! The lid!'

One claw snaked upwards.

Loengard slammed the stopper on it, but he couldn't screw it down with bits of the creature lashing out at him. Hertzog intervened and pushed the claw in with his retractor. John rammed the lid home.

The jar and its writhing occupant was placed on a shelf.

Bach stripped off his glove, the doctor leaned wearily against the table, John sighed in relief. Steele reluctantly holstered his gun. He seemed disappointed there was no killing to be done.

A loud crack shattered their respite.

The creature had punched its tail through the wall of the jar.

Bach grabbed the uncracked side of the container and yelled, 'Open the storage locker!'

Loengard threw open the door Bach was heading for. It seemed to be some sort of fridge with a safe lock. Cold mist billowed. Bach thrust the jar inside. John hurled the door shut and rammed home the locking handle.

The following silence was broken again. This time by Popejoy erupting into the room. He carried another jar.

John regarded it with horror.

Inside was a creature identical to the first. The only difference was that this twin was dead. Motionless and pale, like the other specimens in formaldehyde on the lab's shelves, it swayed in the faint eddying current of the preserving fluid.

Loengard was furious. He shoved his thumb at Grantham's corpse. 'Someone mind telling me how that thing got inside him?'

Bach said evenly, 'I don't know.' He took the jar Popejoy had brought and set it on the surgical trolley at the side. 'But whatever it is, it's a dead ringer for this one here.'

Hertzog strode forward to peer at it, as intrigued as all the others.

'Only we found this *fifteen years ago*,' Bach explained, 'inside one of the Grays at the Roswell crash site.'

The scientist glared at him. 'Why wasn't I told about this?'

'Because you didn't need to know.'

'Wait a minute!' Loengard interjected. 'You're saying you found one of these things in an *alien*? And now in a human being?'

Bach nodded. 'The only question is, how many more people like Grantham are out there?'

8

When Loengard got back from Boise, he thought maybe a bit of humdrum reality would help him settle down before he went home to Kim. Alien creatures and murder attempts had done nothing for his serenity.

Right now he was as jumpy as a frog, so he embraced the comforting feeling of familiar surroundings as he went up the steps to work. He headed to the desk he had made his own in Pratt's suite of offices.

His desk was no longer there. Or rather, the cheap splintered table was still there, but a fresh-faced young man was occupying it, feet up on the blotter. John's posters of Kennedy had been taken down. His personal effects were missing.

The young man stood. 'You've been moved, sir,' he explained politely. 'You have the corner office at the end of the hallway. Do you want me to show you?'

Amazed at being addressed as 'sir', John mumbled, 'No . . . No, that's all right. I'll find my own way. Thanks.'

Everyone he met on the way greeted him differently. Some were effusive, others withdrawn. John couldn't work out what was happening, but it felt uncomfortable.

He found that his name had been painted on the frosted glass door in discreet gold capitals. Even Mark Simonson didn't have a sign like that. Wondering if there had been some mistake, he went in.

It was a wonderful office, decorated with taste and discreet opulence in beige and rich brown. He was impressed, though his pride at such a step up didn't quite mask the guilt he felt at having done nothing to deserve it. Wandering around the spacious room, he admired its solid armchairs grouped around a coffee table, and pondered the status lent by the polished expanse of the desk. He was enjoying the luxurious sensation of an actual outside view when the door thudded back against the wall.

John spun around.

Congressman Pratt let the door swing to behind him. He was immaculate, as if ready for a TV appearance, the neck of his clean white shirt closed by a silver toggle clipped on to his Western shoestring tie. Under the tan from his acres in the San Joaquin Valley the congressman was pale, the skin around his eyes tight with tension.

'I hope it meets your requirements, John.' His tone was bitter, mocking. He slammed the door with his heel. 'I'd offer my condolences, but we both know nobody died. At least, not your uncle.'

John felt his stomach sinking. 'Sir?'

The congressman's lips twisted into a sneer. '*Sir*. Your slick line of crap disgusts me. I was all set to fire you. Then I find out John Loengard's untouchable.'

'What . . . what are you talking about?'

'What am I *talking* about?' He thrust a wad of papers under John's nose, his fingers shaking with pent-up fury. 'Just blackmail. That's all.'

John took the bundle. On top was an admission document from a sanitarium. The scrawled entries read, 'Charles Pratt. Nervous breakdown'. And on the front of the file was a terse, typed note: 'Loengard's untouchable'.

Loengard was speechless.

'So what if I had a nervous breakdown?' Pratt went on angrily. 'I'm fine now. But your friends release that and Charles Pratt will never win another election. Who's behind this, John?'

'All I can tell you is that I'm serving my country.'

Pratt's wrath exploded. 'By serving *me* up on a platter like a damned pig!'

There was nothing John could say. He dropped his gaze, unable to meet Pratt's grey eyes.

The congressman stomped across to the door. He turned to deliver one last shot. 'I don't know who your friends are, but there are forces out there *far more powerful!*'

Then he left, slamming the door so hard it rebounded from the jamb.

The new office suddenly felt less welcoming.

Loengard was glad when five o'clock crawled round and he could leave.

Waiting for the lift, he tried to join in the camaraderie but there was an invisible wall around him and nobody cared to climb over it. He couldn't go home to Kim feeling like this. Instead he made his way to Majestic, and for the first time used the key Bach had given him. Another status symbol he wasn't sure he wanted.

He found Popejoy in one of the underground complex's sparsely furnished rooms. It contained a huge window overlooking a secure laboratory several feet below. Next to it stood a door leading to the lab. Popejoy, laid-back as ever, was smoking the inevitable cigarette as he sat with one leg dangling from the arm of a chair. He was watching Dr Hertzog working in the lab. No sound penetrated the window.

Grey hair as unkempt as ever, the doctor was pottering about between stacks of wire cages where tame rats ate, fought or slept. Against the near wall, just below the window, was a workbench with a microscope and other, less easily identifiable, instruments.

As Hertzog moved aside, a syringe in his hand, John saw a much bigger cage behind him. A chimpanzee sat inside, long arms folded across its knees in a posture that spoke of boredom. Wired electrodes were attached to its head.

The chimp scarcely budged as Hertzog walked over to it.

It seemed familiar with the man in the white coat and beyond opening its eyes a little to check there was no danger, it remained apathetic. Loengard saw that the doctor had kept the syringe out of sight of the primate, only bringing it into play once he'd grabbed the chimp's arm. The needle plunged through its fur. It must have stung, but the animal seemed too lethargic to react.

John noticed that a tripod-mounted 16mm camera was recording the scene.

Hertzog drew a blood sample, patted the chimp absently and turned back to the bench by the observation window. His eyes gleamed in the artificial light, giving him an intensity of expression that showed just how excited he was.

Over his shoulder, John asked, 'What's going on?'

The cloaker shrugged. 'That alien thing they got out of Grantham's body; they're calling it a ganglion now.'

'Ganglion?'

'Yeah. They shoved a chunk of it up the chimp's nose a while back. They think that might be a way of figuring out how it works.'

'Well, it didn't come with a manual.'

'If they wanna know how it works in humans, why inject monkeys?'

'You volunteering?'

Popejoy shuddered. 'Not on your life!'

In the lab, the doctor hastily cleared away some esoteric equipment John didn't recognize. Then he picked up the syringe and came through the door to join them.

'I'm taking these blood samples to be analysed,' he announced. 'Probably too early to notice any behavioural changes but keep an eye out.'

'You got it, Dr Hertzog,' Loengard replied, but the scientist had already rushed off, lab coat flapping.

For a while John and the cloaker watched the ape, but it just sat there, eyes lacklustre, displaying no interest in the bananas and oranges on the floor of its cage. Time dragged and they grew bored. John got out his briefcase and started skimming through a file. Popejoy lit yet another cigarette. John could tell the man was rattled by recent events. The cloaker said, 'So what is this thing they got you working on anyway, Loengard?'

'It's a profile on Patient Zero.'

'Huh?'

'Grantham, the farmer.' John turned over a page or two. Not looking up, he continued, 'Turns out the guy had a "missing time" just like Betty and Barney Hill. Only his friends said he started acting crazy right after it happened.'

'How many of these things you figure are out there?'

'One less than there used to be.' More seriously, he added, 'There's no way to know. Not yet. You've been at this longer than me. What do you think they want?'

'Beats me. I don't think they care any more about us than old Doc Hertzog cares about those animals in there.'

John was deep in the file on Patient Zero. 'Yeah,' he murmured.

Popejoy could tell he wasn't really listening. The cloaker shifted to a more comfortable position and resumed staring through the observation window.

John studied the Grantham case with all the dedication fear could give him.

The night wore away towards morning.

Popejoy was snoring.

Loengard pinched away the sleep gathering in the corners of his tired eyes and straightened. He yawned and glanced through the observation window.

The chimp's cage was open.

'Popejoy!' John yelled. '*Popejoy!* Wake up! The monkey's gone!'

Instantly alert, the cloaker leaped to the window. There was no sign of the chimp.

The chimp with the ganglion in its brain.

'I was just sitting here writing,' John babbled guiltily. 'I didn't even hear anything.'

'We got to get that damn thing back in the cage.'

'It's my fault. I'll do it. Go get Hertzog.'

The cloaker sped off. He didn't need telling how dangerous this might be. Or how furious Bach would be either.

John slid through to the lab, careful to close the door behind him. A sharp stink of animal urine stung his nostrils. The place was warm, presumably for the sake of the live specimens. Or maybe the heat came from the maze of pipework that crossed and recrossed above his head.

He crept down the stairs, looking all around him, but most of the lab was invisible from this angle, hidden behind the banks of small cages. The disturbed rats were scuttling about chittering behind the wire mesh, spilling out litter onto the floor, where it crunched under John's shoes. It was shadowy in the room, except where the light bulb swung above the chimp's empty cage.

The place felt creepy, as though someone unseen were spying on him. He spun around, hoping to catch whoever it was, but there was no-one there. Besides, the 16mm cine-camera was still whirring. At least whatever had happened would be stored on film.

Loengard bent down to examine the open cage door.

The padlock was hanging from it, firmly locked. It was as though someone had released the animal by working out the four digit combination and then pushed home the hasp again. He stooped lower, trying to spot any clue that might tell him who had absconded with Hertzog's experiment.

At that precise moment the experiment landed on his back.

The 100 pounds of frenzied chimpanzee knocked the wind out of him. Its weight bore him downwards, powerful legs locked around his chest. Its horny hands closed around his neck. He felt the air forced from his lungs, the strong fingers digging wickedly into his throat, seeking to crush the larynx. Red fire flared across his retinas. Consciousness was beginning to retreat.

Fear powered him. He managed to grip the wiry arms,

trying to tear loose the ape's stranglehold. The room was spinning and he knew he didn't have long before he blacked out. Lurching to his feet, John threw himself backwards against the cage in an effort to batter the ape into submission. But the manoeuvre had no effect at all. He staggered forward again, the chimp riding him, its hot breath fetid against his cheek. It shrieked continuously.

Pulled off balance by its weight, John stumbled, crashing into the camera on its tripod. Haloed spots sparked in his vision. It startled the chimp, which relaxed its hold just enough for John to gulp blessed air.

There was a rattle of wire mesh as the simian scrambled up towards the ceiling.

John gasped oxygen through his bruised throat. His eyes teared as vision came back.

He looked up and saw the ape worrying at a slender pipe. It pushed and pulled until the weld started to give way and water began seeping through. There was nothing John could do about it; the chimp was way out of reach. Not that he relished the thought of tackling it again in any event.

The water flowed faster now, cascading onto the floor and out into the hallway. John hauled himself backwards on hands and feet, scrabbling to put distance between himself and the torrent.

Metal shrieked as the ape wrenched the pipe free, joint collar still attached, and swung it down at John.

John saw the brass tube approaching just soon enough to duck. The blow couldn't be avoided, but instead of braining him, it glanced painfully across the top of his head. Hands pressed to his cranium, vision blurred, he flattened. Aware that the animal could strike again any second, he began scrabbling for the door.

Footsteps raced along the passage outside and skidded on the pool of water spreading under the door. John drew a ragged breath to cry out a warning. Before he made a sound, Popejoy kicked the door open. John had never been so glad to see anyone in his life. Light flooded in, silhouetting the cloaker crouched in the doorway, his service revolver held firm in a two-handed grip.

The ape swung downwards, the club in one paw. Like a pendulum, all the beast's weight spun around the central pivot of its grip. Every erg of impetus crashed into the cloaker's face with the mass of its club. Popejoy catapulted backwards, his scream of agony muffled by the sound of gushing water. The gun fell and bounced on the concrete floor.

Helpless, Loengard watched as the ape dropped to squat beside Popejoy. It tossed away its brass club and snatched up the revolver by its barrel. For half a second John thought it had no idea what it held. Then it stuck a finger through the trigger guard and aimed at Popejoy.

John screamed, 'Noooo!'

The ape fired. Popejoy's shirt punched inwards, blood spraying out from a gaping hole in his chest.

Then the ape turned the weapon Loengard's way. But it didn't shoot. It jerked up its head in response to further sounds outside. Someone was shouting. Heavy boots pounded nearer.

The monkey fled through the open door, taking the gun with it.

Military police and Majestic men pounded past in pursuit. Not one of them stopped to look at Popejoy or Loengard.

Head swimming and throbbing with pain, John dragged himself over to him. Popejoy's eyelids fluttered, as if he couldn't believe what was happening. He made a feeble attempt to rise. John laid a hand on his shoulder, but it was obvious he was too late. Blood mingled in crimson swirls with the water on the floor.

Popejoy's head fell back and he was still.

A rattle of gunshot boomed in the corridor outside, sealing the monkey's fate.

9

Over Capitol Hill the moon peered coyly from behind diaphanous clouds.

It was long after working hours, and the congressional offices were in darkness. Here and there security night lights glowed dimly, but there were few people about to see them.

Kimberly Sayers walked slowly past the steps, nerving herself to go in. Her face was stiff with anxiety, and there were dark shadows under her eyes that hinted at insomnia. A couple of revellers in evening dress making their raucous way home looked askance at her businesslike outfit. At this time of night the smart camel coat and matching hat she wore to work in the First Lady's office seemed out of place.

It was the last straw as far as Kim was concerned. Bad enough worrying herself sick about John without feeling totally out of place on Capitol Hill. She began to wish she'd never come. But if she went home without even trying to find out what was going on, she knew she'd be furious with herself for being such a lame duck. She gathered her resolve and ran up the steps before chickening out altogether.

It was easy enough to bamboozle the sleepy security man on the desk. He was far more interested in the commentary of some boxing match on his transistor radio. Her White House identity badge was all he needed to see.

'Mr Loengard's office? Fourth floor, turn right as you leave the elevator.'

The door with John's name emblazoned on the frosted glass panel was ajar. There was a light on inside. Anger flared in her. If he was here, why hadn't he called home? Intent on giving him a piece of her mind, she barged in. And stopped, taken aback.

It wasn't John she found. A man with a high tanned forehead and a shoestring tie at the throat of his white shirt sat behind the mahogany desk. He had a mess of papers on his lap. She had obviously caught him rifling the drawers.

He jumped quickly to his feet, dumping the papers unceremoniously on the polished wood.

'Oh! Er . . . excuse me,' Kim stammered. 'I'm looking for John Loengard. He said he has a new office.'

The man came round from behind the desk, holding out his hand and giving her a dazzling smile. 'Charles Pratt,' he said ingratiatingly. 'I'm going to take a wild guess here, but I bet you're Kimberly, right?'

Kim wasn't fooled by his saccharine smile. She kept her distance, coolly accepting his handshake. 'John's told me a lot about you, Congressman.'

A politician, however thick-skinned, couldn't help but notice how frosty she was. He said with a rueful, roguish gleam in his eye, 'I take it not all of it's been good.'

Kim started back for the door. 'I'll just be going.'

In three long strides he was at her side. 'No. Fire away. I insist.'

She raked him with a contemptuous glare. 'Well, your personal life is none of my concern. Except for how you're using John.'

'How *I'm* using *him?*' He shook his head and laughed ironically.

Kim found it patronizing. 'I don't think there's anything to laugh about,' she replied starchily.

His thin lips curved in an unpleasant smile that was at least more genuine an expression of how he felt. 'What exactly is it you think I'm asking John to do for me?'

'Sounds like you asked him to clean your dirty laundry last week.'

He raised his shoulders in a gesture of disbelief and stepped in close enough for her to feel decidedly uncomfortable. 'Hmm. The way I heard the story, his uncle died. Whose dirty laundry are we smellin' here, darlin'?'

'I don't have to listen to this.'

'Course not.' He stroked his fingers up and down the lapels of her coat, flipping her ID into view. 'You can run back to the White House. That must be real exciting. I bet they keep you busier 'n a milk cow.'

Kim sidled away, jerking her coat back across her bosom. Anger and fright brought a becoming flush to her pale cheeks. 'Will you please let go of me?'

He let go, but stepped in again, his nearness pinning her against the wall. 'Open your eyes, woman! I think Johnny boy's got both of us snowed.'

She took a couple of paces sideways, closer to the door, and reached for the handle.

Pratt gave her his arrogant politician's leer again. 'Maybe we should join forces, you and me. Get to the . . . *bottom* of this whole affair.'

Repelled, Kim snatched open the door and ran outside. Her heart beat frantically as she headed as fast as she could for the elevator without actually running. She listened for Pratt following her, but all she heard was his mocking laughter.

It was close to midnight by the time she got back home. The trees and bushes outside the apartment house in Georgetown were full of shadows that wouldn't normally alarm her. But then she wouldn't normally be wandering around so late on her own.

Keyed up, she scurried inside.

Through the door of the flat she could hear the deep vibrations of music blaring out. It was Bobby Darin's version of 'Mac the Knife'. As she let herself in she heard John's new Dansette click and whirr as the needle swung back to the beginning of the record again.

The lyrics made her think of Pratt's toothy leer.

She shuddered and pushed the door wider. The music reached out oppressively. In the room she had furnished with such care, John was slumped on the couch in front of an unfinished jigsaw. According to the picture on the lid of the box, it was of Washington DC. His eyes were red and he held a full glass of Scotch. The half-finished bottle stood on the table beside him.

Her relief at finding him safe evaporated, flushed away by the intense anger her anxiety about him had caused. Her temper wasn't improved by the fact that he scarcely glanced in her direction. He seemed to think the fragment of jigsaw sky he toyed with was more important than her.

She stalked across to the record player and took the needle off the record.

A drunken twitch of his lips passed for John's smile. 'Hiya, Kimmie. Where ya been?'

'Good question,' she said shortly.

He shook his head in exaggerated denial. 'Nah. A *good* question is, do you go for the colour pieces first or do you try to get all the straight edges?'

It was a moment before she regained mastery of herself enough to speak, but even so she couldn't keep a tremor out of her voice. 'You know, the thing I loved most about you, John, was how we could always talk. About anything.' She inhaled sharply, trying not to cry. 'I thought you were my best friend.'

Sensing some measure of her distress, he tried to stand up. He couldn't make it and dropped back on the couch, slopping whisky down his UCLA sweatshirt. Whisky fumes spread a poisonous miasma that stung Kim's eyes in the same way Pratt's innuendoes about John's infidelity burned like venom in her stomach.

'Why have you been lying to me, John?'

'What are you talkin' about?' He obviously sounded unconvincing even to himself, and went back to staring evasively at the incomplete picture of the Capitol.

'I know you're lying. I went to your office and talked to

77

your weirdo boss. You were not working late. Pratt says you told him your uncle died. What uncle?'

John had no answer. At least, none that wouldn't endanger Kim. He sank lower into the couch.

'Are you punishing me because I wouldn't marry you?' she asked in a low voice.

John drew circles round and round the rim of his glass with a forefinger that wouldn't stay on track. Eventually he said, 'I want to tell you everything, but it's just so damn . . . complicated.'

'Well, you're going to uncomplicate things *right now*, or . . . Or come tomorrow, I'm moving out.'

Kim was as taken aback by her own words as he was, but it was too late to unsay them. As the silence stretched out she felt her world wash away in a tidal wave from which only John could save her.

But he didn't. He lowered his eyes and muttered, 'I can't tell you.'

Kim tried to remember to breathe. At last she found words. 'I loved you, John. I really did.'

Still he said nothing.

Kim rushed for the sanctuary of their bedroom and slammed the door.

He could hear her crying her heart out.

Imprisoned in the web of deceit Majestic had woven around him, John could see no way out. He turned his frustration into a kick that sent the table crashing over. Cardboard pieces of Washington fountained into the air, scattering all over the carpet Kim had vacuumed only the morning before.

He lurched to his feet and kicked the table again for good measure. Then he grabbed his coat and stomped out into the night.

The misery should have stayed obediently at home but he couldn't run away from it. It followed him through the streets and out to the Washington Monument.

He sat on the edge of the long dark pool that radiated out from the monument. There were no clouds now. A high cold wind had swept them away.

The blanket of alcoholic warmth had abandoned him and he shivered. He huddled on the grass, staring bitterly at the black waters, wondering how his life had ever got this messy.

If only Kim had married him. If only he'd never got involved with Blue Book, or Bach, or any of it. But it was too late now. He couldn't change anything. And Kim, the most precious thing in his life, was leaving him tomorrow. He couldn't bear it.

All at once a streak of light rippled over the ebony pool. He threw his head back, seeing the shooting star rocket low across the night. It looked so low he could almost catch it in his hand.

The meteor's sparkling trail faded from sight, taking his luck with it.

Even if Kim wouldn't speak to him any more, he craved the warmth of at least being in the same apartment as her for one last time.

More alone than he had ever been in his life, he headed for home.

Kim tossed restlessly in her sleep. A double bed without John in it was the emptiest thing in the world. She huddled foetally under the covers but found no comfort there. Though all the windows were shut, she felt as though a chill wind had robbed the world of warmth. And the darkness around her was impenetrable.

The bedroom lights flickered. A soft buzzing started, as if the record player had somehow stuck and the mechanism jammed. The buzzing grew louder, almost shrill. Its acid pitch set her nerves on end.

'John?' she called.

There was no answer.

Then she became aware that the muslin curtains were

fluttering in the moonlight. She sat up, rubbing sleep from her eyes, and peered across through the dim room. One of the windows was open.

'Funny,' she mumbled, getting out to close it, 'I could have sworn I'd left it shut.' She shrugged away her confusion and padded across the cold lino. Her low-cut white nightdress whipped against her, wrapping itself around her body in a chill draught of air. She stretched to close the sash.

Impossibly bright moonlight danced in her eyes. 'Huh?'

Shaking her head to clear it of the cobwebs of dreams, she looked out again. Hovering motionless above her, a light burned in the sky so fiercely it blotted out the stars.

She slammed down the window and jumped back.

Something was approaching, something that made no sense, that violated reason. It was as though a denizen of a nightmare had refused to stay beyond the wall of sleep.

Kim backed further away, a hand over her mouth to stifle the building terror.

It was in the room with her now.

She tried to scream, mouth wide, lungs emptying every last iota of the breath she'd been holding. But no sound came.

Then she fell into the chasm of its pitiless black eyes.

10

It was near dawn when John tiptoed into the apartment.

He didn't dare disturb Kim. If he did anything to wake her she might up and leave now. Maybe if he just ignored the whole situation it might go away and things could go back to what they had been.

Fortified by this defective reasoning, he collapsed exhausted on the couch, pulling his coat over him like a blanket. Even the Fall cold couldn't keep him awake.

The next thing he knew his head felt like there was a wrecking-crew inside it and he was late for work.

He stumbled into the bedroom. The sash window and the French doors were wide open to the chilly morning. With relief he saw that Kim was still there.

For a long moment he regarded the woman around whom he wanted to build the rest of his life. She looked so innocent in her sleep, her eyes tight shut and her cheeks flushed like a child's. He longed to stroke the soft tumble of her hair from her forehead, but he wasn't sure how she'd react.

Instead he shook her shoulder gently, murmuring, 'Kim. Kim! You're gonna be late for work.'

'Hm?' she mumbled sleepily. 'What time is it?'

'Seven thirty.'

She shut her eyes again. 'I want Chinese for dinner.'

'Seven thirty *a.m.*'

Kim half sat, then rolled back onto the pillows. John

81

went across to shut the windows. Not looking at her, he said, 'Look, I'm sorry about last night. I . . .'

It was no good. He had to go and sit beside her, stroking her hair as if he could melt her by tenderness. 'I just want you to know . . . I'm into something I'm trying to get out of.'

Kim snuggled down under the covers and murmured 'All right.' She was so sleepy she didn't seem to care that they'd had a row the night before. She stretched and pulled the blankets up under her chin as if waking were too much effort. 'I'm so tired.'

Feeling a surge of hope, John leaned over to kiss her cheek. 'Feel better, honey. I'll call your office, let them know you'll be late.'

Again he stood looking down at her, enjoying the swell of love he experienced every time he saw her. Then he took himself off to the Capitol.

In the cosy nest of her bed, Kim tried to come awake, but she didn't really want to. It was too nice where she was. Besides, her head was aching and her neck felt stiff. Then something tickled her upper lip. She brushed it away and saw blood on her fingers.

Kim sat bolt upright. Alarmed, she noticed a patch of blood on her pillow where her head had lain. But there was nothing to explain it. Or was there?

She struggled to remember.

Washington DC
18 October 1962

These days Loengard didn't always go through the pretence of working for Pratt. Some weeks after his near-terminal row with Kim, he still found himself shackled to Majestic.

At the moment, though, he was working on something which fascinated him. He was trying to find some sense in the death of Patient Zero; Grantham, the farmer who had tried to kill him.

Immersing himself in work didn't always succeed in making him forget the awkwardness with Kim, but beyond a certain aloofness on her part things weren't too bad on the home front. She certainly never referred to the argument again, but she was no longer the warm laughing girl he had known.

Maybe it was for the best that nowadays he didn't spend too much time in Washington.

Following weeks of travel and investigation, he drove to Majestic and slotted his turquoise Chevy soft-top into the space reserved for him. By now the MPs on duty knew him on sight. Beyond watching him flip his lapel casually open to show them his ID, they dispensed with security checks and waved him through.

John's double life now seemed normal. It was insidious. The shadow Majestic cast over him was long; he could not even share his terrible secret with the woman he loved, and because of it he might yet lose her. He had come to Washington to stand in the light, to fight for the things both he and Kim believed in, but now he was entangled in a mire of lies and deception.

Bach had been right. The truth did have a price. And it was one John no longer wanted to keep paying.

He walked down the dingy corridors, nodding familiarly at the MPs stationed on every junction. What surprised him most was how good he'd become at living this secret life.

Following Bach's orders, he made straight for the conference room they called the Star Chamber. Passing the inevitable armed guards, he slipped inside. The room was in almost complete darkness. He could barely make out the dozen directors of Majestic seated around the big red horseshoe desk.

The moment Loengard entered, Bach nodded from his place at the curved head of the table and Steele threw a switch. A cine-projector whirred into life, casting black and white images onto a screen at the far end of the room.

Like the bigwigs sitting in front of him, John found the

monkey film unnerving, though he himself had seen it before, not to mention having lived through the latter part of it. He took up a position by Steele and Dr Hertzog near the projector.

As the film wound on, Governor Nelson Rockefeller, Senator Hubert Humphrey and the others present fell silent. Their seats no longer creaked and the embers of cigars and cigarettes dimmed forgotten in the deep ashtrays. Not one of the VIPs moved. The gold braid on the uniforms of the military top brass sparkled under the flickering light.

As the film showed, the chimpanzee in the lab had not been released by any human agency.

Waking, its eyes began to glow with a bright intelligence that hadn't been there before. The ape scanned its cage and appeared to evaluate the situation in which it found itself. It reached up its long shaggy arms and peeled the electrodes off its scalp. After a brief examination, it discarded them as useless, then focused on the combination lock.

Nimble fingers fastened on the casing of the padlock, locating the four wheels that turned the numbers. In less than a minute it had found the combination and snapped the lock open. The odds against that happening by chance were at least ten thousand to one. Letting itself out of the cage, the chimp closed the lock around the bars of the open door.

The film record moved on. Reliving each moment with sick horror, John saw the ape try to kill him, then brain Popejoy and scoop up the cloaker's gun. He had to turn away at that point, but nothing could stop the sight of his late colleague's death replaying itself behind his closed eyelids.

The film ended in a series of numbers and squiggles. Popejoy's replacement put the lights on. The venetian blinds that shielded the Star Chamber from scrutiny by anyone else in the complex were not raised.

Dr Hertzog, looking quite the authoritarian in a smart

brown suit with his hair neatly brushed, announced dispassionately, 'After repeated viewing of the monkey film, we now believe the aliens referred to as Grays may be nothing more than a host organism for a higher intelligence. We are now calling that higher intelligence ganglions.'

Hertzog rose and fell a little on his heels, rather in the manner of an academic lecturing a class of undergraduates. There was not a hint of deference in his manner, despite the august assembly he faced. 'Somehow these alien parasites, the ganglions, have become introduced to the amygdala portion of the brainstems of individual humans. The amygdala is our emotional control centre.'

Briefed in advance to take over at this point, Loengard said, 'One of our latest theories, which we've been testing, is that there may be a pattern to the emotional and intellectual scrambling which seems to take place in recently implanted humans, like this woman here.'

Steele set the cine-projector running again as the lights dimmed. The film leader counted down, then the screen showed the hostile environment of an interrogation room. Although he was invisible in the film, it was John who questioned the subject.

She was a woman in the hinterland between thirty and forty, her hair dark and shining with grease, though it was styled fashionably enough in a French pleat with a sideswept fringe and curls cut short above her ears. A neat shirtwaister completed her ensemble, and should have made her look like what she was; the wife of a well-to-do middle American businessman.

There was something about her, however, that was indefinably different. Although she chain-smoked nervously, she held her cigarette awkwardly not between the tips of her fingers but well down below the level of the first knuckle. Beyond a certain wariness, her dark eyes showed no expression, and her unlined face took a moment or two to react to each statement, as though she had to work out what emotion she was supposed to be showing.

Pulling on yet another cigarette, she said, 'So you guys pick me up like secret agents to find out what movies I go to?'

John's voice, off-screen, answered. 'Actually, the government's very interested in two calls you made to a farmer in Boise, Idaho, named Elliott Grantham.'

Filmed in close-up, the woman's features all but filled the screen. 'I told you. He was just a friend of my family.' She took another puff of nicotine, her movements stilted as though it were a trick she was still learning. With poor timing she said, 'How much longer?'

Hertzog spoke over the film. 'Besides the phone calls to Grantham, we know this woman visited her sister in Midland, Virginia, at a time when there was a documented air-force sighting of a UFO.'

John's voice interposed. 'So, Hilary, do you and your husband go dancing very often?'

The innocent question, oddly enough, provoked her to anger. She stood indignantly, and her voice rose in volume and venom. 'We do not . . . twist the night away on the . . . American Bandstand, if that's what you mean.' She sat, suddenly calm again as if by an effort of will. 'He likes . . . sports.'

'Sports? So when would you guess was the last time that you had a spider mite burrow into you during a golf match?'

The question threw her. She thought about it, obviously trying to come up with the right answer, then said with a deliberate attempt at carelessness, 'He plays golf. I don't.'

'OK. At home, then.'

She paused, then laughed as if sharing a wry joke with which he would obviously be familiar. 'You know. From time to time, I guess. The usual.' Now a real emotion surfaced. Anxiety. 'We almost done?'

Bach nodded and Steele turned off the machine. Without its clatter the room suddenly seemed quieter, though tension filled the smoke-laden air. Bach said, 'What we still don't know is how they get in there. How long the takeover phase lasts. Who are their targets, and why? What is their plan? All we have is questions and no answers.'

He gazed around the people at the table. Rockefeller, the Governor of New York; Senator Humphrey; Secretary of State Henry Kissinger; scientists, admirals and generals, all looked worried.

A man in army uniform, ID badge identifying him as General Arthur Brown, said, 'Do we still have that woman in custody?'

'Yes,' John began, 'she's under observation—'

Bach sliced his hand through the air, commanding Loengard to stop. 'We attempted a cerebral eviction on her last night.'

John knew that meant she was dead. He felt guilty. If it hadn't been for him getting her investigated, the woman would still be alive.

'Why wasn't I informed of this?' he whispered sharply at Hertzog.

The doctor shrugged.

Bach ignored the interruption and steamrollered on. 'We tried to extract the ganglion surgically.' He nodded at Hertzog. 'The patient did not survive.'

Rockefeller slammed his hands down on his briefing book. Outraged, he burst out, 'Experimenting on farmers and housewives! I don't agree with this.'

'And if you'd been a little less tender-hearted, Governor,' Bach said calmly, 'you'd still be chairing these meetings instead of me.'

Before Rockefeller had time to muster a retort at such curt disregard, there was a knock on the door. Chief of Operations Albano came into the room. Silently he handed Bach a sealed envelope. He slit it with one thumbnail and glanced over the yellow handwritten sheet it contained. He passed it to the man sitting beside him, then said formally, 'I'm afraid I'm going to have to ask Agent Loengard and Dr Hertzog to leave the meeting right now.'

John and the doctor left. As the door closed behind them

it shut off the beginning of an argument developing in the Star Chamber.

Still angry about the death of the woman, Loengard vented his feelings on Hertzog. 'I don't understand, Doctor. You said you were working on *another* way! Something about injecting the person with a substance that would kill the ganglion and save the host?'

Hertzog's answer was delivered with scientific detachment. 'Listen to me. ART, the Alien Rejection Technique, is nowhere near perfected. In theory, yes, it should work on the larger cranium of a human being, but so far all I've got to show for it is several dozen dead rats.'

'It just seems so wrong, what we're doing.'

Hertzog looked up at him, not without compassion. 'We must stay focused on the task at hand.'

John turned disconsolately and trudged away along the corridor.

It was dark as he drove home through the streets of Georgetown. The place should have been deserted by now. The rush hour was over, the stores closed, yet crowds of people lingered on the sidewalks and spilled out into the road.

By a hoarding covered with adverts, John had to slow. Across the street was a television store, closed, but still showing its wares through the safety glass. All the TVs seemed to be tuned to the same channel. Two and three deep, people jostled to watch them.

What made John pull into the kerb, though, was Kim. She was drifting along, her coat pale under the sodium street lights, looking bewildered.

He parked and raced towards her. Like the others she drifted over to watch the news on TV. Unlike them, she apparently didn't know why.

President Kennedy was on screen. Usually his slim handsome face was lit by a smile, now he was in deadly earnest. His precise diction was relayed through an amplifier above the shop's door.

John heard him say, 'Aggressive conduct, if allowed to go unchallenged, ultimately leads to war. The greatest danger is to do nothing.' The words rang in John's ears as he pushed his way through the throng to reach Kim's side.

He laid his hand on her arm and she turned to him. Her eyes were red-rimmed with crying, her cheeks starting to blotch. Yet her face was blank, as if all emotion had been wiped from it like a sponged blackboard. All around, men were grave and women pressed hands to their mouths or clutched their handbags tensely.

John slipped his arm protectively around her, asking, 'Kim, what's going on?'

'I . . . I don't know,' she said faintly. 'It doesn't make any sense . . .'

The man next to him interrupted. 'Looks like we're goin' to war. Soviets got missiles in Cuba.'

In a ghost of his normal voice Loengard whispered, 'My God.'

And Kim said, 'What's happening, John?'

11

Deeply disturbed, John shepherded Kimberly back home. Though it was several blocks she hardly said a word.

It was the same in the apartment. He sat her down with a hot coffee and she seemed calmer, but it was an unnatural calm with the world set for damnation. When he took her hand she didn't return his grasp, just let her fingers lie slack in his as though not knowing what to do. If he hadn't known her better he would have suspected she had taken some drug.

John willed himself to be patient. Finally, when she had drunk a second cup of coffee, he said, 'I have to go out for a while. Will you be OK, honey?'

She nodded overemphatically and muttered, 'Sure' once or twice.

He had to be content with that. All the same, he had never made it so quickly to the car before. He had to get back to her as soon as possible. Leaving her like this terrified him.

Scorching along the roads towards Bethesda, Maryland, he cursed at the slightest delay, and there were plenty. It seemed like hours before he turned into a certain street.

This was supposed to be an up-market residential district, the kind where flower borders hemmed in the sweeping front lawns. At this time of night it should have been quiet, a few porch lights here and there, maybe a couple of people out walking their dogs while most folks had their feet up in front of the TV.

Not tonight. People were rushing about in every direction, loading tables and dressers and beds into trucks. One couple were haranguing their wailing tot who wanted to bring his bicycle into a station wagon already bulging with suitcases and bags.

Pushing past a knot of men arguing, he heard at least three radios blaring the bad news. His anxiety threatened to overwhelm him and he felt a bubble of panic trying to break out in his chest.

No-one even noticed him go up the drive towards a beautiful wood-fronted house painted white with a shiny red door. He rapped with the antique knocker and stood waiting for what seemed like for ever.

He had more than enough time to notice the neat clipped plants in pots, the patina on the old brass of the door knocker. Finally the door was opened. By Bach.

He took one look at Loengard and pulled the door to behind him. He was in a sloppy old grey cardigan with a diamond pattern, and carpet slippers. Somehow John had never imagined the Majestic chief in carpet slippers.

Bach grabbed John's arm and pulled him down to the driveway. He lit a cigarette and said, 'There is not a reason good enough to explain why you're here.'

'Well, since the world seems to be going up in smoke, I thought we could bend the rules a little.'

Majestic's chief stiffened with barely restrained impatience. 'What do you want, John?'

'I know it's always changing with you, but what I want is the truth about this Cuba thing.'

As ever Bach's face was closed. 'I am under no obligation to discuss this with you.'

'See, that's what I'm talking about! Who exactly are you obligated to discuss this with? Because I'm watching TV, and maybe I'm naive, but I keep asking myself whether Kennedy has told Khrushchev about Patient Zero. Because if he did, I don't see how they could be threatening each other like this.'

Bach took a nonchalant drag on his cigarette. He looked perfectly cool, even slightly dismissive. 'You're scared, John. Why don't you go home? Be with Kimberly. She's probably pretty scared too.'

It was all John could do not to shake the man. 'We're all scared! You're the only one who's not!'

'Well, they're gonna work it out,' he replied in the manner of a father explaining yet again to his son that there aren't any bears in the wardrobe. 'They have to.'

John stared at him in disbelief. 'President Kennedy doesn't know about Majestic, does he?'

Bach gazed levelly at him. 'I took a big chance taking you on board, John.'

'Oh, so I should be eternally grateful?' He gesticulated helplessly. 'Forget it. Not if I'm being lied to. Now it's a simple question, Frank. Does he know? Yes or no?'

Bach examined the tip of his cigarette and exhaled. 'Kennedy knows what he needs to know.'

John pressed his fingertips to his forehead as though he could blank out the awful truth. His worst suspicions had just been confirmed. 'I knew it.' He bowed his head for a moment, crushed under the weight of it. 'Just tell me this. Who appointed *you* God?'

'Ike.'

Never for a moment had John expected Bach to answer, much less in such a matter-of-fact way. '*Ike?*'

'Ike never trusted Kennedy. He gave us the authority to decide which future presidents should be told. It's all perfectly legal.'

'You don't keep the *President of the United States* in the dark about this. It's wrong!'

'John, look at the panic this Cuba thing's caused.' He flocked away the butt of his cigarette. 'You take God and government out of the equation and you're left with chaos.' He shifted his weight, ready to go back inside.

John was quite prepared to let him. 'You know, Frank, if

you're going to fight for humanity, at least have a little faith in us.'

Then he turned abruptly, leaving Bach standing alone.

All the while John was out, Kimberly sat in one place. She was perched uncomfortably on the arm of the couch, ready to run to the door at any moment. In a way she couldn't define, she missed John. But sometimes she couldn't remember why. Absently she smoothed the short yellow skirt over her knees, monotonously, over and over again. The sounds of sirens and shouts in the panicked streets outside didn't seem to impinge on her at all, yet at the slightest noise on the landing she would raise her head to stare even more fixedly at the door.

Then came something that brought first a glow and then a puzzled expression to her brown eyes.

A murmur of insects, a buzz of bluebottles, a roar like a swarm of bees crescendoed in her skull. First querulous, then fearful, she pressed her palms over her ears as though it would make the mad buzzing stop.

It didn't.

With nothing physical to prompt her, she rose suddenly and went to the door. Though no-one had knocked, every fibre of her being quivered with expectation.

She threw the door wide.

Charles Pratt stood outside.

His manner was wooden. No politician's handshake, no spurious down-home charm. His face was as blank as hers.

'Hello, Kimberly.' He spoke without inflection.

She nodded, unsurprised.

Pratt let himself in and closed the door. Normal social manners would have led to Kim offering him drinks, inviting him to sit, or engaging in light chit-chat. She did none of these things. Nor did she back off, not even after her last beleaguered meeting with Pratt the would-be seducer, though the racket in her ears sounded louder and more sharply focused with him so close.

'You've been expecting a visit,' he stated. 'It's

understandable to experience some confusion. I'm here to help.'

Kim twitched. A slightly more normal expression crossed her face, as though someone had suddenly moved in behind her empty eyes. 'No. I don't want your help.'

She took a tiny step back. The lanky Californian followed her but there was nothing of the congressional lothario about him now. 'I must say something to you, Kim. Are you ready to hear it?'

The pressure in her head broke through into a dimension of pain. She threw her hands over her ears, face crumpling with agony. 'That noise! *Make it go away!*'

Pratt studied her impassively, untouched by her distress. He spoke louder. 'Since John Loengard was not here on the night of our visit, you must watch him until we return. He can no longer be trusted.'

He paused, then added, 'Some day you will experience the joy of Singularity, Kim.'

Now he walked towards the window. It was firmly shut; John had insisted on that before he left because of the panic in the streets. Yet as Pratt drew closer the muslin began to flutter.

Outside was a star. A big star. It glowed with all the colours in the universe and Kim couldn't take her eyes off it. It swooped toward her, dropping down until it burst through the window and the net curtain without piercing either. Somehow it was just . . . inside.

Kim stared at it.

It was beautiful, a ball of pure light that pulsed with rainbow brilliance. Shining curls of rose and violet and amber eddied across throbbing geometrical shapes that melted from one crystalline liquidity to another. Beams of diamond-keen brightness speared outwards in patterns that almost seemed to speak the secrets of the cosmos.

Pratt held out his hand, a falconer calling his hunting bird. The glowing sphere settled gently on his cupped palm. And the buzzing stabbed inside Kim's head. She recoiled in fright.

Pratt stepped towards her. He held out the globe enticingly. 'Just touch it. It'll answer all your questions. Just reach out and touch the light.'

Lured by the siren glow, Kim stretched her hand. Desire blossomed in her. She wanted to stroke the coruscations, play with each dazzling scintilla of light. Her fingertips came closer and closer to it.

Just before she touched it, she snatched back her hand. 'No! I won't! *I won't!*'

Pratt stepped ominously closer. Kim retreated until she was backed against the wall.

Looming over her, the glittering sphere thrust inches from her face, he crooned, 'It's natural to fight it. By now, you know where this must end.' Then he rasped words she had never heard before: 'Klaar si su haar.'

Only it didn't sound like one voice but many.

All the same she seemed to understand. Or her body did, because against her will her hand rose towards the demon sphere again. Tendons straining, she tried to force her fingers away. Her whole arm trembled with effort, but still it brought her closer to the ball of light poised on the politician's palm.

At the last second she threw herself aside. Stumbling against the couch, she half fell, dragging at the curtains floating just above her.

Pratt's face betrayed a monstrous anger. He took a threatening step towards her, then stopped and looked to the door.

A fraction of a second later it started to open. Immediately the flashing orb disintegrated in a thousand points of light that flickered to oblivion. It was as if it had never been.

Pratt pasted on a mock-friendly grin as Loengard came in.

'Hello, John.' His words sounded stilted.

John saw Kim huddled on the floor. He rushed over to her and took her in his arms. 'Kim! Honey! Are you OK?'

She clung to him, speechless. He could feel her trembling.

95

Tightening his embrace protectively around her, he glared at Pratt, naked suspicion in his gaze. 'What are *you* doing here?'

'I came by to check on you,' Pratt answered smoothly. 'What with this Cuba business . . .'

A sob rose in Kim's throat. John looked quickly down at her. Her eyes were brimming with tears, but for a moment she could only shake her head. 'He's in my head, John! Or something is . . .'

'What?' He stiffened, ready for action.

'It's too late, John,' Pratt told him. 'We have her.'

Loengard stared at the congressman, dreadful realization dawning. Pratt met his gaze, his eyes unblinking, almost reptilian in their coldness.

Shielding Kim against his chest, John said brokenly, 'No! Why her? Why not me?' He hugged her to him as though he could take her pain into himself.

Pratt misunderstood the words and the gesture. 'Be patient, John. Your time will come soon.'

It was too much. Loengard gently laid Kimberly against the wall. Then he turned, his face twisted with fury, and launched himself towards the grinning congressman. The ferocity of the tackle sent Pratt reeling. His lanky legs cannoned into the sofa and he fell.

John threw himself at the man, swinging his fists. He got in three quick punches to Pratt's head. Any one of them should have ended it, but Pratt fought back, trading punch for punch. He was the taller man with a wiry strength that belied his smooth manners, and he had muscles once honed by years of wrestling hay bales and sacks of feed. It more than made up for John's youth and athletic resilience.

As John drew back to give him a straight right to the jaw, Pratt brought up his knees and planted his two feet in John's stomach. Loengard was sent flying. He landed hard, tangling with a colonial chair that Kim had rescued from a junk shop and painted a soft green. The chair was solidly made; it lost one of its legs as it crashed to the ground, but it came off better than John. It couldn't feel pain.

He was still scrambling to his feet when Pratt rushed him. Once more John plunged to the floor, the breath knocked from him.

Pratt aimed a savage kick at his throat. Had it landed it would have torn out his larynx, but John rolled aside, tangling in the chair legs. He couldn't get up and out of the way.

Crowding him, Pratt pressed his advantage, leaning forward to pound at his opponent's head. John had neither space nor time to stand. He grabbed the chair and used it as a shield, writhing backwards to give himself distance.

Pratt's fist crashed into the ladder-back, ripping the skin from his knuckles and spraying John with a fine rain of blood. An inarticulate growl rumbled from his mouth and he seized the chair.

It was obvious he meant to raise it above his head and then crash it down on his foe. John wouldn't let him. He kept tight hold of the chair back, jabbing it at Pratt.

In a moment it had become a strange tug-of-war. John thrust out with it, then jerked it back towards himself, hoping to off-balance the congressman. Pratt in his turn tried to pound John with it. He made no pretence at fair play. Savage, barely controlled, he tilted the chair to stab its back leg into John's groin.

But again Loengard yanked it away. Enraged, Pratt whirled and seized the coffee table, using that as a weapon. It was heavier than the chair. The momentum of his swing crashed the table heavily into the chair, which in its turn almost mashed John's stomach. Yet the very weight of the table was Pratt's undoing.

As he struggled to raise it, the cords in his neck stood out. A vein writhed in his forehead but he would not be defeated. With a superhuman effort he boosted it above his head and the weight began to teeter him over backwards.

John seized his chance. In that moment he climbed to his feet and threw the chair at Pratt.

Batting it away with his improvised weapon, Pratt ducked. He began to swing around again. He meant to brain John with the all too solid wood, but John wouldn't let him.

He gripped the rim in a desperate hold. Pratt tried to drag him over.

John let go and Pratt staggered back. As he did so, the lower end of the table tilted. The tilt turned into a wavering swoop and Pratt was impelled backwards.

Trying to regain his balance, he back-pedalled wildly but couldn't stop. He tumbled straight through the window.

The crash of glass rang out at the same time as Kim's scream, but it was too late.

John rushed over to the window. Pratt's body lay on the pavement below. Lying at a crazy angle, his back was obviously broken. He writhed in a febrile attempt to stand, but his limbs would not obey him.

Around him gathered a crowd. Despite the late hour, hundreds of people were still about. Some merely glanced, shock on their faces. John watched as others hurried past. No-one gave the congressman first aid or comfort. They were all too preoccupied with evacuating the city in the threat of a Cuban missile attack.

Heedless of the shards of glass still clinging to the sash, John peered down into the street. He saw blood pouring in a dark stream from Pratt's ears. A thick rivulet flooded from the congressman's nose, bloody froth that bubbled onto the street on both sides of his thrashing head. Yet a manic laughter rose from the mangled throat. Peal after peal of its ugly discord burned into John's memory.

The laughter was only cut off by the congressman's death.

12

'Murder,' John whispered, suddenly backing away from the window. Visions of arrest and trial and public humiliation rioted through him. The headlines burned in his mind: COLLEGE BOY KILLS CONGRESSMAN. He couldn't think straight, but another terror blazed a trail across his mind.

Pratt had said, 'We've got her now.'

Kim was a puppet of the aliens. In one gestalt flash John understood it all: her weird moods, her off-key responses, even why she'd never followed through on her threat to leave him.

There was a ganglion inside her, and it must have been there for weeks.

He thought of all the dead 'patients' he had seen in Hertzog's lab. Agonies of dread anticipation filled him to the extent he hardly cared about his own arrest. Except that it might stop him saving Kim.

In the circumstances there was only one thing to do.

Bulling his way recklessly through the chaos of traffic jams and lemming-like pedestrians, John drove like a maniac, Kim semi-conscious beside him. He headed for an elegant though slightly down-at-heel neighbourhood.

Some of the streets were blocked with traffic. In another, a gang of looters was fighting a retreat against scores of police.

Minutes crawled by as he tried to find the address. He'd taken care to look it up months before, thinking that one day he might need it in a hurry. He hadn't ever thought he might need it for his beloved Kim.

He swept the car round another bend and braked suddenly to avoid a vanful of furniture right in the middle of the road. Kim was slumped against the window.

'Are you all right, honey? Talk to me, dammit!'

'He . . . showed me a light,' she murmured faintly. 'He called it in through the window and the noise it made hurt my head, like there were a million people in there all talking at once.'

John slipped his arm around her and pulled her close. 'Look at me, Kim! Are they still in there?'

She nodded. 'They're not so loud now. Maybe they'll just go away.' After that she seemed to fall into a trance. He shook her but he couldn't wake her up.

Groaning, he pressed her to him, feeling the soft warm curves he had always loved now slack in his embrace. Her bright mind, her laughter. Their future. All gone.

A car behind them hooted. John started, then collected himself, enough at least to battle on to a certain brownstone mansion. The building rose four or five storeys, with white stone lintels over doors and windows. Pillars topped by small statues flanked the wide stoop. John almost drove past it in his haste.

Swinging the Chevy hard over, he pulled up with a squeal of suffering tyres. As he veered in to the kerb Kim tumbled sideways against him.

John leaped from the car and ran up the steps. Fortunately the stained-glass entrance stood open. He ran inside and banged on a plain wooden door.

No answer.

He kicked and pounded at the sturdy oak door until it was opened.

Doctor Hertzog stood with his back to the lighted room, bleary-eyed, with his glasses tucked into the top pocket of his dressing gown. His face looked oddly naked without them. The towelling robe had obviously seen better days. It had frayed loops of cotton and there was an egg stain on the collar.

He took in John's unkempt hair, so out of character, and the flushed mottling of anxiety on his neck. 'John! What is it?'

Breathing hard, Loengard swallowed and tried to find his voice. 'They got my girlfriend. She's in the car. We've got to take her to Majestic. You have to do your ART on her.'

Hertzog shook his head. His hair, newly washed, fluffed out around his head like a cotton-wool Santa's. 'That's impossible.'

At the end of his patience, John grabbed his sleeve. 'Let's go, Doctor! Now!'

'No. You've seen the protocol. The directive prioritizes the collection of live specimens of the ganglion. If we take her in, I will be forced to do a cerebral eviction.'

'You mean you have to cut it out? That'll kill her!'

Hertzog patted the hand John had laid on his arm. The gesture was fatherly, sympathetic, but not so sympathetic that he would agree. 'I have no choice.'

Loengard felt as though someone had kicked him in the solar plexus. He knew the old doctor liked him; it had never occurred to him that Hertzog would refuse to help in such a terrifying crisis. He pleaded desperately for Kim's life. 'Say you'll do it. Please!'

'No, John. Don't put me in this position!'

Mild-mannered college boy or not, John forgot all the rules of polite behaviour. He grabbed the doctor by the neck of his robe and dragged his face up close. He didn't recognize his own voice. 'I'll do it myself. You just tell me what I need to know. And make it quick.'

John was sickened by the fear he had put in the kind old man's eyes as Hertzog whispered, 'All right, all right. This way.'

Fretting and fuming lest Kim be attacked by the unstable

mob outside, John was glad to grab the equipment Hertzog had amassed for him. Not ten minutes after his arrival, John rushed outside with his arms full and all but threw himself behind the Chevy's wheel.

Kim was a little more awake, peering with fuzzy anxiety into the driver's mirror, pulling open her mouth as though to see the thing which had invaded her.

When he said, 'Kim?' she started. He could tell she wasn't sure whether or not to trust him, but so far humanity was winning.

Her head swung pendulously towards him. Slack-lipped, she asked, 'What are you doing?'

John took a handful of Alka-Seltzer tablets and began stuffing them into a milk bottle filled with water. He covered the neck with his hand and shook the bottle vigorously. White froth seeped out, dripping and fizzing down his arm. 'This is gonna work.'

'What *is* that?'

He could barely make out her thread of a voice. 'Hertzog says this will raise the pH level in your body, which'll help get this thing out.'

'I thought we were going to . . . that place where you work.'

'No, we can't, Kim. We've got to find someplace else and do it on our own.' He held out the bottle to her.

She seemed fascinated by the snowy bubbles, but didn't have the will to take the bottle.

'All right, drink this. C'mon, take it.'

Kim made no move. Slowly her gaze travelled down to the hand nearest him. Unbelieving, she said, 'My hand. It won't move.'

John shoved the bottle into her grip, tightening her fingers around the wet glass. Then he guided it towards her mouth. 'You have to fight this while you're still in control.'

Her hand shook with the effort of resisting her paralysis. 'It's too hard, John.'

'Drink it! You have to! It'll help, I swear!'

The cords in her neck standing out with the strain, she

forced the bottle to her lips. She managed to gulp five or six mouthfuls.

Fear struck her. The bottle fell from her nerveless grasp and her head rocked on her shoulders. Horror writhed across her face, tightening it into a grimace of utter dread.

She mouthed, 'Oh God!' and clutched her temples. 'It's *moving* in my head!' Her eyes pleaded for release. 'It's moving in my head, John.'

In answer he started the car and jammed his foot on the gas. The Chevy rocketed away.

Through the night-dark streets John circled the area while Kim whimpered white and sweating beside him.

At last he found what he wanted. He slammed the brakes hard and jumped out of the car, racing round to help her stand. She tottered upright, hardly even noticing where she was.

What had caught his eye was the For Sale board outside a deserted house. It was big, double-fronted, the windows boarded and half hidden by trees. 'C'mon, honey. This'll work. Nobody will find us here.'

Too engulfed by dread, he never thought to hide the car. He led her between the iron railings and up the drive. Drifts of dead brown leaves crackled underfoot. The midnight air was cool enough to make him glad he had helped Kim change from her short dress into cream trousers and a long-sleeved blouse.

It didn't take him long to crack open the larder window and let her in. The house was dark and smelled vaguely of abandonment. Their tread echoed on the bare boards, softened only by yellowing magazines and crumpled paper. Dust motes gleamed like silver smoke in the thin light that filtered between the planks covering the windows.

He found a couple of rickety wooden chairs that had been left behind, unwanted, and helped her across to one. She collapsed gratefully onto it. But when he sat opposite and plunged Hertzog's syringe into the neck of a smaller bottle, Kim sprang up in alarm.

Apprehensively she regarded the bottle on the dust-streaked table between them. 'That's nail-varnish remover!'

John came to her. He wrapped his arm round her shoulders and forcefully sat her down again. 'The main ingredient is acetone. I have to inject the organism with something that'll attack it.'

She looked at him doubtfully.

'With your pH off balance, it'll want to leave your body.'

Enough of her awareness remained intact for her to know the risks. If he missed, the acetone would get into her brain. That in itself might kill her, or leave her mentally crippled for what was left of her life. Or he might stab through into her spinal cord and she'd be truly paralysed.

'What happened to the other people he did this to?' she said faintly. 'And no more lies.'

John hesitated. 'It's . . . never been tried on a person.'

'So unless I want to live with it—'

'You *can't* live with it, Kim!'

Not to be deterred, he came round behind her and tenderly swept the hair from the nape of her neck, exposing the vulnerable hollow he loved to kiss. Knowing the risk they ran, he paused, syringe in his hand.

Leaping to her feet, she powered herself backwards at him.

It was totally unexpected. He dropped the hypodermic. Throwing his arms around her, he tried to catch her, but the weight bore him down. He couldn't break their fall. He toppled heavily to the boards. The crash rattled his teeth and set his ears ringing. Kim landed on top of him, the impact knocking the breath from his lungs.

She scrambled hand over hand to her feet. Through the dust clouding his sight he saw her race to the door.

He hauled himself up and ran towards her. She tightened her grip convulsively on the doorknob, turning it, wrenching it, but it was locked.

Grabbing her from behind, he yanked her away. Her

hands pulled free from the knob and she tried to beat at him, but he had wrapped his arms firmly round her ribcage.

She doubled over, lifting her feet from the floor to pull him off-balance. He tottered a few steps forward.

Kim swung the soles of her feet against the boards on a window and thrust out with all her might. John fell, trying to hold her. His shoulders collided with the table. It fragmented beneath him. The bottle of nail-varnish remover flew up and arced through the air to crash against his ear. Broken glass lanced into the side of his head, drawing blood that streamed down onto his shirt.

Rolling frenetically, she pulled loose and turned on John. Wild with animal panic, she hurled herself at him, fingers clawing for his eyes. Rabid fury contorted her features. No longer human, she was a sickening parody of herself, snarling bestially and kicking out at him.

For a second revulsion held him back. The idea of hurting his beloved, even with her like this, was anathema to him. He felt so bitter he couldn't move. But he had to do it.

Rolling and scrabbling, he grappled her to the ground. She fell prone and he leaped astride, pinning her down with his weight. Still she bucked, but he was bigger and stronger.

All at once the fight went out of her and she gave up the battle. Iron rigidity seized her muscles, making them stand up in ridges. She arched until he feared her spine would snap. A faint, gut-wrenching mewl forced itself from her throat. The sound was scarcely human. It set his scalp crawling.

Once again he brushed the hair from her neck. Now he could see the lumpen scuttling flicker of movement under her skin. Not giving himself time to think, he plunged the syringe into the ganglion.

Hours passed. John crouched beside her chair, glad of the cramps that racked him. They were some slight atonement for what he had brought upon her. At first he had crooned to her, words of love, the gentle endearments that had always bound them together in intimacy, but her body stayed slack, her eyes rolled up in her head.

The blood had clotted on his scalp and stuck his shirt to his shoulder. He shivered continuously in the pre-dawn cold. And still she didn't wake.

Time and again he felt for her pulse. It was hardly there, an erratic flutter that could have been his imagination. Yet her body was hot. It was his only sign that he hadn't killed her outright. Perspiration sheened her skin, plastered her forehead with seaweed strands of hair.

But now and again the ganglion twitched subcutaneously. Then guilt and dread spilt acid into his veins. He was as close to praying as he had ever been in his life.

Outside, the tumult in the street had died down. All he could hear was the creaking of the old house settling on its foundations, or the distant rumble of a car. And the all but imperceptible sigh of her breathing.

For safety's sake he had bound her to the less fragile chair with the cords that Hertzog had given him after his staccato instructions. She slouched, head lolling, and in what little light there was she looked ghastly.

Kim began to mumble wordlessly. Or rather, in words that didn't sound like any he had ever heard. Alarmed, he stroked her forehead and patted her cheeks. 'Kim, honey, it's me, John.'

Her eyes flickered open. She blinked and gradually focused on him.

He tried to smile but his face felt stiff. 'Everything's going to be OK.'

Kim's answer was not what he wanted to hear. 'You have to let me go, John.'

'Not yet.'

Her smile was as unbelievable as his. 'I'm OK.' She must have known he wasn't convinced because she added, 'Really. It worked.'

'Not yet, Kim. I am sorry. I just can't—'

'*I hate you!*' she snarled. 'Let me go!'

'That's not you talking. You have to keep fighting it. Please.'

Her rictus of hate melted. Now she looked like a whipped child, eyes large and fearful. She cowered back in the chair.

The feeling turned like a hacksaw in his stomach. Then it got worse.

Tears welled from her eyes and great liquid streams of misery rolled down her exhausted face. She wailed, 'Honey, please, I just want to go home. Please take me home. Please. Please.'

John turned away, sickened by his own cruelty. But Kim sobbed on and on, pleading with him until he had to cover his ears against the dreadful sounds. Still she wouldn't stop.

He swore.

She choked on a whimper and retched.

He stepped quickly over to her, brushing her hair off her face, comforting her.

The gagging stopped. John was relieved, until the pleading started again. He explained once more that he couldn't turn her loose because the thing was still inside her. Then she started to cry again and the whole drama repeated itself.

This time, not trusting himself to be strong against her begging, he watched from the other side of the room. Self-hatred gnawed at him, so fierce a regret that he almost gave in.

Suddenly her eyes rolled in an extremity of pain that gripped her with talons of fire.

John couldn't take it. He walked quickly towards her, not sure whether he could watch her suffer or if he would set her free.

Then her whole body spasmed in a violent cough.

Before he could reach her something flew from her mouth.

It plopped writhing onto the floorboards. Small, half

formed, it was not a hand span across, but it was definitely a ganglion, or the beginnings of one. The thing thrashed feebly, leaving a moist, slimy trail in the dust.

John stomped on it. He gave full vent to his fury and frustration, pounding out his hatred of the foul obscenity with every pulverizing stamp. It was the first opportunity he'd had for revenge against this nightmare spawn and he relished it. Again and again he crushed it under the heel of his shoe until it was nothing but a viscous stain on the boards.

Kim was breathing more normally. She was unconscious, but her colour was already better, and when he untied her, she fell forward into his arms.

He had to swallow once or twice and tell himself sternly that there was nothing to worry about any more. Wrapping her in his coat, he lifted her, marvelling at the trusting way she snuggled into his chest. Everything was all right again.

Outside, he laid her gently on the back seat of the car. She sighed and sank deeper into sleep. Just for a moment he looked down at her, proud and joyful at her recovery.

Closing the door with a soft click, he drew himself tall and eased the kinks out of his back. He didn't have a thought for himself, the dull throbbing of the contusion in his head or the blood that was once more trickling down to splash his shirt. All his thoughts were centred on her.

Four figures climbed out of the car that had parked, unnoticed, in front of his. A street light behind them made them into black silhouettes. John knew them well enough by now to recognize them anywhere.

Bach, Steele, Albano and Hertzog.

They surrounded him, Bach and Albano in their navy rig.

John was a civilian. It didn't impress him. Anyway, he'd had enough of Majestic. He glared at the doctor as though he was some kind of turncoat. 'So you couldn't help me, but you go running to them?'

Dr Hertzog knew that he had lost Loengard's respect. 'Please, John, I know how you feel, but it's my job.'

John dismissed Hertzog from his thoughts and turned on Bach. 'Frank, if you're going to follow me, why don't you at least help?'

'We just got here, John. We had to clean up the . . . mess you left at your apartment.'

'I'll bet you knew about Pratt all along.'

Albano cut across. 'We need the girl's body, Captain.'

Bach accepted the statement as fact. He turned a level gaze on John and said, 'Don't let her death be in vain.'

John yelled, 'You guys are like vultures. The only problem is, *she's not dead!*'

13

Another day had broken like an egg yolk over Washington. Then grey clouds swallowed the golden brightness and a dull drizzle began to fall.

Down inside the secret headquarters, it made no difference. Day or night, Majestic's unceasing routine went on.

But in a small, clinical-looking room, Kim lay fast asleep on an iron-framed bed. John sat beside her, holding her hand in his. It was more for his comfort than for her own. She hadn't woken once since he had forced the ganglion from her body.

Electrodes were attached to her temples, to the skin above the rounded swell of her breasts. Drips fed in and out of tubes on her arms. Yet her colour was good and her skin-tone had firmed up to something approaching her normal healthy state.

What worried John was what Dr Hertzog said: 'I think we're safe with her.'

'Only *think*?' John asked. Anxiety had worn him ragged. His tie was skewed, his forehead almost as rumpled as his suit. With eyes that were red-ringed from exhaustion, he looked like he hadn't slept in days.

But Hertzog could tell him nothing more. There was a constraint to him now that John hadn't previously experienced, and his vague assurances did little to soothe John's mind.

There was an observation window to one side of the

room. As soon as the doctor left, Bach tapped on the glass and beckoned. With a backward glance at Kim, John stepped next door.

Bach wasn't alone, but the man was no-one John knew, and Bach made no attempt to introduce them. As far as John was concerned, the man was inconsequential. Yet Majestic's chief never let anyone know anything without carefully vetting the circumstances.

John was too tired to care. All that mattered to him at the moment was Kim's welfare. Sufficient unto the day was the evil thereof.

Without preamble, Bach announced, 'You can take her home tomorrow. If she starts remembering any details, I want her brought back immediately.'

John nodded shortly, then let his gaze wander back to Kim. Like Sleeping Beauty, she lay peacefully behind the glass. Abruptly he said, 'I want out, Frank.'

Bach didn't bat an eyelid. 'You know I can't agree to that.'

'What am I supposed to do? What am I gonna tell Kim?' Even John heard the strain in his own voice.

The Majestic leader considered dispassionately. 'That's your business. My business is to keep you part of the team.'

'I'm twenty-five years old. I'm nobody!' John yelled, then pulled himself together. Dropping half an octave, he said huskily, 'You don't need me.'

Naked emotion seemed not to be part of Bach's equation. 'Look, John, why don't you take a break? Get your life in order. Just remember, you work for us, always. That part never changes.'

As simply as that, John was dismissed from Bach's attention. He might as well have been a fly crawling across the desk.

Yet the warning often rang through John's mind in the days that followed.

You work for us, always. That part never changes.

* * *

One Monday some three weeks later, Kim took a half-day's leave from the First Lady's office. She said it was to have a check-up after her mysterious 'virus', but she had more serious business in mind.

John drove her out to the beautiful suburb of Bethesda. Kim's complexion had returned to its usual healthiness, though sometimes there was still a haunted look in her eyes. She tried not to let him see it, but as the turquoise Chevy drew nearer to their destination he couldn't help but notice that she seemed a little twitchy. The tenth time her fingers strayed to twiddle with the necklace at her throat, John pulled over and turned to face her.

'Are you sure you want to go through with this, honey?'

She nodded. Her mouth firmed and her chin went up, a trait John had always found rather endearing.

'We can always do this another day if you're not up to it.'

'Uh-uh.' When she spoke, her tone was determined. 'We've talked it over often enough. Spied out the land. And whatever that Bach man says, this is one secret that shouldn't be hidden from people, especially not from the president. The security at that Majestic is far too tight for you to smuggle the evidence out. We have to tell Mr Kennedy what's going on.'

'I can do it alone if you—'

'No, John. This is much more my adventure than yours, anyway. I was the one who had that horrible thing implanted, remember? You can't keep me out now.'

'Well, if you're certain . . .'

'Look, this is probably the best chance we're going to get. We know Bach's at home, we know his routine. Stop flapping, John, and let's get on with it.'

He would have protested again but she stilled his mouth with a kiss. John started the car again, proud that his woman was one of the new generation who wouldn't stand idly by, begging for help from a man when a problem arose. Not five minutes later, he drew up a few blocks along from Bach's house.

After that, all they had to do was wait. Now it was John's turn to get as jumpy as a landed fish. Kim grinned mischievously at him and settled down for a snooze.

At a quarter to nine, he was ready to explode. Impatience had built in him to a degree where he could hardly sit still. His fingers tapped restless patterns on the steering-wheel and every time a door up the road opened he tensed.

With sheer relief he finally spotted Bach's two children coming out onto their front porch. They were grade-schoolers, with cute little cartoon-character sandwich boxes swinging from their hands.

'Kim. Kim! Wake up! There they are!'

Now Bach and his wife had come out to see the kids off. First the girl and then the boy kissed their parents before tripping off merrily down the drive.

Kim sat up and whispered, 'I can't believe that man has children.'

John had already opened the car door. 'All right, when I wave at you, you go.'

She nodded, more than a little fed up with his fussing, but it wouldn't help to say so. She watched him dodge the morning traffic as he crossed the street and cut around the side of Bach's house. He disappeared into the lilac bushes and popped up a minute or two later halfway up the elm that grew alongside the porch. Once he had taken up position on the overhanging limb of the tree he waved.

Kim waggled her fingers back at him, then slipped on a pair of big sunglasses and tied a colourful scarf around her head. She checked herself in the driver's mirror.

With the scarf pulled forward to hide her red-gold hair and the dark lenses covering half of her face, no-one would recognize her. She hoped.

Taking a deep breath, she let herself out of the car and walked up to the house. Meantime John had shinned along the branch and dropped noiselessly down onto the roof of the porch that ran along the sides and front of the stately building.

Kim walked with a no-nonsense tread up the stairs to the shiny red front door and knocked. She knew that upstairs John would be letting himself in through the landing window that stood ajar in the warmer weather.

From inside, a woman's voice yelled up the stairs, 'I'll get it.'

John tiptoed along the polished parquet. Ahead, in the angle of the landing, a door stood slightly ajar. A little steam was escaping, scented with masculine soap. It carried the cologne that he knew Bach always used.

John heard the crisp clack of Mrs Bach's heels heading, he hoped, for the front door. The sound of traffic drifted up to him. John heard Kim say in a high, tight voice, 'Hi. I'm sorry to disturb you this early in the morning, but my name is Charrisse Rich and I'm a substitute teacher at Willow Elementary.'

'Yes?' Mrs Bach queried.

'I've got the directions but I must have taken a wrong turn somewhere.'

John walked as silently as possible towards the bathroom. Half his attention was on what was happening downstairs, so he didn't see the toy truck until it skidded from beneath his toe. It rattled across the wood and bumped quietly against the skirting. Cursing himself, he froze.

Either Bach didn't hear it or he didn't think it was significant. The noises of shaving, a tuneless whistle, the slosh of the razor through the water in the sink, carried on. John moved gingerly towards the sounds and hid behind the half-open door.

The conversation he could hear from downstairs confirmed that Kim was doing a fine job with her lost teacher routine. Up here, the gush of running water told him that Bach had turned on the shower.

John risked poking his head into the bathroom. And bolted straight back onto the landing. Bach hadn't got into the shower yet.

Gingerly, John peeped through the crack by the hinges.

He saw Bach, a towel around his waist, taking the chain from his neck and laying it aside.

He only hoped Kim could keep Mrs Bach talking a while longer. If they discovered him here, John had no doubt that Bach's men would find a way to silence him. Permanently.

Bach was in the shower now, a faint, flesh-coloured figure veiled in steam and half obscured by the water running down the frosted glass.

Stooping low, John crept into the bathroom, reaching up over his head to grab the metal container off the counter. The chain slithered, clinking against the can of shaving foam.

He held his breath, his hand closed tight around the locket. But Bach seemed not to have heard anything over the splash of running water. Quickly, before Mrs Bach could make her escape from the garrulous stranger at her door, John fumbled with the catch on the flat steel box.

Maybe it was the condensation, or maybe it was the nervous sweat on the palms of his hands, but it seemed to take for ever to get the container open. At last the triangle of transparent metal floated free. Before it could drift off he snatched it out of the air and hastily slid the container closed.

As quickly as he dared, he went back along the landing. This time he was prepared for the little blue truck and stepped round it. Within moments he was through the window and dropping down from the gnarled old elm, the precious alien artefact safe in his pocket.

Kim saw him from the corner of her eye. She beamed at Mrs Bach and launched into the last part of her prepared speech. 'Are all the neighbours as nice as you?'

Bach's wife smiled coyly. Maybe under other circumstances Kim would have liked to chat with her, because she was obviously a lonely woman with her husband away so much, but right now she just wanted to get away before that husband came downstairs and caught her.

'Oh, you're sweet,' Mrs Bach cooed. 'We get along. All except for Mrs Crutchfield across the street.'

Kim turned her head a little, as if looking for Mrs Crutchfield's house. What she actually wanted was to see John getting back into the car. That was exactly what he was doing.

As though she had just remembered it, Kim checked her watch and exclaimed, 'Goodness! Just look at the time! If I don't get a move on, they're going to need a substitute for me.' She took a step away and said over her shoulder, 'It was really nice meeting you.'

Mrs Bach nodded and said, ''Bye!' She closed the door, still smiling at the pleasant young teacher who'd be at her children's school today.

Kim was due back in the White House after lunch. Having changed into clothes of the high standard of elegance the First Lady expected, she hung around in the park not far from the Jefferson Memorial. She was beginning to get worried. John was supposed to meet her there but as yet hadn't shown up, and it was almost two o'clock. Since she'd taken the morning off, she didn't dare leave it much longer.

All the same, her anxieties had sharp, relentless teeth. She couldn't stop thinking that if Majestic had somehow discovered their plan, John could be lying dead in a gutter somewhere. Or have been 'vanished' from the face of the Earth. Maybe Bach had even ordered one of those ganglion things to be implanted into John so they could observe him.

An icy fist clutched her heart as she tried to banish the ghastly picture that formed in her mind's eye. The thought of having the man she loved snatched away by one of those unholy creatures was almost more than she could bear. Taking deep breaths to calm herself, it took Kim a full minute to get her emotions back under control.

She sighed, gave an encroaching stranger a fierce look that made him reconsider putting the moves on her, and looked again down the avenue of trees. A Fall breeze sent dry leaves skittering over the sun-drenched grass, so she didn't hear the footfalls approaching behind her.

'Kim?'

Turning, she saw John hurrying towards her, coat-tails flapping over his business suit as he broke into a run. He carried a large envelope openly in his hand, hiding it in plain sight.

He plumped down on the slatted bench and greeted her with a kiss. 'Sorry I'm late.' Catching his breath, he went on, 'OK. The signed affidavit's in here. The material is inside the specimen bag. Everything's ready.'

'I guess it's up to me now?'

He stroked a finger lovingly over the back of her hand. 'You don't have to do this you know.'

'Of course I do. We both know that.' She kissed him on the cheek and stood to go. 'Wish me luck.'

John gazed at her ardently, full of pride and love. 'Hey,' he called after her.

She looked back at him and saw him hold up his crossed fingers. With a flashing white smile, she headed off to the White House, determination in every taut line of her body.

Not giving herself time to back out, Kim went in through the staff entrance and headed straight for the executive reception suite. Kim knocked on the executive secretary's door, then entered hesitantly.

The woman behind the cluttered desk had an unmistakable air of authority. A discreet nameplate of gilded lettering on mahogany read 'Evelyn Lincoln'. She was of a certain age but her dark hair had not a single thread of silver, and she was beautifully made up. At home in her office, the president's secretary was as elegant as her setting. She wore a V-necked burgundy dress and her single-stranded choker had the soft iridescence of real pearls.

Kim instantly felt that her own heavy beads were cheap and overdone. Clutching the all-important envelope to her like a shield, she took a deep breath and went over to stand in front of the desk, as nervous as a schoolgirl before the headmistress.

'Mrs Lincoln?'

'Good afternoon.'

'I'm Kimberly Sayers. I work for Alicia Burnside.'

Mrs Lincoln relaxed fractionally, the severe lines of her face softening. 'Yes. I remember seeing your name on the staff list. How can I help you?'

'Um, the First Lady would like the president to review the Hyannis Port redecoration plan.'

President Kennedy's executive secretary reached for the envelope. 'Here. I can attach it to his daily briefing.'

Kim held it closer to her chest. 'She told me to make sure only the president saw it.'

For a heartbeat it hung in the balance, then Mrs Lincoln smiled again. She said conspiratorially, 'Well, if I've learned one thing in all these years, it's to let the wives call their own shots. I'll see to it that he gets it *alone*.'

Kim knew that was the best offer she would get. There was no sense in pushing her luck. She summoned up a smile and said, 'Oh, thank you. I'm sure that'll really be appreciated.'

Mrs Lincoln stood gracefully and headed inside the Oval Office.

Just before the door closed, Kim heard her say, 'Mr President . . .'

14

For two long days Kim and John fretted. Neither of them knew what response to expect, but if the president had seen the material and the affidavit, surely he would have done something? The longer they waited, the more time Bach had to discover that he'd been robbed of the priceless alien artefact. Given Majestic's warlord mentality, reprisals could be fatal. Small wonder that neither John nor Kim could sleep.

On the third day, John dragged on his dressing gown as usual and stumbled downstairs to pick up his newspaper. Kim, equally lethargic, was making coffee in the kitchen. Its rich aroma welcomed John back inside.

He sat at the table and smiled his thanks. He was too tired and too wound up to talk. Kim drifted off to the bathroom and he leafed desultorily through the broadsheet.

Abruptly he yelled, 'Kim! We've done it!'

She put her head round the door. 'Huh?'

He flourished a sheet of paper above his head. 'Look! We've done it! This was hidden in the newspaper!'

'What?'

Gone was his apathy. 'See? It's a note from the Attorney-General's office.'

Kim snatched it from him and scanned it quickly. 'Robert Kennedy wants to meet you! And this way the president's kept safe.'

'Maybe they're not sure if we're nuts. I mean, it sounds pretty weird, doesn't it? But that transparent floating foil . . .'

'And they're picking you up at nine o'clock. You'd better get moving, John. I wish I was going with you.'

'I'll tell you all about it when I get back, but you're right.' He ran for the bathroom door, grabbing her round the waist and spinning her joyously aside. 'First dibs on the shower.'

'You rat!'

John was less unnerved by black limousines than he used to be. Still, when the long sleek car pulled in through the security gates and up the sweeping drive of the Hickory Hill Mansion, he had a whole butterfly farm in his stomach. He couldn't get over wondering whether he had solved all their problems, or created a whole new set he could scarcely imagine.

He hadn't decided when the driver pulled the car silently to a halt in front of the Arcadian portico. Slowly he stepped onto the gravel drive.

Robert Kennedy, the Attorney-General himself, left the breakfast he had been enjoying on the terrace and came forward to greet him. John's mouth turned into a desert. Looking at all the muscular aides escorting the president's brother didn't help calm him either.

Casual in slacks and a hand-knitted grey jumper, Robert Kennedy stopped in front of him. 'Mr Loengard?'

John ducked his head awkwardly in a slight bow and worked a little juice into his mouth. 'Sir. It's an honour.'

The face that John had seen a thousand times on television, rounded, with high Irish cheekbones and dark eyes that shone with intelligence, opened to him. 'The honour's mine. If what I'm beginning to believe is true, you've put a lot on the line to get here.'

His reassurance unfroze John's tongue. 'Well, sir, there's a lot at stake.'

Kennedy nodded two or three times. 'Let's take a walk.'

He set off, John at his elbow, putting some distance between them and the aides, who hung back a little to give them privacy. The grass was soft under their feet, and little whirlpools of leaves drifted around them.

John found it surreal: the trees, the birds, the rolling hills and the sweet green freshness of the country air, like there was nothing wrong in the whole wide world, and here he was, a college kid from UCLA, walking with the second most powerful man in the United States. But when he drew breath to speak, Bobby Kennedy gently shook his head, seemingly absorbed in the splendour of the sunlit day.

As they drew nearer the earth-coloured water of the river front, the Attorney-General made up his mind. When he spoke, it was decisively. 'We've had the sample analysed, and it's as advertised. We also checked out certain elements of your story, very discreetly, of course, and it seems to hold together.' He gave a hard tight smile. 'I have to tell you, it has made it rather hard to concentrate on such mundane matters as trade enforcement budgets.'

'What is the president going to do?'

Bobby slowed down, keeping an eagle eye out for intruders. 'John, the president has less than a year on his term. He's got to get re-elected if he's going to do anything. The second term, that's when we can get this out.'

John felt the Earth's polarity shifting beneath his feet. What he wanted was instant action, both against Majestic and against the invading aliens, yet it was obvious now he wasn't going to get it. And equally obvious that the Attorney-General was correct. The president's hands were tied.

Maybe there was something John could salvage from the shipwreck of his hopes. 'I can't stay in Majestic, right?'

Kennedy laid a hand on his arm. Its pressure was warm but firm. 'You have to. The president needs someone like you on the inside. You'll be contacted from time to time.' He held John's gaze with his own. 'Will you do this for us?'

Swallowing his disappointment, Loengard nodded.

That evening, Captain Bach made the Majestic conference room off-limits to everyone but himself and Steele. Bach personally checked the security systems, the blinds. He even checked the telephone at the head of the scarlet table before he sat down beside it. The place was as tight as a drum. No-one would know what went on in this room tonight.

Except, maybe, John Loengard. That was what they were here to decide.

With a suspicion of a swagger, Steele dimmed the lights and moved to the cine-projector. His small-irised eyes were half-lidded, secrecy a habit, but even so he couldn't help plugging in the projector with a certain arrogant flourish.

Uncharacteristically Bach snapped, 'Get on with it!' and fidgeted with the water carafe and glasses next to him before lighting another cigarette.

Steele clicked the switch. He didn't need to see the somewhat grainy monochrome film. After all, it had been he who had made it his duty to follow Loengard and spy on his every movement. But he did want to see Bach's reaction. All along, Steele had felt that having Loengard on board was a mistake. Now Bach would find out what his blue-eyed boy was really like.

And Steele would enjoy dealing with it.

Chain-smoking, Bach watched the silent images of John shaking hands with Robert Kennedy, their behaviour, John's reluctant nod that put an end to the long private walk by the river. He didn't miss the paternal pat on the shoulder either as the president's brother ushered Loengard back into the limo and sent him away.

Impelled from his seat, Bach cast a giant shadow over the screen, his body blocking out huge sections of it as though he would blot John out of reality. So caught up in his thoughts was he that he didn't even notice he was speaking aloud.

Steele did. The cloaker repressed a smile of satisfaction and listened avidly to his boss.

'You don't get to the Attorney-General unless he wants you to. Unless he's already seen something incriminating . . .'

Bach's voice trailed off as he considered the possibilities. His unfocused gaze swept around the room, a reflection of his mental search. Then he looked downwards at his chest. His fingers trembled as he loosened his tie, undid his top button, and feverishly pulled the locket out from around his neck. He stared at it a moment as though he didn't want to uncover something he might not like. Finally he fumbled open the container.

It was empty.

He ripped the thing from around his neck. Squeezing, bending, wrenching at the metal as though he were throttling an enemy, he sought to destroy it, but it was too hard for him to do more than dent it. He slammed it onto the blotter. It thunked dully but that wasn't enough to assuage his passion. Seizing the telephone receiver, he hammered it over and over again. Out of control, he was maniacal, dark blood suffusing his face that was contorted with killing rage.

Steele pretended not to watch but he was silently enjoying every minute. Once more his privileged position inside Majestic would be unassailable as soon as Loengard was destroyed. To give himself something to do he fiddled with the projector, secretly revelling in the sight of his commander racked with anger.

Bach hurled the receiver aside. It swept the locket from the table and smashed several glasses to tinkling shards. Grasping for shreds of self-control, he grated, 'See to it.'

At around the same time, John picked up Kimberly from work and told her all about the meeting with Bobby Kennedy. Exciting as the news was, they still had to eat, so they detoured to the supermarket. It was about half-past seven when they parked the car outside the apartment house and went inside with their arms full of grocery bags.

Outside the flat, John juggled with the carriers so he

could hook out the keys. He was sure they were in his coat pocket. 'So, you gonna let me cook tonight?'

Kim grinned at him, captivating in her pink crochet beret that brought out the colour in her cheeks. 'You don't like my lasagna?'

He laughed at the playful exuberance in her face, and tried another pocket. 'Why not? I haven't felt this optimistic since we moved in. Remember that? It seems so long ago . . .'

The keys turned out to be in his jacket. He unlocked the door as Kim answered, 'I seem to remember you asked me to marry you—'

She stopped, and he couldn't blame her. The open door showed that the room had been trashed. Even the pictures on the walls were skewed, and the couch they'd had cleaned only a month ago had big dirty smears across its cream upholstery. Furniture had been pulled this way and that. The contents of the drawers were one lumpy mess over the carpet, and the standard lamp had been pulled over. Its bulb was flashing unevenly, half under the tablecloth.

Jaws clamped, John moved gingerly inside, but there was no-one here now. For the moment they were safe.

Kim walked warily into the room, subdued by the shock and wanting the comfort of his nearness. As she glanced around, she couldn't see that anything had been stolen, not that they had much worth taking in the first place. But the apartment seemed tainted with the intruder's malign presence. Her heart beat fast with the thought of someone going through their possessions.

Something crunched under her shoe. Bending to see what it was, she found the photograph of John and her on the steps of the Lincoln Memorial that first day in Washington. She could have cried, for the glass hadn't been broken accidentally. Someone had deliberately ground his heel over their faces as if to destroy them. Voice trembling, she held out the photo and asked uncertainly, 'What does this mean?'

John didn't answer. He had stooped to right the standard lamp, and as he straightened, he happened to look out of the window that gave on to the street.

Moving quickly to stand behind the drapes, he peeped outside. A dark sedan had just drawn up behind his Chevy, and two men in black coats were climbing out. What really troubled him, though, was that they didn't slam the doors as people normally did. They closed them softly, as if not wanting to be heard.

One of them slid a hand under his armpit. Once John would have thought only that the man had an itch, but he had spent too much time around the cloakers in Majestic to have any doubt what the man was doing.

The two men turned away a little as a passer-by crossed in front of the car. John knew it was so that the man couldn't witness seeing their faces. They glanced up at the window where he was hiding. Then they headed towards the apartment block.

Frozen with shock, John mumbled, 'Albano!'

Kim had trailed into the bedroom, but that too had been wrecked. She was sitting numbly on the bed, torn between wanting to tidy up and vague ideas that the police wouldn't want her touching things at the scene of the crime.

John leaned in through the door. 'Quick, Kim! They're coming up here.'

She was fast, he had to give her that. He stationed her in the middle of the living room, as though sorting through the debris of their lives, and arming himself with an ugly cut-crystal vase that Kim's aunt had given them, he stationed himself behind the door.

Through the panels he heard the soft footsteps, then saw shadows under the door. Even though he was prepared, the sudden crash of splintering wood churned his stomach.

The cloaker stumbled into the room, off-balance from kicking the lock out of the door. Behind him was Albano, a long-barrelled automatic held level in his right hand. The hand that was closest to John.

Swiftly the cloaker moved in on Kim, grabbing her shoulders as she straightened. He shook her, his fingers jabbing into the muscles of her arms as he grated, 'Where's John?'

Kim didn't have to feign her shock. She said nothing, and the cloaker shook her again.

Albano came towards her. The barrel of his gun seemed as long as a locomotive and it was coming to get her.

As soon as Albano stepped forward, he was within John's range. John pounded once, savagely, on Albano's wrist. The vase shattered, spraying glass splinters, and John heard Albano's grunt of pain. He saw the gun spin away into the mound of jetsam on the floor.

For a second the cloaker was distracted. With all her strength Kim punched him in the stomach. He was too close for her to get a good swing. Retaliating, he landed a short jab on her chin that sent her flying across the room to tumble onto the sofa. Then he whirled to face John.

Albano was game despite his damaged wrist. He snapped a karate chop at Loengard, but his reflexes were dulled by the pain in his arm and John ducked under the blade of his hand.

Stepping in close, John head-butted him, but Albano pulled back and the blow lost most of its force. Albano snaked his hands up in the beginnings of a deadly stranglehold that would crush John's larynx.

Aware that the second cloaker was also closing in, John had no time to waste on the rules of fair play. He grabbed Albano's ears and thunked his head solidly onto the door. Majestic's chief of operations collapsed in an untidy heap.

Leaping aside, John swept up a wooden chair and smashed it over the advancing cloaker. He too fell, not quite unconscious, but John couldn't bring himself to kick a man when he was down.

Pumped up with adrenalin, John yelled at Kim, 'Go, go, go!'

Snatching up her purse, she ran beside him, leaping over the fallen bodies to reach safety.

The good old Chevy didn't let them down. With one stop for petrol and a sandwich, they drove all night, heading south and west through Georgia. Finally, with the sun high and bright in a cloud-mottled sky, they reached the point of exhaustion and began looking for a cheap motel. Problems like getting money and fresh clothing seemed minor in comparison with having to abandon the life they had known. Friends, family, their very livelihood; they were cut off from everything. The whole thing was just too daunting.

But right now what they needed was sleep.

It was just after noon and the shadows of the trees were short. John swung off the highway and headed down a maze of back roads until finally they found just what they were looking for: the sort of quiet, family-run motel that was well off the main drag. They knew they hadn't been tailed: neither Albano nor his henchman had been in any fit state to follow, and even if they had called for support, John and Kim had too great a lead.

The Lazy Acres Motel stretched out sleepily in the midday sunshine, a long rambling building that had been added to at various times over the years. Only one other car was in the lot, an old grey Ford with rust around the wheel arches.

Pulling up alongside, they passed a flower bed with a few late-flowering blush roses sending up a sweet homely scent, and walked sleepily up onto the porch. The wood was silvered with age and creaked gently under their feet. A peach tree was trained against a side wall and there were purple asters starring the flowerpots along the balustrade.

The place was perfect, the manageress discreet. She was the wrong side of forty, her hair a bottle-blond waterfall from a knot on the crown of her head, but she let them have a room at the low-season rate and pointed out the general store a few blocks down the dusty street.

When they settled into the room, which was decorated with pink walls and pine fittings, John made them both a sandwich breakfast. 'Leave the dishes,' he suggested, but Kim was too tense to sleep. She moved restly about the kitchenette, rinsing the few bits of crockery they'd used. Her concentration was turned inward.

For the tenth time she said, 'They know we did it. There's no doubt about that. They know! What are we going to do?'

John sat on the edge of the bed, his elbows on his knees. He had spent almost his last few dollars on clothes for them both. For himself, he'd bought a cheap pair of jeans and a woollen sweater that were comfortable and wouldn't catch the eye like his suit would out here in the wilds. Kim wore pale cotton slacks and a tight button-through top with spots of black embroidery around the edging.

His forehead creased with the effort to stave off sleep. It was almost two and he'd been awake for over thirty hours. 'Well, we can't call anyone,' he decided. 'Bach could be listening. Then he's got a road map straight to us.'

A sharp knock sounded at the door. They tensed. John dived to fish out Albano's gun from under the coat he had dropped on the pillow.

There was a second knock.

Waving her into the middle of the room, John planted himself behind the door. Reluctantly Kim moved to answer it. 'Who is it?' she called.

A woman's voice, rough with suppressed tears, answered her. 'It's the motel manager.'

Kim recognized the voice, but that didn't mean the woman was on her own. Cautiously she answered the door.

It was the manageress all right, and she was alone. Her eyes were brimful of sorrow and her nose was red from crying. In her fingers was a crumpled handkerchief. 'I just came by in case anybody hadn't heard.'

John lowered the gun, though the woman couldn't see him.

Kim was puzzled. 'Heard about what?'

The manageress turned away as if her grief were too private to share. 'Just turn on the TV.' She left, dabbing at her eyes.

Kim closed the door, listening for a moment as the footsteps stopped in front of the next room and the message was repeated. Then she crossed to the television set. It took a time to warm up, and the indoor aerial meant the reception was thin and crackly.

The words, though, were clear enough. A man in the black suit and tie of mourning was addressing a press conference, and for once the pack wasn't shouting.

He announced, 'President John F. Kennedy died at approximately one o'clock, Central Standard Time . . . today . . . here in Dallas.' The government press secretary was distraught, his tone wavering as he sought to blink back his tears. He mastered himself and went on, 'He died of a gunshot wound in the brain. I have no other details regarding the assassination of the president.'

John and Kim stared at each other speechlessly. It was too much for Kim; she sank bonelessly to the bed, and she too was crying as the television went on and on with the news of Kennedy's murder.

John moved to her side, holding her in a protective embrace, but though she clung to him she found no relief. Seeing her suffer only hardened John's anger. Little by little it solidified into a towering monument to the nation's loss.

Kim hardly spoke until the next day, but she didn't have to. Her raw swollen eyes and puffy face said it all. In the speeding car she stared unseeing at the forgotten highway, the ploughed fields and autumnal strands of trees.

In John's mind one thought went round and round with the turning of the Chevy's wheels: he and Kim were completely on their own. Bach had told him they were in a war and that people died in wars. Well, the first real shots had just been fired.

Finally Kim managed to spit out the words that had been choking her. 'We killed the president, John.'

Having spent hours denying it to himself, he gave one hard, emphatic, 'No,' though he couldn't meet her gaze.

'We told him and now he's dead.'

'Kim, you can't know what we know and do nothing.'

'They can't win,' she said in a small voice. 'We can't let them.' Despite her quiet words, her courage rang true.

John heard it and marvelled. After a moment he found words of encouragement for her. 'We have the thing they fear most.'

Kim glanced quickly at him.

'The truth.'

She felt an echo of that truth, a memory crawling in her brain, and shivered.

'Are you cold?'

Shaking her head, Kim answered, 'Just put your arm around me.'

Above the car the sky darkened. And on the radio someone started to sing.

Ugly black clouds roiled overhead, but who knew what was hiding behind them? As John nosed the Chevy up another long rise, he felt as though he was driving straight into the storm.

15

Roswell Army Air Base, New Mexico,
2 July 1947

A few days after his thirty-eighth birthday, Lieutenant Commander Frank Bach witnessed the incident that changed the course of his life irrevocably. He wasn't sure why Admiral Roscoe H. Hillenkoetter had picked him, of all people, to accompany him landside. Maybe he recalled seeing Bach on his tour of duty in the Pacific. Bach knew he had done all right saving his men from Japanese subs that were out to blow his ship sky high, but he also knew many another man could say the same.

Whatever. Seconded to Hillenkoetter's staff, he was ordered to fly out to the harsh New Mexico landscape. You couldn't get much further from the sea than this. Long after sundown, the crumbling earth remembered the heat of the day. As the stars came out one by one, they wavered through the shimmering desert air.

Bach, in his dress uniform and braided cap, waited patiently outside a khaki tent that was big enough to house a small circus. Around him members of all three services went about their duties. A tannoy broadcasting cryptic military instructions meant orders had to be shouted even louder than usual. There were a lot of people here.

Off to one side but well within the heavily guarded

perimeter, a radar dish swivelled, tracking this way and that across the sky. Jerry-rigged screens surrounded it, and operators in shirtsleeves sweated over their controls. Four vast searchlights swept a constant pattern of the heavens. The reflected glow shone off hand-held machine-guns and small artillery emplacements.

The centre of all this activity was a cross of pale green landing lights set out on a patch of cleared scrubland. Dozens of officers, army, navy and air force, kept the service personnel up to scratch, ready for action. And it wasn't just because of the high proportion of top brass. Even the sergeants were nervous, so Bach knew it had to be something big.

As if he hadn't known already. Being on Hillenkoetter's staff, he had made it his job to find out.

Naval secretary James V.Forrestal climbed stiffly out of a jeep and made his way over to the tent, where Admiral Hillenkoetter stood scanning the sky with his binoculars.

Hillenkoetter growled, 'I can't see a damn thing through all these lights.'

Bach said, 'Sir, you probably wouldn't see them anyway until they're right on top of you. Been clocked in excess of seventeen hundred knots.'

Forrestal made a noise of disgust in his throat. 'So we just invite them to a party at the nation's only nuclear base?'

The lieutenant said shortly, 'They invited themselves.' He pointed with his chin at the cross of lights on the sand. 'That is the exact latitude and longitude. This is the time.'

Unimpressed, Forrestal rolled his eyes at the admiral. 'I see Lieutenant Commander Bach's an expert now?'

Hillenkoetter ignored the sarcasm. 'He knows as much as anyone, James.'

A ripple of activity spread rapidly outwards from one of the radar screens. Airman Clark Balfour, its operator, said excitedly, 'Something's coming in fast! I've got a blur streaking in at zero-eight-five.'

Heads pivoted, facing almost due east. The sky was dark

there, with the moon a flattened crescent low on the western horizon.

Then a small pulsing star rocketed towards them. Forrestal drew in a sharp breath.

Admiral Hillenkoetter hadn't got where he was by having slow reactions. He nodded crisply at Bach. 'Frank, get Truman.'

The lieutenant commander squared his muscular shoulders and ducked in through the tent-flap. 'Mr President. It's time.'

A moment, then Bach came out again, stepping aside for an elderly, grey-haired figure in a tweed jacket and bow tie. The little rotund man with the clear-framed glasses was surrounded by generals who glared around as if wanting to make sure there was no mistake.

For a moment breathless anticipation hushed the crowd. Even the tannoy fell silent. Into the vacuum, Airman Balfour said, 'I've . . . it's . . . It's off the scope.'

President Harry S. Truman scowled irascibly. 'Well do we have this thing or don't we?'

Forrestal stalked over to the tech ops. He did not look pleased. Before he could say a word, however, the press officer, Colonel Jesse Marcel, intercepted him. 'Mr Secretary, I think maybe we jumped the gun here.'

Forrestal frowned, then looked respectfully over at the president, giving a slight shake of his head. Along with everybody else, Harry Truman turned his face up to question the skies. He squinted against the flare of the lights on the lenses of his spectacles.

All at once, the scanner stopped arcing. Several radar men burst out, 'It's gone!' 'Can't see a damn thing! My screen's gone haywire!'

Over the babble, the chief of operations said, 'What is this? Tracking is experiencing technical failure. My dials are going crazy!'

Airman Balfour clutched his console, leaning in to examine his screen in sheer disbelief. 'I am in receipt of impossible readings.'

Harry Truman snorted. 'What in the hell is going on here?' he began, then stopped in mid-tirade.

It was audible now, a hum of magnetic force that brushed the skin of everyone present, dragging the small hairs upright all over people's bodies. It grew louder. No-one needed instruments to detect it. A rumble of sub-harmonics vibrated through the ground, singing weirdly through flesh and bone, rattling eardrums as though a swarm of giant cockroaches were marching through everyone's skull.

Abruptly the lights failed. The entire base plunged into a swell of darkness. Only, touching the western hills, the feeble glow of the moon painted a platinum wash across the desert and sparked across the points of bayonets.

What happened next made hand weapons as primitive as bone spears. Out of nowhere a beam of blue light stabbed downwards, spiralling across the area in a blinding search pattern.

It came from a spaceship. A flying saucer that hovered silently some 50 feet above Roswell.

Colonel Marcel gaped at its black metal hull with the circle of light rimming some unknown structure at its base. Three triangular protrusions could have been landing supports.

He was the first to recover. He swallowed and announced, 'We have contact.'

In a silence that iced the sweat on Bach's face, the spaceship descended. At Bach's shoulder, President Harry S. Truman spoke for them all:

'Son of a bitch.'

Now, fifteen years later, waiting at Andrews Air Base for another president, Bach lived the Roswell incident again.

If a president could be gunned down in broad daylight, John and Kim knew that they were in mortal danger. Majestic would see them as loose ends just waiting to be snipped off.

Then the alien danger would never be made known. With congressmen like Pratt taken over by ganglions and Majestic murdering the chief of state, everything Kennedy's administration had stood for could be destroyed. If JFK had been the founder of the spirit of Camelot, Majestic was the murdering usurper who would plunge the world into bloody war.

Unable to sleep, John and Kim fled further westward. Time and again John checked the gun in the glovebox, but they both knew that if any more blood was to be spilled to cover up this alien presence that was called the Hive, it would be theirs.

Taking turns driving, they pushed into Arkansas, keeping the radio tuned for the latest news as darkness swept across the land. At five-seventeen, with the lights of the sparse traffic their only companions, they heard what they had been waiting for.

A reporter, voice thick with grief, described the scene at Andrews Air Force Base. The presidential jet, Air Force One, sat on the tarmac. Massive security held back the hysterical crowd as the bronze casket holding John F. Kennedy's mortal remains was wheeled across under the American flag. An ambulance waiting nearby in the night, its blue light silently revolving, casting bizarre shadows across the flags that rippled at half mast.

Colonel Paul Fuller, the pilot of Air Force One, carried out a meticulous safety inspection of his craft. Security agents in their dark anonymous suits stood guard within a ring of soldiers and airmen.

The radio reporter described Jackie Kennedy coming through, her hair hastily brushed, her beautiful face working as she tried to hold back her tears. She was pale with shock, her eyes glazed with the sedatives that helped alleviate the memory of her husband's murder and his lifeblood splashing over her. Supporting her was Bobby Kennedy.

What the announcer did not relate was the approach of Frank Bach and Phil Albano. They stepped up to Agent

Clint Hill, who was carrying a brown paper sack labelled 'Parkland Memorial Hospital'.

Albano, not even bruised, spoke first. Coming right in close, he said quietly, 'Agent Hill?'

'Yes, sir.'

'Phil Albano.' He handed the agent a signed paper. 'This gives Captain Bach the authority to search the contents.'

Hill narrowed his eyes. He scrutinized the document carefully, wanting a reason not to let these men invade what little privacy remained to the president, but the paper was duly authorized and there was nothing he could do to stop them.

That didn't mean to say he had to like it. Thrusting the bag at Albano, he gestured curtly towards a safe area. Crowding them, he said pointedly, 'Personal effects travel with the body. We don't want to hold President Kennedy here at Andrews any longer than we have to.'

Bach took out the items one by one, peering at them to make sure the alien artefact was not wadded up somewhere in a pocket or a secret hiding place. He laid each one aside as he went: an envelope marked 'Cash', the steel corset the president had worn for relief from his back problems, the blood-crusted suit that had been sheared from Kennedy's body in the hospital. But he didn't find what he was looking for.

As he was feeling his way slowly along the seams of the jacket, the First Lady walked past. She was still wearing the gay pink outfit she had worn for the parade through Dallas. Dark stains made it anything but dashing now.

Wan and angry, she focused on the material in Bach's hands. Staring at the Majestic director as though he were a grave-robber, she said in pained astonishment, 'That was my husband's suit.'

Bach was stricken. Caught literally red-handed, only his years of naval training made it possible for him to stem his blush of embarrassment and guilt. If the First Lady knew what he had done . . . 'I'm terribly sorry about your loss.'

He meant it sincerely. The newly bereaved widow raked

136

him with a bitter look that lingered on the murdered president's clothing in his hands before sweeping back up to his face. 'Yes,' she said caustically, 'I can see that you are.'

Bobby Kennedy put an arm round her and began to shepherd her away. Over his shoulder he said to Agent Hill, 'I don't care what orders these men have. I want them gone now.'

The Majestic man saw trouble brewing. If the Attorney-General went on the warpath, Bach's status would not be enough to save him. He put the president's personal effects back in the bag and handed it to the waiting Hill.

Colonel Fuller, the pilot of AF-1, approached Mrs Kennedy. Bach saluted; the colonel snapped to attention in recognition. Then events moved onward as the late president's party continued on their journey, leaving Bach and Albano behind.

Bach said softly to his aide, 'If he had the item, he left it in Dallas.'

Neither of them noticed the man with the field telephone approaching Robert Kennedy. Chastened, Bach and Albano left to regroup.

But none of this was reported on the radio. In the blue Chevy somewhere in the dark hinterland of Georgia, the only thing that caught John Loengard's attention was the fact that Bobby Kennedy was at Andrews.

Bobby Kennedy. The only man who could save America from the invaders. And incidentally, the only man who could save him and Kimberly.

At the edge of some small town, John screeched the Chevy to a halt and plunged into the first phone booth he saw. Using Kim's White House clearance code, he had his call re-routed direct to Andrews.

Unaware that the head of Majestic wasn't 20 feet away from the portable phone, he asked for the Attorney-General. Robert Kennedy said decisively, 'I'm not taking any calls now,' and took a pace with his widowed sister-in-law.

Then the aide carrying the field telephone hissed, 'It's *him.*'

With a murmured excuse, Robert Kennedy passed Jackie to another aide and answered the call from John Loengard.

'Mr Kennedy, I want to apologize for ever dragging you and your brother into this—'

Robert Kennedy cut across him, saying in that distinctive drawl, 'The president would never accept that apology, and neither will I. Are you all right?'

Terror, assassins, exile from all they had ever known flashed through John's mind. But the man he was speaking to had suffered his own irreparable loss. John said, 'I want to help. What can I do?'

'Our evidence is still in Dallas.'

For a heartbeat John wasn't sure what the Attorney-General meant. Then, in astonishment, he asked, 'You don't have the artefact?'

'He gave it to someone for safe keeping the night before he died. Right now you are the only person I can trust to get it back.'

Steel rang through the conviction in John's reply. 'Yes, sir, I will.'

Bobby Kennedy gave him the information he needed. On the benighted tarmac of Andrews, he saw his brother's casket being loaded into the waiting ambulance and the grieving widow climbing aboard. Emotion welled in his throat, threatening to swamp him. He swallowed and said tightly, 'And, Mr Loengard, I need to know if Majestic-12 did this to my brother. Because if they did, they have not heard the last from me.'

In the lonely phone booth, John hung up and turned to Kimberly. 'Bobby Kennedy says we have to get the artefact back. It's in the Hotel Texas in Fort Worth. Are you up for it?'

Wordlessly she nodded. She knew she didn't have to spell it out. Any reparation they could make would not be enough to assuage her guilt. 'I'll drive.'

Stopping again only for gas, they made over 700 miles by the following afternoon.

Somewhere to the north of Norman, Oklahoma, they watched the shadowed hills crawl by. John was driving his beloved Chevy for what he knew was the last time, and he dragged every ounce of speed from it. This late in November, it was too cold for casual tourists and the road was empty despite the fierce sunshine.

Kim checked her watch and the map yet again and said, 'It's about time.'

John powered around a bend, enjoying the feel of the speed pushing him back into the seat. He sighed. Kim was right. Norman couldn't be much more than a mile or two, and they had a bus to catch. From the last gas station, they had called to check with the Greyhound company. The bus would leave at 3.56 p.m. and it was quarter past three now.

Reluctantly he swerved the Chevy onto the hard shoulder in a flashy handbrake turn that left scorched rubber on the highway. He patted the dashboard once or twice, disguising the gesture as a fumble for the catch of the glovebox, but Kim knew he was making his farewells to the car that had brought them from California to Washington and halfway back again. Both of them remembered the picnics, the trips to the beach, the pure innocent pleasures the turquoise Chevy had brought them.

John got out and fished around for the small valise that now contained everything he owned in the world. Without a word Kim picked up her own grip and followed him out into the dusty weeds.

About 20 yards out, he turned. To Kim's surprise, he was aiming Albano's handgun at his precious car.

She said softly, 'I remember the day you bought this.'

'It's just a car, Kim.'

Both of them knew that was not how he felt.

The gun bucked in his hands. Kim winced at the sheer

volume of the sound, but he fired again and again. Bullets spanged against the trunk of the car, punching round holes in the metal. Taking a more careful aim, he knocked out the light on one tail fin.

Perturbed, Kim said, 'Let's go.'

He shook his head and held the gun butt-first towards her. 'See if you can hit the back window.'

She was not prepared for the solid thump of the recoil. Her first shot whined away into the scrub.

'It's easier if you use both hands.'

Accepting his advice, she fired again. The shatter of glass was somehow satisfying as the rear window crazed. Diamond fragments fell from it. She was getting into the swing of it now, well aware that someday she might need to use the gun in earnest. Encouraged by her success, she took out the driver's side window.

'Go for the tail light,' John told her.

Frowning a little in concentration, she balanced the heavy gun at arm's length, squinting along its barrel just like she had seen in the movies, and squeezed.

The red glass bead seemed to leap loose, like a fish at the end of a line, at the same moment the shot rang out. Echoes of it came back from the purple hills, a reminder that someone might be listening.

The same realization struck John. He went quickly to the car, reaching inside to pick a dagger of glass from the seat. Keeping his face immobile, he sliced the pads of his fingers and thumbs to leave smears of blood on the steering wheel and dash.

Kim understood. He was trying to make it look like some sort of armed robbery or kidnapping. If by any chance Majestic did track them down, it might buy them a breathing space.

Slinging his valise over his arm, he held out his free hand to him. A warm current of love and companionship seemed to bond them even closer together as they set off into town for the bus to Dallas.

They took turns carrying the gun.

16

Right on time, the Greyhound bus pulled up in Fort Worth. The terminal was on a corner, facing a church whose stained-glass windows were dull and featureless in the long shadows of morning. Diagonally opposite was a brown brick building with regular, white-framed windows and a plant-lined entrance. Two doormen in long grey coats with braided epaulettes yawned outside the foyer, their breath smoking white in the chill morning air.

John and Kim took this in as they queued in the aisle of the bus. The driver called, 'Forth Worth. Fifteen minutes,' and stepped on a floor button, making the doors hiss pneumatically apart.

The fresh breeze shook the last rags of sleep from the travellers. They had managed to nap a little through the night but they were still buzzing with adrenalin.

Following the instructions Robert Kennedy's contact had given them over the phone, John walked to the news-stand outside the bus station and bought a local paper. The headline KENNEDY ASSASSINATED jumped out at him, stabbing reality firmly into his mind. Pretending to read the lead article with Kimberly peering over his shoulder, he scanned the broad street but saw nothing out of the ordinary.

Strolling a little, shaking their legs as if to recover from pins and needles after the hours of travel, they glanced up the side street to the left of the hotel. Nothing unusual there, either.

'Looks clear,' John told her.

But they couldn't see the parking lot on the other side where a dark sedan had just pulled up close to the refuse truck. As the garbage men carried the hotel's rubbish bins to and fro, Jim Steele stubbed out his cigarette and went to meet the two men he had been waiting for.

The men who climbed out of the car. Bach and Albano.

Without greeting, Bach raised an eyebrow at Steele. 'No luck at Parkland Memorial?'

Shaking his head, the agent fished in his pocket. 'A nurse kept his watch.' He tossed a gold band at Bach. 'That's it.'

Bach pried off the steel casing, but there was nothing inside that shouldn't have been. He scarcely glanced at the tiny industrial rubies that kept the movements spinning like clockwork, before snapping the watch back together and stuffing it inside his coat. 'What about here?'

Steele shrugged. 'I think you're gonna have to make a run on 'em, Frank.'

Bach and Albano accepted it. Leaving Steele on watch at the side exit, they headed round towards the front.

Meantime, Kim nodded at a phone booth. It was right where their contact had said it would be. She gave John a peck on the cheek, deliberately casual although they both knew how scared she was that something might happen to him. 'If there's anything, I'll call the room.'

He headed across the street, glancing back once at her trim figure in the pale slacks and the voluminous fawn headscarf draped like a shawl around her shoulders. She stood on guard by the telephone, just as she had said she would, his partner in this vale of tears. It was just one more proof that he was truly blessed in love.

The clerk at the hotel desk eyed him briefly, noting the tweed coat over the jeans and sweatshirt, and clucked disapproval at his black sneakers with white laces. It didn't matter. The man jerked his chin towards the elevator and John went up to the third floor, keeping the folded newspaper under his arm and the pistol tucked into the waistband of his jeans, out of sight at the back.

No-one was in the corridor. A deep patterned carpet ran along the centre but showed the floorboards at the sides. Varnished doors punctuated the beige walls between the sorts of pictures only hotels ever seemed to buy.

Stopping at 422, John checked his gun. There were still four bullets left in the clip. He flicked the safety catch to off and knocked.

A man called, 'Who is it?'

Feeling foolish, John gave the coded password: 'I've got the paper you wanted.'

'Yeah. What's the weather report?'

'Dark Skies.'

There was a pause that left John with the sensation that he had somehow been suckered. Then the door opened. On the other side of it was a fifty-year-old man with dark hair lightly frosted with grey. His sharp triangular face was lined, a deep double crease of anxiety rising vertically between thin brows. He wore glasses, the plastic frame paralleling his eyebrows, and his mouth was puckered and small.

Despite the slenderness of his physique the man moved with military precision, stepping aside and looking both ways down the corridor. There was still no-one in sight. He ushered John inside.

Closing the door, he blurted, 'You're a damned kid!' He lifted his shoulders in disgust. 'Hope to God no-one followed you.'

In his months in the congressional offices, John had grown used to the implication that young was stupid. Nowadays he didn't even rise to the bait. 'I'm John Loengard. Mr Kennedy said—'

'Yeah, yeah. Name's Marcel.'

John boggled, his jaw dropping before he recalled himself. 'Jesse Marcel? The public information officer at Roswell?'

The colonel spread his palms. 'Why do you think the

president wanted to talk to me?' Not waiting for an answer, he walked across to the window, approaching it from the side so that he wouldn't be visible to external observers. 'I see a blonde by the bus stop. She with you?'

'Yes.' John didn't want to ask the next question but he had no choice. 'You actually saw the president before he . . . died?'

Marcel sat on the bed, letting his back slump in a most unmilitary way. It was the only outward sign of the grief raging in him. 'Yeah. I wish I hadn't, but yeah.'

A shadow seemed to fall across his face as his unfocused eyes saw again the scene that kept replaying in his head. 'He sat right over there, where you are. Took out this big cigar and lit it with a fancy lighter, sort of silver with gilt overlay.'

John kept his peace, letting the man have time to recover.

'See, he was planning to get a lot of us, the military, NASA, you name it, all to come forward with him, tell the truth about Roswell during his State of the Union Address after he got re-elected.'

Marcel sighed. 'Right after he fired up his cigar, he offered me one. Me, I prefer Lucky Strike, but he passed me his lighter with a special sort of look, you know? No. But I did. That lighter, he meant me to have it, so I put it in my pocket, and he gave that quiet smile, that one that crinkles, I mean crinkled, his eyes up like you see on TV when he's doing those at-home-with-the-kids shots. Gave me his evidence. Said he had a bad feeling about Texas.' The colonel shook his head regretfully. 'Next day, he's dead.' He shot John a piercing look. 'How are you involved?'

It was John's turn to sigh. 'I got the artefact to the president in the first place.'

'Well, you can have it back.' He slipped two fingers into his pants pocket and handed over the silver-gilt lighter. 'I have a wife and kids. I don't want to be a target.'

John took the lighter. It was the kind with the cap that snaps back on a hinge. He examined it, flipped it open.

Marcel said, 'Just pull the lighter part out.'

The works came away with a little tug of John's fingers and thumb. They were still sore from the cuts he had given himself when he dumped the car. He looked into the rectangular case, then turned it over on his palm and tapped it sharply.

Out came the diaphanous triangle, miraculously unfolding itself and floating free of gravity between the two men. John watched it, hypnotized by the strange beauty of the shining foil with its translucent patterns so delicately woven into the metal.

Marcel's features took on the cynical look John was coming to expect. The colonel said, 'You Washington hotshots ever figure out what it was?'

John spun the gauzy artefact with a breath. 'I thought it was part of the spacecraft wreckage.'

Marcel shook his head. 'I was there when they picked up the whole mess, son. I saw some strange stuff but I never saw this.' He sounded annoyed. 'Put it away.'

John obeyed, crumpling the iridescent metal until it folded all by itself, then stuffing it into the lighter.

Marcel stood, his whole demeanour one of dismissal. 'Hope that concludes our business,' he said, turning towards the door.

John didn't take the hint. Staying firmly rooted to his chair, he asked, 'What really did happen at Roswell?'

Marcel said sharply, 'You get the piece. That's it.'

Stowing the lighter in his jeans pocket, John looked him straight in the eye. 'The Attorney-General told me to get the evidence *plus* whatever you told the president. I have to hear your story.'

'They made contact with us, that's what.'

Over Roswell, the saucer kept hovering. Whatever powered the craft, it didn't even stir the sand underfoot. Its bright light strobed down on the high command, on President Harry S. Truman, on Lieutenant Commander Bach and Colonel Jesse Marcel.

The servicemen left their instruments. Not a one of them was working. Electricity seemed to have taken a vacation. Itchy trigger-fingers caressed the mortars, the machine-guns, all the hopelessly outdated war gear that Planet Earth could assemble. Nobody forgot that this was the USA's first nuclear base and it had to be protected at all costs.

But with the spaceship directly overhead, nobody wanted to be the one to start an interplanetary war, either.

Marcel, a young colonel with his oak leaves newly given, stood next to Balfour, the radar operator. He said slowly, 'Maybe we'll all be going to Mars on vacation some day, huh?'

Balfour was too entrenched in wonder to match the colonel's humour. He kept saying over and over again, 'Never seen anything like it. Man, oh man, oh man.'

Without warning a blast of intense white light struck the ground dead on the centre of the landing cross. Marcel covered his eyes to protect them. When he took his hands away, he could just see a figure floating down, limned with phosphorescent brightness, as beautiful as an angel.

When it touched the ground, Marcel's vision had adjusted. The figure was maybe 4 feet high, grey, with a big rounded head and swelling ribs that contrasted strangely with the stick-thin arms and legs. The creature was naked and defenceless, its arms spread wide in a gesture that seemed to embrace all of humanity. Above the huge, dark, liquid pools of its eyes, two depressions that might have been its temples seemed to beat in echo to the pounding of Marcel's pulse.

For a minute or two it stood there, making no move that might be interpreted as hostile. Then it entered the tent. President Truman followed, his face a picture of wonder and astonishment. The top brass trailed uneasily behind. Truman settled in a chair facing the visitor, generals and admirals flanking him. Even Lieutenant Bach went along at a nod from Admiral Hillenkoetter, then the tent-flap shut them off from view. Within moments the power came back and everything seemed as it had been.

Except that the spaceship still sat calmly overhead.

Colonel Marcel had been left behind. He smiled wryly to himself. Dearly though he would love to have been involved, he knew it was a Naval Intelligence operation and he wasn't invited to the party.

But he was there for the fireworks.

He must have waited for an hour or more, listening to the murmurs of gossip and wonder all around him. Nobody knew quite what to do. His own theory was that these marvellous beings had come to earth to warn them not to use the A-bomb again. Hiroshima was not that long ago . . .

Hillenkoetter's appearance put an end to his musings. He shouted with all the authority he needed to make himself heard all over the camp. 'You must evacuate your posts in an orderly fashion. Do so now. This is a direct order from your commander-in-chief.'

Marcel read shock on the faces around him. It mirrored his own. But unquestioning obedience was inculcated into all service personnel. Gathering themselves, everyone began to carry out the command.

The young colonel walked away with Balfour. Under cover of the activity, he asked quietly, 'Why are we doing this?'

But Balfour had no answer.

As the evacuation proceded, the magnetic hum picked up once more. Above, the spaceship climbed slowly, silently, skywards. Then it veered off in a rapid arc that would take it behind the shelter of the nearby hills.

Suddenly the throb and clatter of pom-pom guns burst around the ship. Tracer-fire followed it, two streams of bright shells that bracketed the visitors' craft.

The saucer's trajectory wavered as a direct hit erupted against the black hull. Electrical flares strung briefly across its skin like stranded lightning.

Back on the ground, the noise was deafening. Marcel covered his ears against the roar of the anti-aircraft fire, but his gaze was fastened on the spaceship with those ribbons of killing fire.

The ship was a black-centred circle with a rim of neon light. It dropped like a stone behind a ridge. Then flame crowned the hilltops. A second later came the crash and an explosion so fierce that it swept a fine rain of sand across the watchers at Roswell.

The horror of it still stung Marcel's eyes fifteen years later as he told his story to John Loengard in a hotel suite in Fort Worth. His voice cracked. 'We shot it down, son. They didn't just pick up a crash. They picked up casualties.'

John's eyes showed white rims all around the pupils as disbelief lost to abhorrence. Not twenty-four hours after President Kennedy's death, silence filled the room.

It had not taken Bach long to find out which suite the president had occupied: 850. Now, in the discreet opulence of cream upholstery and swagged curtains, Bach addressed the two local police he had ordered the desk clerk to summon. One at each shoulder, Albano and Steele reinforced his impression of power. In gravelly tones Bach said, 'Officers, I'm Special Agent Clark, with the National Security Council.'

He snapped his fingers at Albano, who stepped forward, producing an official-looking document.

Bach took it. 'When did President Kennedy check out of this room?'

Neither of the Fort Worth men cared for his tone, but before they could protest at his high-handed manner, Steele took out a slim flick knife and began idly tossing it. They watched it glitter as it arced through the air, and gasped almost audibly when Steele caught it without even looking. He was smiling coldly at them.

The taller local cop said immediately, 'His people were out right after breakfast.'

Albano didn't want the local bugs getting above their stations. He stared down his nose at the man. 'We need to search the premises.'

'We've already done that.'

Albano cut him off. '*We* need to do it, officer.' He

stepped in close to the man, who backed away from the hint of menace exuding from Majestic's chief of operations. 'If you'll wait please outside.'

The taller cop was already leaving. His colleague turned to go but Bach stopped him. 'You. I want a complete list of all calls made from this room last night.'

Not a word out of place, but both the local law-enforcement officers were thoroughly intimidated. They left with alacrity.

Bach watched the door close behind them, then nodded at his henchmen. Both Albano and Steele set about the search at once, slitting cushions and ripping pictures from the walls.

The place was a disaster area five minutes later when the younger of the two cops, the one who had drawn the short straw, came back into the room. Seeing the mess, he swallowed but said doggedly, 'Sir, I'm sorry, but there aren't any records of outgoing calls. They all went through the White House switchboard.' He produced a list which Bach took from him. 'All I could get is the in-house calls.'

Bach didn't even acknowledge his assistance. The uniformed officer left in confusion as Bach conned the list, then rolled his eyes in a gesture of contemptuous superiority. 'Three calls to a William Bobo in room 422.'

Albano snorted with derision. 'What the hell kind of name is William Bobo?'

Bach shared his wry amusement. 'It's an alias the boys at Justice use for their informants. They think it's cute.'

'Check outside, Phil,' Bach said thoughtfully.

A moment later, Kim saw the Majestic chief of operations step outside and cross the street. She hunched down in the phone booth, pulling her scarf up over her head. But he wasn't coming towards her. When he reached the far sidewalk he turned to scan the outside of the building.

She turned her back on him and dialled the hotel. With a glance over her shoulder, Kim saw the Majestic man go back into the lobby. She was jiggling up and down in frustration when ten interminable seconds later the receptionist answered.

'I have an emergency call for a William Bobo in room 422,' Kim said.

In Colonel Marcel's room, John started when the phone rang. He strode quickly across and lifted the receiver to hear Kim say, 'John! One of Bach's men is out front. Get out of there now!'

Stunned, John put the phone back on its cradle, then stood with his hand resting on it as he calculated his options.

Marcel sprang up angrily. 'You were followed, weren't you?'

His accusation galvanized John. 'Look, Kennedy trusted me. Now you're going to have to. Let's go.'

There was no profit in delay. Marcel nodded. The pair headed out and along the corridor towards the elevator. Every second was worth its weight in blood. Yet when they reached the lift, the light over its doors indicated that a car was on its way up.

Loengard spun round. 'The fire escape!'

They pounded along to the end of the hallway, the thick carpet absorbing most of the sound. John's hand was already pushing the heavy fire door when Marcel froze.

'My plane ticket! They'll trace it! They'll know it was me!'

Instantly John saw the implications. Marcel sprinted back to his room but the elevator bell rang to say the car was about to draw level.

'There's no time!' John yelled.

Marcel's answer was to throw his car-keys over. John snatched them out of the air as the colonel added, 'My car's a 'fifty-one Studebaker. Pull it around the back!'

For a heartbeat John hesitated, but the old army man shouted 'Go!' in a voice that wasn't meant to be disobeyed. He saw Marcel duck into the room and re-emerge a moment later with the plane ticket in his grasp.

The elevator doors whooshed open and John pelted

down the fire escape. Trapped but determined to hold on to his dignity, Marcel turned to face the men entering the hallway.

Astonishment lightened his features for a moment. 'Frank Bach?'

The Majestic man nodded stolidly. 'It's been a long time, Jesse.'

But Steele saw the movement of the fire door and chased after the escapee.

Barely keeping his lead, John found himself on a metal catwalk outside the first floor. He wrenched desperately at the ladder which should have swung free on its counterweight. The metal was rusted in place. Behind him he heard the footsteps racing closer.

There was only one thing for it. He climbed over the guard rail and jumped the 15 feet which separated him from safety.

By the time Steele reached the catwalk, the only thing visible was a fleeting glimpse of coat.

17

Steele was angry. He showed his frustration in the savage way he manhandled the ageing Marcel into a car. It did not escape the former colonel's notice that the registration place read MJ-9.

Bach calmly closed the door on his prisoner and straightened to fix Steele with a stare that brooked no opposition. 'I want his room torn apart. Same drill as Kennedy. Who'd he talk to? Where'd he go?'

Clenching and unclenching his jaw muscles, the hitman snarled, 'Frank, we're wasting our time here. He handed it to the guy who got away.'

Bach didn't blink. 'Then you won't find anything and we'll keep looking.'

Albano came out of the Hotel Texas and walked over rapidly, a notebook open in his hand. He joined the men by the sedan with an air of suppressed excitement. 'A state trooper just found Loengard's car in Oklahoma. Shot up pretty bad, too. Says there's blood.'

Bach's computer brain clicked straight to the nub of the matter. 'What issue weapon was used?'

Albano saw the point at once. 'Forty-five. He's using the gun he took from us back in DC.'

The head of Majestic nodded, obscurely pleased that his protégé had finally wised up. 'He's playing by our own book. That makes Loengard our mystery man. What else?'

Albano didn't have to consult his notes. 'Dallas PD

thinks there might be evidence of two, maybe three shooters.'

Steele tipped his head to one side. A fleeting grin crossed his face, leaving it once more deadpan. 'JFK had a lot of enemies.'

Bach looked up at his chief of operations. 'Let's get this Oswald transferred out of City Jail. I want an EBE profile as soon as we can get close.'

Albano knew that EBE stood for Extraterrestrial Biological Entity. 'What if he's positive?'

'Then we start looking for the other Hivers who helped him.'

Away down the main street by the far end of the church, a black '51 Studebaker stood facing them. An ordinary-looking youth in a check shirt, jeans and sneakers had his head under the hood. The trunk was open too, presumably for tools. Casing the street, Albano saw that the poor slob was tinkering fruitlessly. The boy kicked the front tyre in frustration, then bent once more to fiddle with the engine.

Not Bach, nor Albano, nor Steele put two and two together and came up with four. But then, they hadn't yet found out that Marcel's car was a black '51 Studebaker, and the former colonel wasn't about to tell them.

Standing beside the crippled car, Kim ducked down to peer through the gap between the chassis and the raised trunk lid. From a distance it should look as though she too was immersed in the repairs.

In the side street, she saw the driver of the Majestic vehicle start his motor. Exhaust gases billowed from the tailpipe like a smoke signal. With a flood of relief she said softly, 'John, they're leaving.'

Loengard slammed his hand against the fender. 'Damn! This coil is shot.' More calmly he crouched over the engine once more and nodded acknowledgement.

Kim asked him the question he'd been trying not to think about. 'What do you think will happen to Mr Marcel?'

'They'll do whatever they have to to get the artefact back. I mean, if they killed the President . . .'

Somberly Kim went back to watching the men from Majestic. She saw Steele straighten and nod curtly at something Bach said. Then he returned to the side entrance of the hotel. Bach and Albano climbed aboard the sedan.

'*Wait!*' she exclaimed. 'One of the agents went back inside. And the car's leaving.'

John risked a glance round the edge of the hood. 'Steele. Perfect. That'll give me enough time to get this thing started. He should lead us right to Marcel.'

Kim straightened, casting a quick loving glance at John's profile against the sun. Reflected light polished the high flare of his cheekbones and lingered on his lips. Drawing a deep breath, she said, 'I'll go round to the front and make sure he doesn't go out that way.'

John nodded his thanks and engaged himself once more with the recalcitrant ignition coil.

In a Majestic safe house on the far side of town, Jesse Marcel leaned tiredly back in a chair. The most visible sign of tension in him was the way his white-knuckled fingers curled around the wooden armrests. But under the fierce lights shining directly on his face, his eyes were dry and red-rimmed, and perspiration dripped down his sideboards and onto his limp collar.

Off to one side was all the paraphernalia of a military-style headquarters: radio receivers, maps, desks littered with coffee cups and sandwich wrappers. The air smelled of stale sweat and old ashtrays. Men came and went all the time, but none of them spoke to him. Marcel had no idea what the time was. Down here there were no windows and no sounds of traffic or church bells or any of the clues that might have told him precisely where he was.

The three constants in this hostile microcosm were the glaring light and the silent cloaker who watched him the way a wolf watches a fat lamb.

The third constant was fear.

A juddering clank told him the freight elevator was coming down. Squinting past the light, Marcel saw that Frank Bach was on his case.

The head of Majestic looked tired, too, but a restless energy burned in him that boded no good. He gestured dismissal at the silent cloaker and pulled a chair close to his prisoner. Lighting a cigarette, he settled back in his seat and studied the slender colonel through smoke.

'Jesse, Jesse, Jesse.' Bach shook his head regretfully, a father displeased with his errant son.

Marcel was having none of it. 'What do you want from me, Bach?'

'You met with the president. Why?'

Marcel shrugged unconvincingly. 'What would the president want with me? I'm just the boy who cried wolf. The guy who couldn't tell a weather balloon from a flying saucer.'

'You swore your silence, Jesse. You took an oath.'

'You mean that gag order you shoved down my throat at Roswell?'

Bach was untouched by the colonel's bitterness. 'Nobody forced you.'

'*Forced?*' Marcel exclaimed. 'No, blackmailed. That's more your style.'

Bach seemed not to have heard. Still paternal, he went on, 'We can work out something, but you have to help us now.'

The prisoner leaned forward until his face was close to his captor's. 'You know, Bach, every day for sixteen years I've had to face my family, my children, my fellow officers . . . myself, knowing that I helped you and the rest of them keep everything quiet. Nothing you can do to me now could be worse than that.'

'Don't be so sure.' Bach smiled nastily, giving the threat time to sink in. Abruptly he changed his tone. 'Who was the man you met with earlier?'

'You're imagining things.' He paused a second before adding defiantly, 'Just like I did.'

'It's a little late to be developing a spine, Jesse. One way or the other, I'm going to find what I'm looking for.'

Marcel laughed and shook his head ruefully. 'I guess sooner or later we all do.'

Loengard knew Steele's mind must be on something else or the cloaker would have spotted the black Studebaker tailing him. Glad of the gathering darkness that hid him, John spent the day driving circuitously around Fort Worth, finally winding up in its twin city of Dallas as the night life was warming up.

It seemed, though, that it wasn't warming up very much. The sidewalks were all but deserted despite the artificial gaiety of the clip joints. John put it down to the nation's shocked mourning for President Kennedy.

He held the Studebaker on the corner of a wide street as Steele braked jerkily outside a seedy nightclub. Peeling limewash was plastered here and there with posters of half-dressed women, and the line of white fairy lights was missing several bulbs. Underneath a street light, a woman with dyed red hair and a gash of vivid lipstick was ostentatiously swinging a necklace. A man in a dark hat stopped beside her, lighting a cigarette in his cupped hands as he eyed up the merchandise.

Maybe the Carousel Club was Steele's idea of a night off, but John didn't think so. The way the cloaker hovered in the doorway looking at his watch didn't seem like relaxation, and Steele wasn't exactly the sort of man you'd stand up on a date.

Kim and John exchanged a glance. 'A strip joint?' Kim said incredulously.

'Probably a Majestic front. Bach's big on using the most unlikely places to set up shop.'

Steele shot his cuff and looked at his watch again. Right then a car with a Dallas Police Department shield on its door stopped and Steele walked purposefully across to it. The officer inside handed something over and Steele held it up to the street light to take a closer look.

From their vantage point, John and Kim saw that it was the sort of small, transparent bag the police used for storing evidence. It appeared to contain three slender, sharp-nosed bullets.

'Looks like . . . rifle shells?' John said in disbelief.

'Maybe he's going to shoot somebody.'

'Maybe not. Look!'

They watched Steele pull out a wad of rolled currency and slip it inconspicuously to the cop in the car. The police vehicle moved away and Steele, pocketing the bag of shells, walked quickly inside.

'Maybe', said John, 'he already did.'

Steele strode through the dim lounge, ignoring the tired stripper and her unenthusiastic routine. Hidden loudspeakers were belting out Peggy Lee's 'Fever', but the few patrons scattered around the tables were more interested in their drinks.

Heading past the stage, without so much as a glance at the woman in the brief spangled costume, the cloaker caught the barman's eye. Knowing what Steele needed without being told, the server nodded towards a private booth in the far corner.

Not a yard from Steele, the stripper slid her fingers suggestively towards her crotch, but the Majestic man took no notice. Pouting, the woman swivelled away to slide up and down a pole which squeaked between her stockinged thighs.

Steele made his way across and sat down facing the Carousel's owner, Jack Ruby.

There couldn't have been more of a contrast between the two. Steele's whipcord figure and intense gaze; Ruby's plump vacuity. The man must have been twice Steele's age. His double chin bulged alarmingly out of his generous shirt collar, and there were crow's-feet that spoke of good humour amongst the lines of dissipation. He wore a suit that was flashily cut to disguise his girth, but not even the best tailor could have made Ruby look other than mediocre, a small-time thug who was obsequious to the police and a bully to his underlings.

Ruby took another slug of whisky from the ample glass before him. He seemed enthralled by the doodles he was making on his cocktail napkin. Under his pudgy fingers strange shapes grew; odd triangles with spiralling curlicues that looked like nothing on earth. Lost in his own private universe, he didn't even register the presence of the Majestic man until Steele said, 'Feeling better today, Jack?'

The fat man roared with laughter as though it were the best joke ever, then stifled it with embarrassment when he saw Steele wasn't joining in. 'I . . . I've been hearing things, Jimmy. Voices. In my head.'

He fumbled his glass to his lips with suddenly shaking hands. 'Real bad thoughts. Can't seem to tune 'em out.'

'Like we don't all get bad thoughts now and again,' Steele smirked. He leaned forward conspiratorially, smelling the powerful aftershave that failed to hide the odour of Ruby's sweat. 'Tell me what's on your mind, Jack.'

Ruby made a half-finished gesture then clamped both hands around his glass. 'I keep seeing Oswald. Clear as day. And I know something bad's gonna happen to him.' Perspiration oozed through the greasy skin. 'Why do I know that, Jimmy?' he whined.

Steele laid a hand firmly on Ruby's wrist. 'Finish your drink, Jack. Then we'll go talk about it.'

In the shadowy alley behind the club, John and Kim scanned the tattered cardboard boxes and piles of drifting trash. The stage door was firmly locked. In this sort of neighbourhood, with junkies and winos hanging around, security had to be tight.

Except way overhead, above a lantern fixed to a metal bracket, a fanlight was open. The fug from inside hazed out into the cold night air: cheap booze, cheap perfume, cheap food.

John glared up at it in frustration. 'There's no way I can get in there.'

'I can. If you give me a hand up.'

He brightened, then his mood turned sombre as he realized he might be sending his beloved into danger. 'Just see if Marcel's in there, then get out.'

She nodded, lifting her foot into his clasped hands. His muscles slid smoothly as he boosted her high enough to grab the bracket. The impetus brought her midriff over the bar, then she swung one knee up. In a second she had slid through the narrow aperture and dropped down out of sight.

John hoped she was going to be OK.

Her sneakers making no sound on the dusty floor, Kim groped her way along the ill-lit passage. At the far end it branched into a T-junction with a flight of metal stairs and a catwalk. From up there came the sound of Peggy Lee; Kim assumed the stairs led to the stage but that was none of her concern.

A couple of yards further along, she stopped at a recessed door marked 'Private'. She pressed her ear against it, listening, debating whether or not to risk going inside. The handle turned gently when she tried it.

Then the music swelled in volume and dropped again to its former level. Upstairs a door must have opened and closed. Footsteps and voices confirmed her fears; the metal stairs clanged beneath shoe heels. She pressed herself back into the recess and risked a peek.

It was Steele. He had a fat man with him, but Kim had no idea who it was. Fear squeezed her heart with icy fingers. She whisked into the room. And stopped.

The scene that met her eyes was too bizarre for words. The place was apparently a disused dressing room with mirrors framed in lights and a slat-fronted closet that filled the whole of one wall. There was a table covered in clutter, and a sagging armchair with two suitcases beside it. But what made the breath catch in her throat was the shrine.

Hundreds of photographs of President Kennedy were Sellotaped to the painted brickwork. Kennedy smiling. Kennedy with his children. Kennedy kissing Jackie. And before them was a candle in a red glass holder, the sort that signified the presence of God in church.

Kim backed up behind the door, her guilt swelling until her chest constricted. Only two days before he had been alive. And she had been the one to cause his death.

She put her hand on the doorknob, but the footsteps stopped just outside.

Trapped.

Kim just had time to jump into the closet before the door opened. Through the slats she could see an old-fashioned radio with valves and lit dials, the sort of thing a ham operator might have. The red light of the shrine shone on a hand-held metal microphone and there was a faint hiss of static in the air.

Steele crossed in front of her line of sight and something about him made the hairs on her neck stand on end. The fat man came with him, taken aback when the cloaker noticed the brown leather cases by the desk.

The Majestic man's lips parted in a cruel grin. He bent and hefted the cases. They were obviously heavy. He turned to the fat man, still smiling like a shark.

'Little vacation, Jack?'

'I need some time, Jimmy,' Ruby babbled. 'To sort things out. Get my head on straight.'

Steele stepped in close, staring down into his eyes. Clearly intimidated, the fat man backed up, his blubbery face whitening.

The slim, menacing figure closed in on him. 'It's time for Jack Ruby to live up to his potential.' He paused, as though listening to unheard instructions. 'All the evidence is gathered. Now the circle must be closed.'

Kim watched the fat man quail. He said brokenly, 'I knew it,' he said brokenly. 'You want me to kill Oswald.'

18

In the dust and murk of the closet, Kim clutched a fold of material. Her mind reeled.

Oswald.

That was the name of the man they had arrested for shooting President Kennedy. She had heard it on the news as they drove Colonel Marcel's car through the streets of Dallas in pursuit of Steele.

It was Steele's voice, strangely husky, that recalled Kim to her surroundings. She listened intently, memorizing the conversation.

As though he were speaking of a third party, the cloaker said, 'Jim Steele's position at Majestic cannot be compromised.'

The fat man back-pedalled still further, edging towards the door. 'Look, just pay someone else! Like we did on the Kennedy hit.'

'Jack Ruby is a friend to the police. It is why he was chosen. It is his destiny.'

'If I shoot him, they'll put me away for ever!' The nightclub owner pulled open the door.

Before he could get away, the cloaker slammed it shut. Ruby cowered before him, 'I like my life, Jimmy. I like my club. The broads. Jack Ruby's not ready to give all that up yet.'

Again the third person. Kim couldn't make it out.

Until Steele said, 'Then we must increase our presence

within him.' His hands shot out with inhuman speed, seizing the fat man's head in an unbreakable grip.

Ruby's mouth fell open in a gape of pain as Steele's thumbs bit savagely into his cheeks. Steele's lips parted in a weird grimace.

Horrified, heart thundering in her ears, Kim saw something squirm free from within the cloaker's mouth. Her diaphragm froze, cutting off her breath as the red and fleshy extrusion writhed outwards.

A ganglion. It had to be. Her skin sheeted with perspiration and her legs threatened to give way. Hands tightening convulsively on the costume beside her, she watched the alien tendril explore the air beyond Steele's lips.

It seemed to scent Ruby. Straining towards him, its obscene flesh flooded with the colour of split intestines.

Steel brought his mouth down on Ruby's in a kiss of death.

Ruby choked, struggled, flailing helplessly in the cloaker's iron grip. His back arched and he wrenched his head free. But the ganglion linked him inexorably to Steele.

The thing slithered worm-like further and further down Ruby's throat. Gagging noises made Kim want to puke in sympathy.

Steele seemed to judge that Ruby had enough inside him to do the job. He bared his teeth and deliberately bit into the ganglion, sucking its milky juices down inside him with relish.

The strand of alien flesh parted and slicked down Ruby's gullet. It was too much for Kim. Her lungs spasmed and sucked in air with an audible gasp.

Bird-like, Steele cocked his head with a swiftness that didn't seem human. He let go of his victim, not looking as the fat man staggered backwards and reeled to the chair where he lay panting, eyes turned back in his head.

Steele took a step in the direction of the closet. Kim held her breath. He moved purposefully towards her hiding place.

Her hands fled to her mouth, unconsciously trying to stifle her breathing. Steele's hand stretched for the closet door.

Then the ham radio burst into life. He spun to answer it.

Kim sagged back against the wall, unspeakably relieved.

Through the flimsy partition she saw Steele open his mouth, but what came out of it this time was a hollow rasping sound. It varied in pitch, but none of what he said was human. She would never have believed that a man could make such sounds. It was more like the rasp of shingle in a neap tide than words. As she became attuned she heard separate syllables that made no sense to her. He punctuated the gritty resonance with names: Jim Steele, Paul Fuller, Oswald and Ruby.

Between the harsh incomprehensibility came words that speared terror into the core of her being: America and Andrews Air Force Base. The murder of Kennedy's assassin was only part of the plan. Kim shuddered at the thought that her entire nation was at risk.

Kim hadn't felt this isolated, or scared, since that dreadful, bewildering night in her and John's apartment. There was a similar nightmarish quality to the scene she was witnessing.

'Ready to go?'

Not until their footsteps had receded back up the ringing metal staircase did she dare come out of her hiding place. The music from upstairs, a different song, equally raunchy but much tackier, swelled and faded, telling her the two implants had gone back into the nightclub.

She fled.

Dropping through the fanlight into the alley, she landed on all fours in front of John.

'I was just about to come in after you!'

She threw herself into his embrace, holding him desperately tight to gain comfort from his warmth.

He stroked her hair protectively. 'Hey, what's all this?'

She told him.

Tersely he said, 'We've got to think of a plan.'

After a heated debate, they gave in to exhaustion and slept for a while in the borrowed Studebaker. They'd had hardly any sleep in seventy-two hours. Unsurprisingly, they didn't wake until well after daybreak.

Next morning, having worked out a plan, they headed straight for the airport where there would be a nice big bank of anonymous payphones. The echoing hall gave them some sort of privacy. Sunlight shafted across it and Kim was glad of her dark glasses.

As John fed the money into the slot, she said, 'Are you sure about this?'

He nodded, cutting her off as the operator at Majestic's Central Headquarters came on the line. 'Listen, I know Bach is in Dallas,' John said. 'Put me through to field ops.'

The man started to argue but John wasn't having it. 'You want to be the guy who has to tell him that John Loengard called about the artefact and you were too stupid to put him through?'

In the Dallas safe house, the subterranean room was alive with activity. Half a dozen cloakers were bawling down phones while a black and white TV played footage of President Kennedy's assassination. Bach, his top button undone and his tie just a little skewed, was going over a field report when his chief of operations approached him.

'Steele says they're getting ready to move Oswald.'

'Good. I've got somebody ready to pick him up on the other side.'

At his elbow, the black Bakelite telephone shrilled. Bach picked up the receiver. After a moment he said, 'John. What a nice surprise.' At the same time he waved to the cloaker on the small switchboard to start a trace.

Loengard had suspected as much. 'Listen, Frank, don't try to make me stay with you, cause I'm not going to let you trace this, understand?'

The cloaker made a circle of finger and thumb as a light

164

flashed, indicating he'd got the first digit. Bach nodded. Into the phone he said, 'Start talking.'

John didn't know quite how to phrase it. Reaching for the words he began, 'You got a problem and it's not me and it's not the artefact. It's Steele. You know where he is?'

Bach's answer was short. 'That's not something we're going to discuss.'

'*Listen* to me! Steele is Hive. Kim's seen the proof. He was involved in Kennedy's assassination. And a guy named Jack Ruby is going to kill this Oswald for them.'

'That's quite a story, John. Maybe we should pick a place to get together and talk about it.'

'Goodbye, Frank. This is the last free one you get.' He hung up.

Bach heard the line go dead. Loengard had talked for less than fifteen seconds. The number couldn't be traced.

At the airport, Kim said, 'You didn't tell him about the radio call from Andrews Air Force Base.'

John tilted his head dismissively. 'Let Bach clean up his own house first. Bobby Kennedy, that's who we have to tell.'

'Then we'd better get to Washington fast if we want to help Marcel.'

They headed through the sparse early travellers towards the departure desk. A shocked ground control worker told them, 'Have you heard? Some other nut just shot Oswald!'

Albano approached his boss but Bach was lost in thought. He had to speak twice before the Majestic chief noticed him, but all he got was a snapped command. 'Get the jet ready. We have to get back to DC right away. And tell them to get the conference room ready.'

As Albano turned away Bach added a rider. 'And Phil, don't tell anybody what it's for.'

Several hours later, Bach settled back at the head of the red horseshoe-shaped table in Majestic's Star Chamber. The grey venetian blinds were firmly shut and, as ever, two MPs stood guard outside the door.

Albano was loading the cine-projector. Bach peered through the blinds at the main operations room below. Everything seemed normal out there. The mix of civilian and military personnel going about their mysterious tasks, the flashing consoles, the transparent maps of the world with the spy satellites' positions blinking across the continents and oceans.

Seating himself once more, Bach lit a cigarette and nodded at his deputy. Albano started the film.

It showed Lee Harvey Oswald, handcuffed to a tall Texas Ranger in a white Stetson. Another officer flanked him as they crossed the underground car park at the Dallas Police Department HQ. Oswald wasn't bad-looking, with dark eyes and arched brows. Though jug ears stuck out from his short hairstyle, somewhat spoiling the effect.

The press pack was there, barking questions, making the concrete structure seem like the centre of a lightning storm with their camera flashes.

From off-camera, a nervous, rotund figure came into view. The policemen looked; neither seemed surprised. After all, Jack Ruby was a stool-pigeon who dropped by quite frequently whenever he found out something that might do him good.

Suddenly Ruby lurched forward. Jerking a gun out, the fat man pressed it to Oswald's stomach. Before anyone could stop him, a shot rang out.

It was shocking. Stupid. There was no way Ruby could escape. He didn't even try.

Oswald sank to the ground, blood spreading from the wound.

Inside Majestic, the phone at Bach's elbow rang. He snatched at it, not taking his eyes off the flickering images on the screen. 'Yeah. We just got back. I'm looking at it right now. Hold on.'

He looked over his shoulder at Albano, the phone seemingly forgotten in his hand. 'Run it back.'

The chief of operations didn't seem put out at performing such a menial task. He threw the little silver lever on the side of the projector and scrolled backwards.

'Now,' Bach told him.

The film rolled forward through the sprockets again. Bach took a deep drag on his cigarette, holding the smoke in his lungs.

On-screen, merging with the mob of pressmen, was Steele.

'Not two feet from Oswald when he got shot,' Albano observed.

'Freeze it right there.'

Steele's image, captured on celluloid, stared back at them. The cloaker wore that familiar, slit-eyed, mocking smile and exuded an air of detached, almost amused confidence that Bach knew so well.

'You get his phone records from Dallas?' he asked.

His chief of operations nodded. 'Clean except for one incoming call.' He paused. 'It was from the payphone at the Carousel. Jack Ruby's club.'

It wasn't what Bach wanted to hear. He spoke sharply into the telephone. 'Get the lab ready. Thirty minutes.'

19

National Airport, Washington, DC
24 November 1963

Late that afternoon, the plane banked over the city lights and circled in to land as the sun sank over the Capitol. As soon after touch-down as they could, John and Kim headed for the bus to the city centre. Between them they carried everything they owned in the world.

Usually the crowds going into Washington would be bright and lively, chattering excitedly as they listed the attractions they wanted to see: the Lincoln Memorial, the Jefferson Monument, all the trappings of the capital of the free world.

Now, though, faces were grim. Despite the slanting Fall sunshine, tension rippled uneasily through the atmosphere, an unfocused anxiety that had everyone wondering where assassins might strike next if even the president wasn't immune to such terror. And many of the citizens wore marks of mourning: black suits, or sombre clothing with black armbands.

With the death of John F. Kennedy, the air of sparkling optimism that had characterized Washington had changed to a profound gloom. The late president's funeral was scheduled for the next day.

As they headed away from the terminal, John and Kim

heard an announcement over the public address system: 'The next bus to the Capitol rotunda will be leaving in ten minutes.'

They exchanged a glance. Time was too short. Kim hailed a cab that was just drawing up at the kerb. She checked her purse. Her White House ID badge was still safely in its side pocket.

'Hopefully I can get back into the White House,' she told John. 'If I can get to Bobby, I'll give him the evidence and the information.'

John slid the president's lighter into her grasp, disguising the action as a simple hand-clasp between lovers. He nuzzled her hair, whispering, 'I'll get to Andrews Air Force Base, see if they've got somebody named Fuller.'

He opened the cab door for her. She hastily scribbled a note, using her handbag to lean on. 'Here. My number at the First Lady's office in case you forgot.'

Then she hugged him fiercely, afraid to let him go. Each of them knew that this might be the last time. The weight of the gun at John's waist was a constant reminder he didn't need, a reminder that Majestic played for keeps and alien implants like Pratt could be anywhere.

Reluctantly they pulled back from their passionate embrace. As Kim was driven away she turned to wave at him, fear stencilled on her brow. John swallowed and waved back, striving to seem cheerful.

When she was out of sight in the traffic, he read the note, his last link with her. Above the phone number she had written, 'I love you. Be careful.'

Despite his worry, a smile twisted his lips.

So much had happened in so short a time that Kim was almost surprised to find her ID got her inside the White House just as it always had. Outside, the dusk was purpling and the first stars were bright in the east, but the presidential palace was swarming with activity.

The First Lady's outer office was busier than ever, with

phones ringing, typewriters clacking, people working in a hushed but purposeful manner. Every one of them wore subtle muted colours.

Kim herself had put on a dress of deep forest green that brought out the highlights in her hair, the discreet gold knot earrings. She stood hesitantly in the doorway, unsure of her ground.

Not so Alicia Burnside, the woman who had first hired her. Alicia was perched on the corner of her desk, leaning across to put a telephone back on its rest. She glanced up and exclaimed, 'Kim?'

Tentatively Kim stepped towards her, but Alicia had no such reservations. Coming forwards, she enfolded her in a sisterly embrace. 'After your call last week, well, I didn't expect you back yet.'

Kim said into the shining dark cloud of Alicia's hair, 'I figured you could use some help.' She paused, wondering if her question would be intrusive. 'How's Mrs Kennedy doing?'

Alicia pulled back, her hands still resting on Kim's arms, and forced a smile. 'Every hour she calls in to see how *we're* holding up.' Patting Kim once or twice, she moved back to sit behind her desk. ' "JFK belongs to the people", that's her motto. And I'm telling you, this funeral is going to be her greatest achievement.'

Kim fingered the clasp of her purse thoughtfully. She couldn't come right out and ask where the Attorney-General was, but maybe she could get a clue. 'Where is she now?'

'The family's sequestered until the procession to-morrow.' Alicia's dark brows pulled together for a moment as she wondered how best to employ Kim. Then she dug among the many papers on her desk and came up with a list. 'I need follow-up calls to every embassy to confirm which countries have RSVP'd.'

Kim nodded, taking the stapled sheets of paper. Crossing to her old desk, she swept aside the newspapers from all over the States. With a pang she saw that all of them bore headlines of Kennedy's murder.

She sat down and started dialling.

Night might have closed in over Washington, but in Majestic's secret headquarters military and civilian personnel carried on their unceasing vigilance.

Bach had put on his naval uniform, the gold banding around the cuffs a bright counterpart to the chestful of decorations he wore. His face was suffused with anger and his lips were tight-set. He strode rapidly past the observation window into the control centre.

Jim Steele matched Bach's headlong pace, and was saying for the fourth time, 'If Loengard's got the goods, he's dangerous. I should be tracking him right now.'

'He's here in DC.'

'Then I want to go and take him out personally.'

Bach stopped a second, his gaze boring into Steele. In a tone of carefully controlled rage he said, 'This is not personal. It's business.' He resumed his furious march.

Steel caught him up. 'We need to stop him before he runs back to Bobby Kennedy.'

'The Attorney-General's got other things on his mind right now. Why don't you let him bury his brother in peace?'

'I think you're taking this way too casual, Frank.'

Bach stopped again, swinging round to bar Steele's path. 'It's my problem, Jim. I'll take care of it.' He leaned sideways, opening the door they'd stopped outside. Its sign said 'Biolab'. 'Right now you've got other things to worry about.'

Steele stiffened, his gaze sliding to the door as if he'd only just noticed where he was. The beginnings of suspicion forced him back a pace. But it did him no good. Bach, taller and broader than the whipcord Steele, grabbed his arm and frogmarched him forward.

Against Bach alone, Steele would have stood a good

chance. But out of the biolab poured four men who swarmed over the struggling agent and wrestled him inside. Phil Albano and the two other cloakers forced Steele into a metal-framed chair. They were all men whom Bach trusted implicitly.

But then, Bach had trusted Steele implicitly.

Steele saw the bare metal arms of the chair and knew they were meant for restraints. He lashed out, kicking furiously, but the cloakers had received the same combat training and, hardly breaking sweat, they thrust him back into the seat.

Only then did Steele think to demand, 'What is this?'

At Bach's nod, Albano lassoed leather straps around Steele's wrists, binding him tightly to the armrests. All the men but one stood close enough to jump on him, but not directly in front; they knew that their prisoner's highly polished shoes hid metal toecaps that could smash a knee or break a leg.

Steele's face contorted in a rictus of rage. He screamed, 'No! You're wrong, Frank! You're wrong!'

Bach was not to be swayed. Resolute, but with a hint of sadness, he stared down at the man in the chair. 'Just relax, Jim. It'll go a lot easier.'

The fourth man wore a white coat. He was young, smooth-faced, dark-haired. Since Hertzog had compromised himself by helping John Loengard and Kim, he had not been seen at Majestic. No-one dared to enquire what had happened to him.

Now the new doctor, whose ID labelled him Halligan, left the cloakers restraining their prisoner and fetched a throat dilator and a bottle of white fizzing liquid.

At the sight of it, Steele renewed his furious struggles. Under his screams an alien cry echoed hollowly.

The throat dilator was a metal funnel, hard enough to resist the most savage bite, and long enough to force its way past the epiglottis, closing off the airway and directing itself straight into an unwilling patient's stomach.

And Steele was more than unwilling. It took Albano and

the other two cloakers to hold Steele's thrashing head steady so Halligan could shove the dilator into place. Veins throbbed in Steele's temples and the tendons stood out on his neck. The threat of asphyxiation should have been enough to keep him still. But it wasn't, and that in itself told Bach all he needed to know.

Halligan poured the frothing liquid into the funnel. It gurgled down into Steele's oesophagus, bubbling over and pouring down his chin like the foam of a rabid dog.

As it hit the pit of his stomach, Steele shoved his toes hard against the floor, aiming to smash himself against the men behind him. He seemed blind to the consequences, arching his back and wrenching against the holding straps.

But Halligan grabbed a hypodermic needle and thrust it deep into a bottle of acetone. Whirling, he thrust his fingers into Steele's hair from behind, forcing his head uncomfortably forward. The legs of the chair crashed down onto the ground.

Halligan plunged the needle into the base of Steele's head. As quickly as he dared, he depressed the plunger.

The captive seemed to have a fit. The dilator flew spit-drenched from Steele's mouth and he literally snarled at the cloakers around him, trying to inflict a bite that would certainly have drawn blood. But he could not shake free the hypodermic at the base of his brain.

For a second, the rigidity left Steele, leaving him slack-muscled in the chair. Then with a burst of inhuman strength he tore one arm free of its leather restraint. Snatching the syringe from his neck, he stabbed it straight into the chest of the man closest to him.

It slid between his ribs and ripped into his heart. Instantly the man spasmed in cardiac arrest, juddering helplessly as he tried to pull the tip from his chest. Crimson spread across the front of his shirt but the others had no time to help him.

Launching himself upright, Steele slammed his head back into the doctor's face, then swung the chair by the single leash that tied him to it. It arced sideways, catapulting the other cloaker into a rack of surgical equipment that shattered down over him in a rain of scalpels and glass. The skinny doctor lay where he had fallen.

Bach threw himself into the attack, but Steele's super-human reflexes packed themselves into another scything slash with the chair. The ruler of Majestic jumped backwards, ducking under the murderous slicing metal but careening from an examination table onto the floor.

That left Albano.

The cunning chief of operations backed away, cross-drawing the pistol from his shoulder holster and firing instantly. Even as his bullet hit Steele's midriff, the prisoner scooped up the fallen cloaker's gun and traded a shot of his own that sent Albano rolling for cover.

The wound through Steele's innards should have taken him out of action, yet it hardly slowed him at all. He ran for the door, the leather thong on his wrist dragging the chair after him.

In the passage, he managed to tear loose the binding in time to send the chair hurtling into Bach. The head of Majestic stumbled, then recovered, drawing his own weapon and pounding out into the corridor.

Pausing for a microsecond, Bach orientated himself and pelted in pursuit of the fleeing Steele's blood trail. He turned a corner and caught up with his quarry. Steele had started to convulse. Unable to run, he collapsed supine at Bach's feet. Unearthly mewing sounds poured out of him.

Keeping the muzzle of his gun pointed inexorably at the cloaker's head, the Majestic chief panted, 'You got enough to make things unpleasant for that creature inside you.'

Steele tried to roll over and push himself upright, but he shuddered and collapsed once more as Halligan, Albano and the others came dashing around the corner. Steele coughed, still striving to stand. Bach squatted beside him.

'Tell me what the Hive's up to or we can finish this. Which might kill you.'

Another convulsion wracked Steele. It left him

coughing. But he made no answer. Only the scratchy shriek of the ganglion sounded from inside him.

Bach tried again. 'Oswald's your patsy, isn't he? That's why Ruby had to kill him.'

Still no answer.

'Ballistics show there were three shooters. Who was the third?'

It took every ounce of Steele's waning strength for him to turn his head and fix Bach with a stare of undiluted hatred. Pure malevolence flowed through him, so tangible it made Bach tighten his grip on the gun.

'This is only the beginning,' Steele hissed.

Halligan came through, another syringe in his blood-drenched hand. He dropped to his knees beside the fallen implant. 'Abrahamson's dead,' he said shortly.

Bach jerked his chin at the man who had been his friend and ally. 'Finish it.' He stood slowly, walking away, head down.

Behind him Albano and the other man pinned Steele to the ground. Halligan twisted the neck below him and jabbed the hypodermic into the vulnerable hollow at the base of the brain.

Steele writhed, then lay still.

Albano aimed his pistol at the Hive implant on the ground. Cautiously Dr Halligan touched Steele's throat, seeking a pulse; his own was so rapid he couldn't tell whether or not Steele's heart was still beating. Gingerly he bent his ear to Steele's half-open mouth and heard the thin whistle of air in and out.

Halligan turned his frightened face up to Albano. 'He's still breathing,' he said.

20

While Kim was in the White House, John made good his promise to go to Andrews. Wearing a suit and clean white shirt, he flashed his Defence Department badge to gain access to the personnel department.

The MP who admitted him watched as he went through the swing doors. Then he checked his roster and reached for the phone.

Inside personnel, John showed his ID again. The nervy young corporal who checked it stood to rigid attention.

'I need to get hold of a pilot,' Loengard told him. 'Is it OK if I look through the records?' It was the same story he told the gate guard.

'Yes, sir.'

'No need to stand to attention. I'm not an officer.'

The corporal relaxed fractionally but kept him under close scrutiny.

John began moving along the filing cabinets, scanning their handwritten labels until he found E–F. 'Imagine things have been pretty tense around here,' he said, making conversation to put the younger man at his ease.

'Yes, sir. You can say that again. Sir.'

John pulled open the top drawer. Racked neatly in alphabetical order were document wallets of different colours, lots of them faded with age. Some were crumpled at the corners but the names remained clear.

'Well, this shouldn't take long. My agency just needs to

borrow a coupla flyboys. Emergency UN conflab next week.'

Walking his fingers across the top of the files, he pulled out one which had 'Fuller, Paul' written above a serial number.

The summary sheet had a photograph attached. By now Loengard had caught up with the television news reruns, and had to hide a start when he recognized the pilot who had been running safety checks on AF–1 when Kennedy's bronze casket was transported.

'Got anything good to say about a Colonel Paul Fuller?' he asked, hoping it sounded casual.

Across the room, the corporal shrugged. 'Bumped up to Air Force One in July.'

'Must have been quite an honour to fly President Kennedy around the world.'

'Yes, sir. Absolutely, sir.'

Leafing through the paperwork, a medical sheet caught John's eye. He took time to examine it carefully.

Eight months before, Fuller had taken a medical leave of absence. The symptoms listed were, 'Nasal haemorrhaging, dizzyness, disorientation, loss of memory. Misdiagnosed as a brain tumour. Full recovery.'

Exactly the same symptoms Kim had. Except her full recovery depended on having the ganglion ART'd.

'Man thought he had a brain tumour,' he said thoughtfully, probing subtly for information. 'Guess that was tough for him.'

'Wouldn't know about that, sir.'

John nodded to himself as if he had reached a decision. He was just about to slip the file back into its position when he heard footsteps and the swish of the doors.

He looked up. The base commander stared back at him, flanked by a small contingent of MPs. Trying to brazen it out, John gazed blandly back. 'Is there a problem?'

The base commander nodded, the gold braid on his hat flashing in the electric light. It was the signal for his men to surround Loengard. They stood very close, their hard faces showing no compassion, every line of their bodies taut with the urge for action.

'Mr Loengard, you are hereby under military arrest. I must ask you to surrender your firearm.'

One of the MPs ripped the file out of John's hand while his colleagues frisked him, sliding their hands impersonally under his arms and in between his legs. No sign of the gun. When they went through his pockets, all they found was a handkerchief, some change and his Majestic badge.

They displayed their trophies to the commander. The grizzled veteran shook his head in disgust at Defence's sloppiness. 'How you ever got Majic level clearance is beyond me.' He handed the badge back to John. 'But your boys want you back.'

Which was precisely what John didn't want to hear.

He was driven back to Washington under armed escort. The black sedan's driver stayed ominously silent and John's thoughts were far from comforting as they slid into Magestic's underground car park.

Inside, the tall slender figure of Phil Albano was waiting at the security checkpoint.

'If you're gonna do all this work, Loengard,' he remarked disdainfully, 'you should have stayed on the payroll.'

John didn't answer. Albano jerked his head for him to follow and Loengard walked back into the lion's den.

Bach was alone in the dimly lit Star Chamber.

The Majestic chief sat at the apex of the red horseshoe table. His face was closed and hostile, the lamplight revealing the ravages the past few days had worked on him.

He lit a cigarette and stared across the table. Unmistakably his intention was to intimidate, but Loengard stared straight back at him. After all he'd suffered it would take more than hard looks to make him weak at the knees.

'You gain absolutely nothing,' Bach said heavily, 'for yourself, your country, anybody, by playing this game.'

John stared back at him, stoney-eyed. 'The president's dead, Frank.'

'I don't need reminding.'

'Guilty?'

'Of what? You set it in motion.'

'He had a right to know!'

'That's not for you to decide.'

'It was your secrecy that killed him. Your cover up. Everything you've been burying for the last sixteen years.'

'I trusted you.'

'No! You don't trust *anyone*, Frank! That's why you wore that piece of wreckage around your neck.'

Bach half smiled. 'Wreckage? Is that what it is now?'

'I've had enough! I know what happened at Roswell!'

The Majestic chief said nothing, did nothing.

'They came to talk, but you didn't trust them. You shot them out of the sky, Frank. Isn't that what turned them against us?'

Bach smiled in a pitying, patronizing way designed to infuriate. 'You're so naive.'

'Then set me straight, Frank! What really happened at Roswell?'

As the tent-flaps fell closed, the power around Roswell came back on line. Within the tent, a single overhead bulb shed its yellow light on President Harry S. Truman, Admiral Hillenkoetter, Naval Secretary Forrestal and the two army chiefs. Lieutenant Frank Bach took a folding seat at the corner of the three tables that had been pushed together. The tingling vibration from the spaceship above crawled over the young lieutenant's skin and buzzed in his ears. A slight breeze ruffled the canvas sidings of the tent, bringing him the alien scent – musky, a little acidic – of the creature standing underneath the light.

The Gray.

Though it was only 4 feet tall it dominated the makeshift

conference room. Every man's attention was riveted to its dry wrinkled skin, the flaring swell of its chest, the dark, lambent gaze of its jet-black eyes. The tiny protruding mouth hung open but no speech came from within that shark-toothed maw. Silence extended but for the shifting sand blown against the canvas.

President Truman sat waiting. And waiting. The sharp eyes behind the plastic-framed spectacles observed the lone emissary, but the creature did nothing at all.

'Now what?' Truman snapped, finally losing patience.

As if in answer, the Gray stepped forward, its oddly articulated arm stretching out towards the president. The military men itched to get at imaginary weapons, and the MPs on guard started to unsling their machine-guns.

But all the alien did was open its hand. As the four many-jointed fingers flexed, a tiny flat object drifted from its grasp.

The thing unfolded by itself, uncreasing several times until it expanded to a pellucid triangle that glistened metallically in the light. A spectrum of colours between silver and gold flowed across its surface as it floated gently at the ageing president and dropped onto the table top before him.

He gazed down at it in wonder, but couldn't make head nor tail of the markings that might as easily have been Maori tattoos as hieroglyphs. They were completely incomprehensible.

'What do I do?' he asked.

The Gray held out its hand, curling one bony finger into its palm and pointing downwards with the other three. It seemed to be indicating a triangle.

'I think', Hillenkoetter said, 'it wants you to touch it . . . like that.'

'Mr President, I strongly advise against it,' Naval Secretary Forrestal warned.

Truman stood, leaning over the table with his head forward like a bull charging at a gate. 'The buck stops here,' he grated.

Gingerly, Truman held out his middle and forefinger, and completed the three-sided shape with his thumb. He touched the circular whorls that seemed to shimmer in the angles of the alien artefact.

Nothing happened.

Truman chuckled uncertainly. 'Must look like a damn fool!'

The brass joined uneasily in his merriment. Then a glimmer of power surged visibly across the nodules under his fingers and he jerked backwards. 'My God! That thing just . . . spoke to me!'

A murmur of consternation rippled through those present. It ceased abruptly as the bewildered president added, 'They just demanded our unconditional surrender.'

Silently the Gray took its leave. One moment it was there, the next it had gone.

Lieutenant Bach watched the military leaders consulting urgently with Truman. Or, to be more accurate, arguing furiously. They seemed to have no idea what to do. Time passed. They were getting nowhere.

Finally Forrestal said, 'How much longer do we have?'

Admiral Hillenkoetter checked his watch. 'Just a few minutes.'

Truman exploded, yelling in frustration, 'It didn't say anything! It put the damn thoughts right in my head with that . . . that floating wangy-thing!'

Forrestal tried to calm him. 'At least they came to us first. Maybe we can negotiate some kind of an arrangement.'

The president turned on him. Elderly he might certainly be, but there was nothing wrong with his mind. 'It's not negotiable! It was an ultimatum. Surrender or die.' He shook his head. 'But I am here to tell you, gentlemen, I will not be the first president to lose a war!'

Thumping the table to emphasize his point, Truman glared around the room, daring them to defy him. Within the tent, all was quiet for a moment.

Lieutenant Bach said, 'There's not going to be any war.'

181

Forrestal snapped at the admiral, 'Roscoe, tell your boy to shut up!'

But Truman waved his hand. 'No, I want to hear this.'

Everyone stared at the young lieutenant. Though he might be trembling inside at his temerity before all those men of power, Bach wanted to have his say. Thinking furiously, he began with a question.

'Mr President, did the Nazis develop anything they didn't use against us?'

Truman's brows shot up but he answered peaceably enough. 'Not to my knowledge.'

'And when we developed the A-bomb, what did we do with it?'

'We used it.'

Bach nodded. 'Twice.'

'Point is?'

The lieutenant took a deep breath. 'They're bluffing.'

Forrestal couldn't contain his exasperation any longer. 'Mr President, are we going to sit here and let a lieutenant commander dictate foreign policy?'

Bach's voice overrode him. 'Ultimatums follow action. These creatures haven't shown us anything but some fancy aircraft. I say that's all they've got.'

'Hmm.' Truman's concentration was writ large on his pink-fleshed face. 'God help us if we're wrong. Because we're about to bet the entire human race.' He breathed out stertorously, as though he had just run a mile. 'We're going aggressive, men. And if we live through this —' he pointed at the lieutenant '— I want him in charge of cleaning up the mess.'

In Majestic's conference room, Bach leaned an elbow on the red horseshoe table and put yet another cigarette to his mouth, peering at John through the curling smoke.

'The birth of Majestic,' Loengard whispered.

Bach nodded. 'I was drafted. It was my duty. And I was right.'

'Were you?'

'They don't have the weapons, the army—'

'No, but they have us!' John saw it all now, and it made his head swim. 'One by one they implant us, take us over . . .'

'Make *us* their army. Use *our* weapons.'

'Right. Look at the assassination! They used Steele. But it's not over. They've been waiting almost seventeen years.'

'Why were you at Andrews Air Force base?' Bach demanded.

'If I tell you—'

'Don't try to make deals!'

Loengard thought about it. Much as he hated to admit it, Bach was right. There was no time. 'At the Carousel Club,' he said, 'Steele talked to a Hiver who mentioned Andrews and a name – Paul Fuller. The guy's a pilot. Air Force One.'

'The president's plane.'

'Yeah. But they'd already killed him by that time.'

The same chill confusion mirrored on their faces. It was Bach who voiced the question: 'What the hell are they up to?'

Bach went to the door and stuck his head out. 'Get Phil Albano!' he snapped at the MP standing guard.

He went back to Loengard and shepherded him to the telephone at the apex of the horseshoe. 'Do it, John. Do it for both of us.'

Loengard slid two fingers into his inside pocket and fished out the paper Kim had slipped him at the airport what seemed like a lifetime ago. He dialled the White House and asked for the extension.

She recognized his voice as soon as he spoke. 'John? I haven't been able to get to Bobby Kennedy yet—'

'Kim,' he interrupted, 'I need any details you can give me about the funeral.'

She rummaged through the papers littering her desk. 'I've got the itinerary right here. We start the procession at eleven a.m.'

Bach leaned over to whisper, 'Ask her how many foreign leaders are confirmed.'

Her answer was frightening. 'As of now, two hundred and fourteen.'

John could see where this was heading. 'The military flyover, Kim. What time is it scheduled?'

'Two-thirty p.m. Fifty fighter planes, followed by Air Force One. What's going on, John?'

He hesitated, calculating the distance between him and Bach. Going for broke, he rushed out, 'Majestic's got me. Get to—'

Bach's hand slammed down on the phone rest. 'Your pilot, Fuller. Sounds like he's on a suicide mission.'

Suddenly John's throat was parched. 'They didn't kill the president just to hide the truth. It was a set-up for the big kill.'

Bach headed for the door. 'Thanks for the tip.'

Loengard jumped up and chased after him. He grabbed Bach's sleeve. 'Kim's going to be at that funeral! I'm part of this, Frank!'

The Majestic boss shook him off and walked out. Phil Albano appeared in the doorway.

John could see he was going nowhere.

But he had to save Kim.

21

In a Majestic interrogation cell, Loengard paced. There wasn't much room, what with a table, three chairs and a broad-shouldered MP who carried a businesslike rifle and never said a word. The only bright spot was that John wasn't alone. After the all-night interrogation that would have been just too much.

Colonel Jesse Marcel slumped forward on the Formica table top, his cupped hands propping up his head. Both he and John were exhausted, their faces shadowed with incipient beards. The MP was as fresh as a daisy. He would be.

John was coming to the end of his tale. '. . . We were on the run for three days before the president was shot. We could've gone down into Mexico, South America . . . Anywhere you go, though, you still have to look up at the skies.'

Marcel eyed him, seeing the restless tension that fuelled John's tired muscles.

'So here I am,' Loengard went on. 'Right back where it all started. Trapped in Majestic.'

He swung, kicking the door in his frustration. The MP glanced at him dismissively, deciding he was no threat. He went back to staring straight ahead.

Loengard went to the observation window. Beyond the reinforced plate glass the new young doctor, Halligan, was writing his case notes in the biolab. An MP lay back in a chair, taking the chance to catch up on his sleep. On the examination table, Steele's unconscious body was strapped down by the wrists, legs and chest.

John tutted in disgust. A typical piece of Majestic overkill. If the cloaker's experience of ART was anything like Kim's, the man wouldn't be fit for a week. But then again, hadn't Bach said something about Steele's ART not working?

Marcel rubbed his temples, then ran his fingers over his tired eyes, trying to wake himself up. 'This is one helluva story. All this time I thought those aliens might have been the answer to our prayers.' He stroked the itchy stubble on his jaw. 'Part that scares me the most is they could be anybody, anywhere, and there's no way of knowing.'

John leaned against the wall beside the glass. 'There are give-aways during the takeover phase, but detection's damn near impossible after that.'

'And you're telling me these Grays, they've got this . . . this ganglion inside their heads too?'

'The doctors here think it's some kind of insect-like life form. That's all we know.'

John stopped. He had just said *we*, as though he were still one of Majestic's secretive crew.

Marcel didn't notice. He went on, more to himself than anybody else, 'For sixteen years I've been wishing I was on the inside. With the truth.'

'Only right now, the truth is that some alien race has got all our world leaders together so they can crash a 707 into them,' John added.

'You figure Bach and his boys can stop it?'

Scant miles away, two black sedans screeched to a halt on the tarmac of Andrews Airfield. From the vast hangar in front of them, two ground crew were wheeling out Air Force One. The presidential jet gleamed white in the Fall sunshine. Newly washed, newly checked, she was ready to go.

Colonel Paul Fuller, resplendent in his starched blue uniform, came steadily towards the plane.

Bach shouted, 'Go, go, go!' at his mob of six cloakers. They fanned out, aiming to cut Fuller off, whichever way he tried to run.

Unsure, Fuller began to walk a little faster. He pulled on his helmet, as though to make himself more anonymous.

Behind him, Albano and a muscular cloaker broke into a run. Fuller heard the racing footsteps and started to sprint for AF-1.

A cloaker yelled, 'Freeze!' but Fuller pelted headlong for the steps leading up to the cockpit. If he could get up there he'd be safe . . .

Albano shot him in the back.

Three or four more shots ripped into him. By the time Bach reached him, even a ganglion couldn't have got Fuller's body moving.

Dr Halligan matched blood samples to a chart on the wall in the biolab. The steady pulse of the monitors overseeing Steele's heartbeat and other functions was regular, almost soothing.

Suddenly the pulse changed pitch.

Halligan swung round to scrutinize the figure strapped down to the table. He leaned forward, reaching out a hand to turn back the unconscious man's eyelids and determine the depth of coma.

Steele opened his eyes.

Halligan gasped. One of Steele's pupils was normal, but the other had turned a hideous marbled white, traumatized by the aftershocks of the failed ART.

Before Halligan's stunned brain could send the impulse to his legs, Steele punched a hand upwards through the restraint on his wrist. His face was blank, but in his one good eye there was a ferocious hateful menace.

The doctor finally managed to back-pedal. He hadn't gone two steps when Steele sat bolt upright, tearing loose the leather strap around his chest.

With a cry of panic, Halligan sped for the door and whisked through, slamming it shut behind him. The lock automatically dogged fast. There was no way it could be opened from the inside. He didn't spare a thought for the MP trapped in the room with the implant.

Halligan groped blindly for the alarm, sagging with relief when the hideous klaxon echoed through the building.

Next door, Colonel Marcel jolted his chair legs back down to the floor. The alarm was deafening. 'What the hell's going on?' he shouted.

'I don't know,' Loengard said. 'But they had Steele in a coma next door. Maybe his ART failed.'

Marcel raised his eyebrows. He was unfamiliar with this particular piece of jargon.

'Alien Rejection Technique,' John explained. 'They tried to force the ganglion out.'

Gunfire erupted from the biolab next door. Loengard cast a worried glance at Marcel. The MP unslung his rifle and pointed it at them, wary of an escape attempt.

There was a tremendous crash.

Steele had hurled his own guard bodily through the observation window. The dead MP struck Loengard's and Marcel's living counterpart, who went down under the corpse's weight.

John briefly regarded the bodies, then scuttled for cover behind the upturned table. Marcel was right beside him.

Heedless of the daggers of glass poking up from the window frame, Steele pulled himself up into the room. Blood dripped from his torn fingers.

Steele stepped onto the writhing MP and wrestled briefly for control of the rifle. The MP's back was broken. Steele won the battle and turned the muzzle of the weapon on his opponent, shoving it against his stomach and firing round after round. A stench of powder and excrement filled the room as gunsmoke hazed the air.

Crouching out of sight behind the table, John and Colonel Marcel heard Steele's footsteps crunch across the powdered glass. The rogue agent slammed the door open with the rifle butt, leaving the dying MP groaning on the floor.

For a second they thought their own getaway was clear. But Steele slammed the door. It clanged hollowly into place, self-locking and immovable.

Slowly Marcel and Loengard stood, aghast at the devastation Steele had left in his wake. John knelt to place his fingers on the MP's throat. There was no sign of life.

'Bach and Majestic are still at Andrews. It's up to us now, Jesse.'

Marcel hesitated, then nodded, the shreds of his erstwhile command giving him backbone. John picked the chair out of the sea of shattered glass and used it to clear the window frame.

By now Halligan had come out of hiding. Stepping over the body of another fallen MP, he cautiously opened the door of the biolab. He was astounded when, instead of the implant Steele, Loengard and the colonel burst out of the room.

Following the trail of blood, John leaped over the MP's body. Marcel scooped up the fallen man's pistol and pointed. 'Up there!'

An elevator door was just sliding shut.

'He's going out the garage!' John yelled above the hideous wail of the klaxon.

There was nobody to stop them as they dashed in pursuit.

It had been a long time since John ran the 2,000 yards for his college. By the time he made it through the mile of underground passages to the garage, his legs were trembling and he felt as though his heart would burst. As he threw himself to the ground to take a look around the last corner, he was astonished to find that the colonel wasn't far behind.

Marcel squatted beside him, taking a much-needed breather. Up ahead, Steele was out of the building and zigzagging across the parkland towards the woods.

Knowing he would lose him in the thick cover, John forced his shaking legs to a run. He had only gone 20 yards when a sharp whistle from behind made him spin round. It was Jesse Marcel, beckoning wildly and pointing around the angle of the building at an open jeep.

John swivelled, seeing that he had little chance now of catching Steele on foot. He raced back to the vehicle as Jesse reached under the dashboard to hot-wire it.

As soon as Loengard threw himself into the passenger seat, the colonel stomped hard on the accelerator. The jeep crashed through shrubbery and bounced across the grassy field.

John had to hold on to the windscreen to save himself from being thrown out. Up ahead, Steele's dark coat-tails were just disappearing amongst bright sumac and low branches of scarlet maple.

'If you take off now, you're out!' John yelled at Marcel over the rush of wind. 'You've got no evidence! They won't come after you!'

'I'm seeing this one through!'

Swerving sharply left, he pulled the jeep onto a gravel track that ran between the trees. Grit sprayed from beneath the tyres and John pulled himself down low as branches clattered against the sides of the vehicle. Lances of sunshine slashed through the canopy, throwing heavy shadows into relief.

In a matter of moments they saw light up ahead. A clearing.

Legs pumping as though he weren't carrying four bullet wounds, the Majestic rogue was racing for a sludge-green helicopter on a concrete landing pad.

Jesse barrelled the jeep straight out into the open. The helicopter's rotors started to turn sluggishly. The Fall sunshine glazed the windscreen and they couldn't see who was at the helm. But they had a pretty good idea.

The rotors whirled as the throttle was thrown open. It was still too soon for a safe take-off, but the helicopter crept into the air, bounced, then leaped up and forwards.

Slewing around to the side, Jesse ran the jeep up close to the runners, trying to get ahead of the helicopter and stop its getaway. Now they could see the pilot; a slim youth with a crew-cut and dark glasses. Steele had the rifle pointed at his neck.

Loengard stood on the swaying passenger seat and hurled himself at the helicopter's metal side bar. He barely managed to catch hold, grasping the bar tightly and easing one leg over it.

The helicopter lurched, side-slipping alarmingly, but John held on grimly.

Now the helicopter was level with the treetops, Jesse Marcel 30 feet below. If John had needed an incentive to hold tight, he had one.

Throwing his other leg over the runner, he wriggled into a precarious sitting position. With a painful thrust of his thigh muscles he tumbled in through the open door of the 'copter, groping for the gun in his waistband.

Steele felt the shift in weight and spun around. Swift as an avalanche, and as deadly, he leaped at the boarder, kicking the pistol out into the void before John could bring it to bear.

Kneed savagely in the face, John almost plunged back out of the open door. He felt one leg dangling over the dizzying drop as he clung desperately to the frame.

The chopper had reached the rim of a valley. A thermal dropped the craft. Not a lot, but enough to make Steele clasp his arm around a stanchion as he attempted to draw a bead on his attacker.

Loengard stared into the muzzle. The implant's finger began to tighten on the trigger.

Frantically John sliced his foot across to smash into Steele's shin. Unbalanced, the man half fell, reflexively pulling the trigger. The bullet whined harmlessly out into the wind.

The report startled the pilot. He whipped round to see what was going on and the helicopter yawed.

John pitched forward against Steele. They fell to the deck, sliding inexorably towards the doorway in a tangle of limbs. The cloaker put out his hands to save himself, letting the rifle plummet in his stead. He was horizontal, his feet towards the centre of the chopper, with John lying half in and half out.

Rolling, the implant wrapped his palms round the edge of the heavy door and heaved it along its track. John jacknifed as the metal scythed past him, rebounding against the frame.

Now he had Steele off-balance. Yanking him across the floor, he got a stranglehold on him. The rogue curled up until he could plant his feet in John's stomach, meaning to toss him up and over the edge. But John released his grip from around Steele's neck.

It was Steele's own impetus that propelled him outwards. John snatched at him, trying to bring him back aboard, but it was too late.

Steele's head bounced against the runner as he plunged out of the craft. He spiralled down and crashed through 50 feet of forest.

'Phew!' The pilot turned, smiling shakily, a sheen of sweat overlaying his tan. 'I owe you a free ride, Mister. Where to?'

Kim was going about her duties for the First Lady. Partly from genuine admiration, and partly out of her need to get the artefact to the Attorney-General, she had gone back to the trashed apartment to retrieve a knee-length black suit and coat. Alicia Burnside lent her a smart little pillbox hat with a short veil.

When the cortège left from the White House, Kim rode in one of the staff cars.

The atmosphere of mourning hung dense across Arlington Cemetery despite the bright sun that fell almost gaily on the bronzed leaves of the trees. As Kim climbed out of the black limo, she clutched the silver-gilt lighter John had given her. It was the one thing that made any sense of the president's death. She could only hope John wasn't dead too.

But where was he?

Immaculate preparations had made the funeral run like clockwork. A ceremonial band of air force pipers played the haunting strains of 'The Mist-Covered Mountain' as the procession wound through the mass of graves. Pink roses and auburn chrysanthemums made a brave show in defiance of death.

There were the 214 foreign delegates, princes and premiers from all around the globe, who had come to pay their last respects to the young King of Camelot who had been cut down in his prime. Many of them had tears running openly down their faces, and when the twenty-one-gun salute echoed across the hillside a shudder racked Kim's frame.

A long bugler began to play the traditional 'Taps'. Like so many others who had served in the forces, or been boy or girl scouts, the words etched themselves in her heart:

> Day is done,
> Gone the sun,
> From the hills, from the sea, from the sky,
> All is well,
> Safely rest,
> God is nigh.

The poignancy of the bugle's call was heightened as the bugler faltered not once, but twice during the course of the dirge.

Leaving her white-faced children one or two paces behind her, the First Lady stepped forward, trembling with the power of her grief as she bent to light the eternal flame.

In a silence that marked the depth of the world's respect, she straightened, swaying a little. Her brother-in-law came forward, encircling her shoulders with the reassurance of his arm, and led her back. Back to where Kim was standing with the others who had served the president's wife.

Feeling as though the whole world was watching her, Kim squeezed the lighter with its priceless evidence of the Grays, a prayer in her heart for protection against the alien threat that darkened the skies above Earth. She took a faltering pace forward, closer to the charismatic presence of Robert Kennedy.

Phil Albano slid alongside her, laying his hand on her arm. It looked like a friend offering her comfort, but his fingers dug painfully into her wrist.

She gasped and turned to see who it was, then sagged. Bobby Kennedy walked past, unknowing. Albano smiled tightly and said in a voice like a rusty hawser, 'Time to go home, darling.'

With a wiry strength he didn't look to possess, he hauled her inexorably away. Away from Bobby Kennedy, the only one who could have helped her.

Albano dragged her through the flower-lined walks to a distant, chained-off side path. A heavy screen of shrubs ensured privacy. Ten yards away on the gravel stood one of Majestic's trademarks: a plain sleek sedan with opaqued windows. He thrust her roughly towards it.

John slid smoothly from behind a tree, the pilot's pistol jammed against the small of Albano's back. 'Let her go, Phil.'

The agent had to comply. Kim rushed to her lover's side. 'He took the lighter, John.'

Loengard jabbed the gun into Albano's flesh. 'I want the lighter too.'

Albano started to walk away. 'You're gonna have to shoot me in the back, John.'

For a moment, John and Kim stared at each other in uncertainty. Then he lowered the gun. 'Tell Bach enough people have died over that damn thing.'

Majestic's chief of operations carried on until he reached the car.

When all the big shots had gone home, John and Kim came back. They looked the perfect all-American couple; equals in youth and attractiveness, mind and purpose. The sky was red in the west, the sun a fiery ball that touched the lilies Kim carried with accents of rose.

They knelt to pray by the eternal flame. In life Kennedy had inspired them. His death would have no lesser effect.

Not when the enemy was out there beyond the darkening skies.

In the woods near Majestic's hidden garage, torches flashed as bloodhounds bayed along the spoor Steele had left behind him. Bach and Albano crouched under the broken boughs of the maples, pulling the dogs away from the pool of sticky blood.

But Steele's body, like the truth about Kennedy's murder, had vanished.

22

Biloxi, Mississippi,
30 January 1964

A ruddy moon hung low in the thick humid night. Off to one side of the road, John and Kim saw a red flicker: a vacancy sign, the 'n' missing, outside a cheap motel.

It was getting late. By unspoken accord, Kim pulled over onto the parking lot. Threading through the half-rotted hulks of the other patrons' cars, she brought the yellow, round-winged Ford smoothly to a halt outside the office.

Humidity glued John's shirt to his back and moulded Kim's blouse closely to her body. When they stepped outside the car, a scent of sickly sweet decay rose from the stand of trees behind the motel. Bullfrogs sang from a nearby swamp and night insects whirred through the still air.

In the cheap room they were given, things were no better. The brown linoleum on the floor was lifted here and there by the damp, and the bed sheets, though freshly laundered, had the tell-tale stains of mildew.

Wrinkling her nose, Kim said with false brightness, 'In a place like this, we'll be one more anonymous couple.'

John caught the constraint in her voice, but when he glanced at her, she wouldn't meet his eye. He knew there was more to it than that. She kept insisting that they head south and east, but whenever he asked her why, she answered evasively. Something was going on but she wouldn't say what, and he didn't like it.

Uncomfortable under his probing gaze, she was glad to take first turn in the shower. He moved to the window, hoping for a breeze, and sucked his thumbnail as he tried to figure it out. Maybe the last two months on the road, even with the clothes they'd taken from their apartment and all the money they'd gotten by closing out their accounts in DC, were getting to her.

But it was better than Bach finding them.

All the same, the wall Kim had built around herself was driving him crazy. John turned on the television. The sound came on before the picture. He heard the announcer say, 'The headlines at eleven: President Johnson rejects de Gaulle's assertion that Vietnam should remain a neutral territory.'

Zigzag lines fizzed across the screen, then the monochrome picture came on. Saw-toothed mountains, dazzling white slopes with jagged peaks behind, heralded the Winter Olympics getting underway in Innsbruck, Austria.

Next came an item that riveted John. He sat on a lumpy armchair to watch a rocket standing on a launch pad. The reporter said, 'And another ranger moon probe is launched from Cape Kennedy – the sixth after five previous missions have failed. Will this one finally succeed in sending back TV pictures of the lunar surface? NASA says it's a crucial step towards putting a man on the moon. Details after this word from our sponsors.'

Vitalis hair lotion didn't appeal to him. He crossed to the set and switched the commercial off as Kim came out of the bathroom with a towel wrapped like a turban around her head. Ignoring the diminishing dot on the screen, she said without preamble, 'If we take the new interstate, we can make it by tomorrow night.'

He clenched one side of his mouth in an exasperated negative. 'Interstate's too dangerous, you know that.'

Kim threw the towel aside and got into bed, leaning back against the headboard to study a map. Vertical creases puckered her brow and once again John had that feeling that she was cutting him off.

'Is it this, Kim? The ranger launch?'

Troubled, she flicked her gaze towards him, then bent to concentrate on the map once more. 'I don't think so . . .' She laid the map on the night table as if it had nothing to do with him.

Nevertheless he slid under the covers and tried to get close. Her head turned away from him, though she let him put an arm across her, even squeezed his hand.

But she wouldn't face him.

'Then what?' he burst out. 'Why the hurry to get to Florida?'

'I don't know, John. I just don't know.'

He paused, waiting for her to acknowledge the lie, but silence wrapped them. She might as well have been on the moon. So, compressing his lips, he turned out the light.

Much later, so late the crickets had finally stopped, John fell asleep. Kim lay on her back, staring at the ceiling. Her face crumpled with fear like a child's. Her breathing turned ragged but she couldn't move. Couldn't stop it happening again.

An eldritch glow bloomed beside her, hovering in space. She closed her eyes firmly, trying to pretend it wasn't there. But it was. It burned brighter and brighter so that behind her tight-shut lids it was like a solar flare. Or a searchlight, prying, trying to get inside her, strip her bare.

The radiance was too insistent to ignore. Panting with terror, blood beating so hard in her throat she felt she would choke, she turned her head fractionally to see if *he* was there again.

He was. Floating in a weightless, infinite chasm, wrapped in a flying suit, the dome of a space helmet reflecting back the dazzling beam of light.

Slowly, every movement agonized, he stretched out his gloved hand to her, begging for the comfort of a human touch.

Kim was too frightened to move. If she did, she knew *something* would take its revenge in the pain of her body.

But the man in the spacesuit gasped, 'Take it . . . take my hand.'

She willed herself to resist his plea. Tears of sympathy flowed down her cheeks. His anguish was hers.

'We have to help each other . . . please . . .'

And Kim extended her shaking hand towards his.

All morning they drove without talking. Only the swish of the tyres along Route 66 broke the silence. John tried the local radio station. It didn't improve matters at all when they broadcast Elvis Presley singing 'Suspicion'.

They crossed the state line into Alabama, still heading east, glad when noon took the sun above the windscreen so they at least had a little shade. Heat beat in through the windows of the ten-year-old Ford they had picked up in Arizona. Whatever was going on inside Kim's head, it drowned out the baked landscape of yellowed grass and scrub. She was completely unaware of what she was doing.

John noticed first. For hours he had been trying to think of something that would bridge the gulf between them. He asked, 'Where'd you come up with that?'

She looked down, surprised to find she had been doodling on the edge of the map. An elongated triangle with a widening tail of swirling circles was pencilled in over the Atlantic coast.

The glyph John had seen cut out in the cornfield.

Kim stared at the shape she had drawn. 'This? I don't know . . . it's in my head.' Her face worked as though some cruel bird of prey had slashed her with its raking claws. Then the expression was gone. 'Kinda looks like fish, I guess.'

She thrust the map into the door pocket, scooping up a hamburger wrapper from the floor and shoving it down on top as though she needed the world around her to be ordered, sensible. Normal.

For a moment she stared blindly at the dunes sliding by. Then her hand crept across to take John's, as if somehow he could protect her from the demons within.

Lights flashed in the rear-view mirror. John raised his eyes and cursed as a patrol car signalled him to pull over. 'Where'd he come from?' he said, darting an irritated glance at Kim, who hunched down a little guiltily. 'You were supposed to be keeping an eye out. Was I speeding?'

'Speed limit's seventy-five on the interstate.'

He slammed his palms on the wheel, frustrated at her provocation in a situation that was already tense, then pulled over to the side of the road. The one officer in the patrol car stopped 20 feet short of them, and climbed out, leaving the door of his vehicle negligently hanging wide. He pulled on a high-brimmed hat, banded twice by a gold cord ending in two acorns. The man was a little on the tubby side, his face creased from years of driving along dusty roads, but there was nothing old-fashioned about the heavy service revolver hanging in the holster on his hip.

'What do you think he wants?' Kim asked nervously.

John's pretence of calmness didn't fool either of them. 'Probably the Arizona plates.'

The patrolman leaned in through the window of their primrose-yellow Ford. 'Good mornin', folks. Please turn off your engine.'

Silently John complied.

'May I see your driver's licence and registration, sir?'

'You bet,' John said, fumbling out his wallet from the seat of his jeans. 'The speedometer on this tank's been acting up.'

Not to be swayed, the officer repeated, 'Your license and registration, please.'

John handed his driver's licence over while Kim fished the car's documents out of the glovebox.

'From Arizona?'

John nodded. 'Tucson.'

'And you're going to?'

'Savannah. Visit her folks.'

The square-built officer inspected the papers slowly, moving his lips a little as he framed the words to himself. Then he fixed John with a sharp look. 'Make a lot better time on the new interstate, Mr . . . ah . . . Lewis. Might want to save yourself some driving. 'Scuse me.'

John watched in the rear-view mirror as the patrolman sauntered back to his vehicle and reached in through the open door to pull out the microphone on its long lead.

Kim started to turn around.

'Don't look back!'

'What's he doing?'

'Calling it in.'

'Would he be doing that if . . .'

'No.' John turned the key and the ten-year-old Ford rattled into life.

'We can't outrun him, John!'

'We're not going to.' He slammed the gearstick into reverse. Dust plumed beneath them as the Ford jumped backwards, crashing into the patrolcar's radiator. Metal grated as the cars collided, the shock pounding the seats into their backs. The open door flung the patrolman onto the dirt, steam shooting out at him from under the mangled bonnet.

Loengard jammed the car into first. The ancient Ford hung on for a moment, its back bumper caught in the wreckage of the other car's grille, then leaped away, gathering speed.

Behind them, the patrolman rolled to his knees, snatching out his pistol.

'Down, Kim! Stay down!' He put a hand behind her head and thrust her forward just as the patrolman fired.

The rear window shattered. John ducked, sending the Ford slewing, then fishtailed back onto the highway. As shots beat at her eardrums, Kim gasped, cramming herself lower. John gunned the engine and the car screamed into the distance.

Once out of range, John slowed, needing time for his racing heart to recover. Kim said in a small voice, 'Think he's still got his radio?'

Helpless, John shrugged. 'It's only five miles to Mobile . . .'

With no rear window and bullet holes chipping the yellow paintwork, the Ford fetched less than $90. Glumly John accepted the cash, slogging off without a word towards the bus depot, once again carrying all his worldly goods in a single holdall. Kim trudged unhappily beside him through a neighbourhood that quite frankly scared her.

At the bus station, Kim fled to the washroom to get rid of the grit that scratched at her skin. Without even consulting her, John bought tickets for Houston, because that was the first bus out.

'C'mon,' he said as soon as she reappeared, grabbing her hand and leading her towards the stand.

She hung back, resisting. 'John, stop. I can't go!'

John shook her gently. 'We don't have a choice.'

'We can split up. You take a bus to Houston. I'll take one to Cocoa Beach.'

Baffled, he stared at her a moment, then pulled her out of the line of passengers boarding the waiting vehicle. 'Are you listening to yourself?' he hissed. 'This isn't a game, Kim!'

Like a child peeping up at an angry teacher, she scraped the toe of one sneaker along the ground, but said very clearly, 'I . . . I have to go to Florida . . .'

'Do you think that cop back there was an accident?' Recollecting himself, he glanced round to make sure no-one had heard, then said more quietly, 'He was looking for that car! I can smell Bach and Majestic a mile away. They know where we are, they know where we're headed. We have to change direction.'

'*I can't!*' She couldn't pretend that his distress didn't hurt her, but she went on, begging for his sympathy. 'I know it doesn't make any sense—'

'You're not kidding!'

'I feel . . . dammit, John, you have to understand this . . .'

John said through tightly pursed lips, 'I'm trying. I've been trying for the last week.'

'I have to go.'

He rolled his eyes in frustration. 'I want to know *why*. Whatever it is that's going on . . . *talk* to me!'

Kim's lips parted but no words came out. Her tongue flickered, as if moistening her dry mouth might help, but it didn't. Tears starred her lashes.

Unmanned, John reached out to embrace her, but she shook her head and backed off. He was left with a half-finished gesture that made him feel stupid. 'Kim?'

'He needs me.'

John's universe shattered like a snow scene in a bottle that's been dropped to the floor. He'd taken everything else – aliens, the loss of the life he'd known, Majestic's agents trying to kill them and the slaughtering of President Kennedy – but when Kim spoke of another man, John couldn't breathe.

'Who?'

'And . . . and I need *him*.'

Gravity's laws no longer seemed to apply. John's stomach dropped away into a pit of misery. He managed to say faintly, 'Who are you talking about?'

'The astronaut. The astronaut in my visions.'

23

A different moon shone its light over Frank Bach: a vast, grainy, black-and-white reconnaissance photo of Earth's satellite. In the Majestic conference room, Albano clicked a switch on the slide projector and a blow-up showed the same scene, closer.

It was a shot of the western side of the Mare Nubium, the short intense shadows of the lunar midday all but hiding something Bach couldn't quite make out. Recon had marked it with a white stencilled arrow.

Albano flicked the next slide into focus. This was an even greater magnification of the previous pictures, the arrow still indicating something that might have been a pyramid. Or just another hunk of rock.

Bach leaned forward, staring at the image. Smoke from his inevitable cigarette curled up into the beam from the projector, turning into a ghostly question mark. 'This is the origin of the signal?'

Adjusting the lens, the chief of operations said, 'Ahuh. And it's as close as we can get with a land-based telescope. These came from Palomar.'

Bach swivelled in his chair, having had enough. 'Shadows.' He puffed thoughtfully for a moment. 'Ranger's ETA?'

'0800 Thursday.'

'This time that dog better hunt.'

As Albano turned on the lights, a cloaker came in with a

note. Bach stood up, scanning the few lines on the paper. The cloaker said, 'Got a man on the way to go over the car.'

'Any indication where they're headed?'

The cloaker shrugged. 'Told the patrolman Savannah.'

Bach traded a look with Albano, then shook his head. 'East on Route Ninety means Florida.'

On the seaward side of the recently renamed Cape Kennedy, John and Kim walked into a cheesy motor court, one of several that littered Route 1-A. Above the door was a sign that read in small plastic capitals 'CLARICE BROWN, PROP'. Their footsteps echoed on the bare boards of the office cum souvenir shop.

From the back room drifted a woman's voice, a little cracked, as she said, 'Of course, they don't bother to consult us about changin' the name.'

John looked at the dusty display cases with their heaped gaudy pens and ashtrays. All of them bore the legend 'Cape Canaveral, Florida' and a handwritten notice said, 'Sale – 50 per cent off'. But there were no spaces in the ranks of keepsakes, which, judging by the layers of wind-blown sand, hadn't been disturbed for weeks.

With a sigh, John limped over to the counter as the owner came out of her sanctum. Meantime Kim had gone straight to a revolving stand of postcards showing rockets in space, rockets on the launch pad, rockets by night. On the other side of the stand were pictures of astronauts, some with 'autographs' printed on them.

The owner proved to be a short woman with piled-up brown hair, lime-green earrings and a loud print dress. She peered over her half-rimmed glasses and told them there was no problem getting a room. Still grumbling, she shoved the register over for John to sign. 'Kennedy, Canaveral, don't mean a thing to them. Me, I gotta switch every postcard, ashtray and gee-gaw.'

Still at the display stand, Kim put back the cards with the Mercury astronauts and their comrades on the Gemini missions. Not one of the photos was the man she was looking for. Interrupting the owner's lament, she asked abruptly, 'Is this all you have?'

The proprietor answered just as shortly, 'No.' Then she got back to complaining. 'I got boxes and boxes in the back room. Might as well burn it all and start over.'

Kim managed to get a word in edgeways. 'I mean the astronauts. Are there any others that you don't have pictures of?'

Clarice shook her head pityingly. It was a moot point whether the pity was for herself or Kim's naivety. 'If they're in the space programme, they're on that rack.' Hope lightened her face for a moment. 'I got a signed John Glenn for thirty bucks.'

Neither of her customers answered. Shrugging, she took out a rag, polishing a stack of toy rockets on yellow cardboard boxes.

John crossed to Kim, the lines under his eyes showing his continuing concern. His heart twisted inside him at the loveliness of her face and she shook her head.

Soft-voiced, she murmured up into his ear, 'There wasn't even a mission then. This card says Schirra was up on the third of October 'Sixty-two.'

'You were abducted on the twenty-first.'

Almost tranced by the recollection, Kim whispered, 'Lost time, isn't that what you called it? No memories of what happened. Just a feeling, a terrible feeling . . . A hole in your life.' She stared blindly out through the fly-specked glass door. 'He has something to do with it, John. I know he does.'

Aching, John nodded. 'Maybe. Or maybe he's just a bad dream.'

Clarice had come out from behind her counter. 'It's all a bad dream to me. You want to sign this register?'

Loengard went over to write 'Mr and Mrs Lewis' on the ledger, but Kim creased her eyelids a little, squinting to see – something outside. There was a buzzing in her ears, but neither John nor the garrulous proprietor seemed to have noticed anything odd.

Clarice rambled on, 'Hasn't been a manned mission in almost a year. And they say there's a year to go before Gemini.'

The sound built up, piercing on the hum of a carrier wave. As if it were some sort of aural fish-hook, Kim was drawn towards the source of it. Nose pressed up against the glass, she searched up and down the wide crossroads beyond.

Past the single tree on the traffic island roared a motorcycle, black and powerful, its gas tank scratched as though the bike had seen some hard use. Its rider was a young man in a white T-shirt and jeans. His windswept hair was short. Sunglasses masked his tanned face. Kim drew in a sharp breath.

He slid the bike to a stop outside a bar a little further down the street and hauled the Harley onto its side stand with ease, his muscles sliding easily under the skin-tight shirt.

Electrified, Kim opened the door, glancing back once, guiltily. John was too busy trying to stem the flood of the proprietor's volubility to notice. The door fell quietly shut behind her.

Clarice was like a gusher. 'Oh, they're testing boosters — got one this week. But if a man's not riding the Roman candle, nobody bothers to watch it burn. Business is as bad as a tick on a toilet seat. I put you kids right up front in number seven, by the pool.' She reached into a pigeon-hole for the key.

John turned towards Kim. Only she wasn't there.

Stomach constricted, he crossed to the door in two hasty strides. Shading his eyes, he squinted urgently against the glare.

There she was, walking rapidly across 1-A, heedless of the traffic. He yelled after her but she didn't so much as break stride. A truck screeched and careened around her, the irate driver bellowing at her through the window, but she didn't seem to hear. She stepped up onto the wooden sidewalk, the shade swallowing her up.

John darted across the highway, dodging cars that hooted at him. At least he was aware of them as he leaped out of the road. He yelled, 'Kim! Where are you going?'

She didn't turn. He saw her, neat green top and pedal-pushers outlining her slenderness, running her fingers caressingly over the black leather seat of a Harley. Then she went into a bar.

Standing at the doorway, she peered into the room. Idle chatter washed out at her. A dozen off-duty airmen lounged around a pool table. At the far end of the bar, a tall figure in white sleeveless shirt and jeans took a mouthful of beer from a bottle, grinning at the waitress as he slid a cue out of the stand.

'Keep 'em coming, Eileen. Figure I got fifteen minutes 'til they drag me out—'

Suddenly he froze, head cocked to one side as though listening to something no-one else could hear. In slow motion, he wheeled around and stopped.

Poised in the doorway, Kim felt the weight of his gaze. Behind her the sun burned, liquid gold limning the slim curves of her body, haloing her hair so that she looked like a saint from some orthodox triptych.

All his bravado fell away from the rugged young astronaut. Backlit, the vision came hesitantly towards him. Inside the building, the golden aura faded. Now he could see her for what she was.

And who.

Transfixed, he rushed over towards her, carried by a force he didn't completely understand. As they came closer, each of them reached out a hand that trembled with the hurricane force of emotion. At last their fingers touched, the completion of the gesture they had only essayed in Kim's dreams.

For now it was fulfilment. Each stared at the other, devouring the actuality that had merely been foreshadowed up until now. The astronaut breathed, 'You're real . . .'

Unnoticed, John leaned against the door. He saw Kim and the astronaut, hand in hand, locked in an intimacy that excluded him. John sagged, only the wall at his back keeping him on his feet. He felt as though something inside him had been broken.

The harsh scream of overrevved engines shattered the moment. From the corner of his eye, John could see a jeep and a sedan screech to a halt outside the bar.

He would have recognized the grey suits and dark glasses anywhere: cloakers from Majestic. By the same token, they would recognize him. Bach had found him.

But the broad-shouldered young man in the jeep waved them to stay where they were as he leaped out of his vehicle. He walked with the rangy stride of an athlete, calling to the cloakers, 'I'll get him.'

John pulled back, hunching lower so that the light from the open door didn't strike his face. But the minute the guy saw Kim, there'd be trouble.

Only the guy didn't even glance at Kim. He went straight over to the man standing next to her.

Before he could speak, the astronaut said in wonder, 'Gator, it's her! This is the one!'

Gator, the guy from the jeep, slid a piercing look over her from head to toe. Obviously the words meant something to him but he shrugged it off. 'Yeah, well, some other time, huh? Those boys are outside, Ty. You know how nervous they get.'

Ty broke away from Kim, seeming to come out of some entrancement. He ducked his head a little as if in embarrassment, and said apologetically, 'My handlers.' With a pen from the counter, he scribbled something on a napkin. Shoving the paper at Kim, he added, 'Please . . . I need to see you.'

John heard it, the pain in his heart turning to an irrational flame of anger, but Ty headed out with the driver of the jeep, who was saying, 'Man, you pick the weirdest times to wig.'

The man from Kim's dream spread his palms, a picture of the right stuff but full of mischief. 'Suits can't take a joke.'

Their footsteps clumped across the boardwalk. They didn't so much as glance at Loengard, nor did the cloakers come fully into the bar, though their careful gaze took him in.

John asked the barmaid, 'Astronauts?'

She shook her head, her dyed hair bouncing on her shoulders. 'Naw, just air force pilots. Nothin' but trouble if you ask me.'

He couldn't have agreed more. Thanking the barmaid with a curt nod, he walked up to Kim. She was staring raptly at the serviette in her hand.

'Mind if I see that?' he said.

Unshed tears sparkled in her eyes like dew in a sunny dawn. She passed him the napkin, saying over and over in amazement, 'He was with me, John . . . he was up there with me!'

The rough print on the crumpled paper said only, 'Beach Road – 2300 hrs'. But underneath it was a crude drawing, vaguely triangular, with a widening tail of coiled circles.

It was late afternoon near Savannah. Sweat stained the patrolman's dark shirt and gummed his hatband to his head. All he wanted to do was go home to a cold beer but Control had radioed him that some government bigwig, FBI or something, they'd said, wanted to meet him outside the Alabama Vehicle Impound. So the patrolman put his dreams on ice and drove the 30 miles through the sweltering heat haze. Of course, he'd had to borrow another patrol car to do it, and the ribbing he'd got at the sheriff's office hadn't done his temper any good at all.

Cursing officialdom in general and the man in the black suit in particular, the officer waited by the shot-up Ford in the pound. It was primrose yellow, with Arizona plates, and the rear bumper rattled when he kicked it. That at least gave him some satisfaction after what they'd done to his car.

When the man in black stood against the sun, the

patrolman couldn't see his face. The officer leaned against the car, knowing that combing it for clues yet again was a waste of time. He'd already done it himself, hadn't he? And the owner of the tacky dealership where it had been found wouldn't have left anything worth having, anyway. But when Control said to give the man in black anything he wanted, they'd made it clear they meant just that.

So he swiped a bandana over his sweaty face and waited with all the patience of long-suffering officers the world over while the man in black rummaged through the contents of the glovebox. Bored, the officer said, 'Swear you could fry a catfish on the hood.'

No response from the man inside the car.

'Told me you boys weren't comin' down until tomorrow.'

The man in black grunted and went on with his search. Finally, with the westering sun red in the sky, he stood up empty-handed and leaned against the open passenger door.

This time the officer got a good look at his face. Rat-featured, with a sharp chiselled nose and a permanent sneer, it was not a physiognomy to inspire confidences. But what made the patrolman step back a pace was the white marbled eye that swivelled blindly in his direction.

Steele stared coldly at him through his one good eye. 'Said they were headed for Savannah?'

Sweating afresh, the patrolman nodded. 'Six-hour drive from here.'

A faint sigh of discouragement blew from Steele's nostrils. Then he glanced down, catching sight of the debris left in the door-pocket. He bent a little, scooping out a hamburger wrapper and two plastic coffee cups. Underneath he found the map.

'Got his license and registration in the office,' the officer said, wanting to be rid of his unnerving visitor.

'Won't be necessary.' Steele looked down at the stiff folded paper in his hand. There was a yellow appendix shape of Florida set in the pale blue of the sea.

And there was the circle of glyphs Kim had unconsciously scribbled around Cape Canaveral.

Steele's thin lips parted in a nasty smile. 'I think I've got all I need for now.'

24

Late that afternoon, John drove out along the coast. Low slanting sunshine was riding golden on the dunes. Here and there cane brakes tossed their green feathery leaves above the network of tiny lagoons which fed into the main one. Gilded ripples skimmed across the top of the waters at the whim of vagrant breezes, casting dazzling patches of reflection into John's eyes.

Fenced off from the car park was a rocket, silvery in the sunlight. Loengard observed it briefly through his binoculars. Even just sitting there it was an impressive sight. Imagining what it must be like when the tail-flames roared and the rocket flew up into the heavens, he could easily understand why the parking lot was so big, and so well provided with rest rooms and pay phones. For a manned launch, the whole area would be packed.

Not now, though. At the moment John was on his own, except for a fisherman with a long rod on one shoulder and a whole basket of equipment over the other. The man came closer, a warm-faced African-American under a beanie. He stopped as he walked past. 'That's a Saturn,' he said in his slow Southern drawl. 'Goin' up tomorrow at seven.'

John lowered his binoculars and smiled at his friendly interlocutor.

Encouraged, the fisherman went on, 'No man on top – just a test, but I'll be here. Roar makes the fish go crazy.'

'That right?'

'Ahuh. Bite at anythin' to get outta that water. Mercury Seven? Caught my limit in two minutes flat. You come back tomorrow' – he grinned – 'bring a pole.'

He strolled away, leaving John thinking about astronauts. Keeping his face from showing his emotions, he raised the glasses and scanned the entire area around Kennedy Base.

Several dark-coloured sedans rewarded him. A man in naval uniform climbed out of one of them. Loengard swept his binoculars back to check him out.

Resplendent in dress blues, complete down to the white cap with the scrambled egg, it was Frank Bach.

Back at Clarice Brown's A-Okay motel, John dashed into number seven. He blurted, 'Bach! We've gotta move!' and dumped their holdalls on the bed. Moving quickly, he began stripping their things out of drawers and closets.

Kim just sat there.

John threw an armful of clothes on the bed next to her. 'Maybe the ranger probe. Or your Hive astronaut. Doesn't matter. We're moving to a room in the back where we'll be less exposed.'

Pleating the astronaut's napkin between her fingers, she said quietly, 'He isn't Hive, John,' then, more resolute, she added, 'He needs my help and I need his.'

'Look, if he's an astronaut and he was in the alien ship with you when you were abducted, it stands to reason he was implanted like you were.'

'He could've been ART'd.'

'It was experimental!' he snapped. 'You were the first.'

'You don't *know* that.'

'Yes I do. And it doesn't change anything. The men who picked him up today were Majestic. I could smell 'em a mile off. Bach is at Mission Control. Isn't that enough? It's too risky to meet him tonight. It could be a set-up.'

She shook her head. 'But it's *not*. I know it. I feel it.'

'Kim, we can't . . .'

'I can.' She drew a breath and said quickly, 'It may not

214

make sense but it's all I have to go on. It's the only way I'm going to find out what's happening to me.' Her eyes met his squarely for the first time in weeks. 'I'm going to do this, John. I'm going to meet him. With you or without you.'

Nothing he could say had the slightest effect on her. In all the years he'd been with her she'd never been so intractable. He toyed briefly with the idea that she still had some kind of alien presence within her. But it wasn't like that, even though he found a menace he'd dealt with once less unnerving than her obsession with another man.

That night, much against his will, John drove her out to the coast in yet another cheap, second-hand car. On the rear window the remains of flaking white shoe-cream still read 'For sale – $150'.

The headlights pierced a bright yellow tunnel through the darkness of the deserted road. Finally the tarmac petered out amongst swelling dunes to the north of the Cape Kennedy complex.

John turned the motor off, but his fingers were reluctant to let go of the key in the ignition. He stared through the windscreen at the grass blowing in the offshore wind. 'Look, Kim, we can still turn round and drive out.'

He was peripherally aware of her opening the door. 'I want you to stay in the car,' she said.

Giving her an old-fashioned look, he climbed out himself.

'Then at least hang back, John. All right?' Without even waiting to see, she plunged off across the sand.

Away from the road, the untamed landscape possessed her. She shivered. On the far side of the sand spit the ocean roared. Overhead, the black velvet of the sky was pierced by cold unwinking stars. As soon as she had left the comforting brightness of the headlights behind, the immensity and isolation of the night closed in, leaving her feeling vulnerable. Still she wouldn't turn back.

Loengard watched her tiny figure diminishing until she was almost out of sight. He checked his gun, its weight companionable in his hand, before starting to follow her. Soft sand swallowed the sound of his feet as he cautiously crested a dune. He started down the other side.

Something slammed against the back of his head. It sent him sprawling. The figure kicked away his gun, but John scrambled up and tackled his assailant.

The unknown fighter was skilled and John was hard-put to hold his own. Rolling, they traded vicious blows as they tumbled back towards the road, landing winded.

In the glow of the headlights John got a look at the man's face. It was the astronaut.

Enraged, John launched a murderous uppercut but the man was service trained, in fighting trim. Ty rode with the punch, seizing John's arm and pulled him down onto the bonnet.

Pinning him in a savage hold, the astronaut quickly rifled John's pockets, hissing, 'Who the hell are you?' He bounced John's head on the metal. 'Who?'

Dragging out John's wallet, Ty found the Majestic ID and released his crippling hold. 'What the hell are you guys doing with her?'

John wiped the blood from his mouth. 'I'm not with them any more.'

Twenty yards away, Kim came running towards the pool of light. 'John? Oh my God! What happened?'

She sped straight to John's side, hanging onto his arm protectively.

The astronaut saw her and froze, mesmerized by her presence in the flesh. He flashed John's identity card and shame-facedly muttered, 'I thought he was a suit.'

'No. He's my fiancé. He's here to help us.'

Ty stared at them both. 'Tell you the truth . . . I don't know what the hell it is we're doing.' His broad shoulders hunched a little, helplessly. 'I don't even know your name.'

Loengard studied the man, weighing him up, trying to guess whether this was the confusion a new Hive implant might feel. Yet the man's surprise seemed to be a genuine emotion, on track with reality. Besides, if he had been implanted at the same time as Kim, he'd have been pure Hiver by now.

Kim didn't suffer from the same uncertainty. She said, 'Kim Sayers.'

'Ty Yount.'

John saw them look at each other as though nothing else in the world mattered. He felt again the connection between them that locked him out, and jealousy spiked through his stomach. 'Where were you on October the twenty-first, nineteen sixty-two?'

Unnerved by the question fired so suddenly at him, Ty turned to John, wearing an expression of friendly idiocy that sat ill with his speed of reaction. 'Hell,' he said, like a down-home farm boy, 'that's over a year ago. You expect me to remember?'

His eyes betrayed him. John saw that he was covering something up, and stared meaningfully at the sky. 'You were up there, weren't you? In outer space . . .'

The astronaut looked uneasily at Kim. 'That's crazy!' But he lacked conviction.

John pressed home his advantage. 'Is it? Is it crazy for me to think you're an astronaut? An astronaut engaged in some kind of a Black Op?'

That was one Ty had been trained to counter. 'That's classified information.'

But he hadn't been trained to counter Kim's appeal. 'You have to trust us, Ty. Trust *me* . . .'

Standing on the dunes, the astronaut said thoughtfully, 'Y'know, fear has always been something I spat at.' He clasped his arms tightly across his chest. 'Not now . . .'

The shadow of remembered terror suffocated him. Face working, he stared out towards the distant boom of the breakers.

Taking pity on him, Kim stroked his arm. 'You're not alone.'

As the moon rose, silvered and ethereal, Ty began to speak, hesitantly at first but with growing confidence when he realized that these people were really listening to him.

'Shepard, Grissom, Glenn – they're the glory boys with the presidential phone calls and the ticker-tape parades. But they're not the élite.'

He looked up at his listeners. 'You ever hear of Midnight Wing?'

Searching their faces, he saw no sign of recognition. 'Didn't think so. We're a small group of space jocks that fly Black Op military missions. The best of the best.'

Kim nodded her understanding. 'You were up there, weren't you?'

'Yeah. Me and Gator. Augatreux, that's the guy who picked me up at the bar, we were launched out of Vandenburg on the morning of the twenty-first in a Gemini prototype.'

The scene had painted itself ineradicably in his brain. As he talked, he felt again the creases of his spacesuit, the invisible hand of G-force smashing him down into his seat until he feared he would be crushed. Around him the capsule shuddered as gales swept the thinning atmosphere. The voice on the radio seemed like the only lifeline to Earth for him and old Gator Augatreux.

Mission Control said across the backwash of static, 'You are A-Okay. All systems Go at T plus forty-five seconds. Coming up on primary separation in five, four, three—'

A thump and jolt hurled the cockpit sideways, then guidance systems locked them into a polar orbit.

On the windy beach, Ty relived his nightmare. 'Our mission was to seek and destroy a Soviet spy satellite called the Black Knight. They told us it had something to do with the missile crisis in Cuba. That we were very close to another world war.'

John didn't like the way Kim leaned in to the tortured astronaut. 'Did Kennedy know about you?' he asked abruptly.

'If he did, I never got my thank-you note. And I think it's

safe to say even we didn't know the whole story. What we saw up there . . .'

Internal reality conquered the outside world. His hands locked around his upper arms and the muscles of his back stood out in ridges.

Kim brought him back out of it. 'The Black Knight?'

He nodded, trying not to fall off the very edge of terror. 'It was . . . huge. As big as a football stadium. This long black triangle . . . I mean, my God! I kept thinking what the hell did the Russians use to get this thing up? It must have come up in pieces . . .

'And Gator just said calmly, "Roger, Houston, we have it in our sights." We came up on it real slow. I remember counting it down to eighty-five hundred metres. I could feel my heart beating like a baby's when Houston told us to go to deploy.'

Yount was panting, perspiration beading across his forehead and dripping into his hair. Every fibre of his body was as taut as a bowstring, quivering. He swallowed and said, 'We had a space-launched missile. Prepared it to fire, then—'

The memories, so vivid, seemed to have deserted him. He huddled down like an abandoned child. 'It was so strange . . . so unexpected . . .'

Kim stroked his arm. 'Ty?'

He shook his head in disbelief, a repetition of that moment when up in space he suddenly seemed to wake out of nightmare. 'I . . . I looked over at Gator. He didn't seem quite with it, either. I checked the mission clock.'

'What, Ty?' she prompted.

'Like suddenly it was two hours later and we were on the other side of the earth . . . and the Black Knight had *gone*.'

Silence pressed down on the trio on the beach. The waves washed hissing along the sand while the sea-breeze brought them the cool tang of salt.

After a while John asked, 'Do you remember anything about the missing time?'

The astronaut's body formed a single shrug. 'Gator

thought he triggered the missile . . . remembered a power surge. Houston said they registered an explosion and thought that maybe it damaged the capsule. Figured we'd been knocked out.'

'But you don't believe that.'

Yount turned his tortured gaze on him. 'I don't know what to believe. All I know is I wanted to get the hell down.'

'Did Majestic debrief you?'

'Up one side and down the other. Gave us a clean bill of health and put us back in the flight rotation. Gator's already flown another mission.'

'But you haven't?' Loengard said delicately.

Ty's head shook like a rag doll's. 'Until now.'

John and Kim exchanged a glance pregnant with meaning. 'The unmanned Saturn launch . . .'

Ty opened his mouth twice before he managed to say, '. . . is gonna have Gator and me riding on top.' He pressed his hands over his face as if unwilling to make his final confession. When he spoke it was with barely suppressed panic. 'And I am scared. I am scared out of my mind.'

He grabbed Kim's hand. 'Why do I see you? Why do I see you reaching out for me in the middle of the night?'

'Because I was up there, Ty. I think I was up there with you . . .'

John could see that Kim's own dark terror was back just beneath the surface. But it wasn't him she turned to, but the astronaut of her dreams.

And he seemed to find the solution that had eluded John. 'Then there's someone I need you to see.'

25

John just hoped the lateness of the hour gave some credence to their story, otherwise they were all in for some of Majestic's more unpleasant fun and games. As he slowed for the guardhouse outside Cape Kennedy, he wished he'd never allowed himself to be talked into this.

Beside him, slumped apparently happily against the car window, Ty Yount grinned like a fool. He reeked of beer, which was hardly surprising. They had detoured to an all-night liquor store, buying one bottle which Ty downed in record time, and another which he had mostly poured down his shirt.

In the back, under John's jacket, Kim huddled in the footwell, fighting the urge to sneeze. John had his seat adjusted way back to give her cover. Plus which, it made him look cool even if he didn't actually feel that way.

He stopped at the red-and-white barrier, trying to appear bored as the airman on duty shone a flashlight into the car. The beam from the torch hit Yount, showing his inane, wet-mouthed expression, and the guard straightened. 'AWOL again, huh?'

Loengard nodded, flashing his Majestic ID, and flipping it out of sight again as quickly as he dared. 'We're thinking about putting a leash on him. Traded his bike for this beater.'

The guard's face cleared. 'That was going to be my next question.'

'At least he'll be easier to catch.'

Leaning on the counterweight the MP said, 'Yes, sir. Amen to that, sir.'

Then they were through. Driving across the open compound to a low sprawl of buildings, Loengard turned to the astronaut. 'You're sure we can trust her?'

The answer was crisp and clear. Yount pointed out the house he was aiming for and said, 'With my life.'

John could only hope the man was right, because he was trusting the unknown woman with his life and Kim's too.

Dr Gould's home looked perfectly ordinary, pictures on the walls, little knick-knacks on a hallstand. Until they went into her consulting room.

Along one side was a brown leather chaise longue, just what you'd expect a psychiatrist to have. Above it her certificates hung reassuringly. A pretty chintz sofa filled another wall, and a cluttered wooden desk sat squarely in front of the curtained window.

Dr Gould came out of the kitchen with another mug of coffee and sat behind her desk in a big black padded leather chair. Her hair was smooth and blond, though escaping a little untidily from the chignon into which it was twisted. John would have put her age on the shady side of thirty, and she was slender though not particularly well co-ordinated. The long quilted white dressing gown served for modesty rather than elegance. At the moment she seemed far too businesslike to worry about that. Her narrow, black-framed spectacles confirmed his impression of a woman fighting for her place in a male-dominated profession.

Though it was way past midnight, Dr Gould had been hard at work, but she shoved her case notes aside when Yount explained his predicament. Too restless to sit still, he strode back and forth as he spoke. He even told her all about the way he had smuggled two civilians onto the military base, but she didn't reach for the telephone.

Hearing him out, she finally said, 'Mr Loengard, Miss Sayers ... I consider myself a Freudian, which means I place a great deal of emphasis on dreams.' She paused. 'Frankly, I don't buy into flying saucers and little green men, but I do feel that there's some significance to their mutual dreams of each other. And that may hold the key to Colonel Yount's fear.'

She leaned forward, her bathrobe parting a little over a bosom that had no right to be so beautiful if it belonged to a professional psychiatrist. Intent, she went on, 'There's a technique that I've been experimenting with, called hypnotic regression.'

Leaning back against the wall, arms folded cross his chest, John nodded. This part he understood. And if it helped Kim cut loose from the wild-eyed astronaut and her cockamamie nightmares, he was all for it. 'You hypnotize a subject and have them relive their dream, or a moment in their life, eliminating the memory blocks that may be caused by fear or inhibition.'

The doctor lifted one eyebrow at him. 'Psych major?'

'UCLA.'

She nodded her approval. 'Good school.' Turning to the astronaut, she went on, 'I've tried the technique several times on Colonel Yount, trying to get him to remember the dream where Kim appears. And it does seem to begin with the incident in his last mission.'

Ty seemed to come out of a daze. 'Except I can't get past the point where I lose consciousness.'

Tapping a pen on the desktop, the psychiatrist paused thoughtfully. 'He comes out of the hypnosis.'

'Which is common in extreme cases,' John said.

'Yes. Whatever happened – he's terrified of it.'

Kim leaned forward on the flowery couch. 'And I may have gone through the same thing?'

'I believe that's what you're telling me.' The doctor sighed. 'Look. My job is to make certain that astronauts are mentally fit for flight. Period. I don't have to reveal details. And no-one has to know you're here. But I would like to find out what's happening to Ty, and if you believe you were there, Miss Sayers . . .'

'You'd like to put me through this regression,' Kim finished for her.

For perhaps half a minute they considered the option. John noticed that once again Kim and Ty were staring at each other as though they were opposite poles of a magnet. That tension between them still shut him out.

The doctor said, 'This is your decision, and your decision alone. You have to want to do it.'

John took Kim's hand but she never even glanced at him. 'We can walk out that door, Kim. Whatever you want to do . . .'

That did get her attention, but she nodded at Dr Gould. All the same she couldn't help adding, 'I'm afraid, John.' Though her eyes were wide pools of fear, she moved to lie on the couch.

John watched her with mingled trepidation and annoyance, but he said with all the reassurance he could muster, 'I know, honey. But I'll be right here with you.'

The room grew deathly quiet once Dr Gould had slowly tuned Kim's attention to the sound of the sea. Little by little Kim's mind entered the pleasant realms of relaxation that the psychiatrist made so alluring.

Only then did Dr Gould lead her into the dream, inviting her to focus on the way her body felt, the breath in her lungs, the smells and then the sights around her. She let Kim take a minute to orient herself. In the office an air of expectancy built until John had to force himself not to squeeze Kim's hand too tightly.

'Where are you, Kim?' the doctor said.

Sleepily Kim answered, 'In our apartment . . . on the balcony outside the bedroom.'

'How do you feel?'

'Upset . . . I'm angry at John. We just had a fight.'

Beneath her closed lids, Kim's eyes darted from side to

side as though something stood beside her. Along her arms the tiny hairs stood on end and her hand clutched fiercely at John's. Suddenly her eyes opened and she seemed to be looking at something above her head. She said in a tiny voice. 'I'm afraid.'

The doctor asked calmly, 'Why, Kim?' and checked that her big reel-to-reel tape recorder was still running.

'There's something. Something in the sky.'

She twitched, her legs flinching as though she had run away. Her breath came faster now. 'I'm back inside . . . but the window . . . the window's rattling.'

Her arms sketched a vague movement as though she had slammed the window shut, but the others couldn't see what she saw. Frustrated, they could only watch her twitching on the couch and listen to the disjointed tumble of words from her lips.

On the soft brown leather, her head turned abruptly. Fear stretched her skin over the bones of her skull. John felt the pulse racing through her wrist and the sound of her ragged breathing was harsh on his ears.

Suddenly Kim said in panic, 'Oh my God! They're here! He's looking at me . . . I'm so scared . . .'

'Who's there, Kim?'

'They are!' Kim was plainly terrified, the blood beating visibly in her temple. Her jaw worked as she shrieked, '*They* are! Oh John, please, make him go away! He's looking at me! John? John!'

Kim had no awareness outside her private world. John stroked her arm, patted her, but his comfort didn't reach her. It made him feel singularly useless when she went on, panting in mental and physical agony. 'Oh no! It's on the floor . . .'

Dr Gould said, 'What is?'

'The green . . . it's on the floor and it's coming . . .' Kim thrashed her limbs, her body stiff with terror. 'Oh God! It's on the floor and it's coming at me.' Her voice rose to a shrill scream. 'It's me, it's on me! Get it off!'

Her free hand beat at herself as though to brush

something away, and the hand John was holding jerked in his grasp. 'So wet . . . it's so cold . . . It's all over me! Let me out! Let me *out!*'

Kim's eyelids slammed shut as though a cruel light was dazzling her. Her face was locked in the rictus of a silent screech.

Her body jerked as though she were dropping at terminal velocity, then she reacted as though she had slammed back down onto the couch, the sort of fear response that happens sometimes in dreams of falling. White-faced and beaded with perspiration, she breathed in short juddering gasps.

Even more alarmed than he had been, John searched for comfort in the faces of Ty and Dr Gould. He found none.

Trying not to sound scared herself, the doctor asked, 'Where are you, Kim?'

Eyes open, staring at the ceiling as though she saw something else, Kim didn't answer. Her jagged breaths rasped out in the quiet room.

John squeezed her hand gently and said, 'Kim, it's John.'

She pulled her hand out of his warm clasp, saying petulantly, 'You're not here with me.'

Hurt, he locked his hands between his knees, looking once more to the doctor for reassurance. Dr Gould gave him a tiny nod, as if to say that at least Kim was still communicating with him, so he tried again. 'Tell me where you are, Kim.'

Like a four-year-old in the clutches of demon dreams, she said in a thread of her normal voice, 'I don't know. It's dark . . . I feel like I'm floating.' Her gaze stayed locked on the space above her. 'I'm afraid to look. I can feel them around me.'

The astronaut shuddered, as white-faced as Kim. His dark eyes were unfocused as though he too saw something beyond the solace of the doctor's cosy office. Something that scared him beyond the point of reason.

Dr Gould watched him, trying to keep her face impassive, but the atmosphere of unseen terror was wreaking its effect on her too. She nodded at John to continue.

He leaned forward. 'What are they doing?'

Kim's gaze darted to a spot above her as if something there magnetized her attention. 'Shadows. Shadows moving. It's like ... it's like spiders on the ceiling. Hundreds of them.'

He said again, 'What are they doing?'

Her hands came up to cover her mouth as though she didn't want to say it. Or as though she were afraid the spider-people might come down and slip in through her parted lips. 'I ... don't know. Only ... no, they're not shadows! They're people with huge great black eyes, watching me ... and it's like their arms and legs are all kind of locked together, crawling over each other.'

Again her breath shortened in dread. 'They're moving ... Oh, they're up there! I can see them now. They're up there watching us! I don't like their eyes ...'

The word hit John like a cannon ball: *us*. As if her fear didn't hurt him enough, the syllable rubber-banded him back to his insecurity. 'Is there someone with you?'

Kim squinted suddenly as though something stabbed at her eyes. 'The light! There's a bright light ...'

She turned her head aside, fixing her gaze on something off to her right, her brows contracting and her eyelids almost closed against the light that seemed to pierce right through her. 'They're shining it down on us.' A sob racked her. 'Shining it on me. Oh, I feel it! I don't like this ... they know everything ... I feel so naked! Take it off me!'

For a moment her torso arched as though in extremis. Then she slumped back on the couch, shattered by her experience. With relief she mumbled, 'It's on someone else now.'

John had to make himself ask, 'Who, Kim? Can you see?'

Her head turned on the brown leather. 'He's glowing ... It's a man in a spacesuit ... an astronaut. What's he doing here?'

'Is it' – John licked suddenly dry lips – 'Ty Yount?'

In Gould's consultation room Kim swivelled her head towards Ty. The man from Kennedy Base stared at her transfixed, white rims showing all around his pupils. Sweat was pouring off his rigid body.

Gould's pen skipped furiously across a pad of paper as she noted her observations. John glanced at her for help, but she was concentrating on the girl on her clinician's couch.

'The light's scanning him . . .'

John had to know. 'Is it Ty?'

So frightened she could hardly shape the words, Kim whispered, 'It's Ty . . . he's reaching out to me! He's saying, "Take it . . . take my hand . . ."'

In agony, Kim slowly extended her trembling fingers. But not the hand closest to John. Instead she reached out to the astronaut on her other side.

Full of wonder, Ty stretched towards her. He was shaking too.

Their fingers barely touched, but John could see relief in both their faces, in their relaxing postures.

Kim stiffened. Her hand dropped and the mouth puckered in a moue of distress. 'Oh, no!'

'What happened, Kim?'

Almost crying, she answered, 'They're taking him away. They don't want him.' Once again her whole body spoke of abandonment.

'How do you know that?' John asked her sharply.

'I . . . feel them telling me. He isn't right for them. He's just . . . getting further and further away. Drifting out into space . . . They want—' Now she wept from unbearable horror. 'Oh, no! No, no. Why?'

Tears thickened her voice and coursed down her into her hair as she said over and over again like a child, 'I wish they didn't want me . . . I'm so scared! Why do they want me?'

John mirrored her distress. It was as if he were forced to watch her being beaten and raped. He wanted to fold her

228

into his loving arms and keep her safe. But she wasn't with him. She was still trapped inside the nightmare of her abduction.

Tortured, her body elongated. Her head tilted sharply back as though someone, something, had yanked it hard from behind. In strangled tones she mumbled, 'It's coming down from the ceiling! Like a spider on a thread . . . only there's no thread.'

Her limbs splayed, acting out the imprisonment of tendrils whipping around her arms and legs, holding her motionless. Her breath rattled rapidly in and out of her strained throat. As though she were having some sort of a seizure, her eyes rolled back in her head.

John blurted, 'Kim! What's happening?'

'Oh . . . oh . . . oh, they're on me. They're all over me. What are they doing?' Her voice rose in a squeal of animal hysteria that brought even the aloof Dr Gould running over to the couch.

Across Kim's skin, suction marks appeared, winding around her wrists and ankles in circles of ruptured capillaries. The raised weals showed a dark and bloody red.

The psychiatrist gaped in a thoroughly unprofessional way. 'Oh, my God . . .'

John possessed himself once more of Kim's hand. 'I'm here, baby. I'm here.'

She didn't even hear him. 'Oh, I see him! I see him now . . .'

'Who do you see?'

'He's coming *down* . . . It's in his hand, all dark and wriggling . . . oh, it scares me . . .'

Her head snapped sideways, only a fraction as though something were restraining her. 'Stop . . . stop the screaming! What are they doing to him?'

'Who's screaming?' John whispered.

'I can't see him . . . something in front of my eyes . . . white . . . shiny. What are they doing?'

Again her head wrenched painfully back. Screams of abject terror ripped from her, the sounds bruised by her constricting larynx. Her shallow fractured breathing seemed to abrade her throat in a paroxysm of weeping. 'No . . . no. They have my head . . . Oh no! Please stop, please . . . please. He has the tip of it. It's wriggling . . . it's alive! His eyes are black. So evil. He's right on top of me! What's he going to do with it? What's he going to *do*?'

Kim whimpered. Her eyes seemed to focus on something that came ever closer to her face. 'Not there . . . please . . . not *there!*'

Abruptly she sat bolt upright. Her whole body was shaking with the sobs that overpowered her. A slow trickle of dark blood welled from one nostril.

For a second she stared wildly around the room as though she didn't know where she was. Then she cast herself into John's arms, crying as though she would never stop.

He was wanted. Relief drenched him and he stroked his strong hands up and down her back, revelling in the simple fact that it was him she needed after all. 'I'm here, baby, I'm here. It's over now,' he soothed. 'It's all over. I'm here.'

Across the room, the astronaut was rocking backwards and forwards, hugging himself. Slowly he became aware of the present.

It was all out in the open now, no more hidden dreads. He drew himself erect, new confidence in his posture. Looking across, he met Loengard's eye.

'You were there with her,' John said.

'Ahuh. But they threw me back, didn't they?' For a moment he seemed puzzled. 'Why didn't they take me instead of her?'

'With their technology, why don't they just come down and take over the world?'

It was Ty's turn to look blank.

One cheek tightened in a lopsided grin, John told him, 'We ever come up with the answers, I'll let you know.'

Across the room, a click drew their attention. It was Dr Gould switching off the tape recorder. 'I'm not sure what to make of this. But whatever Kim and Ty went through . . . they're going to need further professional help.'

26

Over Kim's bent head, John stared at the doctor angrily. 'How can you doubt us after what you've just—'

'I'm a trained sceptic, Mr Loengard. I like to keep my mind open to all the possibilities until I have some proof.'

The astronaut stood, his whole demeanour subtly different. He no longer looked like the class rebel but once again like the colonel he actually was.

John indicated him. 'He's your proof. The mission he's supposed to fly in the morning? If Majestic's involved, it has to do with the Grays.' He turned to Ty. 'It's the ranger, isn't it? Something to do with sending pictures back from the moon.'

'I can't tell you.'

'After what she's just been through?'

'It's classified,' Yount said.

'So was your Black Knight mission. Did they tell you what you were up against then?'

Ty Yount glared back at him. 'It was "*need to know*".'

'And you don't think you deserved to be told? You don't think the people on this planet "need to know"?'

'I'm a soldier, Loengard, not a crusader.'

The anger faded from John's eyes as he realized he had to respect Ty's position. Still within the circle of his embrace, Kim moved a little. He loosened his clasp and she pulled back a little, still leaning against his arms. She looked lovingly at him, though pale with exhaustion.

John smiled. 'Hey, baby . . .'

She smiled back gamely, then put her knuckles to her lip investigatively. 'My nose is bleeding!' she said in surprise.

Dr Gould handed her a tissue from the box on her desk. From the wall outside the consultation room the phone began to ring, and the psychiatrist moved to answer it, not bothering to close the door.

'Dr Gould,' she said into the receiver. 'Yes, he's here.'

Ty called out to her, 'Tell them I'm flying, Helen!'

The psychiatrist leaned back into the room, checking him over with one swift appraising glance.

He looked exactly as he should be: strong, purposeful, his mind at one with his body despite the edge of fatigue. Grinning, he said, 'If Kim can face her fears, I can face mine.'

Helen Gould spoke crisply into the receiver. 'He's certified for flight. We were just talking over some personal issues.'

Hanging up, she came back into the consulting room and gathered John and Kim with a look in which there was growing suspicion. After a moment's hesitation, she came down on their side of the balance. 'If you two value your freedom, you'd better get off the base before his people arrive.'

John nodded and swept Kim protectively under his arm. 'C'mon, honey . . .'

Outside, the air was still and grey, the cool time of the morning before night had completely faded. Stars still twinkled, but off in the east flags of cloud above the horizon were tinged with the first hint of pink.

Yawning, Ty showed them the place where he sneaked off the base. He waved them goodbye and headed back to his quarters for a little shut-eye, while John, with Kim almost beside him in the old jalopy, headed back onto the road.

At 5 a.m., with the rim of the sun a fiery gold that just crested the skyline above the cape, the doorbell of the A-

Okay motel sounded. Clarice, who always said she slept on a hair-trigger, sat up on the edge of her bed behind the shop. As she slid her feet into her slippers and dragged on her grubby dressing gown, she figured that it had to be that nice young couple in number 7, up front by the pool. They must have been out on one hell of a bender because here it was dawn and they hadn't come in yet.

She stood, wondering whether it was worth giving them a piece of her mind about losing the key to their chalet. Shuffling over to the door that led from her bedroom straight into the office cum shop, she decided she'd do just that. She could hint that next time they shouldn't go out without checking they'd got the key. They were both polite little things. It would be safe enough, not like with that filthy trucker who'd come through here last week.

But the man outside the door was on his own. He wore a dark jacket, and the brim of his hat was pulled way down over his face.

Unsure, Clarice called through the dusty glass, 'What do you want?'

'Just a room, ma'am.'

He sounded civilized enough, though she couldn't tell what he looked like. She opened up cautiously, ready to slam the door in his face at the first sign of trouble, but he was charming. Quite charming.

As he apologized for disturbing her well-deserved rest, she checked him in. She couldn't read the signature when he bent to scrawl in the ledger, but that was no worse than a good half of the patrons who flocked here whenever there was a bird to be launched from Canaveral, or Kennedy, or whatever the hell the place was called this week.

'See,' she told him, 'I don't like to leave sheets on beds cause of mildew, so when business is bad like it's been, I only make up a few rooms. Gave the last made-up one away at midnight. Young couple. You knew what *they* were gonna do. Which is why' – she pulled a key on a long tag out of a pigeon-hole – 'you'll hafta gimme fifteen minutes to set it up for you.'

He straightened, sliding an expensive fountain pen back into his pocket. She saw with a start that he had a gotch eye. Its dull white marble surface made her flesh creep, but he was so sweet it made her sorry for the trials and tribulations he was going through. Glad now that she hadn't been rude to him, Clarice left him in the shop while she shuffled off across the court out the back.

As she passed him, the young man smiled and said in the friendliest way, 'No hurry, ma'am. Take your time.'

The minute she was out of sight he ran his finger down the list of names in the resgister. When he got to J. and K. Lewis, he smiled like a wolf.

Out on the parking lot by the edge of the lagoon, John left Kimberly dozing in the beat-up car and took his binoculars over to join the rest of the crowd. There were station wagons and Mercedes, every sort of car from just about every state in the Union. Children ran about, eating cotton candy and chasing dogs, dodging in and out of the people who were setting cine-cameras on tripods. Down below, in the creeks between the sandhills, insects were chirruping and occasional seabirds protested at this invasion of their territory.

A creaky old truck pulled up next to John's car and the fisherman from the day before got out. He was still wearing his beanie and a suede jerkin to which fish scales clung, winking silver in the light of the new day. Over his shoulder he loaded his fishing rod, touching his broad stubby fingers to his hat as he passed John with a cheery, 'Mornin'. Got your pole?' He didn't wait for his answer but made for his favourite spot down among the swaying reeds.

Through the security fence, John trained his binoculars on the giant rocket cradled in its gantry. The same Majestic transport stood in the places they had occupied yesterday.

From a tourist car near John, the local radio said tinnily, '. . . *carrying a ten-ton unmanned payload into space. The countdown is at T minus thirty minutes and counting.*'

* * *

Inside the buildings of Mission Control, the ranks of operators sat at their consoles. Screens alight with flashing colours or columns of symbols keyed everyone to fever pitch as the result of months of hard work came closer to being tested.

Above them, looking down through the glass windows of a booth on the level above, were four men. One wore a navy captain's uniform, the flat white cap with its braid laid aside on a desk. The second wore an expensive suit as though it were a sagging old cast-off draped over his chubby frame. His high forehead was covered in the parallel tracks of worry lines, and dark-framed glasses kept slipping down the bridge of his nose. When he spoke it was with a guttural German accent. It was another of Majestic's directors, Henry Kissinger. Of the other two, one was General Brown, high up in the chain of command at Cape Kennedy. And the fourth man was Phil Albano. Cut off from the hubble-bubble scene of activity below, Albano monitored a tape recorder on playback.

Kim Sayers' voice said in terror, 'He's coming *down* . . . It's in his hand, all dark and wriggling . . . oh, it scares me . . .'

Bach dragged deep on his cigarette, squinting through the smoke. Kissinger stood abruptly, leaning forward to place his palms on the desk as though to hear more clearly as the recorded voice went on, 'Stop . . . stop the screaming! What are they doing to him?'

Cutting across the recording, Bach met Kissinger's eyes with a bland look of his own. 'Yount and Augatreux were EBE'd and declared clean, Henry. This doesn't tell us anything new.'

From the tape spooling through the playback head, John asked quietly, 'Who's screaming?'

'I can't see him. Something in front of my eyes . . . white . . . shiny. What are they doing?'

Her strangled screams of terror made Dr Kissinger close his eyes in sympathy. His knuckles whitened as he gripped the edges of the desk.

On the recording, Kim's shrieks gave way to piteous weeping as she gasped, 'No . . . no. They have my head. Oh no! Please, stop, please . . . please. He has the tip of it. It's wriggling . . . it's alive! His eyes are black. So evil. He's right on top of me! What's he going to do with it? What's he going to *do?*'

Deeply affected, Kissinger bowed his head, Kim's suffering resonating within him. He muttered, 'It sounds awful . . .'

Bach coolly hit the rewind button. 'We'll ship it up to Hertzog for analysis.' Then he switched it to playback again, trying to work out just who Kim was talking about when she begged, 'Stop the screaming . . . what are they doing to him?'

In the dented car on the dunes, Kim sank lower in her sleep. Out by the fence, John was watching Cape Kennedy through his binoculars, waiting among the rest of the tourists for the dramatic launch of the Saturn.

The sun hit the wing mirror of the beat-up vehicle, bouncing the light straight into Kim's eyes. It triggered again the dream that was so fresh in her mind after Dr Gould's hypnosis.

Still dead to the world, she reexperienced her inner scenario on the alien vessel, the fierce beam of light probing her. Her lips moved as she mumbled, 'I can't see him. Something in front of my eyes . . . white . . . shiny . . .'

She jerked upright, suddenly wide awake. Kim knew exactly where she was. The car's cracked upholstery was real around her, the blue of the sky and the bright morning over the dunes.

Throwing open the car door, she hurled herself across the parking lot to where Loengard stood between cameras and spectators.

'John!'

He heard her desperate shout and swept her into his arms. 'I'm sorry I left you,' he said, nuzzling her hair. 'This was driving me crazy.'

She shook her head, struggling to get her meaning through to him. 'The regression. I was dreaming I was in the ship again—'

'It's OK. I'm here.'

'No!' she said impatiently. 'I saw more this time. I remembered.'

'What?'

Wrapped up in the urgency of her explanation, Kim unconsciously dug her nails into his arms. 'The man screaming next to me, the one I couldn't see? It was an astronaut helmet that was blocking me from seeing him!'

'Augatreux!'

'They were implanting him, John! He has to be Hive!'

Out on the launch pad the Saturn rocket was poised ready for flight, and over the radio came a voice anouncing, '*T minus twenty minutes and counting . . .*'

John raced for a payphone, practically dragging a teenager out of the kiosk. His hands were trembling with anxiety as he fed the coins into the slot. From a dozen radios he heard the mission announcer say, '*We are T minus fifteen minutes and go for gantry* roll-back.'

Fuming at the delay, he squinted south-east through the fence. Sure enough, the prep crew had just emerged from the base of the towering iron framework that held the rocket.

Tapping his fingers, unable to keep still, John heard the ringing tone. It seemed to go on and on while he stood a thousand yards away, helpless.

Brrrrrrrrr . . .

The radio said, '. . . *launch area is now being cleared of all personnel. All systems are optimum and go for launch.*'

Kim shaded her eyes against the bright, almost horizontal sunshine. Mission Control did not know what they were firing into space.

After endless moments, the base answered.

'It's Loengard. John Loengard. I need to speak to Captain Bach at once.'

Frustration tightened his lips as he shouted, 'Don't *tell* me he's not there! I saw him this morning. This is a matter of national security, do you understand?'

A pause, then Kim heard him say forcefully, 'I'm a Majic-12 operative. Does that mean anything to you? No, I do not have the authorization code! . . . Look, then just get a message to him. Tell him the launch could be sabotaged—'

He slammed down the phone and stepped outside. 'They hung up.'

One arm draped over her shoulders, he stood and watched in frustration as the Saturn launch ticked inexorably closer.

She asked, 'Do you think Ty would've gone if we hadn't found him?'

'You can't think that way.' He pulled her to his side. 'And maybe it's OK. Maybe they didn't implant Augatreux. He was EBE'd. Majestic cleared him.'

Kim said simply, '*Who* in Majestic cleared him?'

It was a quarter to seven. Clarice finished making up the bed for that nice young man with the weird eye and headed into the shop. ''S all yours,' she told him, handing him the key. 'The one on the corner.'

And Steele tipped his hat to her with old-fashioned courtesy, glancing slyly behind him to make sure she'd gone into her quarters. Out in the back, he settled his sunglasses on the bridge of his rat-like nose and strolled past the tiny pool. It was blue in the early morning. Peaceful.

Steele appreciated the irony as he headed for number 7, the room John and Kim Lewis – read *Loengard* – had checked into the day before.

All he saw, when he silently picked the lock and let himself into number 7, was that there was a mound in the rumpled bed. Drawing out his .44 Magnum in the scant light that came in through the drapes, he screwed the silencer onto the barrel. He took careful aim at the people-sized bump under the heaped-up quilts and the gun kicked satisfactorily in his hand.

A noise from the bathroom told him they hadn't both been in the untidy bed. Steele swung his pistol to cover the door. Clad in a towel, a woman came out. It certainly wasn't Kim Sayers.

He shot her anyway.

27

Kim's single question – who in Majestic had cleared Augatreux – sent John racing to the beat-up car, his fiancée right beside him. Gunning the engine, he set off with a squeal of tyres, weaving through the spectators and barrelling down the road to the Kennedy gatehouse.

Slamming on the brakes, John waved his Majestic ID, glad to see that it was the same, friendly, flat-cheeked guard that he'd met last night. 'I'm in kind of a hurry this morning. Gotta get in for the launch,' he told the man.

'Yes, sir . . . would you please step out of the vehicle while we run an ID check? Should take just a minute.'

Through the plate-glass windows of the guardhouse John spotted the other guard unholstering his gun.

'Must have tumbled to me,' flashed the thought through John's mind even as he trod hard on the gas. The ancient car crashed forward, splintering the barrier. Kim just had time to duck as shards of wood smashed against the car.

He swerved right and left around parked vehicles, heading for the control tower that stood head and shoulders above the cluster of buildings, but he knew the gate-guards must have called in because from a side road swept three Jeeps, loaded to the gunnels with armed MPs.

Whatever happened, though, he had to get to Bach.

As yet unaware, Captain Bach was standing to peer through the windows of the booth at the activity in

Mission Control below. Remote from the packed control area, even he could feel the tension in the flurry of movement and bright flashing lights. Yet it was in his nature to play it cool.

Flicking his lighter at the tip of yet another cigarette, he turned his head only slightly when Dr Kissinger said, 'The capsule will intercept the ranger signal before our Soviet colleagues do?'

'We have a hundred million dollars riding on it.'

Ponderously humorous, Kissinger regarded him. 'I often wonder if Nikita realizes how much we use him for cover.'

Bach couldn't quite hide his smile. 'It's quid pro quo.'

'Whoever thought the Cold War could be convenient?'

And over the loudspeakers the mission announcer said, *We are at T minus five minutes. All systems are go for launch.*

This close to the giant sheds, John couldn't see Mission Control. He took a corner hard, trying to out-race the MPs, but more of them poured from an alley between two blocks.

The little green car sideswiped one of them which skidded, sending metal trash cans rolling across the road. Luckily the jeeps had to dodge them. John gained just a fraction of a second. Speeding in and out of the maze, with Kim keeping lookout, he managed to thread his way through to a clear space.

'How many minutes?' John yelled over the sound of his labouring engine.

'Just over four! There's a guy behind us!'

He checked his mirror to see how close the pursuer was. Too close. 'Damn! Just when I've found Mission Control!'

Worse than that, as he faced front again, he saw two sludge-green vehicles sliding sideways to block all access to where he wanted to be.

Instead of slowing down, John floored the gas pedal. At the last moment he cranked a hard left and jumped the kerb. Suddenly he was bouncing across an expanse of grass then he clove noisily through a white rail and onto an access road.

'Where are we going?' Kim shouted, but the next bend answered her question.

They were headed straight towards the Saturn rocket.

John jerked the car to a standstill right at the base of the gantry. The rocket seemed to touch the sky, rising taller than a cathedral, and the painted spars of the support were the pillars climbing towards the heavens. He switched off the engine.

They were alone. No army trucks, no jeeps, no armed MPs. Completely on their own.

Kim looked back. Their pursuers had stopped well out of range of the columns of fire that would shortly roar from the nozzles not 5 yards from where she sat.

A tannoy crackled, making them both jump, then the announcer said, '*We are at T minus one minute nineteen seconds and counting.*'

John climbed out of the car, coming round to Kim's side. She too stood, smiling uncertainly as he said, 'They'll have to hold the launch.'

They saw the countdown clock at the base of the gantry. Red numbers dropped moment by moment.

A jet of superheated steam hissed deafeningly, then subsided enough for Kim to yell, 'They're not holding!'

Mesmerized by the mass of metal, John tried not to think of the thousands of tons of fuel it would take to carry it beyond the well of gravity and out into space. Fuel that in one minute and seventeen seconds would belch flame hot enough to melt steel across the huge concrete wheel on which he and Kim were standing.

Fear and guilt commingling, he stared at her, aghast. In the seconds left to them they couldn't run fast enough to escape death. Defeat stretched wider than the jaws of hell.

Kim saw it too. Fresh terror drained the blood from her face and John knew beyond all doubt that he had killed

243

her. She clung to him and he pressed her head down into the illusory haven of his chest.

'We're gonna be fried.'

From the safety of his desk inside Mission Control, the commander was the first to react. He tore off his headphones and jumped to his feet.

Bach saw at once that there was something wrong. He grabbed a headset and jammed it over his ears in time to catch what the man down there said.

'Main gate's ID'd them as a couple in their twenties. He has a Majic ID – name John Loengard.'

He looked up at Bach for guidance, adding, 'Sir, they are now in the no personnel launch area. I'm going to have to put us in a hold.'

Bach gazed down at him deadpan. 'How big is our launch window?'

'Thirty-two minutes and closing.'

'Is it possible for them to damage the rocket out there?'

The mission controller stared at him as if he were insane. 'The danger is to them, sir.'

'Then kill the pursuit and continue the countdown. This is our last shot.'

'We are at T minus one minute, eleven seconds and counting.'

Suddenly Kim pointed. John sprinted across to the emergency headphones she'd seen dangling at the base of the gantry. He said urgently into the mouthpiece, 'This is John Loengard. Get me Bach *now*.'

A huge plume of venting gas shot down from the rocket as the Saturn started to come to life.

Bach's irate voice said over the headphones, 'Mr Loengard, in forty seconds it's going to be several thousand degrees where you're standing. I suggest you remove yourself.'

'Augatreux is Hive, Frank. Kim remembers him from her abduction.'

Bach didn't give an inch. 'I listened to her regression tape. There was nothing on it.'

John resented them spying on his fiancée but he wasn't about to give in. 'She remembers more, now. Her view was blocked by something white and shiny. It was an astronaut's helmet.'

'T minus thirty seconds and counting.'

Bach sounded more annoyed. 'He was EBE'd. He was clean.'

Scalding gas erupted downwards at Kim. She leaped aside. 'John, we've got to get out now!'

'Who EBE'd him, Frank? Who went out and did it?'

And one by one the giant fuel lines disengaged, the heavy valves clunking free as the thick metalized tubes crashed loose.

Beside Bach, Majestic's chief of operations was already skimming the pages of a folder. Down below, out of sight of Albano, the young mission commander was sweating. He waved his arms in a gesture of frustration, muttering to anyone who could hear him, 'What the hell are they talking about?'

'T minus twenty seconds . . . ignition sequence has started.'

Albano blenched, his hands shaking as he held a single leaf of paper. 'Phillips was having knee surgery . . . It was—'

The skin of Bach's face tightened. 'Steele.' He grabbed up the headset again and spoke imperatively into the mouthpiece. 'Hold the launch. *Hold!*'

Exhaling sharply, Bach allowed himself one look at Kissinger, then proceeded like it was all routine. He rapped out orders to the mission commander as though he were still on the bridge of his warship.

'Tell the astronauts there's been an oxygen malfunction and that we're pulling them out. I need Augatreux's back-up suited *now*.'

He turned to Albano. 'Meet him with a full security detail. If he makes a move, terminate.'

Staring commandingly at the mission controller once more, he said, 'We have to do this quickly, gentlemen. We have a window.'

Albano paused on the threshold. 'What about Loengard and Sayers?'

The man with the German accent butted in before Bach had a chance to say a word. 'They just saved us a hundred million dollars, Frank. And then there might be a problem with the Attorney-General.'

'Countdown is on hold at T minus ten seconds.'

On the launch pad, at the mercy of the rings of fire that might shoot down to consume them at any minute, John held Kim tightly to him. White-faced but just as determined to die well if that was what it took, she clung to him too. The headphones stayed obstinately silent.

Both of them watched in terrible fascination as the red blinking lights of the clock dropped second by second. Twelve . . . eleven . . .

Ten.

Unbelieving, they saw the numbers freeze. And stay frozen.

Kim whooped, 'They're holding!' She danced up and down, still holding John's hand, feeling a surge of joy through that tiny contact that meant she would live to enjoy him for . . . as long as their future was.

John cupped the earphones, his apprehension mounting.

Then Bach's familiar grating tones crackled into his hearing. 'Mr Loengard?'

'You letting us see the launch, Frank?'

The instant of pent-up breath was the only sign of Bach's irritation at such flippancy. 'I'm letting you live. Now co-operate with security and get the hell off this base.'

Behind them, engines revved. But it was only the petrol-driven engines of the guards' jeeps creeping somewhat timidly towards them. At the rim of the launch pad, a tall MP was beckoning them with his rifle.

John and Kim walked with a spring in their stride towards freedom. To have been under sentence of death by fire and reprieved made the sea air more salty, the smell of the rocket fuel a zesty tang that gave flavour to the warm golden sunshine.

Yet as the vehicles escorted the old jelly-bean car away from the centre of the world's attention, John couldn't help looking back. The guards, however, made it impossible to see just why men were suddenly scurrying across the compound towards a shadowy door at the base of Mission Control. It was frustrating to have been a part of something without knowing exactly what that something was. And why an 'unmanned' mission had two astronauts riding the Roman candle.

As the jeeps herded them round a final corner, they both saw a flash of white in the shadows. Blinking, they saw the whiteness salute.

'Ty!' Kim exclaimed, and both of them waved at the figure in the spacesuit before their escort steamrollered them out of sight. Like Yount, they were soldiers operating in the dark, unsure of their allies, knowing only that they were committed to fight.

Shepherded out onto the public highway, John didn't even have to stop and think. He knew Kim felt the same way. He drove right out to the observation point on the dunes where they joined the holiday crowds watching the distant rocket that seemed not murderous, but toylike from back here.

Standing with his arms around Kim, he saw the vapours rising from the tail of the Saturn. He heard the killing roar as the primaries ignited, then the impossibly bright cone of flame that slowly, slowly lifted the rocket clear of the land.

Kim leaned back into his embrace, pulling his arms tighter around her waist as she too saw the metal bird ride its comet of fire up and into the heavens. Into space . . . into the dark skies above the protective blanket of atmosphere.

Around them the crowd was applauding, shouting excitedly. But John and Kim shared a smile of secret exultation before heading back to their room.

The bird flew. Bach and Kissinger watched it from their glassed-in booth while below in Mission Control victory cries gave way to the serious business of guidance and information retrieval. The huge screen on the far side of the room showed the first ranger moon photos coming in line by line.

Slowly, inch by inch, the picture formed in black and white. Familiar craters drew their ragged outlines as the stark mountains rimmed them in. Seas of dust lay fallow, sown with meteors that had fallen through the ages.

Bach's gaze was drawn to the tip of an ebony triangle at the bottom left corner of the viewscreen. He waited impatiently for the next line of image to be decoded. Then the next.

It had to be the shadow of some prism-shaped peak. It had to be.

The photo was three-quarters complete.

Seven-eighths.

And clear as a woman's teardrop, the picture did not lie. The triangle was no shadow, but a spaceship.

Bach stared appalled at the Black Knight hovering above the moon.

Stunned disbelief imprisoned the workers at Mission Control as they saw beyond doubt the mark of alien presence. It took the mission commander several attempts before he could gasp, 'My God!'

Unflappable, Bach spoke through his headset. 'Mission Control is in a state of lockdown until everyone is debriefed.'

Tired but triumphant, John and Kim drove up to the A-Okay motel. Full of new *joie de vivre*, they could hardly wait to be alone.

But a crowd of gawking bystanders outside the place

made them slow uncertainly. Bewildered, they saw the police cars and the men in dark-blue shirts cordoning off the area. Beyond, a fat doctor came out of one of the rooms, taking his stethoscope off and jamming it in the pocket of his soiled white coat. An ambulance crew came out with a fold-down gurney. It carried a still figure covered head to toe in a blanket.

John called through the car window at a man watching the proceedings with ghoulish interest. 'What happened?'

Glad of an audience, the man drifted over. Somewhere in the doldrums between fifty and sixty, his tired baggy face held eyes that sparked with interest at this interruption to his dull routine. 'Some guy shot up a young couple while they were sleeping.'

Kim found her tongue apparently under a fur ball. She managed to mumble, 'You know what room number they were in?'

His morbid fascination only thinly veiled under a patina of civilization, he suppressed a gleeful smile and said, 'Lucky seven.'

In shock, they packed their meagre possessions and got back on the highway as soon as they could. It didn't matter where they went, just so long as they got away. Both of them knew that seven had been the room they should have been in. That the other couple had taken bullets meant for them.

As they drove north, nightfall came to engulf the optimism of the day. And on the local radio the newsreader said soberly, '*The space programme suffered another setback today as the sixth ranger probe failed to send back pictures from the moon. NASA officials say they will postpone further ranger missions until corrections can be made.*'

Above the battered car, the moon hung full and threatening in the dark skies.

28

John and Kim figured that since back in the summer they'd
told the patrolman they were heading for Savannah,
Georgia, that was the last place anyone would look for
them. Going under cover, taking jobs as clerks or petrol-
pump attendants, they holed up for the winter. Sooner or
later Majestic would track them down.

Or the Hive would make its next move.

Until then, Savannah was a good place to drop out of
sight. What they didn't know was that way up north in
New York City, the aliens had already cut loose.

Where 34th Street met Herald Square, a brand-new
Ford pulled over to the kerb not far from a news-stand. It
was dusk, the lights of shops and offices burning beacon-
like in the gathering darkness. Commuters were already
fighting their way home through the biting cold, but the
January sales were over now and there were fewer people
out on a spending spree when it meant trekking into the
teeth of an icy wind.

Inside the bronze metallic Ford, two men sat talking.
The driver, Ron Burnside, was dressed like a typical ad
man: dark suit and narrow tie. A smile of ersatz friendli-
ness lit his face but not his eyes, which were curiously still
and piercing in a plump net of lines. Just a tinge of grey
touched his short dark hair.

The other person was little more than a boy. Perhaps
twenty or twenty-two, he seemed younger. His curly

brown hahr had been dishevelled by the gusting February air, and he wore his pale cords and wine-coloured shirt with panache.

Turning to the graduate student in the passenger seat, the driver said, 'We really appreciate your help on this, Christopher. You've been a very willing subject.'

Christopher smiled back, but his pleasure was genuine. 'Oh, no problem. Watching those TV adverts was the easiest fifty bucks I ever made.'

Burnside nodded a shade too impatiently, then gave a broad grin as if to make up for his mistake. 'Now, Christopher, in this second phase of the experiment, all you have to do is buy the first magazine that attracts your attention.'

The student was no fool. He nodded briskly. 'Just don't take longer than fifteen seconds to decide. Got it.'

Burnside took out a twenty-dollar bill from his bulging pig-skin wallet and handed it to the young man. 'You keep the difference for going the extra mile with us.'

Christopher beamed openly as he pocketed the note. 'Hey, call me any time. Grad school's costing me a fortune.'

Speaking fast, as though to get rid of the young man in his car, the ad man said, 'Remember! No more than fifteen seconds.' Pulling a steel-cased stopwatch from inside his jacket, he clicked the timer knob. 'Go!'

Christopher opened the passenger door and walked hastily to the kiosk nearby. It had photo reviews pinned overhead, and all along the front of the shelter stacks of papers were weighed down with bricks against the wind.

As soon as the youth came close enough for the vendor to see him through the purple dusk, she slid her eyes sideways as though looking for something.

Her gaze met Burnside's as he sat intently in his car. He nodded once to her; she gave a fraction of a nod in return and switched on a tape in a portable recorder. It was green and white, the latest design, curved at the corners like a valise and with a neat carrying handle set on the side.

Guitar chords started up: a smash hit by that group from England that everyone was going crazy over. Christopher liked it: in the students' lounge he'd danced to that only a couple of days ago.

The Beatles were singing 'Money'.

Darting little secret glances at the student, the pretty woman busied herself with flattening down the wind-rifled papers. She was a little older than Christopher, dark-haired with black arching brows that gave her a bright-eyed look. As he came forward to glance at *Harper's*, *Newsweek* and *Galaxy*, she smiled mysteriously.

Somehow the song echoed in his head. It seemed to vibrate through him, thudding inside his chest until his heart beat like Ringo's drums. A strange veil misted his sight, as though he really weren't in Herald Square at all.

Christopher shook his head. He didn't like it, didn't like what the music was doing to his brain. But shaking his head didn't dislodge the claws of the tune.

He lurched sideways, then spun as if to cross the road. Bumping into a man in a long raincoat, Christopher all but fell to his left, but found his feet again momentarily. In three strides, though, he stepped down from the kerb, spinning a little, walking as though he were drunk.

An oncoming car swerved to avoid him. Blindly, he carried on across 34th Street, not even noticing that the car which had shot into the opposite lane to avoid him had now slowed to a halt facing the other way.

Two other cars screamed to a stop, just missing it. A third careened across the road, the driver trying desperately to keep out of the pile-up.

But focused on the skidding traffic, the driver hadn't seen Christopher. His front bumper tossed the young man up into the air. For a second the victim seemed to hang there, falling in slow motion.

Then the windscreen crumped into him, sending him flying a dozen yards to smash down upon the ground. Blood rivered down his face as he lay bewildered. It drenched his maroon shirt, blending in. But a different wound gushed from his midriff, soaking into his cream-coloured cords. For a second the road and the buildings danced around him in a whirl of coloured lights, then nothing.

As shocked passers-by ran to help the student, the news vendor looked down to hide her sudden triumphal grin. Folding the lid of the tape recorder down, she abandoned her news-stand and carried her smart machine briskly away from the scene of the accident.

Not far, though. In a matter of seconds she had reached the bronze Ford. Ignoring the bystanders' shrieks of horror as they converged on the bloody dead youth, she smiled happily up at Burnside, who had climbed out of the vehicle to greet her.

He had already stopped the timer. 'Twenty-seven seconds,' he told her, then turned and began to stride rapidly past the bright display windows.

In the distance, the sirens of police cars and an ambulance dopplered towards them.

'Fastest yet.' She turned and fell into step beside him.

Savannah, Georgia,
6 February, 1964

Yet another motel room, yet another identity. John and Kim continued grimly playing the deadly game of hide-and-seek. At least at night they could drop all pretence and just be themselves.

Right now it was late and they were fast asleep. The room was dark but for the pink and blue neon lights shining in through the thin drapes, but over in one corner there was a steady red glow and the hiss of an empty carrier wave.

As the period of mourning for the late JFK faded, they made one hard decision: from now on, they would be the hunters rather than the hunted. Since that time Kim had heard the Hive contacting Steele by ham radio at Jack

Ruby's place, they had invested in a set for themselves, not to broadcast, but to tune in on any other alien communications. Only up to now there hadn't been any.

Kim lay peacefully with her head pillowed on John's shoulder. Their slow breathing patterns intertwined in harmony.

Then from the radio set on the cheap vanity unit, a deep hollow voice said: '. . . gh: baa-y-sa-wa. Daang gwa.'

Kim sat up abruptly, wondering what had woken her. The hideous sound of Hive-speak resumed: different tone, an answer to the first speaker.

Tugging down the hem of her nightdress against the draughts through the poorly glazed window, she stumbled to a notepad and pencil that she had left out on the table for just this eventuality. 'It's them!' she said, sharply enough to wake John.

He sat up as Kim began to take notes of the conversation. Amongst the first speaker's hoo-doo sounds were words in ordinary American: One-six-nine-seven Broad Way. Zhaan Sun Day. WN2-DMJ.'

She glanced briefly at John, seeing how the light polished the smooth muscles of his naked chest and highlighted his collarbones. His eyes were alert. Kim said excitedly, 'It sounded like, "One six nine seven Broadway, Sunday."'

Listening curiously, he caught half words he almost recognized, then the transmission cut off as abruptly as it had begun. Even the carrier wave had ceased. 'Some words must not translate,' he said, sliding out of bed and padding across in his sleeping shorts. 'And that call sign was out of New York.'

Already he was breaking down and packing away the ham radio.

In tune with his thinking, Kim pulled her lacy nightgown over her head and began throwing on her beige trousers and a warm jumper. 'We'll have to fly to be there by Sunday. It'll be expensive.'

John flashed a grin at her. 'So we sell the car.'

'Not exactly how we planned to do New York.' But their ironic smiles only sealed their unspoken accord.

The next day, ears throbbing to the roar of braking thrusters, they landed in New York, only to see that someone was taking down the 'Idlewild' sign above the terminal and hanging a new one that read 'Kennedy.' As the plane taxied along the runway, the building momentarily disappeared from view. When the Boeing turned to approach the disembarkation area, Kim, who was closest to the window, saw thousands of open-mouthed girls waving banners over the edge of the flat-roofed terminal. She asked John what it meant.

Until they were on the steps to the ground, John couldn't enlighten her. Out on the wind-swept tarmac, blue-uniformed police tried to form a cordon to hold back the mob of screaming girls. It was pandemonium. Nobody could hear a thing over the sound of the teenage throng, but the hysteria spread its miasma over everyone.

There were enough police to fill a sizeable hall. John squinted into the wind, fascinated by the sights all around him. 'Beatlemania!' he shouted. 'Look at this security. These guys could turn out to be bigger than Elvis.'

Kim felt the excitement tingling through her as they pushed through the seething crowds. 'Yeah. It looks kind of fun . . .'

John smiled down at the slight indomitable figure matching him step for step. 'You got a thing for these guys, don't you?' he teased.

'Well, they are kind of cute.'

He stopped dead in his tracks.

Thinking that she had hurt his feelings, she halted beside him and added hastily, 'Like you. I meant, they're cute like you.'

She scanned his face to try and read his emotions but he lifted his chin slightly, as if to indicate something up ahead. When she turned to see what it could be, there was Steele.

The rogue Majestic agent was pacing along, not slowly, not fast, but his path would intercept them in a dozen steps. As if preternaturally sensitive, Steele craned his neck until he stared straight at them through his dark glasses.

He changed direction, coming at them quickly now, an unpleasant smile stretching his bloodless lips. A man bumped into him. Steele shoved the man ruthlessly aside, not wanting anything to get between him and his prey.

'Get ready to run!' John said, grabbing Kim's hand and beginning to pull her along.

Yet Steele was quicker. He took off his trademark sunglasses the better to see them, and his other hand dived under the front of his jacket.

All at once, Kim hissed, 'This way!' at John, dragging him into the surging swell of Beatles fans. The crowd began to drag them willy-nilly in their wake . . . right towards Steele.

'Kim, he's coming straight for us!'

She didn't swerve. Mouthing, 'Just trust me, John,' she waited for Steele to get almost within striking range before she pointed and yelled at the top of her lungs, 'Oh my God! It's *Paul!*'

The mob turned, then poured like a human torrent in the direction she indicated. Pounding almost rabidly into the terminal, they swept Steele along with them. Jostled, shoved, almost trampled underfoot, the implant didn't stand a chance against the stampede.

Quickly heading off in the other direction, it didn't take John and Kim long to get safely to the taxi stand. A waiting cab drove them to the heart of the Big Apple.

Meantime, Majestic's operatives slaved unceasingly. In Majestic's Washington HQ, Bach followed the young scientist, Dr Halligan, toward a workstation in the biolab. Arcane equipment, both scientific and medical, glinted from glass cases against the wall, and benches and metal-topped counters held microscopes and the like.

Halligan swept back his copper hair and polished his

spectacles, psyching himself up for his speech. He fixed Bach with a proud stare. 'We're in uncharted territory here, Captain. Like Louis Pasteur or Madame Curie . . .'

Before he got properly launched into his oration, Phil Albano burst in and gestured to catch Bach's attention.

The captain said dismissively to Halligan, 'Thirty seconds.'

Walking meekly to his microscope, the doctor busied himself, head down, pretending not to listen.

Albano jerked his head, bringing Bach over to the far corner, where the chief of operations whispered, 'Frank, we've got a fix on Steele. He landed in New York yesterday. He's still using that doctor's credit card – the one he jumped in Alabama.'

Bach's lips widened in what could only be a smile of approval, though his eyes were as calculating as ever. 'How many men do we have in place?'

'Three. Already got them dragging the city.'

'Keep me posted.'

Albano nodded and went out as the Majestic leader moved across to see what his latest protégé was up to.

Wearing a jeweller's loupe wired onto his eyeglasses, the scientist hunched over a metal tray which was encased under a thick acrylic lid. Into the side of the clear-topped cage, two fine, steel-mesh gloves tipped with chrome pincers were built in, so that a wearer on the outside could safely manipulate objects inside.

Swiftly, so his audience wasn't snatched from him once again, the doctor stuffed his hands inside the gloves. With delicate skill he unwired the seal of a small rectangular box under the lid of plastic, then he flipped open the box.

As the lid fell back a messy skein of tentacles appeared, writhing and seeking to get a purchase on anything within its range. Unnerved, Halligan shakily pressed down with one of his metal pincers, trapping the flagellating mess. 'This is what was inside your Hive astronaut.'

A ganglion.

29

The chequered cab drove through the honking traffic of New York City. John and Kim craned their heads, rubbernecking at the sights they had hoped to see on some fabulous vacation. It seemed that this was the closest they would get: a rush-trip to defeat aliens, with the ever-present Majestic creeping up behind.

Inside the sweltering vehicle that stank of exhaust fumes, the driver tuned his radio. 'It's three-thirty p.m., Beatle-time!' the disc jockey said, his words high-pitched and machine-gun fast with his excitement. 'The Fabulous Four arrived at Kennedy Airport earlier today and it's a countdown to Sunday night. The temperature outside is thirty-one Beatle degrees and this is your host, Murray the K.'

Pulling up outside a theatre with a big canopy spreading right to the kerb, the driver waved a hand out of the window.

John checked the address Kim had written down from the Hive translation. This was it: 1697, Broadway. He paid the cab off. Hand in hand he and Kim walked over to see what was attracting the crowd waiting outside the locked glass doors.

Almost all of the people in the queue were girls, anywhere between ten or eleven and mid-twenties. Some of them were blue-lipped and pinched with cold, but they showed no signs of wanting to leave. Talking, giggling, stamping their feet inside their tight, knee-length boots, they looked as though they might wait for ever. The line stretched around the corner of the block.

Slipping around the front past the cases full of posters, Kim and John fetched up outside the entrance. Here too was a display of the group from Liverpool.

John checked the address again. 'This can't be right!'

Kim had wandered away a few steps towards the ticket window. It was shut up, no clerk in sight, and there was a big crayoned sign reading, 'Absolutely no tickets left for Sunday's show.'

'Maybe not . . . But everybody's talking about how big the Beatles are.'

John smiled down at her, incredulously shaking his head. 'Oh, come on! The Hive's not going to go after a *rock group!*'

His fiancée shrugged. 'Maybe they want to take away anything people feel good about.'

'I don't know enough about them to say you're wrong.'

She glanced appealingly up at him through her lashes. 'I could try to get inside.'

'Uh-uh.' John indicated the chattering teenagers with their beehive hairdo's and eyes that never left the doors. 'See all those girls? They all want to get inside. You've got no chance. Let me give it a shot.'

Kim pulled a moue of disappointment, but she could see he was right. She sighed and took the notepad out of his hand. 'I'll make some calls, see if I can put a name to that radio call sign.'

John patted her arm consolingly as she turned to head down Broadway to a phone booth. For a moment he watched her: shining dark blond hair swinging across the shoulders of her brown velvet coat as she walked jauntily along, never letting anything get in the way of her determination. He was smiling as he walked around to the side of the theatre.

*   *   *

Flashing his Majestic pass, he was almost surprised at the ease with which he gained admission. The stage hand closed the crash-door against the knot of voluble girls who were hanging around outside, and John could feel their envy as the door closed behind him.

For a minute or two he wandered around the maze of dressing rooms and props stores. The dusty old place was shaking with the sounds of music. That loud, it had to be coming from the stage. All he had to do was follow it.

In the event, he must have taken a wrong turning because he found himself halfway back at the side of the darkened auditorium. As he opened the door, guitar chords crashed against his eardrums. Opposite, tiers of balconies rose, their gilt decorations belonging to an earlier age. Lines of plush seats curved away into shadows, but down and to his right, coloured spotlights danced across the four-man group.

He stood, breathing in the atmosphere of make-up, stale perfume and sweat that he remembered from old concerts before life got this hard, and watched the Beatles, not too old to appreciate the catchy rendition of 'All My Loving'.

It was a soundcheck, not a real performance, and three of them, Ringo Starr, Paul McCartney and John Lennon, were chatting in between riffs, clowning around, having fun. Their hair was longer than most men's, a kind of fluffed-out pudding-basin cut with heavy bangs across the forehead, and they wore high-necked, collarless suits with tight trousers and over-long jackets.

What really gripped John, though, was the simple magnetic force of their personalities. At the back, round-shouldered behind his drum kit, Ringo sat hard at work. His hands caught the light as he beat his drumsticks almost faster than the eye could see.

The other two both played guitar, but one of them – Paul, according to the adverts in the cases outside – was left-handed and played it back to front. His eyebrows were real arcs set over down-drooping eyes that sparkled with mischief even as he sang. To the side stood John Lennon.

Lennon was getting bored, his irritation coming out in pointed little quips that had a sting in the tail. He particularly tormented a tall, thin man standing off to the side, a guitar slung uncomfortably over his shoulder. This was Neil Aspinall, and the running order suggested that he was the duly appointed stand-in for George Harrison, who was back in the hotel, sick with the 'flu.

John Loengard sighed as the optimism of the music faded into discord before starting up again twice as loud, and set off along a row of seats. He had nearly reached the centre aisle when a young man with a bright-coloured tank top and a belt full of tools shouted from the dimness, 'Hey, you!'

Not liking the suspicious look the man with the English accent gave him, John turned to face him with his most confident expression.

It had no effect. Still hostile, the man said, 'This is a restricted area.'

John reached into his jacket for his Majestic badge. 'I'm with building security. And who are you?'

It did the trick. With the tables apparently turned on him, the Englishman pointed nervously to the ID tag hanging around his neck. 'Parkinson, Kenneth. I'm with the BBC.'

'What do you do with the BBC?'

'Tech ops. In charge of gettin' the broadcast fed back to England. I'm just runnin' a line tap.'

Playing the steely-eyed lawman, John held out his hand for the ID and gave it the once-over, though it was too dark in the body of the hall to read any fine print.

Kenneth went on trying to justify himself. His cheeks were thin, flabby triangles of flesh, his chin receded, and John got the impression he had probably been bullied at school. Fiddling with the screwdrivers and claw hammer at his waist, Kenneth said, 'Er, sorry about givin' you a hard time. We're supposed to be on the lookout for gatecrashers. Photographers and birds, mostly.'

John handed back his ID briskly. 'How can I find out who's in charge of arrangements for the band?'

'You want Mr Epstein. He's their manager. Down at the

soundcheck.' He pointed towards the speakers on the floor to the left of the stage.

'Thanks. Where can I find you if I need to talk to you again?'

Feeling safer, Kenneth tried to make himself sound like part of the trendy scenery. 'Oh, I'm around. Just follow the cables.'

John nodded and moved on towards the brilliance down at the front. The red and blue lights held the focus of his attention; he didn't notice a man in the brown overalls of a janitor staring coldly down at him from the upper tier.

On the stage, Paul crossed to sing a harmony with John Lennon. There was a shriek of feedback that brought the soundcheck to an abrupt halt, then the group played the last bars with a flourish before unplugging their guitars.

Two men in everyday business suits burst into view from behind the speaker. They were arguing, the shorter man storming across in front of the stage and heading up the centre aisle like an outraged prima donna.

'Mr Sullivan. Mr Sullivan!' The voice was English, the 'u' of the star's name coming across almost like an 'a'. John presumed this was the Beatles' manager, Brian Epstein, trailing after the chat-show host like the tail of a comet.

Catching up, Epstein gave the TV personality a piece of paper. The Englishman tried to force his anger back, saying through gritted teeth, 'I would simply like to know the *exact* wording of your introduction.'

John Loengard could hardly believe it. The shorter man, not 5 yards ahead of him, was Ed Sullivan, the most famous interviewer in the Western world. Sullivan screwed up the paper between his two hands as though he wished it were the other man's neck, then slammed it back at the Beatles' manager. He was almost shouting, 'And I would simply like *you* to get lost.' Sullivan stomped away, elbowing past John Loengard.

Seizing his chance, John went down to the other man, saying hopefully, 'Excuse me, Mr Epstein?'

The bony Englishman stared at him disdainfully, then

dumped the crumpled paper into John's hands, leaving in a state of simmering indignation.

From the stage, John Lennon jumped down and came towards him almost sympathetically. 'Don't mind Brian.' The Beatle's voice see-sawed up at the end of his sentence. 'He's like that with everyone.'

'How do you put up with it?'

Lennon shrugged and grinned cheerfully. 'Got me friends to 'elp.' Taking the paper from the American's unresisting hands, he flattened it out and did a quick Biro sketch of himself, signing it with an individualistic scrawl.

John watched him bemusedly. 'Look,' he said slowly, 'if you have a minute with your manager, you might want to tell him to double-check the security arrangements.'

Lennon looked at him.

'I'm in that business.'

The Beatle's quick mind sorted the implications. 'You think our security's bad?'

John shrugged.

In a mercurial volte-face, Lennon grinned. 'They let you in, didn't they?' He folded the paper crisply and dropped it into John's hands, leaving the American staring after him in amazement.

Outside, John found Kim pacing up and down in the draughty back alley, blowing on her hands to keep warm. She glanced up as the crash-door opened, and came over with the notepad.

'Nothing suspicious,' John told her, a twinkle lurking in his eye. 'But I saw a rehearsal, and I talked to one of the Beatles personally.'

Kim goggled. 'Which one?'

'John Lennon.'

He could have laughed to see the awe on her face. 'John Lennon!' Her gaze slid away as she flushed. 'Sorry, I know how serious this is but . . . he's my favourite.'

'Draws pretty good.' He handed her the souvenir. 'So, how'd you do?'

Abashed, she stowed the paper away, glad to get back to business. 'Called the FCC. Took a little convincing, but I got them to give me the name and address of the mystery ham operator.'

John took the page she held out to him. Appreciation radiated in his smile. 'You hit gold, Kim. Let's make a house call.'

At around the same time, Dr Halligan had managed to catch Bach once again and lure him down to the Majestic biolab in the recondite tunnels beneath Washington. The clear plastic case with its ganglion imprisoned waited on the counter, and everything else was ready.

With a slightly theatrical flourish the young, red-headed doctor plunged a hypodermic needle into a container of serum while the captain looked on. Pulling the plunger up, Halligan drew the ruddy liquid into the syringe and spun round to lecture his chief.

'We know that not everyone the Hive abducts gets implanted with a ganglion. Some are rejected – your so-called "throwbacks". The question is, why? The hypothesis is, there's some biological incompatibility.'

Bach gave the man the reaction he wanted, like a straight man feeding a comedian. It cost nothing and it kept Halligan working like a demon. 'And you've found the incompatibility?'

'Not exactly . . .'

The Majestic chief caught a glimmer in Halligan's eye though the young man turned away to hide it. Bach knew that this was what the doctor was really after.

Halligan studied the writhing, flesh-coloured monster. 'To really prove anything, I'd need a throwback to dissect—'

Bach cut him off impatiently. 'When we find a dead one you'll be the first to know.'

Dr Halligan hunched a shoulder and fed the hypodermic into the glass case via a vacuum-seal port. Then, slipping his hands into the steel-mesh gloves, he picked up the syringe once more. 'This ganglion was cerebrally evicted from a Hiver. I'm now injecting a non-Hive blood sample from a throwback.'

Despite himself Bach leaned forward, his pouched eyes alive with interest. Inside the glass case, Halligan's steel-enclosed hands slid the needle into the ganglion.

The beast thrashed furiously. Halligan and Bach stepped hastily back, but this time the case didn't shatter. Inside it, pink and glistening moistly, the ganglion flailed, almost turning itself inside out with the agony of the foreign blood inside it. A green vapour exuded from its abdomen. Flopping, battering its tentacles noisily against the plastic, the alien writhed in extremis, high-pitched shrieks rising to a piercing crescendo before the monster literally exploded.

Torn flesh shot up to impact against the clear acrylic, sliding down again with a soft fleshy slithering that smeared viscera all over the inside of the case.

Bach and Halligan watched in horrified fascination as the maggoty slime dissolved rapidly into fine granules of what looked like charcoal. Both of them understood one point if nothing else: throwback blood was another weapon.

Up in New York, Kim and John took their first subway ride. They couldn't believe how noisy and dirty the tunnels were, miles of them worming deep into the earth beneath the throbbing city above, with the rags of posters overlaid with further layers of adverts for shows and films and museums. Both of them wished they had the chance – and indeed the money – to enjoy everything the town offered. But that would have to wait.

Standing on the platform, Kim found it hard not to gasp when the train roared out of the tunnel, fronted by a wind that nearly threw her down onto the live rail. She stepped almost gingerly into the car, John holding her elbow, and no-one got up to offer them a seat. Crammed along the aisle by hundreds of sweating bodies that smelled of aftershave and damp wool, they hung from the straps, but even so they nearly fell when the train jolted into motion.

Still, it was quite an adventure. It rammed the thrill of New York into them through every one of their five senses, and when they stepped out of the carriage at Queens, it was almost a disappointment – though Kim was glad to be out of the grey-faced, silent throng.

Jewish delis and restaurants lined the streets, shoulder to shoulder with Italian grocery displays and liquor stores with the signs in Spanish. John and Kim walked close together through the noisy polyglot people sauntering along. The borough was up-market; the passers-by were well-dressed against the cold in fur coats or chic designer numbers that barely reached the knee.

On a quieter residential street, with the brownstone buildings rising only two or three storeys above them, John found the place they were looking for. It was a private house with its own little front yard behind a low wall. A dim light shone yellow through the curtains of the wide double doors.

He and Kim went quickly up the steps of the porch. It would be good to get out of the biting wind.

The bell was marked 'Weatherly'. When John pressed it, they heard it ringing through the hallway, but nobody answered. They exchanged a glance, then rang again.

A neighbour came along the street, stopping at the gateway to stare at them suspiciously. The woman was short, with a beaver-lamb collar on her coat and a hairstyle left over from the early Fifties. High Slavic cheekbones proclaimed her European origin, but her voice spoke of Brooklyn made good. 'Looking for something?'

Kim gave her a perky smile. 'Christopher Weatherly. My boyfriend and I went to high school with him. We just got in town and we wanted to surprise him.'

The woman's hard face softened, her tone no longer harsh but sympathetic. She caught the brown paper bag of groceries that was slipping from her grasp and said, 'I guess you didn't hear.'

'Hear what?'

'Christopher died last Thursday. He was working two jobs to put himself through graduate school. It just must have been too much for him . . .' She swallowed, a tear sparkling in her eyes, but something in her manner showed that she enjoyed the drama. 'They say he walked straight out in front of a car like he didn't even care.'

'Oh, my God! Why?'

Kim's shocked reaction seemed to be the credential the woman was waiting for. She dropped her voice and whispered conspiratorially to the young couple, 'Nobody knows. You ask me, the whole family's screwy.'

Heads bowed as if in grief, John and Kim came down to the pavement and walked away. As soon as the woman was out of sight, they doubled around the back.

It was shadowy here, the street lights not penetrating around the corner. Under cover of the bushes in the small garden, John crept up to the windows on the right-hand side.

The old-fashioned sash was rattling in the breeze. It didn't take him a moment to slide the blade of a penknife up between the panes and free the catch. He climbed over the sill and helped Kim inside.

A hush enveloped them. No sounds of occupancy disturbed the stillness, not even a TV in the background. The drapes flapped around them as they peered into the dark room. On a high wooden mantelshelf were photos in heavy frames: a toddler, a schoolboy, a high-school graduate in his veledictorian's robes. All of them were obviously the same person; it must be the Christopher Weatherly who had died last Thursday. In the middle was a couple in their forties, not touching each other, staring straight out into the camera with frozen smiles.

'I'll look upstairs,' John whispered, sensing Kim's nod beside him. He tiptoed up to the first landing and checked the first door on the left.

Switching on a small lamp, he pushed the door to carefully behind him. The sight that awaited him was a sad one: blank spaces on the wallpaper where pin-ups and sports posters had been taken down. Someone had stripped the bed, leaving the blankets folded on the bare mattress. A closet door hung open showing nothing but wire hangers inside. Beside the cupboard was a box on the floor with a charity-shop label slapped at an angle on the cardboard. Inside it, clothes and a few forlorn childhood toys were all that remained of the life of Christopher Weatherly.

On the far side of the room was a desk. It bore nothing but a ham radio. John checked the frequency the dial indicated and nodded to himself. Searching the drawers beneath it, he came across a logbook, dog-eared and green.

As he started to rifle through its pages, footsteps sounded on the stairs outside. He spun around in alarm but it was only Kim.

She held out a flyer: 'EARN $ BY WATCHING TV! Synduct Research needs volunteers. Thursday–Saturday, 10 a.m.–5 p.m., 1157 West Tenth Street. Contact Ron Burnside.' 'I found it on the refrigerator.'

'Addressed to Christopher Weatherly,' John said softly.

Kim pointed to the word 'Thursday', circled in red ink. 'The neighbour said he died last Thursday.'

'And he's got a ham radio set to the same waveband we were listening to. The guy was definitely Hive.'

Downstairs the front door slammed. The two intruders froze, Kim clutching John's arm. For a moment they relaxed as the steps led to the back room, then a woman's voice with a slight accent called, 'Did you leave the window open in here?'

A man answered, 'Why would I do that?' Immediately his heavy tread thudded up the stairs.

Heart pounding, John snapped off the lamp. Stuffing the logbook and the flyer in his pocket, he moved swiftly to the window and helped Kim out of it. As she shinned down the drainpipe, he slid outside, holding onto the guttering to pull the window shut.

In moments they had crossed the little garden and were

running hand in hand up the side street, skidding to a halt behind a garbage unit on a corner. Panting, they took a moment to recover from their alarm. Burglary was not something they were used to, and it made them uncomfortable.

When Kim got her breath back, she said, 'We finally track down the mystery man and he's dead. We're right back where we started.'

'Not exactly.' He pulled the booklet from his suede coat and handed it to Kim. 'This logbook has the names and call signs of everyone Christopher Weatherly talked to on his radio. There's three more names here in New York we can check out, see if anything leads us back to the Sullivan Theater.'

Moving a little to squint at the writing in the dim glow from a distant light, she suddenly pointed. 'Look at this, John!'

John moved across to see. It read, 'Ron Burnside – WGM – 9RS, New York.' The name rang a bell. Comparing it with the flyer, she smiled in triumph. 'Mr Burnside has a ham radio, too.'

Neither of them noticed that in Christopher Weatherly's bedroom, a stocky, slab-faced man was staring out at them, his expression chill and menacing. It was the cold-eyed janitor from the Sullivan Theater.

As John and Kim walked away, he picked up the microphone in his late son's bedroom and said, 'CQ, CQ, WGM 9RS.'

30

After a night in a flea-pit hotel called the Albert, John and Kim went to the address on the flyer. It was in a mixed district of homes and shops. Here and there evergreen bushes grew, and there was a bench by a bus stop right outside.

A group of people, almost all students or high-school kids, stood in line on the sidewalk outside a basement. They were holding forms that fluttered in the breeze, forms headed 'SYNDUCT RESEARCH INC.' just like the sign above the basement.

'Kim, if this turns out to be a trap . . .'

She turned to reassure him, though she was well aware of the risk they were running. 'We're *both* going in.'

A cute preppy teenager jumped off the bus that pulled up alongside the line. Running to the back, she found herself next to Kim and John. With a quick glance down at the flyer she was carrying, she smiled and asked, 'Is this the line for the experiment?'

Kim grinned back. The girl was fresh-faced, with her dark hair in a smooth page-boy cut that fell to the shoulders of her sheepskin-lined jacket. No-one could have been less threatening, so Kim nodded, answering, 'Yes.'

Almost hopping up and down in excitement, the teenager said, 'I hope I'm not too late. They said this is the last day. I came all the way from Albany. It was a three-hour ride and I hate taking the train.'

John looked down at her, feeling suddenly much older. 'You came all the way just for this experiment?'

Giggling, she replied, 'Well, not exactly . . . I was going to use the money to try and buy someone's ticket for the Beatles show tomorrow night. Some people are actually selling them!' She leaned confidentially towards Kim. 'I'm staying at my girlfriend Claire's house – her parents are out of town and my parents don't know it. See, my father, he hates the Beatles. Thinks they're just noise.'

All at once the girl stopped, her fingers going to cover her lips as though she'd only just realized she'd been talking a mile a minute. 'I'm sorry, I didn't even introduce myself. Marnie Lane.'

Kim patted her arm as much as if to say, 'Don't mention it.' Then she shook hands. 'Jill Porter. This is my husband, Russ.'

John shook hands too. 'You must be quite a Beatles fan.'

The girl's shoulders cuddled her ears as she ducked her head in a gesture between pride and embarrassment. 'The biggest!'

Glancing significantly at the green flyer, Kim asked, 'You got one of these in the mail too?'

'Uh-huh. My dad says they get your name on lists to try and sell you things. At least I make money on this one.'

A ripple of movement along the line attracted their attention. Like the others, they looked over the heads in front to see what was happening. A dark-haired woman wearing a coat over an emerald-green dress was coming up the stairs from the basement. Christopher Weatherly might have recognized her curving eyebrows and wide stare from the news-stand. But Christopher Weatherly was dead.

'We do apologize for the delay,' she said in a cool businesslike fashion. 'Now that you have your forms completed we'll start the testing.' She half-turned then swung round again to add, 'Oh, and I almost forgot. Anyone who got a mailed invitation in your own name, please note it on the form. Thank you.'

Leading the way back inside, she took the small but

hopeful crowd down to a basement. In a small lobby they laid aside their coats and scarves, then headed to a larger room with one window set high in the wall. A venetian blind covered it, with heavy drapes hanging in folds at either side. Beyond the close-packed chairs was a screen on a folding stand next to a desk. At the back a projector stood on a high-legged table.

The room was too cramped for what was going on, and it held a faint musty odour as if it hadn't been long in use. Taking their seats in the middle row, John, Kim and their young friend Marnie found that their knees were touching the backrests in front of them.

A slick, smooth-talking man made his way to the desk. He wore a dark suit and a narrow black tie, and there were deep crow's-feet around his eyes. Presumably he was the Burnside mentioned on the flyers because the woman in green deferred to him and at a nod from him pushed her way over to the projector to thread the film.

Leaning the fingers of one hand casually on the desktop, Burnside gave them his best PR grin before launching into his patter. 'Hey, we want to thank you all for coming out. I can't guarantee you'll like all the spots you see, but at least it's warm in here.'

He paused, but no-one laughed. His audience of twenty or so were too busy trying to figure out what the catch was.

'Hey, that was a joke,' he said. Faint, awkward chuckles were his only reward. Raising his brows to invite them to share his apparent good humour, he went on, 'Now, we're just going to run a few of these commercials, and then we'll pick your brains afterwards. Any questions?'

Kim put her hand up. 'What is this being used for?'

Burnside had obviously been expecting this one. Unhesitatingly he gave his white-toothed, artificial grin. 'Well, our clients sink a lot of dough into marketing, and they want to know how the elements in the spots grab you. You know, like the music and the copy.'

Marnie raised her sparkling eyes. 'You mean, what'll make us want to buy stuff?'

'Exactly. Now, how about we get rolling?'

With the lights out and the projector whirring, the place seemed snug. On the screen a cartoon boy made mm-mm noises of appreciation as he stroked a giant-sized packet of potato chips. Burnside stood at the side of the room, arms folded tightly across his chest, watching the subjects' reactions.

Another scene, nothing special, housewives improbably coiffured sitting elegantly around a tea table eating the same potato chips while managing to praise them without spluttering crumbs.

Marnie flinched. Since their arms were touching, Kim felt the girl recoil. She suddenly felt strange herself; disorientated and a little light-headed. A fleeting sense of unreality held her for a split second, then as quickly passed. The commercials rolled on.

Burnside observed them dispassionately.

The prep student and the new 'Mrs Porter' went back to watching the screen as if it magnetized them. Kim could feel herself being drawn into . . . something. It touched a part of her that was buried deep: the part that remembered how it felt to have the aliens commanding her helpless body. She couldn't tear her gaze from the film though she could scarcely have said what the commercial was about.

Beside her, John noticed nothing out of the ordinary. Bored, he wondered how soon it would be until he could grab a cup of coffee.

Marnie's breathing accelerated, so did Kim's. The pair of them leaned forward intently, not blinking, mesmerized. For Kim, the soundtrack of cheery housewives faded. She turned her head a fraction as if trying to tune in to a more distant message. A message that seemed scratchy, its very roughness pegging it ineradicably into her brain. For just a second she saw again the Hive glyph: the fishtailed triangle with its swirling arms.

Her breath lodged in her throat. She had no idea that Burnside had clicked a stopwatch as he noted her reaction. All she saw was the screen with its insignificant advert standing between her and the hidden thing she wanted to uncover.

With relief she caught it: a different glyph this time. She exhaled, more relaxed now, seeing again the alien symbol, but overlaid with dollar signs this time and a snatch of that Beatles tune, 'Money'.

It flickered out of view and Kim shook her head to clear the buzzing from it. Marnie lurched to her feet, teetering as if she might fall at any minute. 'I . . . I have to get some air.'

Her blue cardigan snagged on the back of her seat, but she wrenched it free and pushed past the knees of the people between her and the exit. Worried, Kim turned to watch her. Steps uneven, balance erratic, Marnie cannoned off the wall and made it through the door on her second attempt.

Kim whispered to John, 'You stay here. I'm going to see if she's all right.'

Grabbing her black fun fur coat, she ran outside to see Marnie bent almost double, clinging on to the bus stop as if afraid to let go. She put her arms around the girl and asked in concern, 'You OK?'

Marnie looked up, her face the colour of dirty snow. 'I think so . . . I just felt kind of sick all of a sudden.'

'I got a little dizzy myself.'

Raising a feeble grin, Marnie said, 'My dad always says too much TV will rot your brain.' She pulled herself upright but didn't let go of the pole. 'I should get back to my girlfriend's.'

Then she began to totter across the street to the bus stop back out to the suburbs. Except she only made a couple of steps before she listed sideways, almost sagging to the ground.

Rushing over to the half-unconscious girl, Kim supported her to a bench that stood a little further down the pavement. 'I don't think you should be going anywhere until you feel better.' She sat, her arm maternally around the teenager's quivering shoulders.

Marnie held back for a second then let herself slump into Kim's sisterly embrace. Eyes closed, she murmured, 'I'll be fine. It always just takes a few minutes.'

'You've had this happen before?'

The girl opened her eyes wide, scanning Kim apprehensively before she decided she could trust her. Hesitantly Marnie began, 'It usually happens when I have this one dream. I can't run fast enough and . . . and I get this same feeling like I'm going to be sick.'

Gently Kim stroked her back. 'Can you tell me your whole dream?'

A man walked past. Marnie waited until he was out of earshot before saying, 'You're not gonna think I'm weird?'

'No, I promise.'

Now the girl's apprehension solidified to remembered fear. It seemed to grip her anew as she focused on something that wasn't this New York street.

'See, it starts out . . . I'm in the car with my Aunt Hazel. It's night and we're driving to Niagara Falls for the weekend to meet my cousins. We're right out in the country, miles from anywhere.

'Anyway, then we have this stupid argument about the radio. There's a song I like playing and I want to turn it up . . . It's the Beatles.'

Marnie's hands were twitching. Her whole body tensed as though to run away; she gasped out the rest of her story. 'Then all of a sudden there's these bright lights right above us, and the radio starts going crazy. The motor cuts out and the whole car's just kind of shaking and the antenna right in front of me just sort of wobbles and tilts and then it snaps right off the car and flies up to the lights . . .

'Then I can see it.'

Just recalling it made Marnie shrink down on herself. On the verge of uncontrollable panic, she clung to Kim so hard her nails dug into the older girl's hands.

Kim said as calmly as she could, 'What can you see?'

'It's like . . . a saucer. It just comes closer and closer, so I jump out of the car and start running for the woods.

There's all these spooky shadows and I can hear things rustling all around me. It's really creepy.' The words tumbled out of her as fast as a river in spate. 'I look back and I see . . . they've got my aunt and they're pulling her up toward the ship with sort of a blue light.

'Then they come after me. I'm running, but I'm not fast enough because all of a sudden there's this little guy in front of me. He's all grey and wrinkly and he's got these huge black eyes that just kind of look right inside me and it's horrible!'

The girl seemed so terrified that when she opened her mouth again, Kim thought she might scream. Pulling her into a tighter hug, Kim rocked her, trying not to think of the night the Grays had forced their way into her bedroom. It was for herself as well as for Marnie that she soothed, 'It's all right. It's OK. It's over, it's over now.'

At last Marnie blinked the tears from her eyes and gave a childlike sniff. She looked about ten years old instead of the teenager Beatles fan of minutes before. Hiccuping, she asked the question that frightened her the most. 'I don't know how much is really a dream, Jill. See, I did go to Niagara with my aunt, about six months ago.'

With a little start, Kim realized that 'Jill' was her fake identity. 'When did you start having these dreams?'

'Maybe a month back. They started off as little flashes, even when I wasn't asleep . . .' White and fearful, Marnie stared beseechingly at Kim. 'Am I crazy?'

Kim knew how bad that felt. With a reassuring smile she said warmly, 'No, Marnie. You're perfectly normal.'

'Really?'

'Really.'

A bus pulled up over the road. Marnie said, 'That's my bus. Maybe . . .'

Kim nodded. 'You should go back to your girlfriend's. It won't be so bad watching the Beatles on TV.'

Reluctantly Marnie sped off, gazing back once at the only person she'd ever dared tell . . .

Not 3 miles across the urban sprawl, a stubble-chinned doorman waddled out of a hotel. It was a rundown neighbourhood, the grit swirled along the wind-swept pavements. As he loitered, aimlessly taking the air, a man in a trench coat came towards the cheap dive and intercepted him. Wordlessly extracting a photo, he held it out.

The doorman glanced without interest at the monochrome picture. It showed John Loengard and Kim Sayers, but the fat man shook his head. 'Never seen 'em before.'

Pocketing the photo, the man in the trench coat crossed the name of the hotel off a handwritten list. He was wearing dark glasses though wintry clouds hid the sun, and there was an aura of menace about him that made the hardened doorkeeper wary.

But the man in the black glasses did nothing frightening. He merely walked along the street, apparently heading for the next place on his inventory.

Calling after him, the doorman asked, 'They some kinda criminals or what?'

Taking off his dark glasses, Steele, the man in the trench coat, turned back. He had one useless white-marbled eye but the other bored into the doorman like a stiletto. Apparently he found nothing to concern him because he only said with a twisted smile, 'They're very dangerous.'

Then he strode into the distance, wiping the copious sweat from his chiselled face. Shuddering, the doorman sought the safety of the lobby.

In a little while, Kim saw John coming out of the Synduct basement amid the rest of the crowd. She was glad he was safe and it was with relief that they hailed a passing chequer cab. At least they'd earned 100 bucks. Now things wouldn't be quite so tight for a while.

Talking low so the driver couldn't hear them over his radio, John said, 'Marnie's either Hive or she's one of those people who got thrown back.'

'She's not Hive.'

John studied her measuringly. 'She got a flyer in the mail, just like Christopher Weatherly. And we *know* he was one of them.'

'All she remembers is being abducted, not being implanted.' Kim saw his irritable scepticism and went on, 'What was I supposed to do? She's a kid, John. She wants to see the Beatles and have fun. If I tell her the truth, she loses everything.'

John could see that Kim was not just talking about Marnie. Understanding how her life, like his own, had been changed irrevocably, he took her hand. The simple clasp reassured them both.

More calmly John said, 'Well, nothing else happened in there that I could see. But there's got to be some connection to the Sullivan Theater.'

On the radio the music stopped for the disc jockey's link. 'This is Murray the K. The countdown continues to tomorrow night. That's right, baby! The Beatles on Ed Sullivan. Gonna be more people watching that than any show in history. But if you can't wait that long—' He put a needle in a groove, and The Fab Four sang, and 'Money' rang out from the radio.

Abruptly Kim sat forward until her head was just behind the cabbie's. 'Could you please turn it up?'

Hoisting his shoulders indifferently, the middle-aged man with the greasy hair obliged. Loud and clear the Beatles performed their hit, its driving beat belting out through the tinny speaker as the car sped along. As they started on the chorus, Kim flinched.

Painted on her retinas she saw the Hive glyphs, not just the recognition pattern, but the others that had underlain the commercial she'd seen not half an hour ago.

Reality seemed to pale around her. She had to do something. What was it? Oh, yes. It was over there . . .

Blind to her surroundings, Kim leaned across and opened the cab door. Tarmac rushed by beneath the spinning wheels of the car. Cold air rushed in as she hitched over, already starting to swing her leg forward and step out . . . right onto the road that hurtled by underneath. The car must've been doing well over thirty down the street. That fast, the fall could rip her apart.

The chill wind made John turn to see what had caused it. Fear prickled in his chest as he saw Kim trying to climb out, one foot already dangling over the sill.

The cabbie glimpsed her in his mirror. She was half out of the taxi, on the point of killing herself. Slamming on the brakes, he yelled in alarm, 'What're you doing, lady?'

John grabbed Kim's coat and hauled her bodily back inside as the vehicle fishtailed to a halt. He put his arms around her rigid frame but she didn't respond.

The driver stamped round to throw the passenger door wider open. 'That's it. Outta my cab.' His face was purple with fury.

John didn't even try to explain because he couldn't. Helping Kim out, he was as shaken as she was. He stood holding her but her confusion was obvious.

When the taxi screeched away she wandered apathetically after it, but John pulled her back. With the anger of reaction sharp in his voice he said, 'You almost got yourself killed!'

Slowly her gaze travelled up to meet his face. She blinked, seeming to come back to herself, but John could tell she was scared half out of her mind. 'I don't know what got into me . . .'

31

Taking refuge in their hotel room, Kim felt a pit of panic yawning all around her. John was just as scared; he had almost lost her, and neither of them understood why.

She hunched down against the bedhead, her hands clutched around her knees as John paced back and forth on the small square of carpet. The place wasn't big enough to swing a cat; their ham radio occupied most of the vanity unit, blocking out the lower half of the mirror, and everything else they'd brought was dumped anyhow beside it.

Every time she moved the ancient iron bedstead squeaked. Both of them felt hemmed in. Through the small window the only view was of a blank brick wall beyond a rusting fire escape. It did nothing to relieve their nervousness.

Kim broke the taut silence. 'I think they did something to us in there. You know how they used to plant subliminal messages that made people want to buy popcorn or candy bars?'

John's whole demeanour spoke eloquently of his disbelief. 'Or try to jump out of a car?'

'Maybe.'

'Only I was in there too!'

Testily she snapped, 'You've never been abducted, John. But I was, and Marnie was.'

'And Christopher Weatherly. But if he was Hive . . .'

'I know. Why would Burnside want one of his own to kill himself?' Struck by a sudden thought, John picked up the logbook from the clutter of their things. He flipped through it, his eyes widening as he examined the inside cover. 'Check the name on the licence.'

She took the book he held out, but all it said was, 'Christopher Weatherly'. 'So?'

John's finger stabbed at the cardboard cover. 'Senior.'

'It's like the astronauts! One was implanted, one wasn't.'

'Christopher wasn't Hive. It's his father who was on the radio!'

Kim knelt up on the bed, eager to explore the new idea. She lifted her face to John, about to speak.

He caught a flash of something reflected in the mirror and yelled, 'Kim! Down!' Already he was flying across the room to tackle her to the floor behind. A shot cracked out, smashing into the headboard.

Huddling against him in the narrow space between the bed and the wall, Kim hissed, 'What is it?'

'Steele. I saw him on the fire escape.'

A thunk, then more glass crashed to the floor as Steele swept the windowframe clear and climbed through. He must have seen where they went because they heard him come straight around the bed towards their hiding place.

Quickly they crawled underneath. Hearts thudding, they saw Steele's feet stop, then take another step into the space beside the bed. He halted, obviously puzzled by their disappearance, then bent down to peek under the hem of the blankets.

John skidded out the other side and kicked both heels against the bed, slamming the iron frame against the rogue's knees. Crushed against the wall, Steele screamed, the pistol dropping from his grasp.

It fell onto the pillow. John dived headlong to scoop it up, but the implant recovered and pulled himself free. He threw himself across John's back, trying to get a strangle-hold on him.

Face down on the covers, John could hardly breathe. Struggling to buck Steele off, he knew he was fighting a losing battle. Weakness sucked at his limbs. Red fire stained his vision as the rogue's hands tightened inexorably around his neck.

With a desperate heave, he managed to turn over, but he fell to the carpet, hitting his head against the skirting board as Steele dived at him, grabbing John's throat in one hand. John felt the powerful fingers digging in, ready to rip his throat out, while with his other hand the implanted cloaker grabbed the gun and brought it round until the muzzle gaped cavernously before John's eyes. He seized Steele's wrist, but his angle was wrong. Little by little, the implant was winning.

The next thing John knew, a mighty clunk sounded and Steele slithered limply off him.

Poised over the semi-conscious man, Kim had the radio in her hands, or at least, what was left of it. Bits of Bakelite littered the implant's chest and there was an angry crimson thread running across his gotch eye. He mumbled to himself in Hive-speak, his body twitching spasmodically until he fell silent.

A dial flopped loose from the shattered casing Kim clutched, and sparks sprayed across the bed.

They grinned.

Twenty minutes later, they straightened to survey the results of their labours. Steele lay in the stained bathtub, perfectly dry but imprisoned with leather belts cinched around his wrists, elbows and feet. Dried blood crusted his cheek and brow. He was totally out of it, but still breathing.

Kim brushed her hair back. 'We keep saying we need proof of the Hive. Well, here it is.'

'If we hand him over to the authorities, they'd just think he's some freak.'

'Until they cut his head open.' Her words echoed eerily from the crumbling tiles.

'That's just it. Without proof, they're not going to cut his head open. Only Majestic'll do that.'

Steele's eyes flipped open, his stare preternaturally calm. 'They already tried, college boy.'

John aimed the revolver at the trussed-up implant. 'What's happening tomorrow night at the Sullivan Theater?'

'Like Bach says, that's "need to know".'

Mustering the meanest expression he could, John cocked the gun not a foot from the rogue's face. 'Answers, Steele. Or I'll cut open your diseased head myself.'

In the grim tub, Steele smiled enigmatically, but there was a cold malevolence in his gaze.

John tried again. 'Who's Ron Burnside?'

The rogue gazed blandly at the shower curtain.

Frustration overmastered John. He poked the gun barrel hard against Steele's neck.

Silence.

Kim felt the same intense build-up of anger as she looked down on the man in the tub. 'What are you doing here? All of you . . .'

Still the Hiver said nothing and she lost her temper completely. Face contorted, she hurled her questions like missiles. 'Where are you from? What do you want?'

Infuriatingly, the man smiled. 'You'll find out soon enough.'

John tightened his finger on the trigger, the urge to shoot burning through him.

All the rogue said was, 'Go ahead. Jim Steele's life is of no consequence.'

For a moment it hung in the balance. Murderous fury boiled through John's veins, but on the brink of exterminating the loathsome Hiver, he released the hammer. 'Yeah? Jim Steele is wrong.'

He stalked out of the bathroom, tossing the weapon aside as though it were contaminated. Instead he picked up his wallet from the dresser and headed for the phone.

Kim followed, wondering what he was doing.

Dialling a long number, John grated, 'It's time to play our trump card.'

'Who are you calling?'

'Maybe the only friend we've got.' He paused, listening to the receiver, then said, 'Attorney-General's office . . . Mr Kennedy please. Tell him it's John Loengard.'

Alone, John set out for the address one of the Attorney-General's men had phoned through. The only comfort he could offer Kim was a rendezvous for the Beatles show the following night. If everything went according to plan, he'd meet her outside the Sullivan Theater. With that, they had to be content.

When he stepped out of the cab a half-hour later, the place turned out to be a warehouse in the desolate district around the East River. It was late, around midnight, and the area was deserted. One electric light lit up the street, showing shadows where scraps of torn paper swirled in the breeze.

He checked his watch and approached a heavy door. Surprisingly, it swung open when he knocked.

Beyond, he took in a scene of pallets and fork-lift trucks between stacks of crates, though it was hard to make anything out in the gloom. As his eyes became accustomed, John moved cautiously inside, calling softly, 'Mr Kennedy?'

'Over here, John.'

Bach stepped out of the shadows. A little more grizzled, a little plumper, but just as confident. From other points Phil Albano and a couple more cloakers came forward until John was surrounded.

That deep familiar voice said, 'Lesson to be learned: never trust the telephone. Even the Attorney-General's.'

Loengard scanned the area but there was no way out.

The Majestic chief stepped in until he could have reached out and shaken John's hand, but he made no gesture of friendship. Instead he stated flatly, 'You have something you wanted him to see.'

'What makes you think I'd show you?'

Coming in close, Bach thrust his face right up to John's. 'What makes you think you have a choice?'

Knowing he was trapped, John reached reluctantly inside his jacket.

Three guns clicked in unison as Albano and the toughs drew a bead on him. He froze.

Swiftly Albano reholstered his weapon and frisked John thoroughly. 'He's not carrying.'

Bach nodded.

Dignity ruffled, John hauled out the dog tags with as much aplomb as he could manage. The Majestic chief took them, studying the inscription in the faint light. 'It's Jim Steele's. He alive?'

'If you can call it that.'

'Where?'

It was the only lever John had and he wasn't about to throw it away for nothing. 'You get Steele when I get what I want. Manpower and Halligan.'

Bach flicked a glance at Albano, who muscled in, pinning John's arms painfully behind his back.

John shot his former boss a smouldering look. 'Go ahead, Frank. It won't do you any good. You kill me, Steele rots.'

They had only let John call Kim briefly to tell her they'd be picking her up in the morning. Then Albano cut him off. He sweated all night under Majestic's debriefing, but when daylight came they fed him coffee and a doughnut from a cheap joint near their safe house while Bach laid out his plan.

Just after nine, they set off in two of Majestic's plain sedans. John was relieved to see that the ginger-headed Dr Halligan was in the other car. Stopping by the hotel to pick up Kim, they cruised off once more.

Throughout the ride John and Kim held on to each other while John brought her up to date on what had happened. A while later, they came to a stop around the corner from the Synduct building.

Glad that his sleepless night had made him look the part, John went to the main door, the one on street level, where he found an intercom button, just like the heavies had told him. He rang it.

A woman answered, 'Can I help you?'

John recognized the voice: it belonged to the Synduct secretary, or whatever she was, the one in the emerald dress. Burnside's assistant. He found the *speak* button and said, 'I'm here about the experiment.' Behind him the cloakers moved down to the door in the basement with a set of lock-picks that would have opened Fort Knox.

She said coldly, 'The experiment has been concluded.'

'Have a heart, lady!' John had to keep her talking. He went on with his sob story, 'See, I just lost my job and I could really use the money—'

'Then I suggest you get a new job.' The receiver clicked down.

A second later John heard a crash of splintering wood, followed by a barrage of shots. He leaped down the stairs into the basement to find that the door to the inner room had been kicked down. Behind him Kim, Bach and Halligan clattered down the steps.

The woman from the experiment was wearing a beige cashmere twinset now, but that wasn't what horrified him. It was the crimson stains that flowered beneath her ribs.

Legs spraddled, arms outflung, she tottered back to collapse against a tumble of cardboard boxes, and now that John had a chance to look around he saw that the place had been stripped of just about everything. Two of the cloakers covered her with their guns but she was dying, an alien word hissing from her mouth: 'Ma-jux!'

Albano reappeared from another room. He snapped an order at his henchmen. 'Side door. We're going after him.' They hurtled away on Albano's heels and John could hear their footsteps recede.

Dr Halligan pushed past, kneeling beside the twitching victim. Breath rasped in her throat – then stilled. The doctor checked that she really was dead, then took

286

something brown and metallic out of his black bag.

The thing would have been a cube if it hadn't had quite so many angles. Flicking open two or three catches, Halligan opened it out beside the dead woman's face. It seemed to be some sort of a box.

Aware of his audience, the doctor looked up briefly and said with justifiable pride, 'GCD. Ganglion Containment Device.' Then he strapped it around the head of the corpse, covering mouth, eyes and ears as well as the back of the skull.

Kim shuddered visibly, imagining the mask trapping it inside her. Her stomach churned, making her almost retch.

Not so Halligan. He closed the fastenings securely and said with a cheerful grin, 'Last thing we need is a wiggler loose in here.'

Bach gave them no time to mourn. He ripped down a curtain and threw it over the corpse, then, grim-faced, said, 'Find that film you told me about.'

They set about searching through the boxes, emptying them higgledy-piggledy on the floor until files and books and flyers lay like a garbage dump on the carpet. Kim flatly refused to touch the ones with blood staining the cardboard. All the same it was she who found the projector and the round flat can that held the key to her suicide attempt.

John took out the filmstrip and held it up to the fluorescent light. Yards and yards of trite commercial spun through his fingers to land in a shining black heap on the floor. The cartoon kid, the housewives . . .

'Here.' He showed them the single frame with the Hive recognition glyph, then sorted through the rest of the film until he found shots with other glyphs printed pale under inky dollar signs and the words MONEY MONEY superimposed on a white background. 'And that's the trigger,' he said to the people craning over his shoulder. 'Kim heard it from the song on the radio.'

Dr Halligan nodded decisively. He was more sure of

himself nowadays. 'It's hypnotic suggestion, all right. The symbols could be some sort of built-in coding. Anyone who's abducted gets exposed to some sort of mental programming that, when triggered, causes confusion, bewilderment –' he glanced at Kim – 'like you felt.'

'Built-in?' Bach said dubiously.

It was John who answered. 'Yeah. They're creating a bunch of self-destructing time bombs. Like Christopher Weatherly.'

The Majestic chief added his mite. 'Albano says father and son were abducted last August. We think the Hive is targeting throwbacks.'

Wanting to think, Kim drifted away to kneel by herself on the cluttered floor. There was something bugging her but she couldn't quite put her finger on it. Maybe something in the Synduct files would give her a clue.

Behind her, Halligan continued his exposé. 'The theory is that every throwback gets programmed with normal-seeming events to cover their actual abduction experience.'

John said, 'So why are people like Marnie remembering real events?'

The doctor shrugged. Once it would have phased him to admit ignorance, but not now. 'It's unclear. But it appears these so-called "cover memories" are fading faster in young people.'

A noise from the outer office sent Bach's hand snaking towards his shoulder holster, but it was Albano and his thugs who came in, panting. 'We lost Burnside. He got down into the subway tunnels.'

Albano and his chief went into a huddle in one corner, but John wanted to pick the scientist's brains. 'I still don't understand. Why would the Hive go to all this trouble to kill a few people?'

Sitting on the floor with an open folder lying across her outstretched legs, Kim said worriedly, 'It's more than a few.' She scrambled to her feet. 'These must be the names of throwbacks who got mailed Burnside's flyer. Look.'

John and Halligan came to peer at the list she indicated.

'Look. Three names are checked off, with the dates and times of when they came in here. All three names are marked *deceased*. Christopher Weatherly was one of them.'

'That was their experiment!' John said. 'Test the self-destruct code to see if it works.' He gazed at Kim, wondering how long it would be before she tried to kill herself again. And if he would be there to prevent her . . .

Halligan caught their meaning. 'According to research, subliminal programming is only good for about thirty-six hours. So you're safe.'

'But all those others!' she said, pitying them.

The scientist was unmoved. 'No hint of foul play, no murder investigations. It's brilliant.'

'Why the Ed Sullivan Theater?' Bach asked sceptically. 'That audience can't all be throwbacks.'

John glimpsed the reflection of his thought in Kim's perturbed eyes. 'Seventy million people are supposed to be watching the Beatles on TV tonight. It's not the concert, it's the broadcast. They're trying to kill *all* the throwbacks.'

32

Broadway was jammed. Thousands of fans crushed forward, desperate to be let into the concert, each of them sure that if only Paul or George or one of them knew, she would be his girlfriend for ever. Not all of the teenagers had tickets. At the edge of the crowd, touts preyed on those who hadn't. It didn't need the sign over the canopy, 'BEATLES HERE TONIGHT' to tell the world what was going on. The chanting alone would have done that.

Two sedans finally made it to the little road at the side of the theatre, but the throng was almost as dense. Nevertheless, Majestic was here in force: Bach, Albano, Halligan and four cloakers pushed their way through the mass of clamouring fans, with John and Kim in their wake.

Albano shouldered aside a couple of girls, who protested noisily. Ignoring them, he flashed his Majestic pass and shouted above the din, 'We're here with security.'

The burly usher sneered. 'Yeah, and I'm Ringo's cousin. I heard 'em all tonight.' His gaze flickered to the badge. 'What is this anyway?'

Moving in close, Albano turned from the waist to let him see the butt of the gun tucked under his jacket. 'It's all you need to do your job.'

Frightened, the man backed off, fumbling open the door. Albano smoothly reholstered his pistol and saw the rest of his party inside before slipping in himself. The door slammed shut behind him but he could still hear the squeals of protest from the girls in the alley. 'Hey, you let them in! What about us?'

And at the back of the mob of fans was Marnie with her friend.

Even in the heart of the building the shrill chant hurt the ears. 'We want the Beatles, we want the Beatles!' The only quiet place was inside the soundproofed broadcast booth that Sullivan had had built.

Clustered around two projectors, the Majestic men fast-forwarded through all the advertisements booked for tonight's show. So far, every one of them was clean.

Frustrated, John peered down through the glass wall into the auditorium. Below him roadies, pages and stagehands scrambled around making last-minute preparations. The three guitars and the drums sparkled under the spotlights, and the empty seats seemed to be holding out their arms in welcome to the crowds outside.

Halligan said to the harassed technical director, 'Could you go back two frames?'

The tech man spoke into the mouthpiece of his headset. 'Back two.'

Albano came in, his gaze seeking Bach. 'Frank, we can't keep these people out much longer. The show goes on in thirty minutes.'

'What about the Weatherlys?'

'Their place was cleaned out.'

John looped the film he had been examining back around the reel and stood. Up to now desperation had been a spur to hold fatigue at bay. Now he was overwhelmed by the thought of the thousands around the world who were going to get orders to kill themselves. He said wearily, 'You can't take a chance, Frank. You've got to stop the show.'

The Majestic chief hardly even shook his head. 'That raises too many questions.'

John's fists clenched in frustration. 'Innocent people might die!'

'Only if they see the trigger-frames.' Bach gestured at Halligan, who replied, 'We've been through every commercial spot. No spliced-in shots.'

'We could be missing something,' John pleaded.

Implacably matter-of-fact, the Majestic chief said, 'We don't risk compromising the whole agency over one limited action. That's "acceptable losses", John.'

'Acceptable losses? You're crazy!'

A new voice spoke. 'Son, you took the words right out of my mouth.' Over by the doorway, Ed Sullivan was forcing his way into his own control booth, escorted by his beefy security team. Resplendent in a brocaded dressing gown of brown and gold silk, the little man took over by the sheer force of his personality. 'I want to talk to whoever's in charge here. I will not have my control booth held hostage.'

John stared beseechingly at Bach. 'Frank, stop this.'

For a moment he thought he had won. Then his ex-boss turned to the star. 'Mr Sullivan, we're all through here. Thank you for your patience.'

He swept out as though it were his own idea, followed by his people. John and Kim reluctantly fell into step behind them. John slammed the door on his way out.

Downcast, he didn't notice the significant look Bach gave Albano. Nor did he see the canny chief of operations dogging him as he took Kim down the stairs to the concert hall.

Hurrying, on fire to see if they might yet discover the mechanics of the plot, John and Kim talked urgently. Their footsteps rang on the granite stairs. 'We should have told Mr Sullivan,' Kim said.

'Told him what? Aliens are using his broadcast to try and kill people?'

'Maybe we can pull the plug ourselves. There must be a way.'

In front of her, John suddenly stopped. She bumped into him, but they steadied each other before they could tumble to the landing. He said, 'Wait a minute. Line taps!'

'What?'

'That technician I talked to said the broadcast gets fed out of here to go all over the world. We need Kenneth.'

At the front of the auditorium, stagehands were rushing this way and that, busy about last-minute preparations for the biggest show of all time. John grabbed one and asked loudly, 'Anyone seen Kenneth Parkinson? The BBC guy?'

Someone pointed to the cluster of speakers across the hall. Slumped on a chair nearby, Parkinson was bleeding from a wound above his ear. Another tech man was pressing a clean handkerchief over it to stanch the flow.

John went swiftly to him. Bruised and beaten, the Englishman turned glassy eyes to see who it was.

'Kenneth! What happened?'

'I found an odd cable, followed it up to the rigging on stage right. Next thing I know, I'm laid out like a codfish.' He struggled to stand.

Together John and Kim lifted him out of the chair. He swayed, clinging to his friend, and mumbled, 'I'm fine. You go and find out what those blokes are up to.'

They raced backstage behind the curtain. From a discreet distance, Albano followed them.

The curtain was still down, but not for much longer. Fanatical chanting throbbed through the walls and roadies dashed here and there, clutching bits of scenery, harmonicas and mikes.

Picking their way through the snaking nest of cables, John and Kim headed to their left.

Squinting up into the darkness of the rigging, they saw nothing that they recognized as untoward. But both of them were well aware that what they knew about sound-engineering could be written on the back of a match book.

Kim pulled the curtain aside at the wing but there was nothing hidden behind it. What she did see, though, was the janitor right at the back of the hall. Indistinct in his overalls, he was bending, dropping to his knees to do something she couldn't make out, but the green light of an exit sign gleamed on his cheekbones. He scanned the hall quickly to make sure no-one was observing him.

She gasped. 'John, look! That photo at Christopher's house, remember?'

The janitor was Weatherly senior, the implant with the ham radio. They saw him turn abruptly to glare chillingly down the centre aisle, somehow aware of their scrutiny. Getting quickly to his feet, he ran for a side exit.

John leaped after him, calling back, 'Look for the cable, Kim!'

Thirty years younger and a former track star, John hared through the side door not fifteen seconds behind his man. To his left a door batted to and fro on its hinges. He blasted through it and found himself in the service road at the back of the theatre.

No-one. Just trash cans and empty popcorn cartons. Light fanned from the doorway in a yellow arc. John moved warily beyond it, staring into the darkness. There was no sign of Weatherly ahead. Maybe he'd gone around the corner . . .

Treading softly in his sneakers, John edged forward. Suddenly something grated against the tarmac behind him. He spun even as the older man launched himself through the air.

Weatherly crashed down on top of him, sending them both clattering into the trash cans. John got the worst of it, cushioning his attacker's body with his own. Head ringing against metal, John grabbed the older man's sleeve and rolled, pulling him off, but the Hiver grabbed a trash-can lid and slammed it into John's face.

Then Weatherly took off, running. Groggily John scrambled up after him.

Before he could reach the janitor, he heard a muffled crack. Weatherly threw up his hands to save himself but he couldn't outrun the bullet Albano had put in his back. Staggering a couple of steps, he fell headlong.

The Majestic operative moved up alongside John, theatrically blowing the smoke from the silencer on his gun. He said coolly, 'I've got to get him out of here before that ganglion pops.'

Footsteps raced towards the door. Turning, John saw Kimberly and swept her up into his embrace, but not swiftly enough for her to miss the sight of the murdered man. But there was no time for reaction. She pulled John back into the theatre, saying, 'That cable has been routed off. I think they're dropping the images right into the programme.'

In the rabbit warren of passages behind the stage, it wasn't hard to find a ladder. John grabbed one and brought it over to where Kim stood sentry at the bottom of a long black wire. The cable dangled from a grille set high in the breeze-block wall.

He started to climb. Below, Kim ran a couple of steps then turned to say, 'I'll go get Bach. We'll come around through the front.' She shot off again.

The air vent was loose, held in place only by two shaky brackets at the top. John slid easily inside, finding himself in a conduit that must have been for the central heating, because it was hotter than Hades and twice as dark. The thin metal creaked and sagged alarmingly beneath his weight, and the heat in the aluminium scorched his flesh.

Keeping the cable between his fingers as as guide, he crawled into the blackness ahead. Someone must have opened the theatre because he felt the metal vibrating around him to the pounding of thousands of feet. In here the sounds were both muffled and magnified, and the fans' shrill screaming struck at him with almost physical force.

Rounding a corner, he saw a little shaft of light striking up through an air vent. He slowed, holding his head down because the tunnel was so tight. As he inched towards the grille, he saw that the space below it was empty. The cable led him onwards.

He passed another vent just as cautiously, but at the third the cable wormed down into the room below. Once again he crept nervously forward until he could just see through the grille.

There it was! The hidden control room lay underneath him, the cable feeding into a bank of jury-rigged electronic equipment with red lights blinking and a spider's web of wires connecting it to a slide carousel.

The place seemed to be unoccupied. John stole close enough for his fingers to touch the screws holding the grille in position. They stood proud, hardly connecting at all. It wouldn't take much to dislodge them.

Then Burnside walked into his field of vision. The implant moved to his console, checking over the relays. All at once he froze, his head coming up as though aware of someone watching him. His head turned upwards.

John held his breath, pulling back a fraction in the hope that the Hiver wouldn't see him, but their eyes met. Burnside spun on his heel and disappeared from view. Horrified at being spotted, John began to crawl to safety as fast as he could. There wasn't space to turn around and he had to go backwards.

Metal grated behind his feet. He twisted onto his back to see and another vent clanged upwards into the duct. It smashed down on John's chest, momentarily pinning his arms. Burnside had punched it up and out. Now he wriggled through as John wrestled with the grating, trying to disentangle himself.

The Hiver scooted forwards as John managed to throw the grille aside. He tried to sit up in the low duct, but that was literally playing into Burnside's hands. The man started to throttle him. John slipped his wrists between Burnside's arms and knocked them aside, but the implant recovered with frightening speed and came at him on hands and knees. His momentum carried them both forward, his body dropping down onto John's, pressing the air out of his lungs.

Struggling, John rolled aside, jerking Burnside under him and thudding his head against the metal.

Their combined weight was too much for the aluminium ducting. The loose grille over the cable fell out and spun away into the relay room below.

Unsupported, Burnside followed it, crashing face down onto his console. His flailing limbs ripped a power line loose, trapping it under his neck and the implant's body juddered helplessly, writhing in a fountain of lethal blue sparks. Long after the man was dead his corpse continued its macabre jig.

The door burst open under the impact of Albano's shoulder. Behind him Kim dashed into the room, her eyes widening as she saw the dark-suited cadaver in its dance of death.

Clinging to the sides of the conduit above her, John looked down and grinned lopsidedly. He said, 'Hi.'

Below, Bach came into the relay room and surveyed the wreckage. Into the silence came the voice of a TV linkman. 'And now, live from our studios in New York, the Ed Sullivan Show!'

Bach let them into the broadcast booth. Or maybe he just didn't trust them out of sight. Whatever, John and Kim stood at the back with Halligan, Albano and the Majestic chief, watching the technicians work their magic. A TV monitor showed the small dapper Sullivan in front of the stage curtains. He was saying, 'Now yesterday and today, our theatre's been jammed with newspapermen and hundreds of photographers . . .'

Bach turned to Loengard. 'If we're going to work together, John, we do things my way.'

'This was a one-shot deal, Frank.' He pulled a long hotel key fob from his pocket and handed it over. 'Steele's in room three-zero-four.'

The technical director cut the show to *live* at the touch of a switch. He said into his mouthpiece. 'Taking camera two . . .'

On the monitor, Ed Sullivan said excitedly, 'The Beatles!' and the opening chords of 'Money' crashed out over a tidal wave of screams. In the control room, everyone's gaze was drawn to the screen. The camera panned over the frenzied audience as Lennon sang.

Kim's face was blank with shock. Numbly she took a step towards the TV.

John saw it and blenched. Poisonous thoughts of Halligan boiled through him as he sprang to hold on tightly to Kim's waist. Hadn't the little weasel said the hypnotic suggestions faded after thirty-six hours?

But Kim said faintly, 'It's Marnie!' The only girl in the top tier not screaming. Slender, a clear-cut figure in her black pinafore dress and white shirt, Marnie stood, face slack, utterly still.

Loengard shot a desperate glance at Bach. 'She's one of the throwbacks, Frank. Already programmed. Help us get her out of there!'

Bach eyed him with a faint supercilious sneer on his lips. 'You said it yourself, John. The deal's done.'

Keeping hold of Kimberly, John backed slowly towards the door. Suddenly they whirled and bolted.

Albano started after them, but the Majestic chief placed a hand on his chest. 'Let him go.'

John pulled Kimberly along by the hand. As she recovered, they darted up the stairs towards the highest balcony. Breathless, they burst through the doors and into the auditorium.

It was bedlam up there. They split up, John pounding towards the centre aisle and Kim peeling off to the side. Around them fans were leaping and gyrating. Some wore heavy mascara and it smeared every time they wiped hysterical tears from their cheeks. The rhythmic beat of guitars shook the hot air around them, and their outstretched arms flailed in ecstasy.

Kim found the right row and began pushing past the line of girls. John, meantime, had seen that the throwback had begun to move as if bewitched. Her back ramrod straight while her hands grasped at something retreating before her, she drifted step by step closer to the edge.

On stage, no-one had noticed, but now Lennon looked up, catching sight of that black-and-white figure climbing onto the parapet. Around Marnie the girls squealed anew, thinking that he might be looking at them.

John had to elbow his way through the pack of lust-crazed teenagers. He saw Marnie turn, facing outwards, her feet perched tiptoe on the narrow rail.

Slowly, inexorably, she arched forwards, poised for flight.

Unable to get to her in time, Kim screamed, 'Marnie!' her terror forcing through the din.

The girl stopped. Looked back.

But her dive had already begun. John hurled himself at her, snatching her arms as they started to cartwheel into space.

Her weight catapulted his midriff into the balustrade but he leaned hard against it and Kim finally helped him haul the youngster to safety, while all the time the Beatles played, the focus of every eye.

Huddled on the steps, with the crowd frenetic around them, Kim hugged the frightened teenager to her. Little by little, the girl's hazy eyes focused and she began to come out of her trance. 'What happened?' she whispered shakily.

'Just another dream, that's all.'

Later, from the wings, they watched Ed Sullivan say, 'Thank you, Topo. And now, won't you please welcome back for the second time this evening, the Beatles!'

John stood a little behind Kim, his arms clasped lovingly around her. And Marnie stood in front of them, gazing raptly at the stage. The band began to play softly.

Loengard and Kim watched the historical moment, knowing that they had helped shape it in ways no-one would ever realize. For those few moments, the Beatles made both of them feel like everyone else in the country – hopeful, optimistic, glad to be alive.

John's eyes lit when he leaned forward to kiss Kim tenderly on the forehead. They weren't ignoring the fight.

They were drawing the line between humans and Hive. That night, they felt like they could win.

At the Albert hotel, Albano let himself into room 304. Gun in his hand, he led two cloakers into the bathroom.

He paused. The doorway was smeared with blood. A broken shaving-mirror testified to what had happened. Dripping with blood, shards of silvered glass lay next to Steele's severed bonds. Of the Hiver himself there was no sign . . .

THE END

ABOUT THE AUTHOR

Stan Nicholls is an author and journalist whose interest in science fiction and fantasy began in the 1960s when he edited the award-winning small press magazines *Stardock* and *Gothique*. He has also managed a number of specialist SF, fantasy and comics bookshops and was research assistant for Dennis Wheatley on his *Library of the Occult*. A full-time writer since 1981, his journalism has appeared in publications as diverse as the *Guardian*, *Time Out*, *Rolling Stone*, *2000 AD* and *SFX* while his most recent books include the first volume in *The Nightshade Chronicles* and the authorized biography of Gerry Anderson (with co-author Simon Archer).

Stan Nicholls hosts a monthly conference web site dedicated to SF, fantasy and horror on the CompuServe network.

THE SHIFT
George Foy

'Something wholly new: a gritty urban science fiction *noir*' Thomas H. Cook, author of *Breakheart Hill*

Alex Munn is a burned-out television writer for a soap opera called *Pain in the Afternoon*. Then he's introduced to Virtix, a virtual reality technology so good that the viewer can't tell the difference between real life and Real Life, a Virtix show filled with sex, adventure, and violence. But what really captures Alex's imagination is a story line he's created for a programme he calls *Munn's World*. It depicts a New York of the 1850s, complete with horse-drawn carriages clip-clopping down grimy, poverty-ridden streets. Here a serial killer called the Fishman is on the prowl, disembowelling victims on the Bowery. His main nemesis is a lone cop named Alex Munn.

What happens next is impossible, unscripted, and absolutely terrifying. For the Fishman has somehow escaped and followed Alex into the present, turning Alex's world into a virtual nightmare.

'Absolutely terrifying' *Publishers Weekly*

A Bantam Paperback
0 553 56611 0

MOUNT DRAGON
Lincoln Preston

'A slam-bang medical thriller – swift, gruesome
and wickedly clever . . . a masterful story'
Richard Preston, bestselling author of *The Hot
Zone*

Mount Dragon: an elite desert laboratory belonging
to GeneDyne, one of the world's foremost biotech-
nology companies. For scientist Guy Carson his
transfer there is the opportunity of a lifetime – the
chance to work alongside some of the country's most
brilliant scientific minds on a permanent cure for a
common, but dangerous disease. Success would
guarantee enormous profits for GeneDyne – and a
Nobel Prize for the Mount Dragon team.

But something very strange is happening at Mount
Dragon. The hidden lab harbours a ghastly secret that
puts the entire world at horrifying risk. And by the
time Guy Carson makes his hideous discovery, it may
already be too late . . .

'The writer that scared the willies out of readers
with *Relic* returns with a second, equally gripping
novel of techno-terror . . . It's a grand and scary
story' *Publishers Weekly*

A Bantam Paperback
0 553 50438 X

THE RELIC
Lincoln Preston

When a team of archaeologists is savagely massacred in the Amazon Basin, all that survives is a solitary box of relics. From boat to boat, from port to port, the battered crate drifts. It finally reaches New York City – only to be locked away in the basement of the New York Museum of Natural History, lost and forgotten.

But the black heart of the Amazon never forgets. On the eve of the Museum's massive new exhibition, someone or something other than tourists and school-children is roaming the echoing halls and dusty galleries. People are turning up savagely murdered and rumours of a 'Museum beast', never far from the surface, rise again among the Museum staff. But then Margo Green, a graduate student working in the Museum, uncovers a link between the killings, the failed Amazonian expedition, and an odd figurine that will be displayed for the first time. Will she be able to put the pieces together and stop the deadly menace before terror strikes again?

'High-concept, high-energy thriller ... the narrative builds to a superbly exciting climax, and then offers a final twist to boot ... First-rate thrills and chills' *Publishers Weekly*

A Bantam Paperback
0 553 50496 7